A Feast

'I have seen things which disturb me,' she said softly, raising liquid eyes to his.

'And do you enjoy being disturbed?' His hands slid down her front, running over the arc of her breasts, lingering on her naked skin.

'I do not know,' she whispered, shaking her head with inexpressible anguish.

Slowly, he pulled her towards him and, like a dark tide, she felt his body melt into hers. But when she lifted her parted lips for his kisses, he instead nuzzled her hair and the smoothness of her brow. Then, with uncanny tenderness, he kissed her eyelids, first the left and then the right.

'I am glad that what you see disturbs you.'

She could feel the stiff wetness of the tip of his tongue rubbing the lids of her eyes. It made her weak, made her lean against him for support. As she pressed against him, she could see the pulse at his throat beating fast. She knew that he, too, was extraordinarily agitated.

A Feast for the Senses

MARTINE MARQUAND

BLACK
lace

Black Lace novels are sexual fantasies.
In real life, make sure you practise safe sex.

First published in 1998 by
Black Lace
Thames Wharf Studios,
Rainville Road, London W6 9HT

Copyright © Martine Marquand 1998

The right of Martine Marquand to be identified as the
Author of this Work has been asserted by her in
accordance with the Copyright, Designs and Patents Act
1988.

Typeset by SetSystems Ltd, Saffron Walden, Essex
Printed and bound by Mackays of Chatham PLC

ISBN 0 352 33310 3

*All characters in this publication are fictitious and any
resemblance to real persons, living or dead, is purely
coincidental.*

This book is sold subject to the condition that it shall
not, by way of trade or otherwise, be lent, resold, hired
out or otherwise circulated without the publisher's
prior written consent in any form of binding or cover
other than that in which it is published and without a
similar condition including this condition being
imposed on the subsequent purchaser.

Chapter One

She was almost blinded by the glittering snow. Peering out of the dimness of the coach, Clara could see nothing but flat vistas of sparkling whiteness, punctuated by a long row of gigantic windmills, their sails icebound in the winter air.

'How long will it take?'

She could see the driver in conversation with the postillion as they huddled around the front of the coach, where the wheels had sunk almost completely into the detestable snow. With a shake of his head the surly driver turned to her.

'The wheel's cracked, madame. It must be replaced. We will not move before sundown.'

With an indignant jolt, Clara threw herself back down on the narrow seat. Her new companion, Tresa, eyed her coldly. Clara felt forced by the silence to make some kind of pronouncement.

'Sundown! How can we sit here until sundown? We will freeze to death. If only your master had not suggested such an inclement time of year for this ridiculous journey. I can assure you, the weather is never half so harsh in England. And, in England, there would be people one could send for, to help one. What are we to do, I ask you?'

1

Languidly, Tresa smoothed the fur of the ermine muff she wore to match her midnight-blue velvet pelisse. The coils of black hair which escaped her fur-trimmed tricorne hat revealed her Mediterranean ancestry. Lifting an arched brow even higher, she addressed Clara as if she were a child.

'If you had only listened, Miss Fairfax. The coachman did advise we take a sled for this final stretch to the capital. If you regret that decision, I am afraid you have only yourself to blame.'

It was true. When the man had advised they hire a sled and proceed along the icebound canal to the heart of the United Provinces, Clara had scoffed. No, of course they could not leave the count's coach to be conveyed on to them in Amsterdam at a later date. Just the thought of sliding all the way along their route – it was quite ridiculous. What would people think? Such ideas were never put about in England.

Unable to take much more of Tresa's arrogant stare, the girl pulled on her woollen cloak and carefully edged down into the snow.

The road from the port of Helvoetsluys had at first been tolerable. It was at the abominable inn at Utrecht that Clara had been faced with the decision about how to proceed. Unsure whether she or Tresa might take precedence, she had insisted they should not abandon the carriage. Little had she guessed what lay ahead of them. Never in all her life had she seen such a triumph of winter.

Climbing to the top of a bank of snow and finding her breath turning to steam in front of her, she gazed about the white land in search of guidance. Only a few hundred paces away ran the silver thread of a broad canal. There, she could see bands of skaters speeding back and forth and occasional sleds pulled by workmen or even goats and cattle. At any other time, it would have been an entertaining sight: but at this moment, all Clara could think of was the pain in her freezing, sodden feet.

'You see, Miss Fairfax. In Rome, one must do as the Romans; on the Amstel, as the Amsterdamers.'

It was Tresa, leaning laconically from the window of the coach. Already, though she had met her only twenty-four hours earlier, Clara felt a growing unease in the presence of this elegant Italian. There were nuances of behaviour Clara could not identify at all. If the count had sent her to be her friend, she was not particularly friendly, nor as a paid companion was she companionable. In fact, thought Clara to herself, she is quite, quite rude.

'Indeed.'

'The count, you will see, is a man of education. A man of sophistication and urbanity. If he cares to do a thing, it is the correct thing.'

'I am so reassured, signorina,' Clara replied, with a little of the warmth of smugness to her voice. 'Then my forthcoming marriage to this paragon must indeed be blessed in heaven.'

As Clara had suspected, a little *frisson* of coldness ran between them at this statement of possession. How interesting, she thought, that she is jealous. And yet how insensitive of this man, then, to choose to send her to meet me.

Clara's speculations were interrupted by a little excited cry from her companion. In a moment, the coachman had been despatched by her in florid Italian and it was with a look of triumph that Tresa turned her scornful eyes back on to Clara.

'Did I not tell you he is perfect? Why, he is even capable of putting this disaster of yours right again.'

Following the line of Tresa's stare, Clara found she was watching a splendid sled as it halted at the edge of the shimmering ice. It was pulled by a matching pair of fine horses, their feather-plumed heads tossing and smoking in the cold air, producing the effect of a gorgeous chariot from a carnival or circus. The passenger of the sled was climbing out on to the ice. He was a tall, richly dressed gentleman. Suddenly, Clara began to feel a sickening apprehension.

It was beginning to snow a little again. Wisps of white snowdust were falling from the sombre sky, sticking to their hair and cloaks. The man, who was boldly striding over to them across the snowy fields, appeared yet more fanciful as eddies of snow whipped about his long black hair, tugging at his gold-clasped cloak.

Glancing down at her own unprepossessing exterior, Clara cursed her practical nature. Whilst travelling, she had followed English advice and worn only her most hard-wearing and modest costumes. This morning, waking in the filthy inn where the ice on the water ewer needed to be cracked asunder, she had copied the dull Dutch women and pulled layer upon layer of woollen clothes on, in an attempt to maintain some warmth. Unlike Tresa, she did not even possess an elegant winter habit. Instead, she wore only her brown quilted silk robe, simple cuffed sleeves and bobbin lace cap and kerchief. Over this was an old jacket with squirrel lining which had once been her mother's. Worse, the lower portion of her skirts and petticoat were soaking wet, her stockings and shoes were similarly drenched. To warm herself, she had slung on her oldest woollen cloak. She knew that, at this moment, her hair hung in unbecoming rat's tails and her face was no doubt an indecorous crimson.

For indeed, it was the count. She had little doubt that Tresa would not be stretching and waving so delicately, were it not the paragon himself arriving with his perfect timing. No, no, no, Clara wailed inside her head. If only there had been time, as she had anticipated, to unpack her better clothes: to curl her hair, to bathe, to change her shoes, to catch her breath!

Scarcely daring to lift her face, she peered through her eyelashes at the rapidly approaching man. She had expected someone older, she decided. A man with more *gravitas*, a man with less vigour. This man was a good six foot tall, but long and lean of limb, with the strength

4

and stride of a soldier. Handsome, too – she could just detect, although the snow had settled on his long dark hair, as it lay casually tied in a broad ribbon at the nape of his neck. There was an angularity about his face she immediately liked – no, more than liked – was almost overwhelmed by. The brows were strong, the cheek-bones high and the lips were wide and manly. He was now but a few paces from them, his high leather boots scarcely splashed by the wet. Taking a deep breath, Clara lifted her face to meet her fiancé for the very first time.

'Signorina Fairfax. An unexpected pleasure.'

He was before her; his fingers extended to hers. With some lack of grace, she thrust her hand towards him. As he pressed those cold, chapped fingers to his lips, she looked directly into his face.

His eyes were almost black, but deep, like starless night reflected in water. As they met her own, she felt his gaze penetrate like a blade cutting inside her being. It was a caustic, piercing look which seemed, for one anguished moment, to assail her with need and potent hunger. Then it was gone. He lowered her fingers gently and a veil covered his eyes, like the second lid of a cat. She could, however, feel the damply burning pressure of his lips still scorching her cold fingers.

'Signorina Bressani. What a pleasure.'

Clara could almost hear Tresa purring as the count pressed her gloved hand to his lips.

'Now, ladies. I must endeavour to have these men bring my sled over the fields to you. Then we can make a speedy approach to the capital and be in our lodgings before the gates are closed.'

With a white-toothed smile and bow, the count left them and began to remonstrate with the coachmen. Somewhat breathlessly, Clara clambered back into the warmth of the carriage.

Her pocket mirror did little to restore her self-regard. The wetness had plastered down her hair in fronds across the flatness of her head. Her nose was a crimson button between two rosy apples of cheeks that any tavern maid would have been proud of. There was nothing to be done, however. He had seen her at her worst. With practical good humour she decided that at least she could only improve in appearance from now on.

Clara's reverie was interrupted by a loud tap at the window. As Tresa had predicted, the count had turned the situation about in a few moments. The coachman would send on their trunks as soon as was possible but, in the meantime, the two women could easily accompany the count on his sled into the capital.

It was a fabulous means of transport – carved with the shape of two swans at either side and filled with animal pelts and cushions to keep the passengers warm and comfortable. There was room enough behind, as well, for the count's manservant – for it was he himself who chose to drive the sled, lifting a pair of red leather reins to guide the horses through the strange traffic which proceeded along the broad canal.

Offering her his hand, the count guided Clara to the seat beside him. She settled into the deep pile of furs, almost immediately feeling the effect of warmth reviving her limbs. On the other side of him, Tresa daintily took her place, laughing and chattering in Italian.

'Well, ladies, let us be on our way.'

In a moment, they were hissing over the surface of the ice; the two horses produced a delightful sound as their harnesses jingled with the sound of myriad silver bells. As they proceeded quickly across the ice, Clara took the opportunity to study her fiancé while he was intent on weaving the sled around skaters and sledgers alike. Although the papers sent to her by her father's executor had stated he was a nobleman of six and twenty years, she saw he still had a boyish streak as he eagerly swept the sled across the ice.

What had she expected? Since her parents' untimely deaths from the low fever and the second, even greater shock that followed when her father's disastrous business affairs were brought to light, Clara had decided to bear her heavy load with Christian resignation. This had not been without the urging of her brother James and her married sister Charlotte. In despair, James had told her that the only money left was a small annuity of a thousand a year which had been settled upon her. Beyond that, the family printing house must close, unless some money were raised quickly. Charlotte, too, had wept at their imminent ruin, should her own husband's income fail along with the business; with two small children, the events spelt almost certain disaster.

Finally, James had called a family meeting and they had met in the now cold and neglected offices where her father had used to run his business. After long consideration Clara had attended, planning to make a sacrifice of her own gentility by taking a post as a governess, or setting up a village school and offering the proceeds of her income to her sister's children. However, James and her brother-in-law Walter had set before her a plan, the implications of which had utterly appalled her.

The major business of the printing house was the reproduction of architectural plans obtained from Italy, for the recent fashions had all been for the classical Palladian style which originated in that country. Their contact in Italy was a Signor di Malibran of Lucca, who had been set up in business by his cousin, a wealthy count named Anton di Malibran. Somewhat hesitantly, James had explained that their Italian business partners were prepared to buy the English business, but the deal was faltering as he and Walter could provide no surety as guarantee of good faith. Indeed, James had outlined, the only money they could put forward was Clara's annuity of a thousand pounds a year.

'But, brother,' Clara had interrupted, 'I will gladly give that up. Let me sign it away now.'

James had licked his lips, looking to Walter for assistance but obtaining none. 'I am afraid, my dearest sister, that the money is irrevocably tied to you under the terms of the will. You cannot give it up.'

7

'Then what can I do? Tell me, James, for I will do it.'

The two men seemed at this to lower their heads. It was Walter who at last broached the terms of the agreement.

'The only way we can honour this arrangement with di Malibran is if we give him the annuity along with yourself, Clara. You see, if your relations with him were to be formalised, your thousand a year would pass to him as a matter of course.'

'Formalised?'

Clara wondered what they could mean – as an employee perhaps, or in some legal sense.

'Let me put it this way,' James interrupted, in a strangely cheerful voice. 'You must picture the two businesses – Fairfax of York and di Malibran of Lucca as merging – almost marrying, in a sense. If you were to – let's say you were to marry this Anton di Malibran . . .'

'Marry?'

'He is wealthy, of good breeding and an age to marry. We have all discussed the matter and in truth, Clara, you could not do better. The family would be eternally grateful.'

She had stared speechlessly at them. Then she had swallowed her protests and submitted. Her only words of surprise were muttered to herself, much later in the privacy of her room.

'But how can he be suitable? He is not even English. The man is a *foreigner*.'

Now, as the sled swept across the sparkling plains towards the clustered spires of Amsterdam, Clara felt the warmth of this strange foreigner as he brushed against her with his sleeve. Foreign he certainly was and, as if to draw her attention to this, he began to chatter to Tresa in Italian.

Her surprise at his rudeness soon turned to discomfiture. Tresa's bell-like laughter seemed to echo off the ice, trilling like a bird who finds all in the world to be arranged for her amusement. What was she telling him?

8

About Clara's arrival, like a drowned sea-rat on the Dutch coast, or maybe her lack of suitably genteel luggage? Or maybe, Clara suspected, she was simply informing the count what an utterly appalling choice he had made. How could he be marrying this dreary, plain English thing? Clara was sure that everyone they passed must assume that the two sumptuous Italians were man and wife. Who would even notice the brown-cloaked figure sitting quietly at their side?

So Clara concentrated on watching the changing scene as it flew past her. As the sky darkened in the east, a golden sunburst reflected against the shimmering snow-fields. A few of the skaters now adroitly carried lanterns, spinning out of the dusk like fireflies, their skates hissing softly across the ice.

Once, she glanced over to her companions and was surprised to notice that the count was watching her from the corner of his eye, although he pretended to turn away when she returned his gaze.

Then, at last, the monumental walls of the city could be seen. Inside, she could see a great assembly of roofs, gables and spires. Already the lanterns of the city glowed warmly out into the twilight. Then she heard the peal of bells: ascending and descending scales; simple tunes and great tolling rumbles. As the sled swept up to the great towered gates, the still air shook as the city called its faithful to cease labour and rest after another industrious day.

The apartments engaged by the count for his party were on the long canal sweep of the Prinsengracht. After being pleasantly surprised by the neatness of the house, with its decorative black-and-white marble hallway, Clara was led by a servant girl up to her own private chamber, where a welcoming fire was lit in the blue Delft tiled fireplace.

As the party had arrived at the steps leading up from the canal to the imposing entrance, the count had at last turned to her.

'I must welcome you to your new home, Miss Fairfax.'

She took his hand in the torchlight as he helped her up the slippery quay steps.

'Surely it cannot be called a home?' she replied, with some abruptness. 'I will only ever have one home.'

'I am afraid that wherever we make a halt on this long journey, we must create a home for you. Your home, from now on, must be a repository of your mind and not your body. We can speak of this later. An interview after dinner would be convenient?'

She could see the glint of those strange dark eyes in the golden light of the torches. Truly, all she longed for was supper on a tray in her room and an early night in a clean bed. However, refusal would be ungracious.

'Very well, Count. After dinner.'

At dinner, Clara again noted that Tresa seemed extraordinarily well prepared for the situation of being left without their luggage. She was wearing a fine gown of blue satin that Clara thought far more becoming than that she had first worn at Helvoetsluys. Clara had looked with despair at the stains on her own brown quilted gown and done her best to dry the petticoat before the fire. Without curling irons, she had only been able to tweak her hair with a comb and rearrange her cap. Looking in the glass she grew convinced of it – the count would reject her.

Soon, however, after servings of wild duck, rabbit and a few glasses of Rhenish wine, Clara's spirits began to revive. The count seemed in less exuberant spirits and addressed himself mainly to the wine decanter, only occasionally raising his head to look at her quite boldly and then turning his head nonchalantly when she challenged him.

Having nothing to say to Tresa, Clara paid large attention to the meal. Although substituting some rather odd little dumplings for potatoes, Clara thought the dinner almost as good as that to be found in England. There was good blue china on the table, fine glassware

10

and fine silver salt cellars and dishes. It was certainly better than the disgusting bread and beer porridge in a cracked dish that she had refused at the inn.

'Miss Fairfax, join me at your leisure.'

With a scrape of his chair, the count was off, with only a quick backward glance at Clara. Tresa halted with a full mouth of food, watching them with interest.

'Is he not perfect?' she hissed, once he had left them.

'He seems well enough.'

'Well enough! You are a cold-blooded creature, God only knows. The saints know what will come of it.'

'Of what?' Clara retorted icily.

'Of this whole situation.' The young woman grinned condescendingly.

With a loud scrape of her chair on the brown tiles, Clara rose. 'Good night, Signorina Bressani.'

'*Buona notte*, Miss Fairfax.'

Count Anton di Malibran was relaxing in his chamber when Clara tapped apologetically at his door. Draped across an armchair, he had removed his coat and was relaxing in breeches and linen shirt; playing with his pocket watch, he stared into the fire.

'Miss Fairfax. Do sit over here, by the fire.'

He waved across to a matching damask armchair. Shyly, Clara sat across from this stranger. He appeared extraordinary to her in more ways than mere nationality. His earlier exuberance was clearly spent; now he appeared distracted, even fighting agitation.

'Miss Fairfax, we must talk.'

'Indeed, sir.'

Here it comes, Clara thought, her heart thumping. He has seen me now. He has decided he cannot go through with this sham of a marriage. I am to be sent home in disgrace to tell my family they are ruined. But in the moment of her telling herself this, she became aware how much she not only dreaded the shame of such an eventuality but that she would also be rather disappointed. But why disappointed?

'You find it a strange arrangement, do you not?' He looked at her once more, his eyes only a little dulled by wine. 'This marriage. What do you say?'

'I believe, from my family's point of view, it is a necessary arrangement.'

'From my point of view, however, it is not necessary. It is my choice.'

Clara did her best to summon courage. 'And why, sir, is it your choice?'

His face was warmly illumined in the firelight. Now it creased in unexpected amusement. 'You do not know me, English miss. You do not know me at all. I am an adventurer, a man of wealth and power but also of pleasure. You could say – indeed some do say – that I live for pleasure. But the search for pleasure becomes, shall we say, somewhat wearisome after many years. And the creatures who share that same quest – the pretty flotsam who live for delight and self-gratification – why, their attractions begin to pall. So, like many before me, I look to new pastures – to the unblemished – for my amusement. And my search for the challenge of hard, adamantine purity has been successful, Miss Fairfax. I have achieved my aim. You are quite, quite perfect for my task.'

Throughout this speech, Clara found herself growing more and more agitated. She found his meaning incomprehensible. He was speaking in riddles, surely? 'Count,' she ventured, 'perhaps it is the translation to English. I cannot comprehend your meaning.'

Rising, he poured himself a glass of liquor and offered her a drink, which Clara declined. As he stood against the burgundy drapes, she could now see a certain wildness in his air. A faint film of moisture shone across his face, causing his dark hair to curl and dampen at his temples. The billowing linen of his shirt followed the broad line of his frame; she could glimpse now the strength of the man and his animal vitality.

12

'That is the heart of it, exactly,' he exclaimed. 'You do not comprehend me. This is perfect. You really are too, too civilised. You truly do not have a warm pulse in your body. What a challenge,' he exulted. 'What an extraordinary task I have set myself.'

'You are correct, sir. There is no fault with your English. It is perfect. There is a fault with the explanation you offer me. Tell me plainly, sir ,what it is you plan for me.'

'Clara, Clara,' he said caressingly, cocking his head for a moment to one side. 'Forgive me. I will explain.'

Crossing the room, he picked up a large leather globe from the desk: a beautiful object on which were carefully drawn all the countries and oceans of the world.

'Listen to me, Clara. I speak only of our journey. For, as you know, we are to undertake a Grand Tour of the known lands.' Here he spun the globe and drew his fingertips across the miniature representations of mountains, cities and deserts. 'Now, you do know the purpose of such a journey, don't you?'

'Why, it is to educate our young people in the ways of the world.'

'Correct. Which is why I have planned such a journey for you.'

Still puzzled, Clara stared at the globe. 'You mean I am to be educated in the arts and sciences, that we are to visit the sites of the ancient world?'

The count gave her a twisted little smile. 'Yes, indeed. But there is to be more than the narrow curriculum of your English tourists to be had on this particular journey. Oh, I have seen them – chinless milords who travel the world but never converse with any but their own nationality in the coffee houses of Europe. No – let me tell you immediately that one of my conditions is that you are banned from conversing with any of your own kind. Our journey is rather to be an inner journey. A journey of the mind, the emotions, the sensations. I will teach you so much, Clara, that you shall be quite, quite

13

changed. I shall show you the world of the senses – let you explore them as few women on earth are able to. '

Clara could feel herself tightening like a wound spring. Her fingers, which appeared so placid upon her lap, were pressed so tightly together the bones ached.

'You must explain yourself, sir, for I fear I am being made a fool of.'

In reply, he strode over towards her, so close she could smell the wine on his breath and another, more tantalising scent rising from the body beneath the loose shirt. With an ineffably affectionate gesture, he reached out and stroked her hair, as a woman might caress a child.

'Clara,' he whispered. 'Do not be afraid of me.' Unwillingly, she lifted her head and looked up into his face. His eyes again wore that piercing, hungry look.

'I am afraid,' she murmured, without wishing to.

Sinking to his knees, his face was barely an inch from hers. She could see the firm arc of his brow, the sheen of his warm skin, the dark centres of his eyes. On a sudden impulse, she longed to feel his lips on hers. It was a strange, unruly impulse which she would not have believed herself capable of. But in a second it was gone and she quelled all sign of it.

Quickly, he stood and straightened. 'There is a second condition, I must explain, to help our little experiment work. In the eyes of the law we are betrothed, and certainly in the lands of the Mediterranean that often means a man and woman enjoy each other's body as if their vows were already made. I see you are shocked, at even the mention of such common truths – how delectable you are! It simply would not do, Miss Fairfax, to weakly surrender to the flesh. Indeed, all the piquancy of the chase would be lost. What do you say?'

'I am almost speechless. Of course it would be out of the question.'

'Excellent!' he grinned. 'For one dreadful moment, then, when your lips parted moistly, I thought you were going to prove too easy game for me. I will, of course, expect you to be impenetrable in your resolve until our wedding. We will marry at the end of the summer. Let us say, the beginning of October. When the nights grow long.'

'I see.'

'And now, the more serious matters having been aired, let me tell you about my regime of instruction. Come here, to the window.'

With the reluctance of a condemned prisoner, Clara crossed to the window where the count had drawn back the drapes to reveal a strange brass mechanism.

'Do not be frightened. It is only a magnifying instrument. Our hosts the Dutch are great craftsmen in the field of optics.'

His fingers caressed the intricate device of glass lenses and brass workings. 'Your first lesson, Miss Fairfax, is to truly see. I watched you this afternoon as you gazed at the scenery. No doubt you feel you have collected many interesting and picturesque impressions already. And yet – what did you truly see? Is not the world but a sham of surfaces, of illusions?'

'No, sir,' Clara interrupted, somewhat annoyed. 'The world is as we see it. You may try to trick me, but I believe I see what I see.'

He smiled, and beckoned her closer to the instrument, which was set up at the window with its lens pointing out into the night air.

'It is a clear night. Look out and see the sights of this city. Is it not clean and industrious? Neat and restrained? Here – before dinner I caught a fine example.'

Guiding her to the eyepiece, he placed it against her eye.

At first she could see nothing as her eyes adjusted to the darkness. Then she saw the light of a candlelit room, quite clear across the night sky. A little sofa stood as precisely before her eyes as if it were here in the room in front of her – she could see every detail of its pattern.

'Very gently, guide the barrel,' the count said, sliding her hand around the main piece of the telescope.

Now she could see more of the room. And people. There was a man in a chair, an old man in a night-gown. Before him stood women. Naked women. Immodestly, they paraded before him. She could see their full, ripe breasts and rounded hips. Long hair swung freely to their waists as they shamelessly flaunted their nakedness.

Subtly, the count's hand slid around Clara's waist. She was aware of the pressure, like a serpent uncoiling, ready to strike. He was pressing gently against her in a strange, deliciously proximate embrace.

'What you see is the Bishop's Palace,' he murmured gently into her ear. 'Each night the Bishop has a selection of inmates from the house of fallen women sent to his bedchamber. Soon he will choose one – or two. Then the entertainment will begin. We may watch it all from here.'

With a jolt, Clara withdrew from the instrument, removing his arm from her waist as if it were a rotten limb. She turned to him, her face flushed.

'No, thank you, Count. You may wish to debase yourself with such a spectacle – I do not.'

'Oh, what outrage!' he laughed. His white teeth glinted like a wolf in moonlight.

'No, do not go. Let me show you something more to your taste, then. Let me show you the stars.'

She hesitated. 'I wish to leave. Thank you for our interview.'

Grasping her wrist gently, he pulled her towards him. Although she knew she should resist, she let herself be pulled a few paces towards him.

'I am sorry my little joke did not succeed. I only wanted to prove my point: that there is often more to the world than the surface image. In truth, I bought this optic to gaze at the stars. Here.' Putting his eye to the piece, he angled it upward and made a few adjustments. 'Tonight, there is a beautiful view of the transit of Venus. Let me show you, Clara.'

Maybe it was the lingering way he uttered her name.

16

Maybe it was that, or her genuine interest in seeing the planets, but she felt herself relent.

'I promise you,' he said solemnly, like a small boy. 'There is such a view of the stars tonight – you might never see the like again.'

And so, with her head bowed, Clara once more peered into the instrument. And it was there – a pink globe of such unsurpassable beauty that she gasped out loud. How many thousand miles across the heavens was she able to gaze? The image was as smooth as a rose-kissed pearl, a gorgeous sphere draped in nebulaic mists.

Once again his hand slid about her waist. She felt the span of his hand outstretched against the tight fabric of her bodice. With a deep murmur, he pressed delightfully against her frame.

'It is my favourite planet. My favourite goddess. Yet, with the naked eye, she is invisible. Sometimes it is necessary to look beyond the surface of things. To strip the veneer away and grasp the essence.'

She could feel his breath, hot against the nape of her neck.

'Like you, Clara, Venus is a mystery. What beauty lies within a woman, what tantalising secrets? Only a fool judges by first impressions; the wise man knows the true acolytes of the goddess keep their mysteries hidden deep.'

There was much she could not understand of his speech – or his behaviour. Yet, what he hinted at – was it true? Did she really possess this secret allure? But – oh, it was so late. She remembered the clean sheets and quilted coverlet upstairs in her chamber. Unable to stifle it, she yawned.

Disentangling herself, Clara rose from the instrument and brushed her skirts, as if to straighten them. The count reached out to draw her back.

'But you cannot leave yet. There are all the stars of the heavens to show you.'

'Thank you, Count,' she announced as she took her

17

leave. 'You have been most entertaining. And I believe you have met with some small success. Undoubtedly, my eyes are just a little more opened than they were before.'

Chapter Two

Clara awoke quite sure that the sounds of pots and pans from the kitchen were coming from the familiar range in the house at York. For a second she luxuriated, hovering just above sleep, before remembering with a start that her home no longer existed. It had been boarded up and sold to raise money for the business. As the count had said, each stop on their tour must now be her home.

At breakfast, her host announced the itinerary for the day. Sipping a tiny cup of the country's excellent bitter coffee, he outlined the beginnings of Clara's education.

'Today, I am completely at your disposal. I have arranged that we see the best pictures and curiosities in the city. The Hollanders are an industrious and tolerant people, but their capacity to create the greatest feasts for the eyes are unparalleled. First of all, however,' he added, pushing his coffee cup away across the linen cloth, 'I have arranged for a dressmaker to call on you, Miss Fairfax.'

'On me?' asked Clara in surprise, her mouth just filled with toast oozing with the rich yellow butter of the area.

'Yes, on you.'

'And why is that?' she asked indignantly. She could just see Tresa smirking from the corner of her eye

'You must not take offence at what I say,' he pronounced, in a manner Clara felt was bound to cause offence. 'It is just that I have noticed you are – how can I phrase it? – unused to dressing for the rigours of travel. It is usual to wait until we arrive in Paris before buying a new wardrobe but, in your case – well, I am sure even Dutch dressmakers are more adept than their English sisters.'

'What exactly is it you are trying to tell me?' She could hear Tresa unsuccessfully trying to stifle a burst of laughter.

'Exactly?' he retorted impatiently. 'I am exactly telling you that a dressmaker will call at exactly ten this morning. Is that exact enough for you, Miss Fairfax?'

It was. Clara could feel her face burning. How was she to behave with this mercurial, arrogant man? True, he had already appeared self-satisfied but now she detected the gigantic will behind his proud gestures. So – he would not be crossed, would he? Clara's own will burned within her. She, too, was unused to being ordered about. But for the moment she must submit. Later, perhaps, she would assert her own rights in the matter.

In the event, the dressmaker was sent up to her chamber. She was a small, busy woman whose rosy cheeks glowed below her lace cap. With a few words of halting English and many fussing gestures she soon achieved her task with the aid of pins, samples of cloth and a worn tape-measure. It was difficult for Clara to grasp exactly what it was the little dressmaker was intending to create.

'I will deliver the first gowns this evening.'

'But how is that possible? Surely it will take days to cut and stitch the clothes?'

'*Ja*, some – perhaps. But already I had the instructions of His Excellency. Your ball dress is almost complete. A few adjustments and – it is ready.'

But the woman would say no more; clearly, Clara was to expect a surprise. And, although a new wardrobe of elegant clothes was the dream of most girls of her age, Clara instead felt faintly dubious about the whole enterprise.

When alone once more, she lingered awhile in front of the long glass, admiring the stiff brown silk of her grubby English gown. She had chosen the cloth at the haberdasher's in Micklegate with her mother. It was Spitalfield's silk stitched into a good country style, without frivolity or show. It certainly was not refined, but there was something honest about the simple lines and plain fashioning.

Sighing, she decided that it was the rest of her she worried about – the plain oval of her face which lacked the seductive, glittering eyes of a Tresa, the dull corn-coloured hair. Then, there was what lay underneath. Surely the count must think her too thin, with her narrow shoulders and girlish waist? Yet, when he had pressed against her back in his study, she had felt his enjoyment, felt his hand's breadth beginning to explore the arc of her ribs. As she stared at her reflection, she tried to imagine herself through his eyes; then, with a sudden instinct, she saw her reflection bite her lip as if not daring to utter her own conclusions. An image had sprung into her mind – of herself naked, submitting, desirable.

She drew closer to the glass. Her eyes were not black, like Tresa's, but were clear sky-blue with a shadow of violet in the flecked iris. Until now, they had seen so little – the familiar house and family, church and town, a very occasional dancing party.

'What is it he wants these eyes to see?' she murmured to the girl in the reflection. The question alone made her shiver.

The count and Tresa were waiting for her together, cosily chatting in the parlour. The count rose and bowed slightly.

'Ah, at last. The days are short, you know, at this time of year. We must make the most of the daylight.'

She smiled at him as sweetly as she could. 'I am aware of that, Count. I would suggest therefore that we get out on our visits without the hindrance of dressmakers and such like in the morning.'

But any ill feeling was soon left behind them as the party stepped out on to the pristinely swept cobbled street. Until this point in her journey, Clara had seen only the ocean and empty vistas of land. Now, for the first time, the magic of discovering a new world transported her. The city itself was a picturesque mass of high, prettily gabled houses all pressed together around three rings of solidly frozen canals. Fine redstone embassies and churches lined the byways and, as the party ambled along carefully brushed paths, it was easy to marvel at the richness and good sense of this land. It was much like England in its placidity, but so different in its arcane decorations and quiet show of wealth.

Everywhere they looked, the house-proud Dutch women were at work, sweeping passageways and washing windows and doorsteps. Some wore the traditional wooden shoes of the country, with woollen shawls crossed at their waists and twisted gold hairpins stuck into their lace bonnets. But, for the most part, the people were as elegant as any in the world – jewelled and bewigged in fine furs and hooped dresses. By the time they reached the throngs at Dam Square, Clara felt her eyes grow round at the variety of Turks and Ottomans, sailors and peasant folk, all at work in the business of buying and selling. The air, too, was rich with the scent of their trade. Bales and boxes enriched the atmosphere with the scents of cloves, cinnamon, mace and nutmeg.

Jostling through the crowd, the count warned her to beware pickpockets. It was true that amongst all these riches were also less respectable folk. Moneychangers rattled their black tins before the faces of visitors, an impromptu puppet show was in progress at the front of the Stadthuis and buskers and mountebanks fought the chatter and good spirits of the crowd to be heard.

However, this public show was not the count's destination. Leading his party around to an imposing door-way, he seemed only to have to pronounce his name and with some reverence they were ushered forward to see other, more esoteric treasures. That day they saw the great paintings of the Prince of Orange's collection, the silver and instruments of the East India Company, the works of Messrs Rembrandt, Van Dyck and other Dutch Masters. At the Stadthuis, they admired the great marble floor set with maps of the two hemispheres of the world and saw the windows at the Old and New churches, which the Dutch called 'kirks', like their Scottish brethren. After lunch, they strolled along the Mall and eventually found themselves in the Begijnhof, a little circle of ancient houses given over to a group of Catholic Sisters.

Just as Clara had warmed to the signs of rigorous Calvinism around the city, now she noticed her companions grow more eager to converse with their fellow Papists. As the Count graciously questioned one of the poor sisters about the biblical plaques in the place, Clara wandered across the snow-covered area at the centre, breathing in the crisp air and considering that maybe travel was not such a bad thing after all. Indeed, perhaps the count was correct – to be exposed to ever more interesting visual impressions certainly did enliven the spirit. She had not felt so exhilarated, so full of wonder, since she was a child.

It was as she mused over the pretty scene, admiring the quaint gabled houses and evidence of neat patch-work gardens tended by the women, that a wonderfully familiar sound drifted over towards her. A man dressed as conservatively as a Scottish minister was conversing with another more finely dressed, bewigged fellow. All they spoke of were some mutual friends but, to Clara, their conversation seemed like the most eloquent melody. They were speaking in English. Not only that, their accents indicated most strongly that they were of English provenance. As longingly as a child staring into a toy shop, Clara eyed them from a dozen or so paces across the snow. Then the count called out to her that they must be on their way.

It would have been impossible, of course, to approach the men without impropriety; but now that she was alerted, Clara took a little more note of her surroundings. The redbrick church which stood at the centre of the Begijnhof, which she had assumed to be a Roman Catholic place of worship, did indeed bear a sign in English. Beneath the Dutch lettering, which seemed to Clara to look as if a child had scattered the alphabet, removing most of the vowels, was a notice proclaiming that this was the English and Scottish Presbyterian Church of Amsterdam. Making a mental note to herself of the times of the services, Clara hurried back to her companions, holding this fragment of information secretly within her heart.

Back in the warmth of the apartments on the Prinsengracht, the first of Clara's new clothes were delivered after tea. Despite her legs aching from the long day's exercise, she was curious enough to run up to her chamber and open the silken bags which protected a vast array of garments.

'Oh, I cannot believe it. Are they really for me?' she gasped at the little Dutchwoman.

'Ja, ja, we must try them on in a system. Come along. There are some undergarments here.'

Clara let herself be pummelled and pushed; this time, she threw off the brown silk like the redundant chrysalis of a newly transformed butterfly. In answer to the woman's encouraging nods, she reluctantly stripped off all her clothes. Standing soft and naked before the dressmaker, she held out her arms and let herself be dressed like a doll. Firstly a chemise of the finest semi-transparent muslin drifted past her eyes. As light as featherdown, it clung to her curves, outlining the twin points of her breasts and rounded buttocks. Then her waist was lusciously squeezed tight by a pair of lilac satin stays which may have looked delicate, with their clusters of ribbons and rosettes, but the whalebones and ivory busk were as strong as steel. The dressmaker pulled the laces as tight as she was able. There were hoops hung on linen around her waist and, over that, a petticoat of the finest peacock-blue damask. In matching blue were the silk skirts, wide in the continental style with ruches and frills and furbelows falling away to the hemline.

Clara watched herself being transformed in the long mirror; the little woman pinned her bodice, the embroidered triangle of a stomacher and lace sleeves in place, until the whole garment swayed and flounced about her like a shining confection of satin and lace.

'Oh, it is too, too beautiful.'

Now Clara could see that, with the best clothes to set off her white skin, she did indeed look quite lovely. Gone was the bobbin lace cap – instead the dressmaker had produced an *aigrette* to pin in her hair: a little jewelled clasp set with three exquisite feathers.

'Yes, but what will I wear in the day, until the ball?'

The Dutchwoman looked at her with a puzzled expression. 'But, mademoiselle! This is not your ball dress. This is only a day dress for you to wear in the city. *Mijn God!* Do you think this is the best I can create! You can wear this in Paris – it is *à la française*, the latest style – but it is only a day dress.'

And so, a velvet pelisse was produced to wear over the peacock-blue dress, and then another gorgeous gown of deep salmon-coloured sateen worked in a pattern of swans and cygnets.

'Now we must take all this off.'

'The underclothes as well?'

'The ball gown makes its own arrangements,' the dressmaker replied in her quaint speech.

Clara frowned when the final bag was rent asunder. The dress was as sheer as a veil, of midnight black silk net of the highest quality. It floated down from the dressmaker's hands in a cloud of frothy black fabric.

'It is a strange colour for a ball dress.'

'It is very elegant, mademoiselle. It will show off your skin superbly.'

'But what chemise do I wear?'

The old Dutch woman looked at her quizzically. 'There is no chemise, no petticoat to spoil the line. A half-corset here to accentuate the waist. That is all.'

'How extraordinary.'

But, as she was helped into the undergarment, Clara frowned at her reflection in the mirror. A black band of whalebone-stiffened satin pinched suggestively at her waist, flaring wide at her hips, pushing her breasts hard upwards above the stiff fabric. Unlike a conical, long-waisted English corset, the effect was dramatic; her usually pert breasts were forced emphatically outward in two globes of creamy flesh. The pink nipples were framed beneath, appearing oddly voluptuous, like a courtesan offering her wares for all to view.

'I cannot see why there is no chemise,' Clara complained, holding her arms crossed, so the dressmaker would not see how sensuous the effect was. But, as she bent to roll a pair of finest black silk stockings over her calves she glanced again into the long mirror. Was this how her fiancé saw her? Her pale, rounded rear stuck provocatively in the air, thrown into sharp relief by the tops of the black stockings and cruelly laced corset.

'Be careful, now; this fabric is so sheer it may tear.'

The dressmaker carefully fitted the dress to the very curves of her body. At last Clara stood back to see the grand effect. The gown was highly stylised in shape, with a skin-tight bodice and triple flounces at the elbows and hem. But the fabric was almost transparent – the shape and detail of her breasts were as clear as day beneath the film of black silk. When she turned, she could just see the length of her legs moving beneath the skirt. A careful eye could even see the moving curves of her flanks as she pirouetted and the seductive darker patch below the pit of her stomach. She might as well parade naked, only that the tantalising fabric added a powerfully salacious effect to the outfit.

'I cannot wear that! It is disgusting. It is obscene!'

'Leave us now, Frau. I will attend my fiancée.'

Spinning around, Clara found that the count stood at the door. He was leaning against the door frame, observing her with a most mischievous, insolent expression.

'How long have you been watching? How dare you come to my private chamber?'

But, as the little dressmaker scurried away, Anton strode up to her, taking her fingers firmly but gently in his two hands. 'We are betrothed now, my dear,' he uttered firmly, as if to a child. 'Your chamber is my chamber.'

'How dare you!' she cried, her face flushed, her eyes pricking with furious tears. 'When you said that we would not be as man and wife, I trusted you. That means I keep my own privacy until the end of the summer. It is only a promise, as yet. My body is still my own, to have or to see.'

His hands, which had gripped hers, loosened a little. He was very close; she was aware of his parted lips hovering close above hers, of the warmth of his body just brushing against the fabric of the fabulous dress. How she loathed his insolence, his lack of civil manners! Yet, at the same time, she had to stifle a desire running through her like a molten river: to lean against him, cling to him, submit to him. Something in the very depths of her ached, something she had never felt before. When she looked at the vein pulsing at his neck or watched his dry lips, she felt it pound even stronger. What is this? she asked herself. I cannot bear this man – and yet I could melt before him, falling to my knees. To do what? She did not know.

'The dress is magnificent upon you,' he whispered. With a lingering caress of the sensitive palms of her hands, he directed his gaze downward. From the nerves in her hands a shiver passed down her arms and deep inside to her very centre.

The neckline was extraordinarily low, the gossamer fabric barely teasing across the pink outlines of her nipples. Yet it hardly mattered – so translucent was the cloth that the very outlines of her nipples were clear – the pink areolae showing clearly and the pointed bud-like nipples.

'I cannot wear this.' She found that she, too, was whispering. It was as if he had drawn her into a conspiracy against her modesty. 'What will people think?'

'Stand still. I will tell you if it doesn't suit.'

Shyly, she stood as he paced back, pursing his lips a little. Looking down, she could see that the skirts were almost transparent. She might hardly have bothered to put the gown on at all, for the narrow corset and stockings showed through quite boldly. He pursed his lips and she waited.

'It is remarkable. Quite lovely. Exquisitely provocative.'

He spoke in a low, breathless voice. And she could see from his heightened colour that he was agitated by the sight of her. Suddenly, her fury boiled over, smothering her own desire.

'What do you think sir, that I am your rag-doll to be dressed? That you may creep up on me, come into my room, have me pose like a trollop?'

'Oh, yes, yes,' he laughed, his eyes creasing with amusement. 'When you shout, your breasts rise and fall magnificently.'

'Get out of my room,' she shouted, picking up a fan and striking him feebly on the arm. 'I will not be your marionette. Go to Tresa; she would love to dress up for you.'

'Tresa?' he laughed, then thought a moment. 'Perhaps. But she is not of the same type. She would enjoy this, so the effect would be spoiled.'

'I will not wear it!'

'If you are frightened that you will draw attention to yourself, you are wrong. It is a select private party. Most of the guests will be dressed in such a – pleasing manner. You would attract more attention in that old frumpy brown sack.'

He snatched her hand to his lips and she felt again a tremor quake within her, although she frowned peevishly at him.

'Believe me. You look matchless. The black makes your skin glow like pearl.'

Clara was speechless. Catching sight of herself in the mirror, she had to agree that, once the general effect of whorishness wore off, the dress truly did suit her shape and colouring. And the sensation of the tight fabric against her naked skin was subtly pleasing. Seeing her hesitate, the count continued, kissing the soft tips of her fingertips so that little runnels of flame seemed to pass into Clara's blood.

'This boorish intrusion into your room. Forgive me.' His limpid brown eyes met hers and, with a blush, she nodded, lowering her gaze. 'I promise on my honour I will not enter your room again without your permission. Can we be friends?'

'Of course,' she replied, swallowing hard.

'Only – please wear the dress. You see, I have also ordered a costume to complement yours. We will be like the Lord and Lady of the Night. I beg you, do me the pleasure of accepting the gift and wear it for me. Just on the one occasion.'

Clara felt herself impossibly trapped. When she thought of his outlay on even the clothes which had appeared up till now – it was maybe more than had ever been spent on her in her whole life. Was she being ungrateful? In the glass, she could see the back of his coat and black hair as he held her hand, beseeching her. He had made her appear beautiful. It would be cruel to refuse him.

'If you insist. I will wear it the once.'

On the dressmaker's return, Clara asked her to dress her in the peacock-blue gown again. With her hair recurled and the *aigrette* pinned coquettishly to her curls, she saw herself again transformed. But, since the count's departure, her agitation would not leave her.

29

'I am too excited to sit quietly and wait for dinner.'

Glancing down at the brick-paved thoroughfare below, she could see many people hurrying home from their day's labours, some with small hand-carts whilst others loitered in the streets, smoking pipes or warming their hands over red-coaled braziers.

'Shall I call the count to accompany you?' the dress-maker asked as she folded her bags, ready to depart.

'No, I do not want to disturb him again. It would be pleasant, just this once, to slip out alone. Have you never felt that before, when you arrive in a strange place, that to really know it one must wander about alone?'

The old Dutch woman smiled indulgently and helped her into the velvet pelisse.

Once alone, Clara strode quickly through the little byways, occasionally watching out for the tall redbrick steeple of the English church. Tracing her way across a series of bridges which looked to be those she had crossed with the count, she found herself at the church door. Yet it was not the church on the green of the Begijnhof. Tired now, she stretched to peer up above the roofs of the mass of buildings. Many spires of different shapes and hues were scattered across the city. She must have wasted a quarter of an hour, at least.

Slowly circling, trying with all her might to remember the way, she finally fixed on a second reddish spire, quite a distance into the dusk, further towards the thronged masts of the Arsenal. It had been so easy when the count led the way; she had scarcely looked about herself. Now that she was alone, each canal was edged by the same leafless trees, each bridge bore similar crests and finials; and all the pathways were of identical red-paved bricks. Even worse, she could feel her feet begin to pinch with the cold beneath her new overshoes. Suddenly, she wished she had never left the roaring fire at the apartment on the Prinsengracht.

At last, Clara resolved on a plan. She would simply walk to the second church and then turn around and go back to their lodgings. If the second spire was not the

English church, she would abandon the search immediately and try to speak to anyone respectable in the locality; to continue wandering alone at night would certainly be foolish. If it were the church, she could at least ask for assistance in finding her way back.

Now the byways grew narrower still. Entering a part of the city less frequented by wealthy visitors, she could not help but notice that the people paid her greater attention. She passed a low, evil-looking doorway; two smokers made loud remarks as she struggled down a set of narrow steps, greatly impeded by the wide hoops of her skirt. Neither was the high-walled alley at the bottom of the steps any more welcoming. With growing trepidation, Clara walked ahead, dreading turning back to face the noisy smokers and perilous steps again, and yet equally fearful of what lay ahead. Occasional figures flitted by her in the gloom – ragged women and hungry-looking children, a couple of inebriated sailors. Despite the cold, she felt an uncomfortable heat and constriction rise from her throat. How could she get out of here?

There was a fork in the alley. It was impossible to see over the tops of the four- or five-storey tenements decorated only with a few ragged curtains and washing lines. With wavering resolve, Clara took the left fork, guessing she could smell the scent of the sea. Each step seemed to take her further and further into a shadowy labyrinth, surrounded by the odours of long-cooked food, filth and bitter smoke from the unseen inhabitants who lived behind the walls. Then at last she turned a final corner. Before her was a wide thoroughfare, the open air of a broad canal. And there, just visible now in the dusk, was the welcome shape of the English church.

Slipping inside the heavy doors, she silently passed into the gloomy interior, dropping as soon as she might into one of the empty back pews where, at last, she could recover her poise a little.

The service was only sparsely attended that wintry evening; the lack of a large, merry congregation was somewhat galling to her after all her adversities. While

31

the gentleman she had overheard speaking earlier in the gardens of the Begijnhof led the service in the melodic tones of a Scotsman, Clara's fellow worshippers largely collected about the altar – a few elderly gentlemen, a middle-aged couple in the dress of gentlefolk, a younger man and a large family of parents and five restless offspring.

Sitting quietly and unseen, Clara considered that she must make herself known at the end of the service, if only to obtain guidance on her return journey. Outside, the sky had been rapidly darkening and the possibility of a night frost made the return journey rather more perilous than she had at first anticipated. Consequently, as the organist played out the service, Clara stood in the aisle, ready to greet the minister and call on his assistance.

He was a rather severe, thick-set man with black brows and a horse-hair pigtail wig. As he strode towards her, it was only with some timorousness that Clara nodded, extending her hand.

'Sir, may I ask for your assistance?'

The minister started. He had clearly not seen her, coming as she did from the gloom behind the tall pews.

'Assistance?' He peered at her as if she were a specimen in a rare collection. 'Do I hear an English voice? You have the look of a continental.'

'I am Miss Clara Fairfax of York. I should be so grateful, sir, for your assistance. This evening I was tempted out to stroll in the city by a kind native of the city but consequently I have lost my way. Seeing the spire of your church, I came here to beg your help in returning to my lodgings. I am utterly without direction.'

The minister had been joined by the young gentleman, who was showing a great deal of interest in the conversation. Clara nodded to him but he simply continued to stare, no doubt also intrigued by the appearance of a rather showily dressed young Englishwoman appearing without any chaperone or servant.

'Miss Fairfax, you must tell me where you are lodging, for me to be of any assistance,' the minister declared.

'I have lodgings on the Prinsengracht. Number one thousand and fifty-seven.'

'That is not an English lodging house. Do you have connections in Holland?'

'None at all, sir. I am one of a party with my fiancé, Count Anton di Malibran.'

It was not difficult for Clara to detect an expression of some repugnance pass over the clergyman's face. He seemed to look her up and down again as if she already wore that degrading transparent ball gown. How she wished she had kept the simple brown outfit on this evening.

'May I be impertinent enough to offer my assistance?' broke in the young man at this difficult juncture. The smile across his broad features felt to Clara like water on a parched tongue. 'I am on my way to the Westerkirk and can easily take a detour along that stretch of the canal. It would be a pleasure to escort you to your door.'

'Oh, thank you, thank you,' Clara managed effusively, clutching his hand in gratitude. 'You cannot imagine how fearful it can be, wandering alone in such a strange place, knowing none of the language or customs.'

Still she was aware of the minister scowling at her. With a severe compression of his beetle brows, he addressed the young man.

'Very well, John. It would save me a chore if you would escort this young lady back to those who must now be out of their minds with worry at her whereabouts. Miss Fairfax,' he concluded, taking her fingers limply, 'I trust you will take more care than to wander away from your protectors again like this. Even the best shepherd cannot tend bad sheep.'

'Of course, sir. I do hope we meet soon under happier circumstances.'

But the minister was off, clearly anxious to quit his church as soon as he was able.

* * *

The young man was named John Palmer, a native of Boston in Lincolnshire, as evidenced by the pleasant slight burr to his voice. With the greatest courtesy, he offered Clara his arm and together they again set forth into what was now indisputably night. But this time, Clara saw only the surface delights of the city as she and Mr Palmer conversed in an easy and open manner. Even as she listened, she assessed him in the way a woman will. He was not the cleverest of men but seemed kindly and was not above laughing at his own misfortunes on the road. Somewhat broader of figure than the count, his face and nose were also rather wide but his eyes were clear and his mouth was wide, with good teeth. Though he wore powder on his hair, she thought him naturally a fair-haired man. Although his green coat and waistcoat were rather travel-worn his neck-linen was clean, she noted, and his cloak was heavy fur-lined wool.

The second son of a country gentleman, Mr Palmer was also making an extended Grand Tour of the continent as a part of his education, before following family business interests in the county of Nottinghamshire. Clara listened to him attentively as he described his route. For the first time, she realised the pleasure she was missing in not having compatriots with whom to share the perils and pleasures of the road.

'Of course, after Paris, I must get to Rome for the art – but whether over the Mount Cenis pass or by sea from Marseilles, I cannot decide. What route will you take to Italy, Miss Fairfax?'

'I have no idea. It is not my place to be an adviser on such things. The count is well travelled and will no doubt make the right decision based upon his judgement.'

'So it is not an educational tour for your sake?'

'Yes,' Clara murmured. 'It is. But the syllabus is devised by the count. I am entirely at his disposal.'

Mr Palmer halted, for they had reached the final bridge over the Prinsengracht canal.

'Miss Fairfax. Forgive my impertinence if I overstep

the boundaries of our short acquaintance. Only there is something I must ask you.'

His wide face was so serious as he uttered this, his eyes so fixed upon her face, that Clara was for a moment taken aback. 'Of course. Only ask.'

'Are you happy? I mean, is your current arrangement suiting you? I only ask because it is an uncommon situation for you to be travelling alone like this.'

'Am I happy? Why, I cannot assure you of that, Mr Palmer. But I believe I am content.'

He nodded gravely, as if this were a very great matter to him.

'Only make me a promise, if you will. I will sleep happier at night if you tell me that if you are ever not so contented, you will seek me out. In every city, we must register with the consuls, so you might easily find me through that route. In truth, I am fearful for you, Miss Fairfax, travelling alone with foreigners, so far from your English family and friends.'

'Mr Palmer.' It was now Clara's turn to speak warmly. Grasping his hands in hers she looked up into that honest, round face. 'I have no reason to believe I will not be content on my tour and that I will not eventually be content in Italy. But, if it pleases you, I make that promise. I solemnly swear that if I need you, I will seek you out.'

'Thank you. Good evening, Miss Fairfax.'

Tipping his tricorne, Mr Palmer waited as Clara climbed the steps and knocked on the grand wooden door. Then, as the servant arrived with the lamp, she slipped into the warmth of the house, aware of him still standing on the bridge, poised as a statue, looking on after her.

Chapter Three

*T*he count raised his head laconically from his glass of porter. 'Ah, our prodigal returns. I should be obliged if you would wait for me in my study, Miss Fairfax.'

Clara looked about the dining room. Dinner had clearly ended; the candles were burning low. Tresa kept her head low, too, no doubt struggling to stifle her amusement at Clara's disgrace. There was something in the count's studied indifference of voice that alarmed her. She decided to test him.

'I am rather tired, Count. Perhaps we could speak in the morning.'

The look of molten fury he shot from beneath his dark brows was enough to quell any notion of rebellion. She pretended to stifle a yawn and then smiled brightly. 'Very well. I shall wait upstairs.'

With a start, she turned on her heel and scampered up the stairs. Really, what a petty, petulant creature this man was, she said to herself. She had scarcely been gone a few hours at all. Did he consider her a prisoner? Certainly, at least until they married, she would do as she pleased.

The count's chamber seemed itself to be expectant; the fire crackled in the grate, a book lay open on the table, and the ornate grandfather clock solemnly ticked away the time. Clara wandered about the ruby damask walls, admiring the globe with which he had outlined her education, gazing at a fine picture of a bowl of flowers, trying to settle her jolted nerves. This man stirred up the most violently contradictory emotions within her – fury and attraction, derision and gratitude, fear and fascination. Why could he not be more like that plain Mr Palmer? One could immediately see that the Englishman's behaviour was always well within the prescribed bounds of acceptable manners. He would not bark at one and order one off to his study. And he had put it within her reach to search him out if she needed him. He really had been extraordinarily kind.

Idly caressing the telescope still placed at the window, Clara watched the few skaters still gliding down the canal, some carrying lamps or tall lighted candles. Placing her eye to the lens, she tried her hand at surveying the city – getting a sudden view of the spire of the English Church in the moonlight. Then, as she turned the brass screw to focus the image, she felt a pressure on her shoulder.

'What is it you have found?'

'I do wish you would not creep up so silently!' His sudden closeness had almost made her jump out of her skin.

He reached out and stayed her hand from adjusting the telescope. 'Let me see.'

Irritated, Clara let him stoop before her and gaze as she had done, down the telescope. From this close proximity she could smell the fresh scent of pomade that rose from his abundant black hair. Tonight he had not tied it and it hung loose at his shoulders, falling in wild tresses of midnight black. Yet she could not help but notice that in quality and style of dress, he was quite superior to any Englishman. His long frock coat of forest green was worked with lilies and narcissi embroidered in filigree silver lace. From the buckles on his shoes to the gleam of his fingernails, he truly was a man of style.

'How apt. It is the English church you pine after so desperately.'

Clara opened her mouth to make some retort, but again there was something in his clipped tone that stopped her. With a gesture of frustration, he strode to the fireplace, throwing off his coat, standing indignantly in his ruffled shirtsleeves and long embroidered waistcoat.

'Miss Fairfax. You force me to speak my mind. These last few hours, only one question has run round and round my mind, like a horse without a bridle. I am sorry if the liquor now speaks but, lady, you have forced me to the comfort of the decanter. Why is it you detest me? Why do you cast scorn on our betrothal? Why do you despise my generosity?'

Listening to this tirade, Clara found her limbs began to tremble. The man's passion was quite genuine; whatever offence she had committed burnt like fire in his eyes.

'What do you mean?' she asked uncertainly.

'Do I need to spell it out? Are you stupid as well as mischievous?'

Taking a deep breath, she did her best to compose her voice and features. 'Sir, I do not understand my offence. Until I understand it, I cannot explain it.'

With a reckless gesture, the count flung a glass goblet from the table into the fire. Accompanying an alarming crash was a sudden roar of purple flame as the contents of the glass ignited and then quickly died away.

'So, we must speak some truths, must we?' he declared. 'I consider myself to be not an ungenerous man. Today, I felt I discerned some small gratitude in your bearing when I gave my time to show you the sights of the city. I have seen them before; Tresa has seen them before; but to see just one expression of wonder on your face as you absorbed new impressions seemed to me a fully adequate reward.

'Later, you thanked me profusely for the gift of your new wardrobe. Indeed, I believe you said that you had

38

never before had such generosity lavished upon your person in the whole of your life. I do not look for such thanks. But I do demand respect.'

As she listened, a peculiar crawling sensation crept across the skin of Clara's back. Everything he said was true. Had she behaved badly? What if he was right? He was staring at her, his black eyes glittering with affront.

'In the past twenty-four hours, I have made a number of promises to you. To educate you, to respect your person until we marry, and – at your request – to respect the privacy of your chamber. Miss Fairfax, I demand that you reciprocate!'

The beginnings of an uncomfortable understanding were forming in her mind.

'I made only one simple requirement of you. That you would at least respect the aims of my educational system and desist from seeking out other English travellers. Yet we have been here barely one day and off you go, scurrying like a duck to the pond, hanging about with your despicable English cronies.'

'I did no harm,' she succeeded in muttering, as he paused for breath.

'But you have done harm,' he pronounced. 'You have done harm to my reputation. You are under my care but tonight you have dressed yourself in an outfit from your wedding gift, travelled without a chaperone to the one place you have promised me not to visit and picked up an admirer as adeptly as any streetwalker hanging about the Dam square tonight.'

'How dare you speak to me this way!' Clara felt her cheeks burn crimson red.

'How dare you bring a strange man almost up to my door!'

For a long moment, they stood facing each other across the Turkey carpet. Then the count inhaled deeply and composed himself. 'Very well,' he continued. 'For I see we cannot continue like this. I will be generous once more. Miss Fairfax, if you feel you have made a terrible mistake in coming here and accepting this arrangement, you must say so now. I am not an unreasonable man. If you wish to be released from your engagement, no more will be said. I will discreetly arrange for your return home to England.'

Clara's mind whirled with irreconcilable feelings. To return home? But she did not want to return home. What life was waiting for her there? 'No, sir. I will stay.'

'And will you submit to my regime?'

It was not in her nature to do so. With a last spark of revolt, she glared at him. 'Very well. So long as your regime is reasonable.'

'Reasonable it is not. Do you submit?'

She could not speak; her mouth was dry, her pulses racing.

'I ask you again. If you stay, will you submit to my will?'

She could not speak. She could hear the pendulum of the clock as it leadenly marked away the time. The fire in the hearth spat and crackled and then subsided.

'In Italy, a man will not bear such insolence from his wife,' he exploded. 'I fear you are begging me to extend your education in a way you will not much care for.' As if bursting with rage, he began to unbutton his waistcoat and threw it over a chair, so his linen shirt hung free.

'In my country, a man takes action when his woman disdains him. I am afraid the time has come when you must learn a harsh lesson.'

Clara watched him in complete bafflement. Then, striding across the room, he picked up a fine, narrow walking-cane.

'Over to the table, lady. I fear you must learn who is master here.'

'What on earth?' began Clara, unable to comprehend what she suddenly guessed was being planned for her. It was impossible.

Flexing the supple cane between his fingers, the count waited with an ironic smile. Then laconically, he tapped the smooth table-top with the tip of the stick.

'Come along, now; it will soon be over.'

'You cannot mean,' she began, feeling her heart about to burst from her ribs, 'to strike me with that thing?'

'I ask you quite openly, do you wish to stay? If you do, your lesson must be learnt.'

Again, she could not reply.

'I take your silence to be acquiescence. Come here, and this matter can be over quickly and smartly.'

'I cannot. It is against all propriety.'

The count's mouth pursed in irritation. 'In a moment, I will call my servant. It is your decision. I will either instruct him to arrange passage for you to England tomorrow or help me to administer your dues. Personally, I should rather this was just between us, in private – but if you will not come here now, it is no longer my choice. My servant can just as easily hold you still.'

Quaking, Clara took a few paces towards her fiancé.

'Just lean across the table. I promise to be quick.'

Clara stared down at the expanse of polished wood and then into the count's open face. She could see no escape. Certainly, she did not want to bundled off home like an unwanted package.

'What do you mean?' she asked, looking at him for help.

Very gently, he helped her lay her palms straight across the wood, with her face to the side, gazing at the embers of the fire. There was something in his gentleness that unsettled her. It was a quite provoking mix of tenderness and barbarity.

'What are you doing?' she gasped. She could feel him grappling with the skirts of her gown.

'You do not think I can administer the punishment through these? A man must always beat his wife on the flesh.'

At this, Clara began to wriggle but, like a velvet clamp, his hands surrounded her wrists. 'Listen,' he breathed softly, 'it will be over in a moment and all will be paid for. It is not as if I haven't already seen you undressed.'

So she relaxed a little and, with firm dexterity, she felt

41

him lift the heavy damask of her gown above her waist. Then her matching petticoat was lifted and she was acutely aware of his eyes on the thin chemise. With her eyes closed, she could just imagine the provoking sight so close to his eyes – her rounded rear forced upward by the angle of the table, with the thin muslin stretched like a thin veil over the twin globes of flesh. His fingers now seemed more languid as he lifted the final wrapping and she felt the air of the room pass over her bare flesh.

'You are not uncomfortable?' he asked, his voice slightly hoarse. Then, with both hands he gently guided her hips to the centre. Closing her eyes, Clara felt her insides suddenly melt with pleasure. What was it she wanted him to do? She barely knew – only that the ache within her was building to a pain, an agony. Suddenly, she felt herself stretch languorously and, in so doing, felt the very centre of her sex press provokingly against the hard edge of the table. It was all she could do not to sigh with abandonment.

She could feel his eyes pressing against her flesh, admiring the curve of her rump, passing over the plumpness of her thigh before it was pinched by the garters holding her silk stockings. Then, in a voice almost choked with emotion, he asked if she were ready. Quite speechless, she nodded.

The first blow fell – a burning, stinging stroke. With a cry of anguish, Clara bucked beneath it.

'Please, no,' she cried. A moment later, she felt the impact of the blow in a long stripe that stung like fire across her bottom. Hot and sore it was, and then, as the seconds passed, she felt a profoundly sensuous glow pass through her body. It was as if all the nerves of her body were filled with flame, from the tips of her fingers to the depths of her sex. She had just enough presence of mind to stifle an enthusiastic groan as it rose in her throat.

'It is a necessary evil,' she could hear him reply to her earlier cry. Yet his voice, too, was betraying no lack of arousal. Then, with fingers as gentle as a woman's, he caressed her writhing rear, bringing it back to centre. This time, as she heard the hiss of the cane falling, Clara could not help but tense in anticipation. But when it fell, she jolted so violently that again the pleasure exceeded the pain as her body was rubbed ecstatically against the hard wooden edge. Again and again, he let the cane fall and, with each blow, Clara felt a terrifying dam of carnality mount excruciatingly within her flesh. Now she could feel the tight whalebone of her stays rubbing incessantly against her breasts, abrading the stiff nipples, massaging the sensitive flesh to a frenzy. With each blow, a fire burnt stronger in her sex until she wanted more and more.

Now she longed for him to fall on her, to pull her thighs wide open, to take her, to claim her, to force his flesh into hers. Suddenly it was too much – with a sob escaping her trembling lips, she felt him once more pull her hips forward, drawing her throbbing vulva over the hard wood. Something was about to break asunder inside her. With a cry, she felt her fingers rake the smooth wood of the table. She could smell sweat and lust in the air. Closing her eyes, she imagined him forcing his cock into her pliant quim, riding her like the willing beast she was, lifting her on the table and scorching her insides with the explosive impact of his penis. With a moan, she let herself go, ready to slip over into complete abasement. With her eyes closed tightly, she felt herself at the very top of a long, slippery slope. Just another caress, another scorching kiss from the fierce brutality of the cane and she would fall – ecstatic, moaning, convulsed – into his arms.

'Very well,' she heard him announce, as if speaking from a tremendous distance. 'You have taken your punishment.'

With a jolt, she looked about herself. It seemed that the room had righted itself around her. She was aware of Anton offering her his hand, to help her rise. Aching and stiff with pent frustration, she let herself be lifted.

She felt hot, sticky and dishevelled. He, too, was clearly warmed by his exertions; his eyes were black and lustrous as they followed her every movement.

'You must see the results of my art,' he said in a low voice.

Quite docile now, whether from extreme surprise or the floodgate of her feelings, she let herself be led by him. In the corner of the room was a tall looking-glass of the French style.

'Look at the beauty of your suffering,' he breathed, gently lifting her skirts to her waist.

Indeed, looking in the glass, she could see the criss-cross of reddened stripes across her pale flesh. Although the skin had not broken, the weals were slightly raised and the whole area of her rear was smartly heated and crimsoned. A peculiar excitement gripped her at the sight. But why should pain arouse her?

'Is it warm?'

She nodded, quite unable to speak. In a moment, he had returned from the window and, with his hand cupped, pressed something so exquisitely cold against her that the sensation was almost painful in its cool relief. Very tenderly, he was anointing her with freezing snow from the windowsill. Yet, as his fingers spread across her skin, she had to struggle with every shred of her self-control not to cry out and press her pubis hard against him. Gently, she felt his fingers work across the rounded flesh, nearing the sensitive parting that made her want to scream with desire. If he would only go further, press downward, probe into her sex, relieve her of this aching and longing that made her want to throw herself at his feet and press even her face – her lips, even – against the salt of his skin.

'For some, there is pleasure as well as pain,' he whispered. Her eyes were closed now as he rubbed the last of the melted snow into her wounds. 'Are you of that kind?'

Deftly, his fingertips inched between the parting of the two cheeks of her flesh. With mounting anguish she felt him seek out the secret crimson flesh of her sex. With a gasp she felt the very tip of his index finger sink into the honeyed heat where she felt a chasm was waiting, opening for him to take her. Almost swooning as his fingers reached into the wetness, Clara bit her lip hard, ashamed to think he had conquered her so easily.

But he paused in his explorations. She felt him tense and his breath come fast. Then, with a groan, he withdrew. Opening her eyes, she saw that, as they stood face to face, he was watching her reflection in the glass, gaining every particle of satisfaction from the visual as well as tactile effects of his caresses. Searchingly, she looked up into his face as he stared into the mirror. Again, she wanted to kiss and lick and taste him, she ached for the hard pressure of his lips. Suddenly, he glanced down into her face and smiled a sad little smile.

'You will not disappoint me, will you, by proving too easy a conquest?'

'Of course not,' she answered haughtily, with some semblance of composure.

Quickly, he embraced her and, in that moment, she felt again that she might faint against him, so dizzying was her craving for his body. For, at that moment, for a priceless second, she felt the true extent of his own need for her. It was there as he pressed against her, in the hard bulk of his cock, crushed against the pit of her stomach. There was no doubt at all that he, too, was in a state of extremity. Now, with a covert glance, she noticed the protrusion from beneath his shirt. With a rather sluttish movement, she turned around, knowing she pressed against him quite provokingly, so she even heard his breath gasp and a groan catch in his throat.

'I must retire to bed,' she said, with a little more equanimity as she saw her full reflection in the mirror. What a transformation he had effected. Her hair was unruly and dishevelled, her face quite warm and flushed; even her throat and breasts glowed with heat. She could see the count close behind her, absorbing her bright eyes and disorderly undress.

'Yes, I must bathe. But just a simple adjustment before you leave,' he smiled.

Then, reaching down around her, he reached for her right breast. With a look of horror, Clara saw in the mirror that, as a result of her writhing exertions, one of her nipples had worked free of her dress and peeped over the mass of lace and ribbon. Again, with those delicately sensual fingertips, he cupped the pink rosebud of flesh for a second. Like a hot knife, she felt a dagger of desire travel through her skin, making a place deep inside her abdomen cramp and release. Then it was over. He had tucked the sensitive little bead of flesh away and she was left with only empty, languid yearning.

'Thank you,' she whispered.

'Is it only for this simple adjustment you thank me – or for your chastisement, also?' he asked, smiling wickedly.

But, with a frown, Clara pulled away from him. Suddenly, she could no longer bear the torment of his nearness. Primly lifting her skirts, she strode back to her room.

Yet it was not so easy to retire for the night. On a wave of relief at her near escape, Clara clumped back to her room, carefully locking the door behind her. What had he done to her? Throwing off the stiff bodice of her gown, she could see in her mirror that her breasts were swollen and engorged, pouring over the tight restriction of her corsets. How was it he had touched her? Gently, she reached out her hand and brushed the nipple as he had done. Instantly, it grew stiff and hard, almost unbearable to touch. If only he had gone on and on. Tentatively, in the soft candlelight of her chamber, Clara reached up and touched both breasts at once. With a cry, she felt a tremor of excitement grip her as they responded, stiffening and teased, sending sensations of abandonment through every nerve in her body.

When we are man and wife, she daydreamed, he must

caress me like this. On and on she squeezed the scarlet tips, feeling her thighs tremble as the waves of pleasure grew like an unstoppable tide.

Reaching out for a chair, she set herself down, lifting her skirts as he had done, surveying the creamy skin of her thighs and the crimson of her sex, surrounded by a thin covering of golden curls. Now she saw that she was ready and wet and glistening. What was it he planned to do? Bathe?

Closing her eyes, she conjured before her inner eye a picture of him also undressing, anxious to relieve his body of the unbearable poundings of his flesh. She could see the bronze expanse of his chest, well-formed body, long muscular flanks. And what she had felt pressed against her she now imagined – a heavy, fleshy cock, stiff with desire, hot to the touch, throbbing for release.

With her eyes closed, she parted her lips with abandonment. As if with a life of their own, her fingers drifted to the juncture of her parted thighs. She had only to imagine his cock deep inside her to feel a spasm begin, a quavering of desire as her body trembled to have possession. With sweet relief, she let her fingers fondle the wet lips that now felt silky and swollen, eager to possess, intensely pleasurable to her touch. Faster and faster she rubbed at her slowly swelling and glistening clitoris, all the while seeing Anton now in his bath, now similarly unable to resist exploring the delights of his own frustrated body. She imagined his hand gripping his own penis, then instead replaced it with her own. In her mind she could feel the hard muscle, the tautness and flinching desire.

Unable to resist any longer, her index finger found the entrance to her own aching sex and, with some trepidation, she pushed the rounded fingertip onward and upward. With a sigh, she flung her head backwards, feeling a harrowing pleasure as her inner muscles gripped the slender finger, hungry for it but wanting more and more. Now, as she daydreamed of Anton's hard cock, she imagined kissing it, of feeling the magnifi-

47

cent width pass into her small mouth, of his reaching down, squeezing her breasts, picking her up and pulling her on to that hardness that would fill her like a hand forced tight inside a glove.

Oh, she needed more – she needed the fullness of him. For a wild moment, she imagined herself running to his room and presenting him with her wet eagerness. He would have her now, for sure. Yet it was too soon. In the unwritten rules of their contest, that would mean he had won. Never would she be so weak.

The ache in her stomach had become a pain – like a feverish wound, it needed to be lanced. With a shock she remembered the pleasure and heat of the cane's touch; as it fell, her entrance had been stretched wide, her legs pushed wide apart. If only she could feel his long stiffness pushing inside her. Moaning with the greatest craving of her life, she looked about herself.

The candle in the sconce was long and thick: much the size she imagined Anton's phallus to be, if maybe a little smaller. In a delirium of need, she grasped it and snuffed it with a derisive twist of finger and thumb. Then, with her trembling thighs parted as far as they could be, she pressed the pointed end against her slippery entrance. Crying out with pleasure, she felt the hardness press and then breach her entrance. Gasping, she pushed an inch and then two inches of the solid wax into her.

If Anton himself had burst into the room, she could not have stopped herself. Again and again, her hand pushed back and forth, sliding the candle deeper and deeper into her delirious flesh.

Looking into the glass, she was excited and appalled by what she saw. Her thighs were trembling, widely parted, smeared with her own unctuous fluid. The hard white wax of the candle was almost completely buried inside her, smooth and slippery, forced back and forth into her.

Giddily, she thought of Anton beating her. She pictured him above her, arm raised, swollen with frustration. If he were to push against her as he chastised her, surely he could not bear it for long. How she would love to watch – to touch – to feel that moment when he lost all his arrogant self command. It was too much to bear. With a last glance at her own ecstatic body – legs open, nipples stiffly pointed in the air, the glistening white column of the candle – Clara herself lost control. If he were also to weakly succumb over her – that was her last thought. Of his seed falling over her, of the ecstasy breaking over his usually immaculately self-controlled face.

With a cry of abandonment, she pushed the candle in as far as it might go, almost burying in the spasming heat as she convulsed around it. If he were to empty himself into her – again, at the thought, she felt an afterwave of pleasure grip her body, rise deliriously and gradually fall.

Then at last it was over. With a sigh she felt herself relax, the waves of pleasure ebbing and dying, her muscles recovering from this first, dizzying release.

With some surprise now, she glanced at the shameful creature reflected in the mirror. She had never seen herself like this before. It had been a surprise, but suddenly she realised that such a sight was no doubt part of the count's education. He did not need to be present to say it; she was already a willing pupil. He is teaching me, she pronounced to herself, to see myself as I might truly be.

Chapter Four

The sun was setting in a crimson ball across the flat waters of the polders as the count's party set off for the Witteburg Paleis. Only the great rows of windmills, black as giant sentinel towers, punctuated the twilight. Still the frost had held, so Anton had enquired and found that the entire route was still passable across the ice. Now, as Clara warmed herself within a nest of furs inside the sled, she was pleased to hear her companions chatter in Italian so that she could at last retreat, alone with her thoughts. All day she had attempted to maintain a haughty reserve, trying her best to forget the indignities of the previous evening. That very morning as she woke at dawn she had for hours turned in her bed, seriously reconsidering her decision to stay. Surely, she had thought, I should escape this man? If she were to only tell John Palmer half of what had happened, he would insist that she be returned at once to her family in York. Her previous narrow experience of life had in no way prepared her for such an onslaught. And yet, in the end, she had taken no action, only waited to see how matters would settle.

After lunch, the count had been all composed courtesy when he sent for her to ask if she wished to see a gem-cutting workshop in the town. Together, arm in decorous arm, they had strolled together down the neat, tree-lined canal paths, watching goods being lifted by pulleys into the tall houses, admiring the industrious people as they carried goods to and fro. It was as if, Clara observed, she had won his respect through her fortitude. When they arrived at the diamond shop, he was most attentive, finding her a chair to watch the little Dutch-man at work as he ground and polished the fabulous gems. Then he had helped her put the eyepiece to her eye and, as before, when she had viewed the beauties of Venus, here was again another strange world when viewed so close. The pretty, sparkling diamond now seemed to be a living thing of rainbow fire: a strange, unearthly star that radiated sparks of burning light. Always, before, she had disdained showy, flashy jewels. But, at the gem-cutter's shop, she understood their beauty as rare and precious mementos of eternity.

Now, as Clara watched the flat landscape rush past her, listening to the sprightly jingle of the horses' bells, she found herself toying with the simple diamond hang-ing at her neck. The count had bought it as a gift – it was neither large nor flamboyant but already she loved it. Just a simple teardrop of flashing diamond, it was simply set in a claw of gold on a fine golden chain, as delicate as thread. As she touched it, so close as it was to the pulse at her throat, she noticed Tresa casting her a curious glance. For the first time since their meeting, Clara glared back provokingly with raised brows and then glanced down, making a great show of the jewel. Tresa turned away abruptly, clearly in a fit of pique. It was evidently not difficult to provoke her companion to jealousy.

Their journey continued, racing past humble skaters and lesser sleds pulled by goats and oxen and even large dogs. Soon, they ascended the bank of the canal to a snow-carpeted road that passed through a dark wood that the count told her was the hunting park of his friend, the Baron von Amstel. Eventually, they reached a long drive; and ahead of them, at the end of an avenue of dark trees, lay the Paleis.

How could he ask if I would return to England? Clara exclaimed privately to herself. The building was lit like a fairy-tale castle in the violet dusk, with flambeaux set into its ancient stone walls and lights sparkling at every window, from the vast leaded windowpanes on the ground floor to the tiniest arches in the many snow-capped turrets. At the wide portals, liveried servants flocked about them, seeing to the horses, handing them out of the sled on to immaculately brushed stairways. Then at last they were inside: in the heat and the glowing light, in the high frescoed walls, below a vast chandelier of rainbow-coloured Venetian glass.

'Miss Fairfax?' A stoutish man with rather round blue eyes and a white curled periwig lifted her hand to his lips.

Clara immediately disliked the wetness of his mouth on her skin.

'How are you, Pieter? Have the goodness to keep your eyes in your head, will you?' Suddenly Clara realised that, since a flunky had taken her black hooded *domino*, she stood only in the thin diaphanous ball dress. Yet, in the candlelight, it was merely suggestive rather than indecent. And, as she looked about at the massing crowd wandering about the marble reception hall, it was true that she did not feel half so self-conscious as she had expected to.

Some were in fancy dress – clowns and pierrots and the obscenely masked Punchinello. At a second glance, some of the less attractive women she guessed to be men in tall wigs and hooped skirts; while others, whether in male or female dress, she could not place at all with regard to gender. Bare-chested youths were draped in grapevines and thin togas whilst ladies old enough to be their mothers paraded in the traditional bare-breasted gowns and crimson hair of courtesans.

Clara would have liked to simply find a quiet corner to watch the crowd. Certainly, it was like nothing she had ever seen in England, but it was at least – well, interesting. But no sooner had a glass of wine been placed in her hand by one of the richly garbed servants than the count motioned her to join him.

'These are but dull souls,' he sneered. 'Pieter is holding a more intimate soirée in the private rooms upstairs.'

With a quick glance, he summoned Tresa and, together, the three ascended the elaborate gilded stairway that curled magically around the turret of the house. Now, as he walked, she could see that he, too, wore a new costume. In a black silk coat with spangled waistcoat, the count appeared as striking as ever with his dark, saturnine looks. The white linen at his throat had been replaced by an elaborate ruffle of black gauze that matched the fabric of her own dress. She mused that, if only Tresa would leave them alone, they would look a very fine couple indeed.

Upstairs, the rooms were indeed smaller and more intimate. Small parties were gathered around card tables, intent on gaming while others lounged on delicate French sofas and gilded chairs.

'Come along, Anton,' exclaimed the Dutch nobleman, suddenly coming upon them as they loitered over a game of *vingt-et-un*, 'you must see the new additions to my collection.'

Down a tapestried corridor he led them, until they reached a chamber so crammed with paintings and glass cases and shelves of curios that Clara thought she had never before seen so many objects in one room.

'Look, Clara,' began the count, 'here is a work of art after my own heart. It is an allegory of the very lesson I am trying to teach you.'

It was with some trepidation that Clara crossed to his side, imagining God only knows what horrors to be exposed across the canvas. But, when she looked, it was only a very interesting picture.

'This was commissioned by the Habsburg Prince Rudolph – a connoisseur after my own taste. It depicts

53

the "Sense of Sight". Do you begin to appreciate my lesson?'

The painting revealed a room just as crammed with beautiful objects as the one in which they stood. But, in the allegory, a beautiful woman – quite naked, save for a thinly draped sapphire cloak – was admiring a painting held by a winged seraph. All around them were globes of the earth, telescopes, paintings, jewels, statues. And when Clara peered into the painting held by the winged child, she saw it was a painting of this whole allegory. And within that painting was a further tiny painting – the whole effect went on and on, tinier and tinier, like looking through a telescope the wrong way.

When she drew away from the canvas and looked around herself at the room full of real objects, Clara laughed.

'For a moment, then, it seemed to me that even this room was not real. That we are simply in a picture too and, outside us, giants peer into our little tableaux.'

The count laughed, too, and it seemed for a moment that they could genuinely form a liking for each other, if only he would lose his arrogant constraint.

'I have something to show Miss Fairfax, if you will allow me, Anton.'

It was the unpleasant Pieter, seeming to eye her from top to toe as he held out his arm. With a desperate glance to her fiancé, Clara found herself unable to politely decline his invitation. Coolly, Anton turned to Tresa, pointing out the intricacies of the allegory to her. Clara swore to herself she would return as soon as she was able.

'I know my friend to be a connoisseur of the fairer sex, but I must congratulate him on his choice, on this occasion.'

Was this supposed to be a compliment? The way this fat oaf was staring so hard at the bodice of her dress made her want to hold her hands up in shame. How she wished now that she had not let Anton persuade her to wear the sheer fabric. Glancing down at her neckline, she could see the rounded points of her breasts pressing against the fine fabric. Below, the half-corset pulled her waist in tight above the flounces of her skirt.

'Is it true then, that you are an entire innocent?' he leered.

Clara was truly lost for words.

At this point the Dutchman halted, opening a further chamber door with a key fumbled from his breeches' pocket. Hopefully, she stared back the way they had come, longing to see her companions follow. But, with a lecherous smile, Baron Pieter ushered her inside.

With some relief, Clara saw that it was only another collector's room; for the last few moments, she had dreaded finding herself in a secluded bedchamber. This man might be her host here, but already she suspected him of trying to do his best to stretch the laws of propriety.

'Here is one of my finest books,' he began. Affecting only the coolest interest, Clara glanced over his shoulder. The picture, at first glance, was of a typical mythological kind. A half-dressed damsel stood before a satyr. But, a moment later, she noticed that the half-man, half-goat was obscenely endowed with a wand-like phallus and the maiden was clearly welcoming him with eagerly parted thighs.

'I am a member of the Society of Arcadius,' the Baron continued, flicking through the book to show other strange configurations. 'One of our interests is this mating of the gods and mortals. Do you not believe, Miss Fairfax, that such myths hint at certain possibilities which the commonplace mind could never aspire to?'

She was staring at an illustration of a naked woman astride a marble statue as she clearly reached some kind of ecstasy. As he turned the page to a scene of a woman caressing the under regions of a bull, she looked away, truly shocked.

'I think you are a beast, sir.'

'Exactly my point,' he laughed. 'All of us mortals are beasts – yet only the more unrestrained can also be truly god-like. Does that challenge not interest you? Here, if you do not believe me, only look.'

Still, Clara glanced hopefully at the door but, as yet, there was no sign of the count. How could he leave her alone with this old lecher? All of her new regard for him drained away, replaced by fury.

There was a little doorway at eye-level fixed into the wood panelling on the wall that he now opened and, for a few moments, stared into. Then he ushered Clara over to see. Hesitantly, she peered into the square of light beyond.

She was looking into what appeared to be the next chamber. A perfect view had been captured of a large, cushion-strewn bed and an even better view of its attractive inhabitants. The couple were barely twenty years old; he had long curls falling over his milk white skin and she was even paler, dressed only in her flouncy *chemise du matin*, surrendering gracefully to her lover's kisses.

'It does not seem right, sir, to spy on young love.' She frowned at her clammy companion, who had quickly taken her place at the shutter.

'You would be surprised, then, Miss Fairfax, to learn that our pretty *amoureuse* is quite aware of our watching her – indeed, she welcomes it. This young chit is my ward – a troublesome girl, but of a certain appetite which enjoys such spice added to her sport. When she wants to add a little extra animation to her *amours*, she takes them to this particular room, quite aware that she will have an audience. At this moment, there may be half a dozen gentlemen absorbed in her performance.'

'I cannot believe you,' Clara retorted. 'I hope you have not used this girl badly – for, if you have, I will see she is rescued!'

'Really, Miss Fairfax, you are extremely amusing. If you don't believe me, just take another look.'

Clara did so, peering into the little window, quite ready to cry out to the poor girl and accomplish some kind of heroic rescue. But what she saw quite unfortunately supported the Baron's description. Now the youth lay recumbent on the bed and the pretty girl was removing her gorgeous chemise. As she pulled it seductively from her perfect, rosy breasts there was a proudly self-conscious expression on her face. Tossing back her hair, wriggling her smooth hips suggestively as she climbed on to the supine youth, there was something clearly theatrical in her movements. There could be little doubt. She was cavorting with more than half an eye to her audience.

'There is no point in calling out,' the baron added, although Clara had already decided it was no longer appropriate. 'They look close but are, in fact, quite a distance away in the house. The whole effect is brought to you by a series of pipes and mirrors.'

She glared at him. Of course, the whole scenario had been silent.

'At least you do not listen, then? Your guests have some small privacy?'

'But what should they hide from me? No, of course I can listen if I wish.' Setting a long, snake-like pipe to his ear, the baron listened for a few moments. Then he offered it to her.

Declining haughtily, Clara only agreed when the baron told her she might learn something to her advantage. Frowning, she placed the pipe against her ear.

The sounds emitted were clearly amorous: sighs and moans, pleasurable gasps and little cries of delight.

'Who is it?' she found herself asking, before she had time to check herself.

'We shall find out later.'

Instead, the baron guided her arm towards a second little shutter in the wall. Opening it, he peered in. 'Ah, you will like this.'

'I am sure I will not,' she retorted, no longer concerned about what he might think of her. 'I should like to find the count.'

'Would you?' the man leered at her again. 'Oh, don't worry about him. He will be amusing himself.'

'I really should prefer it.'

It was becoming quite warm and confined in the little chamber with this horrible man.

'Very well; I can see you are not interested in my private collection.' He affected a particularly unattractive sulking air. 'But just indulge me in one particular before you go. Will you?'

She ignored him and he asked again. Impatiently, Clara spat out a reply into the ensuing silence, simply to get away. 'Very well.'

'Certainly, you will like this.' He motioned her towards the small, open shutter. 'Or, if you say you do not, I am sure I will not believe you. I believe it to be every woman's dream. Perhaps you can see your own future role enacted here. If you leave now, you will always wonder what that is.'

Cautiously, Clara edged to the opening on tiptoes. It was at first difficult to discern the details, so gloomily lit was the room. A few candles in sconces stood in the corners around a raised dais. On this was stretched a person, whom Clara only slowly distinguished as being a tall and very well-formed man, bound by his wrists and ankles. Into this scene suddenly swept a woman, seen somewhat in shadow from the back. Unlike the man, whose rippling olive skin flinched as she caressed him, the woman wore a tight, short-dressed costume like a dancer in a ballet.

Quite fascinated, Clara watched as she produced a short-fronded whip and caressed the long line of his back and muscular flanks with its gentle tip. She could see him struggle, though whether from revulsion or desire she could not tell. Then, with a gentle swipe of the lash, she gave him a stroke to his bucking rear end.

'I see you also bear some scars of love,' the Baron whispered from just behind her. She had been strangely intent on the scene, quite unaware of him sidling up against her as she stood. Glancing back at him, she saw that he was peering through the filmy mass of her skirt, identifying the marks still apparent from Anton's work on her rounded flesh.

'I should like to have seen that done,' he muttered. 'Or perhaps you would care to do me the same service as our lady friend is performing?' She ignored him, watching what might happen next.

Indeed the man was clearly fervid with lust. As the woman rearranged his bonds and rolled him over with the tip of her pointed shoe, Clara could see the beating had only made him wilder. Now the woman taunted him, dragging the tip of her scourge across the stiffened flesh of his cock, making him flinch and beg. He seemed entirely vulnerable, entirely at the mercy of the shadowy woman.

She became aware of the baron's breath now close to her neck, as he too peered into the little frame. Seeming to steady himself, he gently grasped her shoulders. But she was too intent on what might happen next. Would the woman allow him release, or simply torment him some more? She was aware of the delicious question hanging in the air, of the man's need and the woman's scorn. Yes, maybe that was a woman's dream – to have power over those who so often had power over them.

Very, very slowly, the woman was beginning to undress. Now, as her breasts toppled forward, full and bare from her bodice, Clara watched how she flaunted her body, driving the bound man wild. With the gentlest touch, she kissed him, caressed him, licked him, stroked him. Then, as she lifted her skirts, the man writhed with desire as he finally saw her sex, hungry and enticing beneath the lace and frills.

Clara was only half aware now of the baron pressed beside her. But as his fingers gently stroked her shoulders, she shook herself without thinking, as a horse might shake off a fly.

At last the woman was naked, save all but her corset and, though teasing him right up to the very last second, she finally knelt between his spread legs and began to kiss the now stiff flesh of his cock. Clara could feel her breath grow short as she watched, and a renewal of that strange tingling between her legs. Barely aware of what was happening, she suddenly noticed the baron's hands sliding across her shoulder to cup her breasts. They were covered in only the thin filmy fabric; the sensation was thrilling as he began to squeeze the roundness with his palms, deliciously pressing against the nipples. She had barely time to be aware that her body was betraying her as her nipples sprang erect to his touch.

Yet it was impossible to take her eyes off the frenetic pair. At last, the woman straddled the long, reddened prick and, in a sympathetic gesture, Clara felt her own inner muscles throb and squeeze around aching emptiness. Still the baron was teasing her breasts. She knew without looking that they must now be forced taut against the fabric, so exciting was the sensation of silky tightness through which he kneaded her flesh with expert precision.

'Please, just let me see,' the baron moaned softly. She felt rigid with fascination and desire as he quickly lifted her skirt to reveal the reddened plumpness of her bottom.

'I promise I will not touch you,' he breathed noisily. And yet, the irony was, such a fever of carnality flooded through her veins that, at that moment, she would have let him do anything to her. Indeed, as she felt him rearrange his clothing, she even smelt the salty scent released into the air and longed for him to push her forward and ram his cock home deep inside her.

For that was what she could see in the faraway shadowy room. As the woman mounted him, the man threw his head back in ecstasy, in a fit of excitement so powerful it resembled pain. With skill and timing, the woman straddled her lover, tantalising him with the sight of her luscious body, her breasts bouncing as she thrust, pausing and delaying, teasing and squeezing until it was clear that the man would not be able to bear very much more of this torment.

At the same time, Clara was aware of a rapid movement behind her. Right next to her bare flesh, the baron was doing something else she had never seen before. With his hand tight around his own member he was pulling at himself, quite unselfconsciously bringing himself to a rapid climax with one hand whilst the other clawed at her protruding breast.

So thick was the air with the atmosphere of sex that, for a long moment, she felt empty, longing, left out of the fun, as she watched the couple in the room achieve a series of vigorous, frantic climaxes. She was amazed by her own harlotry, as if she had discovered another, more lecherous person living inside her flesh, overwhelming the better part of her febrile mind. For the second time in twenty-four hours, she might unquestioningly have given herself to a man. No – might even want or crave that man, whether he wanted her or not. Her limbs were as weak as her self-command. She was on the verge of falling back on the baron, or seeking out that piece of flesh which could at least temporarily satisfy her.

It was then the woman in the room turned around. The face and hair were unmistakable. It was Tresa. Clara thought her heart would stop. Suddenly, her body felt nauseous and leaden. Not because it was Tresa, but because – she could hardly say it.

'Who is the man?' she finally uttered weakly.

The baron was too intent on his disgusting self-abuse to hear her.

She whirled around, almost pushing him over. 'I said, who is it?'

Now she could see lust close up, with a cool, steady eye. His face was flushed and stupid, his eyes glazed. A film of sweat covered his skin. The cock dwindling rapidly in his hand looked foolish and pathetic.

Suddenly, he smiled, but with malice sparkling in his eyes.

'Don't tell me you don't know him, Miss Fairfax? Now, that would be lying to yourself, wouldn't it? After

61

all, you watched his every move with your very own eyes.'

How she wished that she could wipe out the impressions so resolutely lodged inside her organs of vision. That she had never seen this with her own eyes.

'I wish to go now.'

'Very well. I will see you escorted back to the city. I will let – him – know you have left.'

'Very well. I see.'

But as she was led out to the waiting sled and finally hid herself in the wraps and furs that was not true. Tears welled in those same eyes. Tears of rage and humiliation. She could not see how it had happened at all.

Next morning at breakfast, Clara found only Tresa sipping her coffee in the wintry light. Not speaking, she frostily took a roll and some weak tea from the sideboard and, for a while, they ate in restrained silence.

'I am to tell you he has gone.'

Clara looked up. If her eyes had been able, she might have shot daggers at the other woman.

'Gone?'

'Urgent business in Paris. He will see us there.'

Clara felt the gall rise in her throat. 'See you, perhaps. Not me. I will arrange my passage home today.'

Tresa's dark eyes pondered her over the rim of her coffee cup. They continued in silence, Clara hating the woman with every fibre in her body.

Leaving the table, the Italian woman suddenly turned to her.

'He left you this,' she said abruptly, then turned quickly and left.

It was a letter addressed to her in an ornate, elegant hand. Feverishly, she tore it open and scanned the contents two or three times before she could understand the import.

'What am I to do?' she moaned to herself, shaking her head with frustration. Then slowly, she stood and walked out to the landing, calling up the stairs to her hateful companion.

'Very well,' she called, knowing full well Tresa would be listening by the banister, 'I will go as far as Paris.'

Chapter Five

The noble city of Rheims sprung up from the plain like a great peak of coruscated stone.

'The cathedral of angels,' murmured Tresa, for once splitting the veneer of her elegance to show some interest in the scenes which paraded past the carriage window.

'It has the look of York,' Clara could not help but reply. 'For the Minster at York is the finest cathedral of the north.'

Yet, as the carriage drew closer, she could not help but marvel at the vastness of the portal and the thousands of statues which studded the walls between encrustations of gargoyles and strange mythological beasts. Admitting it only to herself, she had to confess the place was indeed much finer than York.

It was the seventh day since leaving Amsterdam. Confined within a newly hired carriage, Clara and Tresa had borne each other's company with mute and mutual suspicion. Each took up a routine of staring silently from the windows or occasionally dozing as the carriage rolled and heaved over hundreds of miles of roads. Yet now Tresa had decreed that she should like very much to stop awhile and visit the city for a day. The uncertainties of precedence between them had continued. Reason told Clara that, as the count's betrothed, she must have the advantage over a presumably salaried companion. Yet what she had seen at the Witteburg Paleis had profoundly shaken her. Fiancée or favourite, wife or wanton – surely the situation was insufferable. And yet she did suffer it – continually pondering the contents of the count's rapidly scribbled letter. He had begged her forgiveness and said he would explain all when he saw her again.

Finding lunch at the Hotel Lion d'Or, the two women refreshed themselves while the manservants and postillions saw to the horses and other gear. Then, wrapped in cloaks – for the weather was still not mild – they set forth to see the sights of the town.

It was not long before, as she stood comparing the Great Rose Window of Rheims to its counterpart in Yorkshire, Clara heard the elongated vowels of English folk. With a powerful sense of longing, she stared over at a party of six: two rather stout grey-haired ladies in grubby riding dress and the rest comprising wigged and booted gentlemen.

The elder of the two women, whose piercing tones echoed quite without concern up to the roof of the nave and back, was offering a diatribe on the theme of the foolish extravagance of the French.

'I am so heartily sick of these spiced ragouts and over-stewed potages! Why can they not roast a good piece of beef in the simple manner? And this over-decoration of every inch of their churches. And their personages, too!'

Hardly reducing the volume of her voice by a scrap, she pretended at once to address her companions *sotto voce*.

'To illustrate my point, just look at that rude young chit staring at us as if we just fell off the moon! Those ridiculous hoops and shiny cloths – it's a miracle she can get up the aisle. As for modesty –' here she raised her brows and cleared her throat loudly '– well, gentlemen, not much left to guesswork, there.'

Clara's eyes shot to the floor. How dare she? At least

she did not have muddy skirts made of the most inferior, drab cloth on earth. Fortunately, the offended feelings which sprang up within her did not form coherent words. Instead, spotting Tresa sauntering up the nave, she took her arm.

'And what do you think?' she asked in her thick Italian accent.

'Ah, très, très belle.'

Quickly scurrying the other woman away, Clara kept her head down. Once out of earshot Tresa whispered, 'What is it?'

'Oh, just those ghastly people. For the next few minutes, I should rather not pass as English.'

'Ah,' Tresa sighed, rather too knowingly. 'The ones with round red faces and dirty shoes?'

'I am afraid so. Faces like plum puddings and heads containing about the same amount of brains.'

Outside it was a grey winter's day but, amidst the bustle of other visitors, students from the university and townsfolk, the two women set out to explore. Immediate wonders were the famous Roman forum and together they marvelled beneath the Porte Mars. Tresa was anxious to visit the church of St Nicaise where Clara shook her head dismissively when the monks showed their famous trembling pillar. At St Remy, they were also ushered in to see the sacred ampoule which Tresa thought quite a wondrous thing, though again Clara found it was all she could manage to prevent the derision from appearing plain on her face.

Of much more interest were the vines kept by the brothers. Following the urgings of an enthusiastic brother, they were led into the back courts where row upon row of hogsheads were piled against the walls. The monk explained enthusiastically the process whereby the fermented wine is transferred from the casks to bottles for at least another year to effect the miraculous second fermentation.

'Mademoiselles, le champagne pour vous?'

'He wants us to try their local wine. It seems a shame not to.'

'Indeed,' Clara agreed. 'All this walking and staring has made me quite thirsty.'

The monk fetched three glasses and proceeded to pour the wine from a corked bottle. It was a rosy pink colour, fizzing with bubbles. Clara found it quite delightful and refreshing. Soon they were drinking their second and then third glasses. Another bottle had been opened, with a great performance of pulling until the cork flew out like a bullet.

Clara began to laugh suddenly, at the peculiar scene. The monk was clearly growing inebriated and it was hard not to giggle as Tresa gave a long and rambling explanation of the effervescent wine.

'Dom Perignon then shouted, "I am drinking the stars!" He had left the bottle too long, you see, and a second fermentation had occurred.'

'So every bubble is a little star,' giggled Clara, holding her fizzing glass up to the light. 'Then I could swallow a whole galaxy.'

'And me,' agreed Tresa, her usual coldness at last melted by the superb wine. 'I could drink the whole universe!'

It was as they sauntered a little more unsteadily back to the Lion d'Or that they caught sight once more of the English party.

'My goodness, they are staying at our hotel.'

Clara felt a wave of irritation pierce the bubble of her happy mood. Arm in arm with Tresa, it seemed to her that such people really should not be allowed access to the gorgeous sights of France. It would be wasted on them utterly.

'Well, let us move on, then,' Tresa suggested. 'After all, the sooner we leave, the sooner we arrive in Paris. And you will love Paris, Clara – it is like heaven on earth.'

'But where shall we stay tonight? Do you know the road?'

Tresa squeezed her arm in a warm, sisterly manner – albeit a slightly drunken sister.

'Who wants to stay at the Lion d'Or with all those grand tourists, anyway? If we leave now, we can find a quiet little inn and be well on our way to Paris by noon tomorrow.'

The idea certainly had appeal and, when they found the postillion, he reported that new horses had already been engaged. Indeed – if the ladies wished to proceed tonight, they might do so. He also warmed to the idea of reaching Paris all the sooner, for he could then turn around and return home all the quicker.

Yet there was all the trouble of reloading the trunks and cases, and then the servant lad could not be found. By the time the carriage stood ready in the yard, the skies were darker yet and Clara was alarmed to hear the clock strike three. It was not uncommon for night to fall by half past four.

'Tresa,' she asked, in a far more amiable manner than she had been able previously, 'are you sure this is wise? Might we not be better staying in comfortable lodgings for just one more night?'

'With your pudding-heads? Certainly not. Come along, my timid friend, let us be off to Paris.'

And so, with not a few bemused stares from the men hanging about the yard at the Lion d'Or, the count's carriage jolted to life and clattered noisily over the cobbles to the city gates.

It was on a road which wound through a deep forest that Clara first became aware of the rain. It spattered irritatingly at the window but, when they left the shelter of the trees, it seemed that a torrent opened above them, hammering at the roof of the carriage. The road, which had seemed fair on a dry winter's afternoon, began to be filled with large muddy puddles. Peering out of the window, Clara could see runnels of water pouring along deep cracks and fissures. Soon she could bear the situation alone no longer. Tresa had soon nodded off in a huddle of cloaks and rugs.

'Tresa! Tresa! Do wake up. Look at the weather. What are we to do?'

With a start, her companion wakened, frowning at the deluge as it streamed past the window, threatening to burst into their tiny compartment at the seams of the roof. Being suddenly woken did little for her mood.

'Oh, don't be a fool, Clara. We are safe and dry in here. Let the driver take care of it. I advise you to sleep until we arrive. That is what I will do.'

'Arrive? Where can we arrive tonight? Look, Tresa. It is nothing but wilderness and the road gets worse and worse.'

With a dismissive wave of her hand, Tresa closed her eyes and settled back down in her seat. Despondently, Clara watched the darkening sky, aware every moment of the slowing pace of the carriage as the horses picked their way carefully through rivulets of water that were growing into the size of a running stream.

Barely a hundred paces further, the driver decided the matter for them. Halting beneath a group of trees which offered just a little protection, he dismounted and tapped at the door.

'Begging your pardon, ladies, we must stop awhile and take a look at the maps.'

'We are not lost?'

'It is not likely, mademoiselle,' he replied, his cloak soaked black and water dripping from the end of his long nose, 'but it is not advisable to go further without being sure of the way. There is a ford ahead which I will not risk the horses across unless we are sure of an inn at the other side.'

Considerably alarmed, Clara passed down the case of maps.

'If you have a lantern, miss?'

So, with some trouble, a lamp was lit and the driver's wet head and trunk was pushed into the compartment so that he might make out the route. Even then, he called for the postillion, a surly fellow whom Clara now recognised had little aptitude for his work. Together they argued a while, primarily over the significance of a plume of smoke they had seen to the west in a clump of trees.

The postillion maintained that this had to be a sign of their destination, the town of Châlons-sur-Marne. The driver was less convinced, arguing that such a large town would be marked by at least a church spire. He maintained that the wrong road had been taken far back in the woods. Yet, in the end, there was little to discuss as there was no room at present to turn the carriage around. Consequently, Clara heard them agree to go forward in the hope that the marked ford across the Marne near Châlons would indeed appear.

Sitting back in the carriage, Clara felt, not for the first time, the considerable void left by the absence of the count. She was sure, in a trustingly child-like way, that he could read a map far more skilfully than these dolts. It was not only his knowledge and worldliness as a traveller that she missed – she also felt a peculiar excitement in anticipation of seeing him again. Somehow the world had seemed a little less colourful since his hurried departure. And there was something, too, in being begged to supply forgiveness – something that seemed to promise he had at least some regard for her.

The carriage arrived at the ford but, when Clara saw the wild landscape and fast-flowing river, her heart quailed.

'Tresa! My God, we cannot pass through that!'

Together, they dismounted into the rain and were immediately soaked. The torrent roared past them, throwing up a shower of spray. Instinctively, Clara turned backward to look at the road they had travelled down. It now had the appearance of a running stream, splashing down the track to join the seething river. Even Tresa looked a little pale. They were in a valley where water would naturally collect; it could only be a matter of time before the whole area flooded.

The driver turned to them, shaking his head.

'This is not the ford at Châlons-sur-Marne, but somehow the carriage must be got across.'

'But the poor animals,' exclaimed Clara, seeing the drenched creatures shiver in their harnesses.

'Never mind them, what about us?' Tresa wailed, lifting damask skirts already saturated at the hem.

With a somewhat steadfast look at Clara, the driver indicated a line of stepping stones further upstream.

'The best I can do is suggest you try to get across on foot. The smoke indicated some kind of settlement in the woods but I'll bet my life you won't find a sizeable town across there. Really, mademoiselle, that rascal of a postillion should be whipped for this. You can be sure the count will hear all about it from my lips. I am sorry – I can only suggest you finding some kind of shelter before nightfall and I'll seek you out when my work is done.'

Clara nodded at the man's wise words, although Tresa began to utter a stream of invective in Italian so passionate that Clara led her back into the carriage.

'We have little choice but do as he says.'

'No; I will stay. I will not leave this carriage. They are engaged to take us in this carriage to Paris.'

'Then you can sail in it to Paris and drown alone. I am off to find some shelter.'

Packing a few items in a purse, Clara made ready to leave, pulling a second cloak over her shoulders and finding a pair of overshoes in her trunk. At last, Tresa reluctantly did the same.

Trudging through the rain, Clara could not help but remember the well-accoutred Dutch women in sensible clogs and layer upon layer of shawls and wrappers. She could not bear to look at the skirts of the blue damask dress; it was as heavy as lead and doubtless ruined. Judging from Tresa's bedraggled state, it was a very good thing that they had washed up so very far from the eyes of civilised society.

Matters only got worse. The stones across the river, it transpired, were half submerged and even on a fine, calm day Clara might well have declined to make the crossing. Now, with water rushing over many of them, she began to tremble at the very thought of venturing out into that flood. Yet, even as she looked, she could see a clear track emerging at the other side, rising into the woods. Indisputably, the stepping stones had been laid in order to reach a particular habitation.

'Well, there is nothing for it. I, for one, intend to survive this little adventure.'

To Tresa's astonishment, Clara lifted her skirt and untied her hooped petticoat. It fell like a tent to the ground. Then, removing her shoes and stockings, she felt the mud squelch beneath her toes. Finally, she pulled up her voluminous skirts to her thighs, all the better to jump unhampered.

'Come along, Tresa, it is not as if anyone will ever see you. Your skirts will only drag you down into the water.

As ready as she ever could be, Clara set off across the river, glad to be freed of her leather-soled shoes as the stepping stones were green with slippery slime. Using her toes like a monkey, she gained purchase on each rock and then, with all her concentration, made the leap for the next.

After a dozen or so steps, the stones no longer broke the surface and she had to peer into the fast-flowing water to make out the next darkened shape for her bare feet to grip. With a great effort, freeing herself of all the constraints which had kept her sedate since reaching womanhood, she took a deep breath and leapt on to the next submerged stone. With a splash she landed, slipped, righted herself and stood steady, calming herself.

'Clara, Clara, how is it?'

'Not now, Tresa, for goodness' sake.' She did not even dare turn round. 'Shut up!'

The next stone was again submerged. The water round her ankles was freezing cold. She had a great fear that, if she loitered, her flesh would grow so numb that she might no longer feel it. A little whimper escaped her lips as her eye travelled over the long gap between this stone and the next. And yet to turn around would be difficult – she might completely lose her grip on the slippery rock.

It took more than a few moments for her to build the courage to make the next leap. Then, at last, she jumped and her toes successfully gripped the rocky surface, though her legs were wet up to the calves. Now she was in the centre of the river, the water was none too clean, either. Broken sticks and a yellow froth floated on the surface. If she were to slip? It did not bear thinking about.

But now, as she peered into the current, she could no longer see the next stone. How could it be possible? Fearing the worst, she crouched a little, peering into the rushing water.

'What now?' she said to herself, not knowing where to turn next. As if to cap it all, at that moment the wind howled up the river, carrying a freezing spray of rain.

'Which is it to be? Drowning or death from some deadly ague?'

It was no use; she had to stand a while longer and gather her nerves, though tears had begun to gather in her eyes as all courage seemed to abandon her.

Then, at her lowest moment, it was there – stretched in front of her, reaching for her arm. A strong, calloused hand, attached to a broad, hairy arm. Barely a few paces from her was a man, stripped bare-chested: a rough, long-haired young man up to his thighs in water.

He muttered a few words of encouragement in a dialect of the area, impenetrable to Clara. But his meaning was clear. With a rush of relief, she took that calm, steady hand and let him help her from stone to stone, confident that if she missed her footing, he would catch her.

At last her foot reached the harsh stone track and, untying her shoes from her waist, she pulled them on.

Then suddenly she noticed her new companion's obvious appreciation of the length of naked leg below her bunched skirts. With large dumb eyes, he offered her his ragged shirt to dry herself with.

'*Merci, merci,*' she repeated. 'You have saved my life!'

His hand reached out to help her dry her soaking thighs. It seems, thought Clara, churlish to deny him his reward. As he helped her to dry off a little, more than natural feelings of gratitude to a rescuer surfaced in her mind; he was so tall and strong, his nose a little crooked but handsome. Certainly, he was a remarkably agreeable specimen of manhood.

The rescuer's pleasant ministrations were too soon rudely interrupted by Tresa's vociferous cries, as she shrieked from the other side of the bank. With a long, glowing look from his dark eyes, the youth mumbled adieu and set off manfully into the river. Clara's eyes were full of his swelling muscular shoulders, which seemed barely to flinch at the roaring waters, as his stout legs set off once more to steadily negotiate the perilous stepping stones.

By the time Tresa had been carried rather more genteelly across the river, Clara had managed to tidy herself up a little; she had pulled her skirts down and tried to comb the rat's tails of her hair. Dropping Tresa rather unceremoniously to the ground, the youth turned to both women and made signals they should follow him. Trotting to keep up with his striding form as they climbed the track, Tresa turned and whispered to her friend.

'Well, what a savage! Look at those legs – if that is what honest toil can do to a man, it should be compulsory.'

Clara coyly pretended to look away but, as Tresa's brazen remarks quieted, she could not help but cast the odd admiring glance up at their bold Hercules.

Their destination was not, of course, the town of Châlons-sur-Marne. Instead, they arrived in a stony clearing in the woods where stood a tall habitation

74

which seemed to be farm, house and barn all combined into one. Yet, if it were not for the rain and the ever-darkening sky, Clara thought, it might have appeared quite charming. Its construction was of thick wooden timbers, such as the tumble-down old houses in York were made, the squares and cross shapes filled with white plaster, topped with attractive tall, carved gables. Yet when the man led them inside, the interior was far less agreeable than the façade.

The building appeared to comprise only one large room and in that was a little rough furniture, a smoking fire and stalls containing a goat and pig. Sitting on a rough stool, doing something indescribable to the insides of a dead pig, was a fat peasant woman whom they took to be their rescuer's mother, who merely grunted at the sudden apparition of two bedraggled gentlewomen appearing at her door. Only after a distressing period attempting to communicate in simple French words and gestures did Tresa and Clara succeed in firstly getting the fire rebuilt and then obtaining some primitive sustenance.

Eventually, it was only by dangling a gold coin from her purse that Clara found herself sitting by the smoking fire eating a bowl of rough brown bread, goat's milk cheese and slices of disagreeable boiled mutton. With their skirts hung out to dry on pieces of rope about the room, the two women had to make do by sitting in damp petticoats and bodices.

By now, the sun had set and, as no news had been received about the coach, Clara began to look about in the gloom for somewhere to sleep.

'Ask him, not her,' she whispered, eyeing the youth as he sat at a rough table, pretending to carve some wood with his pocket knife. Yet she could see that each few moments, when he thought they were not looking, he darted a glance over at them, trying to see as much as he could of them in their undressed states.

'Monsieur,' began the Italian, *'vous avez de la chambre?'* Here she did a giggling, flirtatious mime of sleep, tilting her head prettily to the parodied pillow of her compressed hands.

The youth laughed too, showing not only a happy humour but fine teeth and bright, excited eyes. With a simple gesture, he pointed upward to the roof. Clara frowned and then, gazing upward, noticed there were some rudimentary haylofts up there. Then she noticed sets of crude, towering ladders.

'My God, what will our next ordeal be?' Clara whispered.

But Tresa was not listening. With a familiar flounce of her petticoat, she stood and held out her hand to the handsome lad. With a grin he took it and led her to the foot of the ladder. With somewhat more misgivings, Clara followed, alarmed by Tresa's brazen behaviour. Never in her life had Clara seen a woman with less modesty or self-control.

Soon leaving the meagre pools of light from the fire and the building's single tallow flame, they climbed up the trembling ladders to a platform piled with mounds of straw. With another irritating giggle, Tresa began to make a mattress by piling up the best straw and then seductively untying the topmost of her petticoats and throwing it over to make a comfortable sheet. The presence of the youth was quite palpable, watching them with round, hungry eyes.

'*Bonsoir*,' announced Clara emphatically, as she stood waiting for him to leave before she bedded down. But he only laughed.

'How do we get rid of him?' she hissed at Tresa, who was literally romping across her bed in a fine display of abandon.

'Why get rid of him?' she laughed

'Oh, I do wish the count was here,' Clara snarled. 'You would not behave like this in front of him.'

'Very well, Miss Prim,' she snapped back. And to the youth she waved her hands dismissively. '*Alors, finis, bonsoir.*'

Reluctantly, he trailed away, leaving them in near

darkness as he took the tallow he had skilfully carried with only one hand, as athletically as a performing ape.

Left in darkness, Clara had to make what she could of the straw on the narrow platform, dragging her makeshift mattress to the far side, well away from Tresa who had rolled over with a loud sigh in a fit of temper.

At last, after much difficulty, Clara made a mound of straw comfortable and, slipping under a pile of her petticoats, she at last lay down after the long day's exertions. It was only now, as she lay alone, listening to the creak of the old house and the odd tramplings and snortings of the beasts below, that she had free rein to let her mind drift freely. How she missed him, she was appalled to find. Though the count had seemed to bring chaotic disorder to her life, yet how much she felt his absence as they foundered alone without the anchor of his worldliness.

If only he were here now – and Tresa were not. Drifting off to sleep, she stretched her aching limbs luxuriously and conjured up a pleasant little dream. If only they were somehow together and had become lost in this picturesque place. With him, she would not believe herself to be in danger; instead, she could enjoy the novelty of sleeping together with him in this quaint little hay loft.

She imagined his lips pressed hard to hers, his tall body crushing her as he covered her in kisses. Yet – he was so delicate, too – her own hand brushed her breast quite lightly as his had done, making her shiver with excitement. Did he think of her? Oh, how she would open to him, yield to him, once they were married. Wriggling and stretching on the scratchy straw, she pictured herself beneath him, his hunger for her as he thrust her legs wide, pounding inside her again and again until both were utterly sated.

Such fantasies even invaded her sleep – for sleep did come quite fast, so exhausted was she from the rigours of the day. So, it was in a state of dazed confusion that she emerged from her slumbers to find her dreams appeared to have come quite true. A warm, smooth body lay next to hers. As she turned her head sleepily, hungry lips were pressed to hers. A hot tongue probed her mouth, while simultaneously two strong hands clasped her, pulling her hard against his body. Such was her stupefaction that, for quite a few moments, she truly believed it was Anton who lay in her bed. As his kisses burnt downward, from mouth to throat, she flung her head back sighing. The mouth reached her breasts as her head began to clear. She blinked. Who was it? As she puzzled, the tantalising lips kissed her breasts, two gentle hands circling them gently, a tongue grazed her nipple like fire. Such a tide of lust gripped her she felt she might immediately faint away.

'No,' she managed to whisper.

In reply, his lips returned to hers, seeking and probing, making her mind spin as his fingers squeezed and fondled her breasts deliciously. Despite the darkness, she could see the profile of the youth – his long hair falling across his manly face, the sudden glint of his craving eyes.

The trouble was – and it got worse, every second of his caressing her – she wanted him so much. Her body was so overwrought with wanting, she could barely hold back the flood. She tried again.

'No, please,' she whispered, though very feebly.

With a charming gesture, he lifted his finger to her lips and bade her be quiet. Oh, he was terrifically handsome, she knew that. And now, his fingers were exploring further, slipping into her petticoat, caressing her stomach, approaching her thighs. Clara felt she might explode if he continued any further. She could see his broad shoulders glistening in the darkness, smell a gorgeous scent of sweet perspiration and clean hair. Very gently, he rolled above her and, at the merest pressure of his iron-hard cock against her stomach, she very nearly cried out loud with desire.

'My God,' she whispered to herself, panting a little. He had begun to writhe a little above her so he could lift her petticoat higher and higher. 'My God,' she uttered again as his hand brushed the inside of her thigh like a tormenting feather. She could no longer think – only feel. He was sucking her nipple now, rolling his tongue deliciously around the stiff bud of flesh. And his fingers still climbed, pushing her thigh further and further back.

Then, as he wriggled slightly, she could feel the pressing bulk of his cock. For a second, it brushed her thigh – hot, taut, damp. Gasping, she felt her hips move automatically towards it.

'No, no,' she whispered, but no one was listening. So this is it, she found herself thinking. I am unable to keep my promise to the count. I am no better than that harlot Tresa. My body is stronger than my mind. I must be satisfied.

With unendurable slowness, his fingers found her sex and, at the first touch, her back arched ecstatically. She was wet now, hot and ready, in an agony of need. Gently his fingers probed, parting her lips as if he had found a rare flower, rubbing the provocative bud of her pleasure, slipping a broad finger into her hungry entrance. Unable to hold back, she began to moan, feeling his cock squeezing hard against her thigh. Feverishly, she clung to his kisses, finding herself wrapping her legs about his, close now to the final moment, lost in a torrent of pleasure.

She was aware of his hand suddenly taking hers. She was utterly his; as he placed it upon his prick she felt such a sharp sensation grip the insides of her stomach, she almost felt sick with need. Frantically, she squeezed the hard flesh, feeling her palm dampen as his cock twitched excitedly. It felt like nothing she had ever touched before – magically exciting, something she wanted to consume with her eyes, her mouth, her body. Moaning, she arched herself submissively beneath him.

His fingers, meanwhile, were exploring her thighs, her lips, her sex. She had no idea before it happened how high she had climbed. But suddenly, as she adoringly

79

circled the massy bulk of his cock and balls with her hand, she felt again that almost painful spasm grip inside her. Panting, she pushed towards him. His fingers, till now so delicately exploring, momentarily slid inside her like a knife into fruit. For a second she cried out; then, as his fingers probed and pushed, suddenly it happened. Like falling far, far, down into a well, she seemed for a moment to lose all consciousness, aware only of the spasms gripping her, of wave upon wave of scintillating pleasure, of the texture of his cock within her small hand and the hard digit of his finger thrusting inside her.

'Oh,' she whispered as the world seemed to right itself about her. To her horror, he was now trying to get astride her, ready to make the final conquest. Released from the massive dam of lust, Clara looked about herself with a sudden lucidity. Yes, he was handsome – desirable, certainly – but now her desire was even partly spent, she did not want the act itself.

Pulling herself half upright, she addressed him.

'I am sorry, but no!'

He looked at her like a wounded animal and she almost relented. But no; when she thought of the count, she felt peculiarly ashamed. He had utterly woken her to this sensual world. Somehow, she felt herself to be his. No, it could not be like this.

'No. I am so sorry, but I cannot,' she said sadly. He looked at her again and, despite the difference of language, she could see he understood.

'Let him come over here.'

Alarmed, Clara looked over to Tresa's pallet. She was a white figure sitting upright, her hair tumbling darkly over her shoulders. Silently, Clara cupped the youth's disappointed face in her hand and indicated with her other finger the availability of Tresa. For a second he wavered, looking greedily down at her body. Then, in quite a gentlemanly fashion for a young peasant lad, he took her hand, kissed it, and slipped silently out of her bed.

For a short while, Clara lay still on her straw bed. Continuous afterspasms of pleasure erupted though her body as she squeezed her thighs together, remembering the deliciousness of the youth's muscularity pressing against her. Still she could smell his scent on her fingers and, even as she dozed, she tentatively licked her palm where precious drops of his fluid had seeped on to her. Just the smell of him almost made her regret not having had him fully.

But as she heard him quickly take Tresa, with much breathing and knocking and little cries from her, she knew she had done well to remain faithful, not only to the count but to herself.

And later, as he crept away, she overheard Tresa grumpily complain to herself in a pique, 'Well, he was a disappointment. I think he had already spent his best.'

But Clara could not agree with her estimation of the youth. He had not disappointed her in the very least.

Chapter Six

*I*t was the smell of Paris which first greeted them. At first, the road had been merely busy: a broad thoroughfare thick with shops and crowds and animals. Then the main road into Paris had broadened; as the houses grew taller and more imposing, the mass of people had become a multitude. Clara had never seen so many people pushing and shoving, parading and purveying, all in one place. And the smell – it was both rich in its deep, sweet textures and squalid in its reek of sulphur, drains and rottenness.

Gradually, as the carriage slowed and then ultimately halted, the smell pressed in against their clothes and hair and skin as privately as the most intimate acquaintance.

'What is it? Why have we stopped?'

Tresa languidly glanced out of the window. 'Oh, this? It is quite common. There are too many carriages for the roads here.'

It was true. As the road narrowed ahead of them, it took only one overloaded cart to spill its load or a fine carriage to break a wheel, and the entire city traffic ground to a halt. And although the procession would speed up slightly upon a paved section of the road, when the next unpaved part of the city was reached, it would once more be swallowed up in the infamous, stinking Paris mud.

There was a sharp tap at the window. Cautiously, Clara lifted the curtain. A dreadful face peered in – toothless, wild-haired, filthy. It was a beggar woman who, the next moment, raised the mud-smeared body of a small child, dressed in the meanest rags, to the window. The knocks grew persistent, the hand stretched aggressively for money. Clara fumbled for her purse.

'In the name of the saints, never give money!' Tresa cried. 'We shall be mobbed.' Fixing the curtain closed, she turned to her companion. 'They are *les misérables*, the idle poor who refuse to work. If you give to one, you will only attract a plague of them. The mob would as soon turn the carriage over as give you thanks.'

'But how have they become like this?' Clara was appalled.

'Who knows? They drift to Paris from their farms and think that begging is a substitute for honest labour. It is sheer immorality.'

Clara looked askance at Tresa's explanation; it seemed particularly ironic that she blamed their dependence on a lack of morals. But the Italian did not notice, so vociferously was she waving a silk and ivory fan before her delicate nose.

To Clara's relief, they moved on a little further, but not before a handful of mud slapped against the window. She began to long to arrive at their apartments at the Hotel de l'Impératrice. Not only was she tired and feeling a little sick after the long day's drive, but each step forward she thought of as bringing her a second nearer to the count. I must be a fool, she mused, but I crave his very presence.

It was almost dusk when the carriage at last rolled between the gates of a tall, elegant residence on the Rue Jacob, just near the church of Saint-Germain-des-Prés. With much relief, Clara finally set foot on the hard ground and ascended to ornately plastered chambers furnished with the finest gilded furniture and mirrors, long gauzy drapes and a golden ewer of rosewater laid out before a crackling fire. Furthermore, the floor-length windows were sealed tight so that the dreadful odour of the city could not invade the building. A maid had been engaged and, with her assistance, Clara began to unpack and prepare for dinner, which was to be brought to the apartment's dining room at eight. With great attention, she washed and changed, her hair was styled and her gown was made ready.

It was with a rapidly beating heart that Clara finally saw the count in the salon. Standing at the window, peering over towards the lighted craft out on the Seine, he turned quickly as she rustled into the room.

'Clara? I trust you have had a good journey?'

His dark hair was gathered back in a black ribbon and he now favoured the French style of dress; his black necktie was held with a diamond solitaire.

She laughed a little too brightly, although his manner seemed unnaturally formal. 'Certainly not. It was quite dreadful. You must not abandon us again.'

But this attempt at coquetry seemed to miss its mark. Instead, he merely shook his head.

'That may not be possible. I have urgent business in Lucca, this spring.' For a long moment he gazed at her, his eyes cool and proprietorial. 'Come here.'

After a moment's hesitation, she walked slowly over to the window. Casually, he placed his hands upon the nakedness of her narrow shoulders and looked into her face. 'Tell me, Clara, what have you seen?'

Beneath the heavy weight of his shining eyes, she averted her gaze. What had she seen? He did not mean the cathedral at Rheims, that was certain. Instead, she remembered the dark silhouette of the peasant boy pressing against her, the frenzied visions of her secret fantasies. That put her in mind of the last time she had seen him, his body contorted and naked; he had achieved a frantic bliss she had not known existed.

'I have seen things which disturb me,' she said softly, raising liquid eyes to his.

His hands slid down her front, running over the arc of her breasts, lingering on her naked skin, then settling around her waist. A spark passed through her for a moment. Unable to stop herself, she felt her eyelids momentarily close in response to the pleasure.

'And do you enjoy being disturbed?'

'I do not know,' she whispered, shaking her head with inexpressible anguish.

Slowly, he pulled her towards him and, like a dark tide, she felt his body melt into hers. But when she lifted her parted lips for his kisses, he instead nuzzled her hair and the smoothness of her brow. Then, with uncanny tenderness, he kissed her eyelids, first the left and then the right.

'I am glad that what you see disturbs you.'

She could feel the stiff wetness of the tip of his tongue rubbing the lids of her eyes. It made her weak, made her lean against him for support. As she pressed against him, she could see the pulse at his throat beating fast. She knew that he, too, was extraordinarily agitated.

'Soon it will be time for your next lesson, Clara,' he whispered, although no one else was in the room. 'Until then, I must exercise mastery over these indulgences.'

And so it was that, as dinner was then announced, he took her arm quite formally. Throughout the meal she noted an air of restraint in his manner. The effect upon her emotions was a profound disappointment, but she succeeded in masking this with a bright, amiable manner.

'I was at Versailles yesterday,' Anton finally began, after speaking only in single words, 'and was quite the tourist, watching King Louis set out to hunt.'

'Was the Queen there also?' Tresa asked.

'No, I believe she is in the country, taking a rest from her husband.'

'You mean avoiding his mistresses?'

'Perhaps,' answered the count, as he raised another glass of burgundy. 'But La Pompadour has even befriended the Queen, I believe. I caught a glimpse of her only a few days ago. She really is a most striking woman. Extremely finely dressed and vital, rather than beautiful. Indeed, I should say she did not have the looks of either of you both.'

He smiled at this, but Clara's heart froze. What were these commonplace flatteries?

'What was she wearing?' Tresa asked excitedly.

'She favours a new style of robe with much in the way of *tâtez-y* or 'touch me here' frills and *parfait contentement* ribbons at the breast. It is quite a provocative style. I can see my wallet is going to be somewhat lighter by the time we leave. What do you say, Clara?'

Tresa squealed with delight but Clara raised her eyes to him solemnly.

'As you wish, sir. I would not have you squander money to please me.'

At last their eyes met directly and a little spark of fire passed between them.

'Ah, but I should very much like to squander my money. It would please me exceedingly.'

The count was as good as his word and barely a few days had passed before boxes and bags of garments were deposited like an avalanche of Christmas presents in her room. There were indeed robes in the style *à la française*: a day dress in pearly lemon with a huge overskirt decked with double frills, braids and flowers. Another salmon-pink robe of heavy brocade was so flounced and frilled that Clara almost felt lost in the massive confection of fabric. With a matching frill gathered around her neck and flowers at her breast, the mirror told her she looked exquisite. There were pretty matching silk shoes and her hair was lifted and pinned beneath an artful arrangement of flowers, ribbons and plumes.

Yet the most intriguing gift in her wardrobe was a simple *négligé*, a dress in the new style made all in one piece to wear in the boudoir. Made of sheerest lilac silk, it fell in rippling flounces down the back and was light and soft and clung to her skin like silky water. With a simple knot at the breast, it fell in a stunningly low décolletage, draping the nape of her neck and shoulders. Yet the strangeness of it was the scent. When Clara first opened the garment bag, the scent that rose had made her close her eyes and breathe the vapour slowly and rapturously. Even as she wore the robe, the scent remained just as powerful, increasing as she moved, or even breathed, as if the cloth itself were impregnated with tiny vessels of the most powerful perfume.

Soon Clara had little time to consider the count's contrary fits of heat and coolness towards her. After all, as Tresa constantly maintained, they were in the most fashionable city in the world. How much finer were all the palaces and *cours*, the gardens and hotels, than anything she had ever seen in England. At the Palais Royal they saw pictures by Titian, Raphael, Veronese and Rubens; but Clara argued with the count that she much preferred the Dutch Masters for their precision to render a face who looked just like the next man in the street, or a bowl of fruit so fresh you wished to reach in and pluck it. Again, with faultless courtesy, Anton showed her the extraordinary sights of the city. They marvelled at the Pont Neuf, the Louvre and Luxembourg Palaces, the factories of Gobelins tapestries and the new coffee houses where the *beau monde* sat to parade their wealth.

And she learned that the smell which had greeted them had in part drifted from the graveyard of the pauper hospital where the flooded Seine had set adrift thousands of wretched bodies. Yet, she mused, the rich continued in their pursuit of pleasure just the same, simply ordering their coachmen to take a different route across the city.

One day, as they strolled through the gardens of the Palais de Tuileries, Clara asked the count what perfume it was in the cloth of her *négligé*, that it stayed so fixedly in the fabric of the robe. They had ventured out to take some exercise alone, as Tresa was indisposed. Together, they were enjoying a slight increase of warmth in the air, gazing at the other promenaders who sauntered back and forth along the neatly clipped hedges and geometric paths. Bending to smell the scent of a miraculously early April rose, she realised that she had never smelled a flower which had the pervasive, pungently attractive scent of her *négligé*.

'You enjoy it, then?'

He was watching her. Sometimes she found he observed her but pretended to look away when she challenged him. Now, alone in the long, shady walk of roses, he smiled as if at some secret pleasure as she spoke.

'I do.'

'And how does it compare to, say, your lavender gloves or jasmine-scented jewel box?'

'However much I love the gorgeous gifts you have given me, there is something almost animate in that simple lilac gown. I am convinced it is something in the scent. What is it? The perfume is like none I have ever known.'

This was true, for what she failed to tell him was that the scent had a powerfully erotic effect. For the past few nights, she had felt a great reluctance to take it off at the end of the evening. She had even taken to dismissing her maid quite early so that she could sleep in the gown without another soul knowing. Then, as she lay there in the vast bed, with moonlit shadows scudding across the high ceiling, her mind wandered down the corridor to the chamber where she knew Anton slept. Feeling the silk meld to every inch of her naked skin, she remembered the sensation of his touch – both gentle and savage. Although the dress was tight it did not cut or chafe; rather, it rubbed pleasantly, squeezing her waist and breasts and teasing between her thighs.

There was an aroma she occasionally thought she recognised in the dense perfume of the robe; it was as deep as incense but less sweet, as musky as burning myrrh or the ashes of scented cedar wood. Then Clara would turn in her bed, aching not to be alone, and another scent would reach her, of fresh myrtle, a scent as fresh as the wind rolling in from an aromatic sea, the hot savour of crushed rosemary spikes. In the centre of the shifting, evocative scent was something she had smelt before – she was sure of it. But each time she felt on the verge of discovering it, it eluded her as subtly as a word hovering on the tip of the tongue.

The count paused awhile, turning on his heels to look at her with a glimmer of mischief in his eyes.

'I have a great interest in the senses, as you know.' Here he glanced at her quickly, and she knew they were once more speaking with their previous openness. 'And Paris is, of course, the greatest originator of scents in the modern world. It seems to me –' and here he hesitated a little, as if he were not quite sure he should tell her this '– that I might set you a small test.'

'A test?' Clara did not like this at all.

'Oh, do not worry. You have passed my *petit examen* with no difficulty at all. I believe you have identified the scent. That is very, very good.'

Clara frowned up at him. 'But that is precisely what I am saying to you. I have not identified the scent. I asked you what it was.'

He took her arm, smiling to himself. 'Would you care to visit one of the great perfumers, this evening? Then the lesson can be of a practical nature.'

'I should love to. But only if the answer to your riddle lies there.'

'It does indeed, Clara. If you wish to learn the lesson, I will give it.'

That evening, Clara was secretly delighted to find that Tresa continued to feel unwell. It was not that she found the woman's presence particularly irksome any more – simply that she very much wanted to be alone with Anton. And, as they left in the carriage, clipping along the paved roads, surrounded by thousands of wondrous street lanterns, Clara once more felt so happy that she had not been denied the chance to see these lovely, long boulevards and sumptuous palaces. She did not need to speak to him about this; she knew that he watched her as she peered out of the window, and that he approved her admiration of the wonders he placed before her.

The House of Parfums Sapphora lay in an elegant street very far from the malodorous stink of the Seine. As ever, when the count rang the doorbell and gave his name, they were ushered quickly inside. Despite the rather plain façade, the reception room was quite lovely; a glittering confection of gorgeous white and gold panelling, lavish chandeliers and arches of dazzling mirrors. In England, her only perfume had been the modest lavender and rose waters bought in plain stoppered bottles; here in Paris, perfume was evidently a far more prosperous business.

'Ah, count, what a pleasure to see you again.'

Madame Sapphora was of middle age, a slender, rather sharp-featured woman dressed in a flowing emerald dress in the exquisite style copied from the paintings of Monsieur Watteau. Her eyes glittered beneath finely arched brows as she took Clara's hand, pressing it affectionately.

'*Enchanté*, Mademoiselle Fairfax. I believe you wish to learn about perfumes?'

'Yes, madame. I am particularly hoping to learn about the scent my fiancé has chosen for one of my gowns. Can you tell me its origin?'

'Of course, my dear,' Madame Sapphora replied, taking her arm and leading her through a heavy door into the laboratories of the perfumery. Clara had only fleeting glimpses of glass distilleries and racks of bottles, strange machines and furnaces. But all about her, as she was led by the older woman, she smelled an immensely rich fragrance, so powerful that she could taste it on the air.

But behind the private doors of madame's own study, it seemed the scent subsided.

'The doors are made of lead,' she indicated with a nod. 'For I must not be distracted by extraneous scents.'

The count relaxed in a brocaded armchair while Clara was led to the delicately scrolled and gilded sofa. The room was pleasantly peaceful, with a fire settling in the grand marble fireplace and shelves adorned with dainty Sèvres porcelain.

'How many scents can you make?'

Madame lifted her slender fingers, heavy with diamonds and pearls, in a shrug of inexpressibility. 'How many paintings could an artist create? For the palette of scents are quite as diverse as any selection of colours.'

Clara knew that her face revealed an expression of some disbelief.

'Like many persons,' began the count, 'Clara believes the sense of smell to be the most inferior and debased of the senses. Many of our modern philosophers would agree with her. They place the sense of sight as preeminent, as the sense of reason and enlightenment. And smell? They associate that with savagery, lunacy, the realm of animals.'

Clara could see their hostess nodded quietly.

'I am not sure you can speak for me like this,' said Clara. 'It is just that I have never considered the matter at all.'

'*Exactement*.' The woman nodded. 'The fifth sense is so devalued no one but a perfumer such as myself cares to even consider the matter. Or a man of discrimination such as yourself, Count.'

She rose and fetched a small wooden box that, when opened, revealed a dozen or so glittering vials.

'My dear, would you care for a demonstration?'

Clara nodded, but was somewhat surprised when she also produced a black velvet scarf. 'What is that for?'

'Your sense will be so deadened that it will help if we remove the distraction of sight temporarily. Don't be alarmed; I shall tell you all the time what I am doing.'

Feeling somewhat disarmed, she let the woman tie the scarf firmly around her eyes. Without her sense of sight, she was for a moment quite dizzy, relying only on the voices of her two companions to judge what was going on around her.

When the count began to speak, Clara found that her sense of hearing was already considerably heightened. She could tell, by the faintest quickness of his breath, that he was more animated, even excited, than before.

'When we saw – many beautiful things – in Amsterdam, it may have seemed to you that their image was readily captured in your mind. And yet those images are but the surfaces of things. To find the true interior, the essential being, the pure essence of a thing, one must capture its scent. So, madame, if you would open one of your vials?'

Here the woman wafted a scented bottle before Clara's face.

'Do you know it?'

The scent was pungent – sweet and rich. It seemed to flicker before her like a myriad collection of the tiny seeds of scents. It was piquant, almost astringent. She knew it was a great collection of aromas collected and bottled and distilled. The topmost layers were unspeakably fragrant, but underneath was another more subtle, binding fixative. The core of the essence was richly noisome, even rank. Yet, she recognised it as a scent she had breathed only within the last few days.

'Do you know it?'

Although blind, she turned her head in the direction of the count's voice. 'It is somewhere here, in Paris.'

He laughed pleasantly. 'As ever, Clara, you speak wiser words than you know.'

'What do you mean?'

It was disarming not to see his expression, even though his voice exposed more than he knew.

'It is a distillation of the whole city,' Madame Sapphora said. 'A tincture of the air and water of Paris.'

Clara marvelled that such a thing could be, but it was true. It had all been there in the glitter of the high notes and gloom of the lower.

'And now for the solution to your riddle.'

Once again, as the perfumer waved a vial before her, she inhaled the gorgeous scent that impregnated her gown. The poignant muskiness was apparent, and the sharp zest of saltiness above. Throwing her head back a little she let her mind drift in the darkness behind the velvet of the blindfold.

'Take your time,' the count murmured softly. And as he did, she suddenly smelt the subtle trace that was him as he moved, so close had he come to sit beside her on the sofa. Then she knew it, but decided on the instant not to say.

'Maybe if I breathe it again.'

This time, as she inhaled the scent it took all her powers not to smile with recognition.

'I should choose this scent for my personal use,' she began, still stifling her laughter, 'only there is one thing I dislike in its mixture.'

There was silence.

'What is that?' It was Anton. With her sight blinded, she could hear the edge of offence in his voice and had to do her utmost to control her face.

'This perfume has so many qualities,' she began slowly. 'It certainly attracts; it is a deep and interesting fragrance. It is not like your flower waters; it is profound and heady but as sharp as the sea.'

'So what does it lack?'

'Something in those deeper regions. Is it true that a perfume attracts at a sublime, animal level? If so, I believe this scent lacks that musky depth that would make it irresistible. To use a rather ridiculous metaphor, if it was the scent of a man, I should say he was charming and attractive. But he lacks that earthy pungency which enslaves a woman.'

The woman was silent. She felt the count fidget near her.

'Tell me, then. Have I passed your test?'

She could sense the count rising to his feet abruptly.

'No. You have failed the test. Let us go.'

'But, Count,' interrupted Madame Sapphora, 'I have hardly begun my lesson.'

'Yes, I should like to continue,' added Clara. 'This really is most fascinating. Please, I should like to stay.'

She could hear Anton sigh impatiently.

'Please, Anton. Now I am here, I should just like to learn a little more. Madame Sapphora, would you continue?'

'Of course I will.'

'Very well,' she heard the count agree, strained to the limit of his good breeding. 'I shall take a stroll across the park and return at the half-hour. But I will not be delayed beyond that time. Good day, ladies.'

With this, he was off, most appreciably not in good temper.

The two women sat in the stillness, listening to the delicate tick of the clock. Finally, Clara could relax and a mischievous smile broke out across her features.

'Mademoiselle Fairfax, I believe you are quite a wicked tease. Tell me, now we are alone, what was that second perfume?'

'It was him. I do not know how you did it, but somehow his very essence was distilled. I just cannot bear this cold arrogance of his. Both you and I know the scent is quite heady enough, it was just too strong a temptation to bait him a little.'

She laughed and the older woman joined her.

'How did you obtain it? It is him utterly. Indeed, I confess to you, it does thrill me already. I can hardly bear to take the scented gown off at night.'

'Thank you. That is a compliment worthy of my labour. I took one of his shirts and subjected it to months of *enfleurage*. Just as in my native Grasse, we layer heaps of mimosa, lavender, jasmine and roses with special fats for months, so I did with your fiancé's linen. Then, when the fat is saturated, the oils are washed out with alcohol and evaporated until a tiny, tiny amount of pure essence remains.'

Clara began to feel uncomfortable, continuing this

conversation still blindfolded. She reached to untie the scarf.

'Listen, my dear,' said the woman as she stayed her hand, 'would you not like me to continue the lesson? Would you perhaps like to learn a few of my more intimate secrets?'

There was no hesitation on Clara's part. She nodded and let the perfumer continue. The first waft of perfume was light, golden, sweet.

'These floral notes are used simply to attract attention. They promote goodwill and make the recipient trust you implicitly. Shall I show you how to wear this?'

Clara nodded and the woman dabbed a little on the pulses at her neck and elbow.

'But if I want to – create a more powerful effect?'

'Everybody asks me, "How do I make him love me?" Well, that floral scent will make him like you and that is a good step on the road to love. But you, my dear, have an advantage over all of them. You see, I have already made his own essence.'

'Ah.' Clara felt she was beginning to understand.

'If you were to use a variation on his own essence, the effect would be almost magical. In France, we have many myths of lovers meeting their own images. This is how it would be for you both. He would be close to you and feel in his heart – I know this woman as well as I know myself. She is as dear to me as my own heart.'

Clara felt her lips upturn into a smile.

'Can you do this for me?'

'Of course. I only ask, do you need it? His fit of irritation just now was only because of an affront to his dignity. I confess I know for sure he only wished it confirmed that you might know his scent – an ancient test of love since the days of the Romans.'

'Oh, I knew his scent easily enough. But he is so arrogant, so severe – so cold. That is why I could not resist teasing him. Please, madame, help me conquer him.'

She heard the woman open a cabinet somewhere in the room and then return.

'And when you conquer him? Will you want him then?'

Clara bit her lip. 'I cannot say for sure.'

'Nevertheless, you must promise me: this is our secret?'

'Of course,' replied Clara expectantly.

There was the sound of tinkling glass and unscrewing of lids. Then Madame Sapphora began her explanation.

'The ancients had great secrets in the arts of scent. If we study their writings we find that most perfumes were not liquids but oils, powders and unguents. The word *parfum*, of course, describes scent carried upon the air in smoke. So, I will begin your preparation with a balm that can be more liberally rubbed into your skin and be retained for a longer period. I will add some of the count's essence so that he will recognise his own self in you, some of the powerful aromas gathered from animals – musk, civet and ambergris.'

Clara was aware of a rich, potent mix rising to her nostrils. The smell made her heart beat a little faster as a warm tingle extended across her face, down to her throat and breast.

'Now, shall I show you how to wear this?'

Nodding, she felt the woman gently lift her hair at either side of her jaw and find two spots at the top of her neck below her ears. Then, with warm, luxuriously slippery fingers, she began to rub the unguent into her skin.

'It is a powerful aphrodisiac, is it not?'

It was true. The perfume essence alone had made her crave the count but now, combined with the dense animal pungency, she felt a pleasurable, expectant wave of pleasure pass over her skin.

'To make him want to touch you further, you must anoint yourself in the right places,' the woman laughed. 'For example, here.'

Her pliable warm fingers slid over Clara's throat and downwards over the twin swellings of her breasts. Then one finger slid inexorably into the cleft between her breasts, massaging the balm into the deepness of her cleavage. The scent was now so powerful she could think of nothing else.

'Shall I show you how to anoint the breasts?'

'Yes,' Clara replied, a little breathlessly. 'What will that do?'

'It will make him want to touch them, of course.'

With a little adjustment, Madame Sapphora loosened Clara's bodice and, with a sudden sense of release, she felt her flesh overflow the tight whalebone and silk. Now the heated fingers gently massaged both breasts, giving each a deep covering of the rich salve.

'It is best if the *téton* is hard, so that every part of the breast is saturated with scent.'

With this, the woman began to pull and squeeze the pointed buds of Clara's nipples so that they stuck out, stiff and exquisitely sensitive. Still blindfolded as she was, Clara found it hard to hide the acute pleasure this treatment was giving her. With a little sigh, she felt the woman cup and lift her breasts.

'Exquisite, my dear. How could he resist? And, for the tongue.' With this, she popped a little lozenge in Clara's mouth. 'Chew it. In a moment, I will test it.'

Clara did so. It tasted of sweet violets and refreshed her mouth considerably. Yet she was still surprised when the perfumer leant over to her, as they sat together on the sofa, and gave her a little kiss. Curious, but also somewhat amorously aroused, Clara let the woman's soft lips linger and, a moment later, they were locked together in a warm embrace, the woman's hot little tongue pressing deliciously into her mouth. And still, as they kissed, the woman fondled her breasts, rubbing the salve into her engorged and receptive nipples.

'And now for my final secret,' whispered Madame Sapphora. 'I must show you where to keep the ultimate scent that will make him crazed to have you.'

With this, her delicate hand slid upwards, lifting the frilled weight of Clara's heavy skirts. Clara docilely leant back. What did they look like? She pictured the two of them recumbent on the sofa in their masses of silk and lace. What a strange sight to see them kissing like that – and even – maybe – pleasuring each other. It was not a situation she had ever dreamt of. Yet now, as it was happening, it felt so pleasurable and soft and gently refined.

Madame Sapphora found the top of her stocking. With a quiet moan of pleasure, Clara let her legs part a little as the hot little hand began to massage her thigh. Still, they leant together to kiss, nipping and rubbing with soft, dainty lips and probing each other's mouths with their tongues.

'Please, I must tell you,' panted Clara as she suddenly broke away, 'you are arousing me most terribly.'

'Do not worry, I have nearly finished,' whispered the older woman, letting her hand snake further up her thigh until Clara gasped with pleasure as it brushed against her hot cleft. 'Let me see if I can accomplish it.'

With this enigmatic statement, the woman probed further, pushing along the silky cleft so that Clara felt she might any moment cry out with abandon. Finding her entrance, the woman sighed, kissing her lightly on the lips.

'Here, I have my greatest secret.' With this, she pushed into Clara's fingers an elongated lump of soft wax, impregnated with the headiest aroma. It was as long as the woman's hand but rounded at the end.

'If I can press it inside you, the material will slowly melt and impregnate your very core with an irresistible scent for months and months. Although your cavern of Venus is well hidden between your skirts, still a discriminating gentleman can detect the scent in a whole ballroom of others. Shall I try it?'

In answer Clara let her fingers linger on the broadness and length of the thing. 'If you are gentle.'

'Here, I will help its entry.'

To her amazement, the woman slipped down from the sofa and, doubtless with her emerald skirts billowing out behind her, pushed between the heavy frills of her lifted skirt. When she felt the woman's lips press against her sex, her back arched with delirious pleasure. The mouth was rubbing, licking, sucking at her slippery entrance. Suddenly Clara felt all control disappear. She could feel a tremor in her thighs as the woman gently pushed them further apart.

'Oh, madame, I cannot bear much more,' she cried.

In reply, she felt something hard pressing against her most sensitive spot. With her throat stretched backward against the back of the sofa, Clara found herself panting loudly. Then, after a moment of pounding resistance, the soft lump of wax parted her lips and was forced inch by inch inside her.

'Oh, madame, I do not know, perhaps you should stop!'

Another inch, and then another. It seemed to press against the pit of her stomach, filling her in a most gratifying manner. Then, with a little catch in her throat, she knew she could indeed bear it no longer. The woman was nuzzling against her shamelessly parted lips, sucking at her unbearably sensitive clitoris. With a loud cry, she lifted her bottom a little and felt the rod of scent impale her to its furthest extent. With a further spasm it was over, her relief so exquisite, her body so miraculously satisfied.

It was just in time. A jingle of bells sounded at the front door. Giggling a little, they could hear the maid clumping along the corridor. She could feel Madame Sapphora adjusting her bodice, straightening her skirts and putting all to rights. There was a tap at the door.

'You must keep my gift inside you until it melts away,' she whispered. Clara nodded impatiently.

'Come in,' called the perfumer.

She could hear it was the count. Indeed, she now wondered if she could smell it was the count.

'We have just finished the lesson,' said the woman, quite calmly. 'I will remove the scarf.'

Suddenly, Clara's eyes were full of light. Blinking, she looked about herself.

Madame Sapphora sat as genteel and sedate as any civilised lady. The count extended his arm to Clara to leave. For a sudden moment, she wondered if she had fallen asleep and dreamt this bizarre encounter.

But, as she stood to leave, the perfumer pouted a secret, laughing little kiss at her when the count was not watching. 'I will send you some samples as a memento of our meeting,' she smiled. 'And you will remember, won't you, not to let my little secret out?'

As Clara walked to the door with the count, she realised that would be impossible. Indeed the perfumer's secret was still lodged hard and provokingly deep inside her.

Chapter Seven

'*I* have a confession to make,' she said finally, as they sat in the frigid silence of the carriage.

'Yes?' He pretended to watch the crowds as they processed along the boulevard.

It was time to be resolute. 'I knew the scent was yours. Not when you gave me the dress. But this evening. It was perfectly apparent.'

'Then why did you pretend otherwise?' His tone was still peevish. How long was it now, he had sulked? An hour? She did not particularly care for him in this temper.

'Because I wished to tease you,' she exclaimed. 'I do confess to being extremely grateful to you for all your time and efforts over my education. Indeed, at times, I am extremely fond of you. But I have come all this way and still you offer no explanation, sir. Your behaviour in Amsterdam was outrageous. All you offer is this desire to control all, to dictate my every response, to subject me to your *petit examen*. It simply won't do!'

Clara had been too busy during this little outburst of heat to pay much attention to the effect of her words upon her fiancé. Now, as she raised her eyes, she blanched.

Anton's fist was squeezed as tight as a ball and he

pressed this to his teeth as if he might chew away the skin of his own knuckle. His face was a deepening scarlet. As he turned to her, she swallowed, wishing she could as easily swallow back her recent torrent of words.

'Simply won't do!' he repeated very slowly and coldly. 'You? You, who have just humiliated me in front of my friend, who have the manners of a frightened peasant girl, have the effrontery to pass comment on *my* behaviour? How dare you? How dare you make a fool of me in front of my friend! Very well, if it is all such a tedious combat of control and examination, I shall retreat from battle!'

With this, he banged loudly on the wall of the carriage with his stick. The horses slowed and, in a moment, he had leapt out of the door.

'I am sorry,' was all Clara had time to call, as the tails of his coat disappeared into the night. They had pulled up just near the bridge at the Tuileries where the terraces were thronged with what the count had in happier moments laughingly described as 'fair votaries of Venus'. Then, as the driver cracked his whip, they rolled forward again and Clara burst into a surprising, violent fit of tears.

Back at the Hotel de l'Impératrice Clara was immediately confronted with Tresa's round and curious eyes. 'Where is the count?'

Clara glared at her quite rudely. 'So, you are better now?'

Tresa was standing on the stairs in her own lace-ruffled *négligé*. 'I feel a little better, yes. You have not lost the count?'

Clara turned away from the candelabra that illuminated the hall. She did not want this woman seeing the signs of her tears. 'Lost him? How could I lose him?' And yet she felt she had. 'He wished to walk back. I am sure he will be home soon enough. But now I am tired and wish to retire.'

'But where did you last see him?'

Quite rudely, she shrugged and pushed past Tresa, who stared back in surprise. Then she added, 'Why are you looking at me like that?'

'Clara, it is just the scent you are wearing. Well, it is extraordinary. I am surprised the count could drag himself away from you.'

'Drag himself away?' she retorted from the safety of the first floor landing. 'He could hardly run away fast enough.'

With few words, Clara dismissed the little maid as soon as she had been unlaced from her costume. Finally alone, she pulled on the lilac gown and threw herself down on her bed. What had possessed her to speak to him like that? And yet, how finely his response illustrated that arrogant, controlling flaw in his nature. What a joke that Tresa believed her so irresistible. Closing her eyes, she imagined him wandering the parks and gardens even now. One evening, he had even joked about those painted women on the moonlit terraces of the Jardin de Tuileries and how it was only his little 'harem' which kept him from calling upon their services. Is that where he would find solace, away from this screaming shrew of a woman whom he had showered with gifts and consideration? Tearfully, she thumped the exquisite silk bolster and sobbed her heart out. What was the point in learning all of those arcane secrets from Madame Sapphora if she destroyed the whole effect with her sharp tongue? Painfully, she listened to the bells of St-Germain-des-Prés chime each quarter hour. There was no sound of his return.

It was the depths of the night when she awoke. Blinking slowly, she became aware of a candle burning unsteadily near her bedside. Peering into the darkness, she saw he was there, standing still beside her bed, the flame casting a reddish glow across his features. She sat up, clutching her upper arms as if she was cold. She was not cold, however, only shivering with surprise.

'You know why I am here.'

Still dazed with sleep, she squinted at his dark shape, rubbing her eyes. Then she saw the long cane twitching in his right hand.

'No. I do not know why you are here,' she began. But his shadowed face remained impassive.

Suddenly, she caught sight of her reflection in the looking glass against the wall. Her tangled hair had fallen down abundantly around her shoulders and pale, round-eyed face. The lilac dress fell in a low semicircle across her bare white throat and shoulders. But she could not see if he stared at her with fury or with lust.

'You have done me a wrong.'

'Anton, sit down. Be reasonable.' She tried to smile up into his impassive face.

'It will not take long. It is the right thing.'

Irritated from being woken, she shook her head. 'For God's sake, Anton. Let us talk in the morning.'

With a darting movement, he caught her left wrist and held it tight – as tight as a vice. After a few seconds Clara realised it was too painful to struggle. Slowly, he lowered himself on to the edge of the bed, holding her wrist fast all the time. Now at last she could see him a little more clearly. He was pale and unkempt, his hair hanging free and his shirt half open. She wondered if he was drunk.

'This is an outrage. Let go of me.'

'Clara, why do you despise me?' His voice rasped with emotion. 'Perhaps this is why I take Tresa. You are not ready yet. But, in time, you will be.'

She could not reply. Despise him? She could not at all describe how she felt about him, now. As she felt his gaze palpably devour her by the light of the single flame, she felt a tumble of emotions: fear, excitement, power and yes, perhaps a little scorn. But, the next second, her delusions of possessing any control disappeared. Snatching her other wrist, he roughly pulled her towards him.

'I cannot sleep,' he murmured hoarsely. 'Such things are best done under cover of night.'

His hands tightened around her wrists and she began to feel the great weight of his will trapping and dominating her. She felt pain, but also the beginning of that peculiarly docile feeling: she had no choice in this; what would happen next was no longer her responsibility. Submission. Her heart began to beat faster.

'It is right,' he whispered, then lifted one of her reddened wrists to his lips. Kissing it softly, he lifted his belt and began to wind it around her wrist.

'What are you doing?' Pointlessly, Clara tried to resist his attempt to bind her. It was impossible. He was far, far stronger than her.

In a few moments, both of her wrists were bound. She looked at him in desperation. 'Let me go.'

He seemed not to hear her. When she saw his face his expression was inwardly absorbed, as if anything she said was of no interest. As he pulled the leather strap tight through the buckle, she felt herself jolted and pulled.

'Do not concern yourself; I have promised myself I will not take you. Only teach you your lesson.' But his glinting eyes were at odds with his professed intent. His gaze moved possessively from her parted lips to her pale shoulders, half naked breasts, disordered gown.

As she struggled, she became aware again of the heavy perfume that now suffused much of her skin, continually releasing its scent into the air. He, too, seemed to smell it; it made him sink his head low, closer to the impregnated fabric. Suddenly she felt his warm brow pressing against her throat.

'I will not take you,' he whispered. 'Only chastise you as you deserve. That is all the explanation I will give you, lady. Move down.'

'This is outrageous,' she hissed.

His reply was physical, as he dragged the end of the belt around.

Reluctantly, she felt herself turned so that she knelt on

the floor at the side of her bed on her knees, with her bound wrists stretched before her across the mattress.

Suddenly, he slipped something around her head. She struggled, then found it was only a scarf tied around her eyes.

Oh, the scarf would make it easier, that she already knew. Without her sight, how effortless it was to sink into the beguiling world of the senses. Without her sight, it was easy to forget who she was, to forget she had a self at all. In the blackness, she was only a creature of urges and responses. Inwardly, she struggled to keep hold of her belief in herself as more than a blind object of this man's lust. But outwardly, as she struggled with the tight strap of the belt, she found herself utterly restrained. She could not get away. Maybe, a perverse inner voice suggested, she should simply enjoy it to the full.

Roughly dragging her rump towards him, Anton knelt behind her. All her sense of hearing was intent on him. She could hear him breathing as he paused; she almost believed she could hear the hammering of his heart.

'You have done me a wrong,' he muttered, seemingly to himself. 'It is only right that you are punished.'

In the interlude that followed, she tried to guess what it was he was doing. Arranging the bedclothes? Pacing around? She could not tell. Blindfold and bound, she wondered why he hesitated.

Then at last, it began. Already, she recognised the orderly steps of his chastisement. With a groan from his throat, she felt him lift the edges of the hem of the lilac dress. If only I could honestly say I do not want this, she thought. But it would be a lie.

His fingertips grazed the soft nakedness at the back of her thighs. Clara had to bury her face in the mattress to stay silent. Very gently, he lifted the skirts of her dress to her waist. She felt a voluptuous thrill as she pictured his gluttonous gaze, tracing the rounded curve of her buttocks in the candlelight. Against all her better nature, she suddenly wriggled, pretending to struggle. It

106

brought the desired effect. His hands sank into her flesh, pushing her against the firm edge of the bed. The thrusting pressure of the mattress against her sex spread fiery pleasure down between her thighs and into the pit of her fluttering stomach. She could hear him breathing raggedly.

'Are you sorry?' he managed to ask, hoarsely.

Maybe it was the delightful tête-à-tête at Madame Sapphora's perfumery, but tonight she wanted to exercise a little power.

'What have I to be sorry for?' she whispered angrily.

His answer came in the long hiss of the cane and burning, stinging blow across her buttocks. It hurt. Uncontrollably, she swivelled away. But then the heat came, the long, slow burning across her flesh, tingling and prickling without subsiding.

Very gently, he reached down and grasped her hips. It made her gasp as his hands reached around her pelvis and pulled her backward towards him again. This time, as she waited for the cane to fall, she felt a deep tremor begin in her bones.

'I will not take you,' he muttered, as he let the switch fall, its flexible end cracking against her flesh. 'But I will watch. I will have that at least. I am a man. I must have some release.'

That was what she could feel; his scrutiny was even more powerful than the blows from the harsh, stinging switch. As she buried her face in her bedlinen, hidden in the darkness behind the blindfold, she could picture him vividly. He was ravenously watching her, eyeing the whiteness of her thighs, the rounded fleshy parting of her rear, the hot, crimson breach between her peachy buttocks. It made her shudder with desire – to feel him so close, with only the thin thread of his restraint holding him back from falling on her and taking her.

As the third and then the fourth blows fell, she slowly became aware of a new scent rising around her, as powerful even as the perfume rising from her anointed body and dress. In the blackness, she let her olfactory sense free, questing for the source of the new fragrance.

It came from him, she decided. As he struck her again, she smelt his sweat, the swelter of his desire. It made her feel weak; it made her involuntarily arch her hips, lifting her parted cleft so he could see it even more clearly. His response was a heartfelt groan. This time, as he positioned her smarting rear, his fingers lingered. As they withdrew, his fingertips tentatively drifted downward, over her reddened buttocks to the inward curve of her thigh. She could feel his hand hovering above her parted cleft.

Again she could detect a salty, bitter scent on the air. Sharper than perspiration, it smelt of the ocean; it was sweetly brackish.

She felt his hand withdraw, and could only imagine what struggle that involved. The cane sighed again and stung like a bitter kiss. Pulling on the leather restraints at her wrists, Clara suddenly became aware of a piece of clothing against her bare foot. In an instant, she realised why she could suddenly sense Anton's presence so vividly by his scent. She had no doubt now that behind her, as she lay blindfold, he was naked.

The idea made her rigid with excitement. What she could smell was the nakedness of his sex. In those first few moments, when she had wondered what he was doing, whether he was rearranging the bedding, he had silently stripped off his clothes. She pictured him naked and glowing behind her. This time, as he reached down to centre her squirming hips, she suddenly pushed backward.

She felt his cock. It was there, naked, only inches behind her. Hot and swinging, she had felt the heat rise as his tautness brushed her. Just to brush against it made her instinctively moan with desire. She wanted it. She wanted it inside her.

'Keep still,' he said hoarsely. 'Just keep still.'

Panting in the darkness, held fast, she was entirely his. When she felt his fingers touch the crimson ridges rising on her skin, she could barely control the violent spasm that erupted inside her.

'Do you like this?' he whispered.

She could not reply. It seemed, after a while, that he did not expect one. With a touch as light as featherdown, he explored the criss-crossed results of his work. Clara held her breath, paralysed in expectation of his capitulation, his need to push his cock inside her. Even more tentatively, she felt his fingertip glide downwards to that parting where the skin changed to a pink sheen. She knew it was heavy and wet, her lips swollen with anticipation.

Then she remembered it. The perfumer's wax! With a jolt, Clara was dragged from her limpid stupor. Any moment now, he would find it. She could barely imagine how to explain how it had got there. And what would he make of her pleasant dalliance with Madame Sapphora?

It was too late. His finger brushed the slippery swelling of her lips. Groaning, his fingers pushed against her flesh, raking at the little stream he found there. Clara could feel it – a little runnel of perfumed juice trickling down her thigh.

'What is that?' he moaned. There was a moment's pause and she realised he had slid his wet finger into his mouth. 'Did my friend play one of her amorous tricks on you? If only I had stayed. If only I had watched.'

He probed gently, pushing the wax even deeper inside her. A spasm of excitement ripped through her abdomen. Deep inside her body, she was pulsing, ready. All she could think of was the heavy, blood-swollen mass of his phallus, jutting barely inches from her eager opening. The air was thick now with an exhilarating mix of fresh sweat and scented wax and animal secretion; it made her want to touch and taste and lick him too.

'Very well. Let me end your lesson with another test. We shall see if you truly know my scent. Let us see if

109

the scent of my manhood can disturb that sanctimonious facade you hide behind.'

She was nothing now, but a repository for her heightened senses. When he knelt even closer to her, she shuddered and moaned. But still, to her surprise, he did not mount her, only continue to stroke her poor, switch-reddened rump. Then, in her fever, she felt something strange brush across her trembling flesh. She could feel his tongue, licking and tracing the pattern of her weals. On and on the heated stiffness of his tongue licked, making her shiver as she pressed her face hard into the bedclothes, stifling her cries.

Now she could feel his naked chest pressed against the backs of her thighs. She was certain he was kneeling prostrate, his tongue tracing the artistry of his blows, his mind completely lost to his desire.

The movement, when it came, still had the capacity to shock her. It began as a pulsating tug as the edge of her skirt was lifted and pulled. It was a gentle, persistent rhythm. He no longer cared. He was intoxicated, his mouth sinking into that receptive parting between the twin spheres of her flesh. In the febrile darkness, she could feel him stroking his own naked cock with the silky hem of her skirt. In her mind she saw it, hot and taut and bursting for release beneath the tantalising, scented silk. He was betrayed only by the steady beat of the muscle in his arm, working back and forth like a piston. Clara felt her muscles contract, felt her need must be almost visible; her body was as needy as his, trembling and ready like a hair trigger, eager for release. In the dark cavern of her imagination she pictured his cock squeezed and worked within his hand and so much did she want it – to possess it and feel its hardness inside her – that she let slip a little cry of pleasure in the back of her throat. She wanted to feel it in her hand, in her hot, waxy cunt, in her parched mouth. Insistently, his mouth bore downward, his tongue nuzzling between her cleft, finding that most secret, second entrance which quivered beneath his delicious probing. She even longed

110

to feel his broad phallus there – massive and pounding into her other, hidden entrance.

He suddenly began to falter in the rhythm of his kisses. Clara could feel a stream of wetness trickling down her thigh. Unable now to hide her frenzy, she cried out into the suffocating pressure of the mattress. Her arched fingernails dragged along the bedclothes. She wondered, suddenly, if just by rubbing that second, burning orifice with his tongue he might bring her to release. She was certainly close, uncontrollably trembling at the edge. All her senses except sight were concentrated on his frantic urgency, feeling his arm continuing to work up and down, up and down. Tugging the sheer fabric along its length, he was masturbating as he drowned his face against her wetness.

He began to pant. Clara struggled and pulled on her bonds. She wanted to reach out and squeeze his agonised cock dry, to fondle that rounded tip that glistened in her imagination. She wanted to feel him spill, to see that moment of utter, spasming release. He was pressing his face now against her, suddenly, involuntarily pushing downward, drenching his face in her provocatively stretched, wax-dripping entrance.

As she heard his moment of climax approach, she thought she, too, might buckle and collapse. His face was buried now in her sex, gasping for breath as his arm jerked frantically. Then his scent reached her. It was too late. With an anguished cramp of frustration, she knew he had released his bitter, pent-up semen on to the dress. With a cry that expelled every particle of breath from his body, he convulsed behind her, pushing his face into her heat, jerking spasmodically. Clara sobbed with a pang of sick, unsated lust.

For a long time after he had released her and gone, Clara lay quietly in the rumpled mess of bedclothes. Then, she angrily pulled aside the blindfold and tore off the dress.

Something hard stubbed against her toe. Pulling it up,

she found it was the count's boot: a tall, leather boot adorned with tiny gold buckles. Throwing herself back on the bed, she voluptuously pressed it to her face. Moaning, she twisted feverishly on the bed. Like the perfume, his boot carried his own unique scent, the musky aroma of his sex. Tentatively, she licked the polished skin, but could not taste him as she might have wished. But as she lay with her back arched in abandonment, she could smell him, and that alone summoned him into the dark arena of her imagination.

Haltingly, she dragged the boot across her breast, feeling the pleasant abrasion as it rasped across her hardened nipple. If only he was here, she wished. Again, she buried her face in the leather, imagining the pressure of his foot compressed into the tight container.

Something inside her was so tightly wound she twisted the leather in her hands, sliding it down across her stomach. The hardness of the sole and heel was painful, but that pleased and excited her. Barely knowing what it was she did, she pressed herself on to the toe of the boot, feeling its unforgiving hardness slide inside her slippery, wax-molten sex. Her response was immediate – a great surge of desire, an overwhelming need for release. Trying her best to stifle her cries, she pushed the toe cap further against her wet lips, imagining he still wore it and pushed at her receptive fissure with the contemptuous toe of his foot. He might then rub it a little, she felt, just to see her squirm. As she pictured this, she thrust more of the inflexible leather against her entrance. She could bear it no longer – for too long she had imprisoned her fever. With a desperate cry she turned over on her stomach and pushed the boot beneath her and barely knowing what it was she did, tried her utmost to mount the long, tapering toe. Gasping, she felt a broad wedge of leather pierce her entrance. Delirious, she pushed on and on, working back and forth, driving the inflexible tip an inch and then two and then three inches into her melting entrance. All the time, she hugged the long leather leg, rapturously inhaling the pungent scent of leather, the man's scent and her own heady, sensual secretions.

Only one thing was missing to reach the very pinnacle of pleasure. Reaching down to the floor, she grasped the lilac dress. Quickly, she found it – a damp, still warm patch of acrid semen. Just pressing her face into the stained fabric, she shuddered as the muscles between her thighs gripped and snatched the thick leather jammed inside her. It barely took a few strokes for her to explode with desire, gripping the hard leather to her stiffened breasts, pummelling her wet sex with the long, waxed hardness. As she did, she felt her tongue reach out greedily, rolling and lapping along the salty cloth. With a spasm of pure pleasure, she felt her entrance contract around the toe of the boot as she pushed it as far and hard inside her as it could possibly go. The scent of his semen pounded her brain. Involuntarily, she bit and sucked the salty fabric. Losing complete control, she felt her spasms eject fluid down her thigh and over the black leather. But she did not care. Somehow, temporarily, her body was sated. That was all she cared about now.

Later that same night, Clara tiptoed along the stairway through the silent apartment. The count's door was closed, but she did not try the door. He had curtly told her he was leaving the next day and she should follow in a day or two. Her civilised self wished she could storm self-righteously back to England. But she could not. He was binding her to him in a way she could not understand.

Instead, she placed the single boot where he might clearly see it, hung askew on the banister at a rakish angle. Laughing silently, she wondered if he would see it was strangely misshapen, as if held in a vice or crushed inside a tight space. And wet, too, though she had tried her best to wipe it dry. Still, she considered, as she tiptoed back to her room, if he does not see I have used a part of him very shamefully, I am sure he might just be able to catch the scent of my wickedness.

113

Chapter Eight

*T*hey were crossing the border. At the frontier of Pont-de-Beauvoisin, for the first time Clara felt a tremor of fear at the enormity of her journey. The Alps were not hills, like the rough-hewn Pennines, or even mountains such as she had seen in pictures of the Scottish highlands. They were sheer, white naked rocks, stretching up to the skies. Jagged precipices cut the rock asunder; huge clefts loomed in the icy granite, as if giants had struck the land with sparking axes.

Waved ahead by surly soldiers of the Duchy of Savoy, their carriage began to wind forwards, deeper and deeper into the mountains. They were alone on the road; no birds sang on the mountainsides scattered with windswept pines. Even the breeze had quieted, so that the only sounds were the horses' shoes and the creak and rattle of the carriage.

In the silence of the mountains, Clara once more withdrew far within herself. In keeping with her physical sense of disorientation, she felt her whole inner self had been cut adrift. Strange changes had come upon her. As if to torment her, the perfumer's wax continued to melt. Always it was there, rubbing and chafing inside her, reminding her of the secret heat buried inside her body. Even as she sat demurely at breakfast or chatted

114

in the halls of inns, she had only to squeeze her inner muscles to define its elongated shape pushing apart the sensitive walls of her hidden passage.

The effect on her mind was worse. Every moment she could, she retreated into her own, vividly indelicate thoughts. How she wished now, that Anton had lost his battle with his embattled will – how she watched that encounter again and again in her fervid imagination. But then, as long weary days of travel passed, she embellished that encounter more and more freely. To add to her excitement, she remembered the violent heat of his cane on her bare, wriggling bottom. Even stranger, she wished she had kept in her possession that hard, long-toed boot. To her shame, she even watched again in her mind that wild, pain-frenzied coupling between the count and Tresa. At those times, she watched Tresa secretly, even enviously.

It was hard not to puzzle over her companion. She was frivolous, voluptuous, immodest. At Lyons they had stopped to buy lighter, more appropriate summer clothes. But this time, instead of only Clara being attended by a dressmaker, they both spent a wonderful afternoon in the private sitting room of their inn, opening bags, being pinned and laced into fanciful new gowns and parading in front of mirrors.

'Here, Clara, this woman will not lace tight. You come and help me.'

The dressmaker had gone to fetch yet more goods from her shop. Tresa was standing, hands on narrow whaleboned waist, before a tall cheval glass.

Laughing, Clara approached the vain Italian, then tried to pull the long laces even tighter through the dozen tiny eyeholes that punctuated her new pair of stiffened satin stays. Beneath, she wore only a gauze-like chemise and Clara suddenly found it hard not to notice the fabric stretched ever tighter across Tresa's pronounced, coffee-coloured nipples.

'I do not think these will go tighter,' she exclaimed,

her fingers growing red with the effort while her face rapidly blushed the same colour.

'Look,' said Tresa, incredulously, 'there are inches of room in here.' Grasping Clara's hand, she pushed it down between the rigid casement of the corset and the soft flesh of her breast.

'Here, I suppose I must show you how to do it.'

Pushing Clara in front of the mirror, Tresa took up her position behind. Unpinning her bodice, in a moment Clara stood only in her own sturdy pink corset and sheer muslin shift.

'No, there is no need,' she began, struggling to get out of the other woman's clutches.

'I will simply show you how it is done. Then you will know how to lace me next time.'

Tresa glared at her reflection in the mirror and Clara slumped, docile beneath her companion's eager fingers. Quickly, Tresa unlaced the back, down to her waist.

'Now, to get a good tight waist, we must get some resistance.'

Grasping both ends of the laces hard, Tresa slipped her bended knee up to Clara's bottom and began to pull, preventing her from falling backward. The laces pulled the ivory busk of the corset deep into her waist. Tighter and tighter the stays closed, like an iron belt, forcing the breath from her body. Next, Tresa pulled the higher laces, her knee still pressing hard against her rear, suddenly slipping between the rounded cheeks of her bottom. The rhythmic pressure against Clara's sensitive rear felt horribly exciting.

'How does that feel? Tight? I love to feel it that tight.'

Clara tried to get her breath. She understood what Tresa meant; it was oddly arousing to feel her body so compressed and straightened.

'See how it pushes up your breasts,' Tresa smirked, gazing at the twin white spheres which threatened to tumble over the rigid satin.

'Shall I see if there is space left for a finger?'

Laughing, she slid both of her hands mischievously

116

up the smooth seams of the corset from her handspan waist to the suggestively low neckline. Swiftly, her elegant bronze fingers slid over her swelling breasts. Clara could feel her nipples tingle pleasurably in response.

'No, no!' Clara spun out of her grasp. 'Just leave me alone, will you?' she snapped, picking up her own clothes and leaving Tresa to face the dressmaker alone.

Back in their room, she had struggled to release herself from the torturous cage of the garment. She felt dirty, she decided. No, it was Tresa who made her feel indecent; even more so when she noticed the liquid wax dribbling shamefully down from her golden pubis to her thigh. There was no escaping the fact that she was hot inside, hot with need.

Between tears and a wretched temper, Clara ordered a bath to be drawn, but only once she lay inside the water, legs luxuriously steaming over the sides of the tub, did she finally feel her heart slow down. Her waist still tingled pleasurably, as did the sensitive little orifice Tresa had unwittingly rubbed against. Tentatively, Clara lifted her hips and began to massage that burning, quivering little spot. Her breasts were slippery as milk beneath the soap, her pink nipples hard and wet. Unable to stop herself, Clara's fingers dipped inside the dripping, waxy entrance between her arching legs. Pressing apart her swollen, aching lips, she found her sex; ripe, plump and burning with need. Stifling every cry of pleasure, even preventing the ripple of the warm, silky water, she teased and tormented her own body and, for the moment at least, succeeded, again and again, in finding a kind of burning release.

Now, looking ahead, Clara could see that the mountains grew ever taller, their peaks lost in the clouds. She was beginning to feel sick with apprehension.

'Have you travelled this way before?'

'I have,' replied Tresa, without interest. 'It is necessary, sometimes, to pass through a little danger to reach a better place. Do not worry yourself; we shall pass quite

117

safely at this time of year. And, when we reach Mount Cenis, the porters are very careful. They are used to carrying big fat men, so you will be no trouble.'

'What? What did you say about carrying me?'

Tresa could not resist a sly little grin. 'Has no one told you? There is no road ahead for the carriage to cross. When we reach Cenis, the carriage will be dismantled and dragged across the mountains by mules. We will be carried in the local version of sedan chairs. It is really quite exhilarating – though it is an extremely high pass and very narrow. The drop down – why, it is best you don't look down, my dear.'

'You are teasing me, aren't you? I have never heard of such a thing.'

'Ask the driver, if you don't believe me.'

'I certainly will.'

Clara found she was twisting her gloves into strings, so horrified was she by this piece of news. It was not that she was a coward – it was just that she could not abide high places. She would feel sick and giddy. If there was a narrow edge, she was bound to slip off into an abyss. Perhaps her legs would no longer carry out her commands if she had to leave the carriage.

When at last the driver called a halt for the horses to rest, she approached him and asked quite directly if what Tresa had said was true.

'Certainly, Miss Fairfax. But it's naught to concern yourself about. The Alpine men carry all kinds of heavy goods across the pass and it's of no trouble to them to carry a lightweight body such as yourself. If I was you, I should just watch the splendid views and enjoy it.'

But this was little reassurance. Wandering ahead of the little group, she stood on a shelf of rock and gazed ahead at the precipitous mountain range. In the evening light, the sun shone on glacial peaks, making the summits appear even more frightening and remote. It was deadly silent; the stillness made her think of the mountains as great crouching beasts, slippery and cold, waiting for her to enter their steel trap. The sheer emptiness, lacking all signs of man or beast, appalled her. Then she heard a sound – a tinny, ringing bell, glancing back and forth between the crags. Peering up into the whiteness, she at last found the source of that penetrating sound. It was there, leaping across dizzying gaps between shelves of rock, a tiny speck of blackness.

'It is only a mountain goat.'

Tresa was beside her, obviously much amused by Clara's horror. As the goat faltered across a gap thousands of feet above them, it sent a small shower of rocks downwards in mimicry of its own descent, should it be less sure-footed the next time.

'I cannot abide such heights and precipices. If only we could stay in the carriage, I might have borne it. If only we had travelled by sea, like the count. If I had known I should have insisted!'

Anton had made it quite clear that his business in Lucca necessitated the fastest route possible by sea. Yet, given the time of year, he had insisted that the boat from Marseilles to Italy would take the two ladies on far too hazardous and uncomfortable a journey.

'Come along, Clara,' Tresa cajoled, taking her arm. 'Think only that, by tomorrow evening, we shall descend into the most beautiful land on earth. Once we arrive in Italy you will find all the perils of the journey quite, quite, forgettable.'

The inn that night was little more than a hut set into the mountainside. Feeling cold and feverish, Clara declined to join the others to admire the views, trying to keep her eyes firmly to the ground as she entered the dirty, smoke-filled room. She glimpsed only that here the mountains were sheer up into the sky and, covered as they were with pristine snow, the setting sun cast a lurid crimson glow across the jagged peaks.

To her, it looked like a landscape of hell.

Her sleep was no better. Sequestered with Tresa in an area no better than an animal byre, she tossed and turned on a scratchy, verminous pallet. Around midnight, in the impenetrable darkness, the wind suddenly rose. Then, instead of the uncanny silence of the mountains, a slow moaning began, as the gusts whipped around the peaks, chasing each other like furious will o' the wisps. Again and again, Clara's mind returned to their precarious position here, up on a mere shelf of stone on the side of a dizzying peak. How sensible were the English, she thought, living in pleasant valleys where the land was flat and fertile.

At last the day broke, pale and cold. A little feverish with tiredness, Clara pulled on all her clothes in layer upon layer, trying to still her shivering limbs. Tresa, meanwhile, produced the winter outfit she had first worn in Holland: the fur-lined cloak and matching fur-trimmed hat.

'Come along, Clara,' she called. 'The ride will make our complexions glow.'

And when the Savoyards arrived, dressed in high boots and feathered caps, she leapt into her chair like a mountain goat, all the sooner to be carried off over the crags. Meanwhile, Clara looked nervously at the peculiar transport. It was a chair of wood, padded with animal pelts but not like a sedan at all. Without a roof, it was open to the elements and the passenger was obliged to sit with her legs extended in front and be tied in with a cord at the ankles and waist. At front and back were four long poles for the men to lift the chair and carry her at the height of their waists.

At first Clara was terrified when the chair rose and began to swing and lurch along, and she was certain she would any moment tumble out and roll to the bottom of the mountain. But soon, despite flurries of snow and the appalling steepness and zigzagging route of the path, she began to understand that she might, indeed, be reasonably safe. And although the sheer faces of rock and crashing cascades around her were terrible, yet she could also discern that after a time the path was rapidly descending. In time, the land grew less precipitous and populated by a lush spread of chestnut trees.

Now that she was not obliged to see the edges of chasms and feel so utterly dependent upon the two sturdy Savoyards for the continuance of her life, Clara could at last begin to enjoy her journey a little more. The sun began to break through the forest ceiling and new, misty blue vistas spread out down below them in the valley.

Tresa, too, was extolling the beauties of nature around them.

'See how the land changes as we approach Italy. Soon we will be able to reach out and pluck oranges and lemons with our hands. Feel it – it grows warmer already.'

It was true. With great relief Clara arrived at the bottom of the pass. They were at least a day ahead of the rest of the party, who were dragging the dismantled carriage across the pass. So, after spending a comfortable night in a rambling old inn by the river, Clara woke with some pleasure to the prospect of a day at liberty.

She had to admit that Tresa's praise had been apt; the weather was pleasantly balmy and the sky a pale, cloud-feathered blue. The women's room, by a prettily rushing river, was quaint and charming to the greatest degree, with tiny gabled windows and brightly painted furniture and gaily woven rugs. Taking an early morning stroll in the sun-dappled woods, Clara stretched her limbs, enjoying the unusual luxury of sun on her face and shoulders. The area was still surrounded by pictur-esque mountains but she knew the worst was over. She had made the crossing. Now, all the beauties and novel-ties of Italy lay before her.

There was no doubting that they had journeyed into the summer. Yet, even as she closed her eyes to feel the sun, an ominous phrase rang in her ears. 'The end of the summer.' By then she would need to be sure about the count, sure that she wanted to spend the rest of her life with him. Yet, looking about at the greenness of the forest and the blueness of the sky, she decided to postpone any wearisome decisions. For the present, at least, she felt driven to follow him.

'Here. Catch.'

It was Tresa. The next moment Clara just had time to reach out and catch a large orange as it was thrown in her direction.

'I told you, in Italy, we can pluck the fruit from the trees. This is my proof.'

It was true, for the orange was large, round and deliciously sweet. Clara felt it must be a good omen.

'I have just had a message from our driver,' Tresa added, making her way down the path. 'There is no possibility of setting off until tomorrow. There are still horses and a new postillion to be engaged at Susa.'

'Oh, I am glad,' replied Clara, yawning luxuriously.

'Is it not the most beautiful country in the world? But of course, it is not one country, but a number of states and, though we are far from the island itself, we are now in the Kingdom of Sardinia. My own homeland in Lucca, that is the most lovely. Listen, what do you say to us taking a little excursion? Not far from here are some ancient caves. There is a legend that those who bathe there may obtain eternal youth. What do you say? We could engage a carriage and bathe there. Come along, Clara; we deserve to enjoy ourselves. No one need ever know.'

She found it difficult to remain angry with Tresa – it was impossible, given her utterly charming gift for self-indulgence. Once she had been assured that the caves were not far and were certainly not up a mountain pass, Clara agreed. Life was easier, as well, now that Tresa could chatter at speed with their hosts, instead of the pair of them labouring over their words in stumbling French. In no time at all, she had arranged transport and a picnic lunch with their Piedmontese hostess.

Delighted to discard the dusty layers of her travelling clothes, Clara pulled out a thin silk gown with a simple muslin chemise beneath. When she joined Tresa, she found she had procured two large straw hats, such as the peasant girls wore in that district. Their transport was little better than a dog cart, but that made it all the pleasanter, to be open to the warm elements instead of jolted in the half-light of a dingy carriage. Soon, as the lovely valley opened below them, rich with fruit and chestnut trees and full of trusting little songbirds, Clara smiled. If this were to be her adoptive homeland, she could be contented here.

Stopping to eat their picnic at the head of the valley above the caves, it seemed they had indeed discovered the Arcadia of the ancient world. Bright blue alpine flowers were scattered in the grass; the simple fare of white bread, soft cheese, hams, figs and wine, tasted as delicious as any banquet. Watching Tresa through half-closed eyes, Clara forgave her much; dappling her fingers in the stream with her voluminous sky-blue dress billowing across the rocks, she looked far more agreeable than when her eyes had flashed avariciously over the luxuries of the Parisian shops.

'Tell me more of this legend of eternal youth,' she yawned, joining Tresa at the stream.

She replied with a slow, dark smile. 'All I know is that the maidens of this area travel to the caves each midsummer eve in all their peasant splendour of embroidered dresses and veils and golden bodkins, and sleep outside under the stars, dreaming of their future lovers. Then, at dawn, they all go inside and bathe in the warm waters, acquiring such beauty from the natural elements of the place to then go forth and obtain whatever they wish. I should call it the country woman's spa, and there will certainly be less charge to take the waters than at the French spas.'

However, when they arrived at the entrance to the cavern, Clara felt somewhat unprepared for her ordeal. An old crone sat alone on a rock and, for a few sou, offered them smoky tallow lanterns. Shuffling inside, they found the floor was unpleasantly slippery and, were it not for a length of rope attached to the clammy wall, Clara might well have chosen not to proceed at all.

Yet, with much laughter, Tresa led the way, her tiny lamp revealing long, shining formations of rock as ornate as cathedral organ pipes, as well as strange patches of blue and green colour that gleamed like freshly daubed paint.

Just at the moment when Clara, growing much concerned about the state of her silk shoes in the many puddles, was about to announce that she would turn back, Tresa shouted out that they had arrived. Indeed they had, for at the end of the dripping passage was a vast chamber, illuminated by flambeaux set into the wall that cast an eerie, red light. Astonished, Clara looked about herself, amazed at the roof that arched as high as any church and the magnificent walls, as strangely carved by nature as if by the most inspired sculptor.

'What do we do now?' she whispered, grasping Tresa's arm.

'I think we came here to bathe.' Dipping an elegant finger into the large pool at the centre of the cavern, Tresa flicked a few drops of the tepid water at her companion's face. Giggling, they began to undress, laying their gowns across the many convenient boulders set about the place. Soon, Clara became aware once more of the voluptuous build of her companion; she could not help but conclude that Tresa had been formed for pleasure. Her lack of abandonment, too, meant she gave no thought at all to modesty. As she stretched in the torchlight, she seemed like some preternatural she-devil, her olive skin glowing redly, casting dark shadows beneath her swinging breasts and the luxurious blackness below her stomach. Clara, meanwhile, undressed beneath the voluminous cover of her gown.

'Oh, it is hot!'

Quickly slipping her limbs into the pool, Clara felt the strangely warmed water slip over her skin like heated oil. There was something heavy about the water, too.

'It is full of natural elements,' Tresa told her, 'which should give a lustre to our skin.'

For some time, they floated and glided about the pool,

exploring the rocky niches at the edge and testing the depth. At the centre, it was too deep to stand, but elsewhere they could quite comfortably lounge across the gently shelved rock. Suddenly Clara felt something grab at her ankle. With a scream, she splashed away. Blinded by the spray, she could not see when again something pinched at her leg.

'Stop it! Is that you, Tresa?'

With a great heave and splash, Tresa rose laughing from the water, her hair and face drenched, water streaming over her face and breasts.

'What did you think it was? A slippery eel?' Mischievously, she wormed her fingers around Clara's waist. It tickled so much Clara almost fell under the water as she doubled over with laughter. 'Did you think I was Anton – worming his way into your dry virtue?'

This time, she slipped her fingers around to Clara's rear end and the English girl had to smack her away, laughing so much she thought she might burst.

'You are a devil, Tresa,' she giggled, dancing about to stay out of reach but not quite succeeding.

'Ah, that is what you wish, is it not? That I am so bad and you are so good?'

'Something like that,' she agreed, regaining her breath.

'That Anton raises you on a pedestal – whilst I am more useful on my hands and knees?' With this, she lounged her dripping arm casually over Clara's shoulder and eyed her with almost unbearable intensity.

'It is not like that,' Clara mumbled half-heartedly.

Tresa lifted a wet corkscrew of hair from Clara's face. Clara was abruptly aware of the other woman's closeness, of her smooth nakedness pressed against her own nakedness, even of the soft bulge of her breast pressing against the side of her body. With a flutter of panic she wondered what might happen next. She felt quite powerless beside Tresa.

'I know.'

Bending only slightly, Tresa brushed her lips softly against her mouth and then, when she met no resistance, returned to kiss her full and hard on the mouth. As her tongue slid into Clara's mouth, Clara found herself reaching out to the other woman, pulling at her shoulders, trying to nestle into her body. There was a shock, but also a rightness to their passion. Clara relaxed into the slippery softness of the other woman.

'I know, because I watch you closely,' Tresa whispered between kisses, stroking Clara's body now, running sensual fingers down her back and flank, caressing her slippery buttocks. Clara remembered the dark tumble of thoughts that had haunted her this last month. The thought of Tresa watching her, now gave her a *frisson* of pleasure.

'You are not quite so prudish as you wish Anton to believe, are you?' she asked, and when she got no reply, for Clara was drowning fast in a flood of desire, she cupped her chin in her hands and demanded to know. 'Are you so prim and unfeeling? Or do you feel as others do?'

With this, she slid her hand between Clara's thighs and Clara felt an ecstatic shock, like fiery lightning-run through her bowels.

'I know Anton wants only to conquer you. It is driving him wild. But, though you hide it well, you feel just as I do, don't you?'

Tresa's fingers jutted inside her. Clara felt as if her insides had turned to hot syrup. It was impossible to deny her excitement. Her thighs loosened, inviting Tresa's fingers to explore. She wanted more, much more. Sliding her hand behind Tresa's head, she sought her mouth and insistently kissed her, driving her tongue hard towards her throat. Her mouth was softer than a man's but urgently responsive too. Eagerly, her hands reached for her breasts and, with a wave of supreme pleasure, she took one in each hand and squeezed. They felt softly resistant within her hands, slippery and almost alive. It was delightful to hear Tresa gasp with both surprise and excitement. Tresa's breasts were firm and lively, too large to cup in each of her small hands.

'Of course I feel,' she whispered sharply. 'But I command my feelings; I do not let them command me.'

But it was hard to stay true to her words. Finding Tresa's brown nipples growing long and hard between her fingers, she reached down and sucked on each, long and luxuriously. The bitter water mixed with the salt-sweetness of Tresa's skin. Every new feeling delighted her. It was as if her tongue had always done this, abrading and flicking the nipple, nuzzling against the luxurious flesh of the woman's breast. In response, she felt Tresa's hips press hard against her, insistently rubbing her pubis against her. With a gentle splash, they toppled back against a ledge of rock. First one then the other was above, feasting on each other's bodies, sucking and nuzzling nipples, licking, kissing each other's flesh and pressing hard now for satisfaction.

Uncontrollably, Clara began to cry out with pleasure, pulling Tresa closer and closer inside her thighs.

At last, Tresa's hand slid back between her legs and this time found her lips parted and slippery, urgently nuzzling against her fingers. In conspiratorial whispers, Clara explained about the perfumer's wax. Tresa was intrigued, sliding her long fingers inside the girl's acquiescent entrance. Clara shuddered, as the movement of the round remnant of wax set off exquisite spasms of pleasure.

Following suit, Clara began to explore her lover's body, slipping up the slender olive thighs, seeking the wet cleft which felt like hot-ironed satin against her fingertips. Slowly, at first, she stroked the other girl's lips until their mutual urgency rose and all modesty was abandoned. Both began to cry out quietly, whimpering with pleasure. Around them, in the flame-lit darkness, their gentle cries echoed strangely, like two wild birds.

Tresa's slippery entrance felt so strange, yet also like her own body when she explored it: yielding and hot to the touch. Their movements were gentle, teasing; nevertheless, their first release was achieved in moments. Almost as soon as she felt Tresa push hard against her, crying with pleasure, she felt her own moment arrive. Wave upon wave of bliss spread through her body as the woman's fingers deftly tickled her clitoris. Finally, she could bear it no more and thrust Tresa's hand away, so unbearably tormenting was the ceaseless pleasure she brought.

Yet she only had to look down at Tresa's long, voluptuous body, glowing redly in the torchlight, to know that they had barely begun. Artfully, Tresa ran her palm across Clara's breasts, enjoying the swell, teasing the nipples until they sprang up hard. Almost instantly, Clara felt the pit at her centre contract with excitement. Suddenly she knew that this had been a possibility between them from the start: a small part of their mutual mistrust and wariness as they secretly took stock of each other.

Smiling like a cat, Tresa ran her fingernails deliciously downward, along Clara's stomach.

'When I saw you with our well-endowed friend, I should have loved to have joined you. Would you have liked that? The three together? Imagine all that pleasure.'

Clara tried to imagine it and sighed. Misgivings about Anton were for another time. Instead, she pictured that exciting young gentleman and Tresa besides in a variety of most delicious postures.

'You needn't have let him have you fully,' said Tresa, 'only imagine if you would, his rather fine endowment pressing here,' and with this she pushed at the cleavage between Clara's breasts. 'Or here,' and she ran her fingernails gently across her throat. 'Or even here.' Tresa's fingers pressed insistently against her mouth. Clara fervently opened her lips to admit entry to the imaginary cock and pressed her tongue hard against Tresa's fingertips.

'And you must picture me, meanwhile, engaged here.'

With a rapid slither, Tresa travelled down her body, kissing her stomach and then lightly parting her surrendering lips. As Tresa kissed her sex, Clara thought she was transported to paradise. With an alarming swiftness,

128

she was again licked and sucked to the doors to gratification. Panting, she lifted her thighs and pressed them involuntarily about Tresa's head. In seconds it was over, in a little flood of waxy juices mixing with the briny water.

As Tresa rose, she stretched to kiss her, tasting her own self on her lips, eager to satisfy as she had been satisfied. Tresa needed no persuasion, and soon they settled, curled around each other like two halves of the same coin. In that heady darkness their tongues and lips and fingers explored every private inch of each other's bodies, inspecting lips and swellings and orifices in a ravenous hunt for pleasure. It seemed that each few minutes, one or the other would shudder and convulse, so long and powerful was their delectation. Never before had Clara's body felt so utterly used and pleasured – she ached with it, yet each climax was like another, even finer, exquisite morsel. Each time she returned for just one more luscious bite. With all the skills of finger and tongue, Tresa teased her, inching from the jutting mound of her pubis to the quivering entrance between her buttocks. On and on, Tresa tormented her mercilessly, until repeatedly Clara had to beg her to push and pinch and – just finish her, again and again.

Finally, they heard the sound of footsteps approaching from the cave entrance. Reluctantly, they sprang apart, Clara feeling she was almost waking from some other world contrived only of sensation. A little shyly, she looked at Tresa, whose face was gleaming and dark-eyed with sex.

'It is time to go,' she murmured, slipping into the water and crossing the pool to their clothes. Silently, they both dressed, as the crone finally shuffled into the cave holding a bright lantern aloft. For a while, she gabbled in Italian and then, when Tresa replied, shuffled off, leaving them the lantern which cast giant shadows against the crimson walls.

'What did she say?'

'She said she thought,' began Tresa, stifling laughter,

'that we were so long we must have secret lovers in here with us.'

'What did you say?'

'I told her we smuggled them in here.' Then she mischievously batted Clara's petticoat. 'And that we hid them under our skirts.'

Chapter Nine

Clara wanted to weep when she heard the little convent children sing at the church of Santa Maria. Arriving unexpectedly early at the Albergo Montane, they had found the count already out for the evening at a concert at the church. But now, as she looked about, she could see no sign of him in the great press of the audience. Then the girls of the convent and the boys of the conservatory began to sing. If the church roof had opened above them to let the voices of angels be heard, it could not have been lovelier.

When she at last saw him, Clara's reaction was physical. The count was to the side of her across the aisle, lounging in a pew but deeply attentive nevertheless. As ever, he was immaculately dressed in black silk with a white linen stock at his throat. His beautiful face was lost in the singing, dark eyes turned inwards in some secret contemplation. Something sparkled in his hand. Clara saw it was a rosary of jet and diamond threaded between his fingers.

How many different aspects could a single person have? Like the theatrical masks of Rome, she contemplated his different personae: narcissist, sensualist, elitist, even prig. Yet also kindly, generous, enlightening and often, as now, disarmingly vulnerable.

It was something she did not consider often – this difference in religion. How she had laughed at his Popish ways when they passed ludicrous roadside statues hung with peasant's jewellery and symbols. A little shamefully, she wondered at her insensitivity. Clearly, in his private moments, he was devout. She wondered if that was why he took their strange promise so seriously.

Clara turned away from him. Perhaps she was prying. For a moment, she glimpsed the utterly different, transcendent world he inhabited. As the air grew thick with incense and the heady scent of lilies drifted from the altar, she surrendered to the moment. Perhaps she had been a sleepwalker all her previous life. Now, even common scents and sights aroused her – not only to lust, but to a consummate, new intensity.

They met in the piazza outside. Quite changed, he strode up to Clara and Tresa, holding out his hands to greet them both the same. He smiled, his eyes bright and quite removed from the transcendent gaze that had fixed them earlier.

'Ladies, you surprise me most delightfully. Your journey – it was comfortable?' They chattered animatedly about their travels – the pleasures of Turin and Genoa, the short and uneventful crossing to Leghorn. Clara wondered if he had the perception to note the change in her and Tresa's bearing towards each other. As they had journeyed, it had proved impossible not to indulge again and again in their mutual pleasurings. Tresa still flirted with nearly every man they met, but Clara could only be amused by that. They were not in love but had become friends, which was so much easier and amicable.

Once they were all agreeably installed at the Albergo, they were free to enjoy the magnificent bounties of the Eternal City. As they visited the antique and modern sights, the remnants of the Old City and the fine new churches and palaces, the count's manner was coolly amiable, just as it had been on her arrival in Paris.

'What would you see today, Clara?' he asked, one morning at breakfast.

She felt like a cosseted child. The sun shone into their breakfast room and purple grapes hung on vines curled about their window. Already, she could hear the litany of morning bells ringing through the clear air and the sounds of horses and streetsellers on the Piazza della Rotunda. Each morning she rose full of bright expectation, ceaselessly marvelling at the wonders laid out before her.

'Whatever you advise. For it is you who control my education.'

He smiled pleasantly, peeling a peach with a silver knife. 'But the pupil must be willing.'

'Oh, I am willing, sir.'

They were alone, for Tresa was making a necessary visit to an old family friend. Suddenly, Clara became vividly aware of this and the quietness of the apartment now that the servants were downstairs.

'Not always, I think.'

Clumsily, she set her teacup on the saucer with a loud rattle. She looked up at him carefully. Never had he raised any difference between them since their confrontation in Paris.

'I only follow my teacher's rules.'

He slipped a piece of fleshy peach into his mouth while she watched his lips. Abruptly she thought of kissing them – how sweet they would taste now.

'Maybe it is time to invent new rules.'

Clara's heart was thumping. 'But I was always taught that learning needs to stand on a firm foundation. Upon the solid rules of nature.'

'Clara, nature can be chaotic and wild. Do you not know that yet?' He was looking at her quite boldly and there could be no mistake as to his meaning. He flashed a glance at her and she felt naked provocation thicken the atmosphere between them. 'I fear your education is incomplete. Come here and show me what you have learnt – so far.'

She stared at him. But in reply, he only raised his brows, waiting, continuing to peel the fruit. With a scrape of the chair, she rose and slowly walked over to his side of the walnut table.

'Well, I am here,' she announced boldly, standing directly in front of him.

She feasted upon every inch of his face with her eyes. That arrogance did indeed enhance his looks even more. Dark brows, fine nose, well-shaped lips, and the long, virile hair now loose to his shoulders. The spell between them was very powerful

'So,' he asked softly, 'what have you learnt of scent?' As he did so, he impaled a slice of dewy peach on to the silver knife. He lifted the morsel to her face so she could smell the ambrosial scent, as sweet and aromatic as any perfume. Before, she would never have smelt it so strongly, had it not been for his lessons. Now much of her journey was like this: punctuated by intense new sights, feelings and scents.

'That it is the true essence of a thing.'

As she answered, she felt his hand slip around her waist. He was pulling her ever so slightly closer, but she carefully hid any awareness of this.

'Well said.'

His eyes were devouring her, watching the pulse at her throat and the burgeoning flesh above her tight damask bodice.

'Here is your reward.'

He lowered a morsel of fruit to her lips and nudged for an entrance. For a second she pouted, frowning indignantly. Suddenly he laughed and she was aware of his white teeth. Slowly she parted her lips in a smile and he slid it inside.

The pulp of the fruit was as sweet as any syrup, the fragrance bursting on to her tongue as she chewed it. His other arm slid around her waist.

'I have dripped a little,' he murmured, indicating a few drops of peach juice upon the smooth ivory of her bosom. He lowered his dark head and she suddenly felt the soft abrasion of his tongue lap across her skin. Her limbs felt weak. Then he raised his face so his eyes were

134

very close to hers, the pupils wide and black, searching her innermost thoughts.

'It is nearly time for your next lesson.'

Her breath was short. 'When will that be?'

Running his hands along her back to her shoulders, she felt she might involuntarily fall into his arms if he would not cease this seduction directly.

'We shall continue tomorrow evening, on our visit to the Villa Barberini.'

Very softly, she heard him exhale, feeling the heat of his breath scorch the sensitive skin of her breasts, his eyes reverently closed. Clara, too, was finding it hard to breathe. Then, on the instant, he sat back and continued his breakfast.

The very next moment, Tresa bustled in, having certainly been detected on the stair by the count. Flustered, Clara straightened her skirts and went to pick up her reticule.

'Oh, and apropos our conversation, I must today visit my bootmaker,' he announced casually as she made for the door. 'It is the strangest thing, but one of my new kid boots is quite out of shape, all of a sudden.'

He was laughing at her, she could see it as she flew through the door. In the privacy of her room, she rinsed her flushed face in the porcelain ewer, trying to cool her glowing face. Outside the sun was rising in a sapphire sky. It was going to be an uncomfortably hot and sultry June in Rome.

The most invaluable of Clara's new possessions was a cream silk parasol, purchased for her by the count as soon as the weather grew warm. Now, in a thin gown of new soft muslin from India, she embarked with her companions in the carriage to see the sights. Through the narrow byways of the old city, they slowly picked their way past the ancient Pantheon on to the broad Via de Corso. The streets were thronged with beggars and flowersellers, artists, friars and red-petticoated housewives. Yet here, thought Clara, there is not the same fearful desperation of Paris. The people appeared well fed and simple but pleasure loving.

Never were they far from music. Song sellers stood on street corners with musical scores pegged on to boards, eager to sing a sample of their wares on request. Blind hurdy-gurdy men, Polish fiddlers, gypsy tambourine players, all set up their pitches in any open space and filled the air with music.

In time, they inched past the ruined grandeur of the Forum where other travellers, guides and artists already wandered, eagerly inspecting and sketching the remnants of Rome's glorious past. Then, Clara caught her first glimpse of the Colosseum, that stupendous monument to the Roman Empire's splendour and folly. Leaving the carriage in the road, they wandered in awe beneath one of its massive arches.

'In the days of bread and circuses, this arena held 50,000 people at one time,' the count informed her, taking her arm. 'In the heat of the sun, a vast canvas awning was stretched across the top held by wooden masts. And at night, a gigantic iron chandelier was suspended above the arena.'

As tier upon tier came into view, still replete with stairways and entrance vaults, her mind was almost overpowered with the immensity of the scene.

'Yet was it not an evil place?'

'Powerful, perhaps. The Romans were self-indulgent but not evil. With their passing went much interesting, esoteric knowledge.'

'Count, I fear you are being a little ingenuous in your explanation. I speak of the atrocities carried out on this ground – the slaughter of Christians, the murder of innocent people by wild beasts.'

'Yes, perhaps our ancestors mixed their wisdom with barbarity. Humanity is not so simple as you believe, Clara,' he continued arrogantly. 'The appetites of the senses can be far, far stronger than the chains of civilisation.'

Consulting Anton's pocket watch, Tresa soon announced that they needed to leave shortly. Both she and the count wished to attend the feast of Corpus Christi at the church of Saint Peter. Feeling a little put out by their insistence that the ceremony was only for believers, Clara became gradually aware of a burgeoning resentment at being bustled off back to the dull confinement of her room.

'I have hit upon an idea,' she suddenly announced. 'While the carriage takes you to Saint Peter's, I will begin to stroll back through the forum. Then the driver can meet me at the other side. That way, you will not be late, and I will enjoy the sights of Rome at my leisure.'

Her companions entreated her with warnings about pickpockets, itinerant guides, poorly guarded excavations, even rabid dogs. But Clara waved them all away. Once the idea had been formed she was resolute. Nothing could dissuade her from the luxury of enjoying just a little time with only her own thoughts for company.

Thus it was that, some quarter hour later, Clara waved her gloves prettily at her companions as they rattled off to the Papal City. With a pleasurable sigh, she set off across the grass towards the glimmering white ruins of the ancient forum. It was now coming towards noon and as she proceeded carefully, the sun beat upon the tight back of her gown like a smith's anvil. Neither was it simple to make her way; though dispensing with heavy panniers beneath her dress in the daytime, still her petticoats and hoops dragged at her waist and invariably picked up heavy dust and dirt. Furthermore, since reaching hotter climes, the tight whalebone of her corsets had irritated her. Like the heavy damasks and velvets of her evening gowns, they were moderately comfortable in the cool evenings. But now, under the unremitting heat of the sun, her unyielding stays felt like steel instruments of torture. With a private groan as she attempted a slight incline, she remembered the Parisian witticism about a lady who complained to her shoemaker that her new shoes had fallen to bits. 'Why, of course,' he replied superciliously, 'Madame has attempted to *walk* in them.'

Yet, as she passed an ornamental pool, she could not complain at the effect. The count had again attended to the needs of her wardrobe and now her reflection in the water threw back a ravishing image of cool, creamy elegance. The new muslin dress was decorated with row upon row of Valenciennes blonde lace in a pattern of arabesques. With her fair hair piled high and topped with a pretty straw bonnet dressed with silk rosebuds, it was not surprising that many of the other sightseers raised their eyes to watch Clara wander amongst them.

'Miss Fairfax? Can it be you?'

'Mr Palmer!'

Striding towards her across the grass was that same John Palmer who had offered his services in Amsterdam. It was with genuine pleasure that she extended her hand to him. His eyes brightly drank in the vision before him: a pale confection of lace and even paler skin, the bright eyes and ready smile beneath the parasol.

'Please. Might we talk? I am sketching – although sketching may be too ambitious a description for my meagre scribblings – over there, by the columns of Castor and Pollux.'

She followed him and found he had set up a little camp by some welcome cypress trees. There she could at last rest while Mr Palmer poured for her some delightfully cool wine and water. For a few minutes, they exchanged opinions of their respective journeys and immediate impressions of the Eternal City.

'And where is Count Malibran today?'

'He is at his devotions at Saint Peter's church. He is a religious man, Mr Palmer.'

The Englishman looked dubious. 'For myself, I would say it is this papistry that is one of the few blights on an otherwise delightful country. Only yesterday, my friends pointed out this Henry Benedict who styles himself both a Cardinal and a Prince of England. It is quite openly paraded, Miss Fairfax, this court of the Pretender, plotting against our sovereign state.'

Clara only nodded pleasantly. It was a secret wish of hers to see Henry's brother, the tragically handsome Prince Charlie who had led the ill-fated uprising in Scotland. Whilst she might be as good an Anglican as John Palmer, yet she had to admit some of the romantic attractions of the Church of Rome.

'Nevertheless, I cannot help but admire such devotion as the count's, whichever church,' she replied.

'But do you not see the hypocrisy of it! As if every dreadful sin can be wiped clean by just a few words to a priest or passing a few beads through one's fingers. Come along, your English sense knows better than to agree.'

'I am afraid, sir, you put me in danger of disloyalty to my future husband. To me, that is the greater sin than disloyalty to any attribute of my country.'

At this, Mr Palmer appeared moved. With a sudden passionate gesture, he took Clara's hand in his. 'Miss Fairfax, you are too good.' He shook his head sadly and then continued to press her hand. 'I only beg you to consider one thing. This beloved husband of yours – is he worthy of your goodness?'

'What do you mean?'

'I cannot pretend I have not heard things that make his papistry a matter of insignificance.' He caressed her hand, staring into her eyes earnestly. 'Someone must tell you, and no one else will. He is known as an infamous sensualist, Miss Fairfax. General opinion believes you to be in great moral danger.'

Clara laughed uneasily, wishing suddenly that she had never set eyes again on the broad, zealous face of Mr John Palmer. 'Come along, I am in no danger,' she smiled. 'I receive every attention. I have clothes, gifts, tours arranged for me, the highest standard of accommodation and attention. Tonight I am to be taken to the opera, and tomorrow out to Tivoli.'

'But do you not know that the operatic stage here is

the centre of unspeakable iniquities? They say there are unutterable practices. I cannot believe it is a fitting excursion for you at all.'

Privately, she began to recoil at the idea of her situation being discussed freely by others.

'Tell me,' she asked sharply. 'Who are "they"? I should like to know whose notions it is make up the general opinion?'

'Your English compatriots, those who care for you. They have no opportunity to meet you, you are jealously kept away from their company. And yet you are obliged to mix with every type of rogue and rake. Even today, I find you wandering here quite unchaperoned. It is outrageous, Miss Fairfax.'

Taking her fan, Clara began to cool her rapidly flushing face. 'You do not know how it is at all, Mr Palmer. I am here against the count's best advice, only because I wished to cross the forum alone. Blame me if you will, not the count.'

Yet, if this man only knew the half! Clara's face was scarlet at the thought of it. Maybe she had been too long without English company. Some of the thoughts that plagued her – and some of the things she had already done – it was impossible to contemplate them here, in a civilised place. Certainly John Palmer's opinions, even though he would never guess the extent of her fall already, had some substance.

'How could anyone blame you?' he suddenly cried with a passion that quite alarmed her. 'You are too unused to the world. You appear here, like an apparition of innocence.' Here, he suddenly flung himself on his knees on the grass before her lap. 'And all the time it torments me that this devil is taking pleasure in the corruption of that innocence. I would save you. I would do anything in my power to protect you. Miss Fairfax – Clara – he is seeking to destroy you.'

Too alarmed to move, Clara sat quite still as the man buried his face in her skirts. He was making himself ridiculous. Yet she found herself wondering how much he truly knew. Or did he only guess at the count's method of sensual education? And was it true? That Anton's cruel aim was only to destroy her innocence? Unbearably hot tears welled up in her eyes and rolled down her cheeks.

'Please, Mr Palmer,' she entreated, her voice broken with emotion, 'do not speak any more about these things. I cannot bear it.'

At this, the Englishman rose, and though still quivering with emotion, succeeded in quelling the greater excesses of his passion. Rapidly fanning her face, Clara was eager for their interview to end.

'I am late,' she announced. 'My carriage will be waiting. I must go.'

'I will accompany you,' cried Mr Palmer, rising to his feet.

And so, arm in arm, they strolled between the massy temples and columns of the ancient forum, their eyes resting on those wondrous objects but neither person particularly seeing what stood before them.

'I will consider what you have said in the privacy of my own thoughts,' said Clara suddenly. 'But, for now, I will not speak of it.'

'Let me repeat only one thing more. If you should ever need help, advice, or the support of a friend, you must call upon me. If you will make me that promise, I will be a happy man.'

Yet as she bid him farewell at the edge of the Piazza, Mr John Palmer did not appear a happy man, although she had agreed to his promise. And though the sun still shone and the crowds were as noisy and vivacious as before, Clara no longer felt happy. Once in the dark stuffiness of the carriage, she found she could not prevent herself from bursting into hot and childlike tears.

Later that evening they entered the dark, smoky theatre of the opera house. The count had a box from which they could look down on the groundlings, who milled and chatted in expectation of the main performance.

141

'I have never been to the opera,' Clara announced, looking about herself with a little apprehension following John Palmer's warning, but seeing nothing to concern her at all.

The count leaned back, smiling in his chair, resplendent in an ivory silk embroidered waistcoat with his coat removed to show thin cambric sleeves caught at the wrists. 'I know. That is exactly why I did not contaminate your brain with French music in Paris. Tonight, the great Angelicco sings. You will never have heard such a voice before and possibly never will again.'

He was explaining the workings of the orchestra, the arias and recitatives when the loudness of the shouting below broke into his discourse. Peering over the balcony, he shook his head.

'In Rome opera is for many their only religion. We have tonight two factions – one for Angelicco, the other screaming for a rival – Gentillini, who sang last night.'

Looking down, Clara could see two angry sets of supporters jostling and pushing, with many angry gestures and happily incomprehensible shouts.

'Look, there is he who some say should be your king.'

Peering across the dusky hall to the boxes opposite, she saw an elderly and a young man together reading a libretto. She could just see that they each wore a tartan band pinned across their chests.

'Is that Prince Charles?' she asked excitedly. The younger man wore powder in his hair and, though she could barely see him, she thought him quite tall and regal.

'You call him Prince, do you? It is Charles Stuart, certainly. Do not let your English friends over there hear you say otherwise – they would call him only the Young Pretender.'

Guiltily, Clara glanced at the large contingent of English lords and ladies gathered in another part of the theatre. She could somehow tell they were English. They were rather pale in comparison with the olive-skinned Italians, and she had to confess that their clothes were less stylish. As good quality perhaps: fine silk sacque dresses in rather muddy colours but with an odd affectation towards lace caps and other such obsolescences. She was suddenly grateful that the count had taken an interest in her wardrobe. Quite without knowing how, she realised she had acquired a modicum of taste.

'See,' whispered Tresa, 'how they stare at their would-be monarch but try so hard to appear discreet.'

It was true. Clara could just see one or two, gazing apparently innocently about them, fixing on the two Stuarts and then whispering to their companions. Even worse, she noticed a couple of women with eyeglasses firmly fixed in her own direction. Quickly, she drew back.

'Why is it, Count, that you will not have me mix with my compatriots?' she hissed. He looked at her, startled.

'Why should you want to keep company with them?'

She was annoyed; they had clearly been expressing an interest in her. 'Why do you always answer a question with a question?' The orchestra was beginning. She flung open her fan with a loud click.

'And why do you?'

Turning her back, she studiously watched the lifting of the curtain, cutting him quite dead.

The first scene was set in a garden. For a long while, Clara simply enjoyed the artfulness of the set and clever way the lamps coloured the stage. The orchestra was beautifully sweet and she did her best to follow the Italian, enjoying a dramatic aria with flutes very much. Then the atmosphere in the theatre grew noisier. It was clear the audience knew something was about to happen.

'Angelicco is coming on,' whispered the count eagerly.

A fanfare sounded. Somehow the lanterns shone brighter, the air grew thinner, the audience hushed. A gasp from a thousand throats greeted Angelicco's approach. Clara felt a spell drop on the theatre as a tall and strikingly beautiful woman sauntered on to the stage. With hair powdered white, her golden skin gleamed exotically. Her eyes were large and black, painted boldly, flashing seduction over the captive audience. With a broad scarlet smile, she welcomed the flurry of roses, love letters and comfits, thrown on to the stage. When she opened her mouth, it seemed a thousand others forgot to breathe. Her voice was as pure as crystal, warm as velvet, voluptuous as over-ripe fruit.

At the end of the piece she curtseyed and, to a collective howl of disappointment, sauntered off the stage again, clearly too colossal a luminary to linger when not performing. The crowd erupted in a tumult. A fight broke out below them. Someone ran on to the stage and threw himself at Angelicco's feet. Clara began to laugh at the whole spectacle of it all, turning to the count with all rancour forgotten.

'You enjoyed my treat?'

'She is divine,' began Clara, but immediately the music began again and they settled down to the next scene.

It was during one of the long intervals when, as they sat eating a dessert of fruit and creams, a knock at their door foretold a visitor. To Clara's amazement, the cloaked and hooded figure proved to be none other than Angelicco herself, once she was safely escorted into their box. She began to converse quite easily with the count, who was clearly on intimate terms with the lady, and served her himself with dessert from the table. Clara found herself growing quite resentful as the exotic beauty wriggled and simpered beneath Anton's courteous attentions. She noticed also that Tresa was a little put out, too, and this was her one small crumb of consolation.

'Now enough of you, Count; let me talk to your *bella Inglese*.'

With a long, sharpened fingernail, the diva summoned Clara to her side. Her beauty was undiminished at close quarters. Her skin was perfect, her painted eyes like dark jewels. Above the satin ruffles of her bodice, her small breasts arched like two creamy pears. Feeling as insignificant as a snail, Clara let her hand be taken, all the time admiring the woman's feminine grace and daintiness. Only one very slight aspect surprised her. It was Angelicco's scent. She wore perfume, certainly, but there was a hint of coarseness to her that belied her scrupulous manners.

'My dear, your hair,' she enthused, caressing Clara's curls. 'It is a very fine colour. Tell me, do you spread it in the sun? They say the juice of a lemon increases the gold. Do you do that?'

With a sharp blow of the elbow, she nudged Anton away. 'We are talking woman talk! Get away!'

Clara saw Anton laugh, shrugging his shoulders. She thought she had never met such a woman as Angelicco. Once the count was distracted, she began to giggle and whisper, stroking Clara's hand all the time, admiring her skin in a quite excessive manner. Clara began to think that perhaps the stage deranged a woman a little. She also suspected that, despite the extraordinary adulation of men, Angelicco was perhaps rather a follower of Sappho. Yet her manner to the count had been similarly cloying.

'And do you love your husband-to-be?' she grimaced coyly. 'For I admit he is rather captivating, and so tremendously rich. What do you say, is he all you desire?'

Clara stumbled over an answer. 'I fear he might hear me praise him and that will do me no good at all,' she whispered.

'*Excellente!*' shrieked Angelicco. 'You are beginning well. When my lovers try to find out from me how I estimate them, there is only one answer – *pathétique*! That way they can never untie their strings – for we must always hold those tight in our hands. By the saints, it is time for some more exercise for my lungs. So, Count,' she continued, holding her hand out to him, 'I look forward to our meeting tomorrow.'

'*Enchanté,*' he murmured, kissing her fingers most

reverently. Then, in a flurry of silk and lace, she had gone.

In this final act, Clara found she could not quite enjoy Angelicco's performance so well, now that she knew she was to be present at the count's lesson the next day. Privately, she admonished herself for these peculiar feelings of what must only be jealousy. For she considered that Angelicco, who was clearly a very old friend, was much more of a match for the count than she was. So beautiful and adored, she must be a great trophy to the man who captured her skittish heart.

It was in the carriage that she determined to establish the count's opinion of the lovely diva.

'Angelicco sang so well tonight,' he began. 'It is no surprise the audience charges the stage.'

'I have never heard a voice like it,' agreed Clara. 'And she is so beautiful too. Do you not think she is lovely, Count? Almost the ideal of womanhood.'

To her profound irritation, this somewhat leading remark immediately prompted an explosion of laughter of a volume and wildness from Anton and Tresa that left her biting her lips with anger.

'What is it?' she snapped. 'Why is it, when I try to express my opinions, you just laugh at me! Why should I not have opinions, too?'

'Oh, I am sorry, Clara,' Anton managed to say, struggling to keep his face reasonably straight. Then he made it worse again by saying sympathetically, 'Oh, my poor girl. What a lot you still have to learn.'

At this, he again laughed uncontrollably, clutching his stomach at the pain.

'Very well, let me in on the joke,' she said through tight lips.

'Oh, I am sorry,' he managed, taking her hand. 'I fear I am a quite dreadful teacher. You are right, Angelicco is beautiful – but, do you not know? No woman is allowed on the Roman stage.'

'No woman? What are you talking about? How is she allowed to sing, then?'

'My dear, you might have noticed Angelicco has followers of both sexes. Beneath his dress he is a castrato, the knife has paid for that gorgeous voice. Quite infamously, he is the *mignon* of Cardinal Barberini. He will be most marvellously flattered to hear your opinion of him. An ideal of womanhood! For he is, quite indisputably, a boy.'

Chapter Ten

As their carriage drove up the long hill to the Villa Barberini, Clara closed her eyes, listening to the tumble of the cascades falling down the craggy rocks, the melodies of birds and the pleasant hum of nature on this warm summer's morning. Then, softly on the air, like Echo singing to her lover, she heard music drift towards her; the soft, silvery notes of a flute and the warmer sweetness of a violin. Not for the first time, she privately thanked Anton for the bounty of the senses he laid before her.

The Villa Barberini was a broad white confection, set on one of the highest crags at Tivoli. Clipped green gardens in the neat Italian style fronted the residence, set about with elegant statuary and bubbling fountains. Never before, when she lived in England, had she guessed that such grace and beauty existed in the world.

As she descended from the carriage on Anton's arm, her new gown rustled and rang with thousands of tiny silver bells sewn into the fabric.

'Anton, I feel like a prize mare in harness,' she complained, trying to smooth the long silk skirts and only succeeding in raising a wild harmony of music.

'But I like it,' he replied. 'You are an instrument of

music in your own right. I can almost hear your every breath.'

Clara frowned at this. It had not occurred to her, when she found the gorgeous silvery dress, that it was anything other than a striking costume for a masque or carnival. But now she recognised it as another aspect of Anton's deliberate policy of control. Why would he want to hear her every breath? Or indeed, as he could now, her every movement?

They were led by liveried servants through cool, marble-floored salons hung with vast mirrors and paintings of saints achieving every type of ecstasy. Finally, they reached an open door leading out on to a tree-lined terrace. There, far above the famous waterfalls, with an awesome view back over the rolling hills of the Campagna to distant Rome, stood the Cardinal's pavilion. It was from this vast, tented chamber, with the heavy curtains drawn back to reveal the view, that the mysterious music had issued. Inside, a small orchestra of strings and flutes was playing a concerto with great delicacy and virtuosity. As they took up seats on low, pillowed chairs, Clara looked about herself with interest, curious to find that everything in this place seemed designed not for sanctity but for pleasure. Oriental cushions, candelabra, crystal flagons and trays of sweetmeats all depicted the Cardinal as a man of Epicurean pleasures.

The Cardinal Barberini himself only waved the ring on his fat fingers at her to kiss and began to speak to the count. He was a bald, rather florid man of perhaps fifty years. Apparently, when at home, he refrained from religious robes and today wore only a silk dressing gown and Chinese cap. Scarcely had she settled in her seat, however, than Angelicco appeared, this time dressed in man's clothes, though few men would have suited the gorgeous embroidered rose waistcoat over a loose cambric shirt.

He sauntered across and kissed her as softly as a woman on her cheek. Clara was suddenly extremely pleased to see him again. Throwing himself on to a low divan, he stretched his long booted legs out in front of him and pouted.

'What is the matter?' she asked.

'He will not let me sing for you,' he sulked. Judging from the inclination of his head, Clara assumed he meant the Cardinal. Even in a fit of pique, he was exquisite. Though wearing boy's clothes, still he wore a little paint and powder in his hair. His eyes flashed even in the daylight like two sultry sapphires. Clara could see why a man like the Cardinal, who loved beautiful things, would place Angelicco at the centre of his collection.

'Do not worry yourself. I heard you sing last night and will treasure the memory all my life.'

'Angelicco!' called the Cardinal, twisting his bull's neck around from his low chair. 'You must save your voice for Milan. When will you learn that your gifts will disappear if you squander them?'

'But she is my new friend,' the boy sulked, whining like a child. 'I wanted to play my game.'

'Do not worry, she is quite seduced already,' laughed the count, setting down his glass of wine. 'Clara, may I tell them of your misapprehension?'

'Oh, I suppose so.' It was her turn to be churlish.

Still, Angelicco was in raptures when he heard of her mistaken opinion, squeezing her hand and kissing her cheek with delight. 'Let me show you the grove,' he whispered. 'It is my favourite place.'

Questioningly, she looked over at the others, who were now engaged in a debate with the Cardinal conducted in extremely rapid Italian. The musicians had retired and, from the hurried comings and goings of liveried flunkies, Clara guessed the main performance would not begin for some time.

'Angelicco will just show me the view,' she quickly blurted and, at the count's preoccupied nod, they rose and slipped out of the curtained pavilion as silently as they might, given the chiming chorus of Clara's dress.

Walking hand in hand with him across the green velvet of the lawn, Clara felt her own heart sing a little to be alone with Angelicco. How foolish she had been to feel jealous of him. The danger, she was quickly realising, ran rather more in her own direction. However, she consoled herself that though it might be delightful to dally awhile with this fabulous creature, his cruel operation had surely lost him the power to play the man in all but costume.

Approaching the furthest walled edge of the terrace, they leant there awhile, gazing at the blue hills and distant spires and domes of the city that glittered in the sunlight like scattered jewels. Angelicco turned, lounging with his back to the wall, stretching like a self-satisfied cat.

'How old are you?' he suddenly asked.

'I am twenty in September. And you?'

'Twenty in December. We are of an age, then. At last – a playmate not old enough to be my parent.'

He smiled, showing his brilliant white teeth. She knew what he meant. The Cardinal was no doubt old enough to be his grandfather. And, for herself, though she liked it mostly, the count was an old man past twenty-five. Even Tresa would not see twenty again.

It was impossible not to stare at him. Even here, in the open air, where many a complexion shows its coarser side, Angelicco's skin was as flawless as gold-tinted porcelain, his curling lips a limpid cherry red. As a woman, he was beautiful – more beautiful than any thousand women. As a boy, he was simply a work of art.

He caressed her hand in that familiar yet childish manner of his. 'Do you want to see the grove?'

She nodded and, with a rattle of her thousand bells, they were off hand in hand down one of the winding white paths. The grove, when they arrived, did not disappoint. She guessed it to be modelled on some pagan place of worship. The statues were of strange half-beasts, naked forms writhing in copulations and other pleasurings. The scent of lilies was very thick in the air, producing an oddly church-like atmosphere. At the centre of the circle of statues was a fountain and, before it, a bed of stone. Clara admired it, for it was not merely a plain slab of marble. The pillows and drapes had all been skilfully carved to represent a gigantic, elaborate reproduction of a bed. Around and about it were candle sconces and even chandeliers suspended in the trees. It appeared to be used both day and night.

'Here, sit on the edge,' her companion suggested. With a welcome ceasing of her musical skirts, she sat quite comfortably on the hard stone, caressing the lifelike rippling that mimicked rumpled sheets.

'Are you not sitting too?'

Secretly, Clara had guessed that he had led her here for a quiet little embrace away from the others. She was quite disappointed when he stood back, shaking his lovely head. It would have been innocent fun to kiss those pouting lips and for the count to never guess.

'No. We must play the game.'

'What game?'

He rapidly pulled the white linen stock from round his neck and approached her.

For the first time, a sense of misgiving flashed into her mind. Angelicco was charming, she was sure. And a little innocent dalliance with this lovely boy was certainly to her taste. But she remembered the hint of derangement she had noticed, the previous night. Now, as he tried to place the cloth around her head, she struggled against his surprisingly masculine grip. Paganism, sinister games – he might be mad and about to strangle her.

'What are you doing?' she fought back.

'Listen, silly. I am only going to sing to you.'

'Ah.'

'And for that, I wish you to be blindfold. I know it is an indulgence, but if I sing for you alone, I should like you to concentrate. Is that too much to ask?'

She shook her head apologetically.

'You see, they will not let me sing until I go to Milan.

But I like all of my new friends to come here and let me sing a story for them. *Bella Inglese*, will you indulge me?'

He looked into her eyes with all the yearning of a beloved pet hound. Silently, she nodded assent.

With his curiously soft hands, Angelicco wound the white cloth around her eyes. Suddenly in darkness, Clara waited.

When he sang, he did so very, very quietly. Quite disarmingly, his voice was like neither man nor woman. As brilliantly sparkling as a choirboy, it yet had the suavity and facility of a great female soprano. Blind-folded, Clara listened attentively.

Gradually, she became aware that the angelic voice was telling the story of a castrato.

'Son giovin, Italiano, amoroso,' he sang, 'I was young, Italian, amorous.'

Losing any sense of her surroundings, she listened as the tale unfolded of the young hero who unwittingly attracted the erotic attentions of his singing master. In order to continue their affair, the youth took to visiting his teacher in the clothes of his sister, which tormented the lust-crazed teacher even more. One day, just after the master had frenziedly taken the boy on all fours on the floor of his studio, the local Abbess called. Hearing our friend's marvellous voice, she claimed the girl for her convent choir.

As she listened, Clara began to wonder at the nature of Angelicco's song. Here, in the quiet of the grove she could hear every pause and tremolo, the perfection of every turn and trill. Yet he sang *pianissimo*, and she could feel the warmth of his sweet breath on her face and naked breasts.

At the convent, she learnt, the castrato modestly pulled on his dress and allowed the nuns to brush his luxuriant hair. But in the dormitories, at night, he found himself staring at the girls' naked breasts and thighs, slyly straining to peep at their virginal clefts of Venus. Then it was that he became aware of the pulsing of his cock, jabbing at the fabric of his dress between his legs.

Angelicco's voice lingered here, phrasing the notes *dolce*. She could feel his breath was hot. He longed to kiss the young novices, he sang. Then, in the natural pause, Clara thought she felt his lips brush hers, as soft as featherdown. The castrato longed to touch them. This time Clara was sure of it; a gentle caress at her throat. She felt weak and limp, in desperate need of those lips against hers; but instead, she sat like a statue, her heart pounding. Then, in a supremely sensual gesture, Angelicco raked his fingers through her hair, from her temples upward, so her chin lifted a little and met his lips. An involuntary gasp left her throat.

Angelicco continued his song. The castrato hero was discovered by one of the girls as he tried to relieve his bothersome cock of its unhappy habit of rising at unexpected moments. Curious, she encouraged him to continue his peculiar exercise with her feminine assistance. Soon, all the girls were enjoying the pleasures of this prohibited commodity. It is a miracle, he tells them, that, as he is snipped, they may fornicate until eternity and there will be no disagreeable consequences to show for it.

As Clara listened drowsily, feeling an insinuating pleasure growing within her body at the amorous details of this strange story, again the gossamer lips brushed hers. This time she could not help but respond, tilting her head a little in compliance. Again she was left unsatisfied, but a moment later felt those same moist lips brush against her throat. From the scent of his hair beneath her, she knew he bent and kissed her there, then moved down to bury his face in the flesh pushing over the tightness of her bodice.

It was impossible to hide her excitement. Though she continued to sit motionless, her breath was fast as she felt both lips and tongue nuzzle between her breasts. Then, as if this interlude had never happened, he continued again, singing very low, moving closer she felt, towards her. She could also hear the infernal bells on her gown shifting very slightly as she breathed. Despite the blindfold, she knew he watched her keenly, watched her pulse, the flicker of her tongue across her dry lips, the rise and fall of her breasts. He was such a sweet and skilful seducer. Blind as she was, even to his beauty, the more so was she lost in a dark place where all that pounded through her veins was anticipation.

As Angelicco depicted the final chapter of his story, he delicately moved forward, at last brushing against her knees in a gesture that filled her with fire. As he told her of the love the castrato youth engendered in the great Procurator of the city, he tenderly laid his fingers on her shoulders. Pressing his face to her cheek, he lasciviously whispered the end of his song. She could feel his breath, the smooth skin of his face, the softness of his hair. Now her ear vibrated softly to his voice as it dropped in *diminuendo*.

The man invited the boy to his apartment; he sang, much to the fear of our castrato, who knew his falsehood would be shamefully unveiled. The boy's treacherous heart pounded as the man trapped him in a kiss.

Here at last, Angelicco cupped her shoulders and kissed her lips, long and passionately, exploring her slack mouth with his sweet tongue and pushing himself neatly into the gap between her pliant legs.

Then, holding her tight to his heart, he sang the very last verse.

Se maschio son o femmina? the Procurator asks angrily, as he feels a bulge grow beneath his hand as it moves up the boy's skirts. 'Are you male or female?'

But when the boy guides the Procurator's hand around his ardent cock, he cannot believe his luck. He is a fortunate man indeed to have the pleasures of both sexes in one he cries, falling on the castrato with frenzied lust.

Eagerly, Clara felt Angelicco lift her skirts high and his fingers pass expertly upward over her stockings and garters. Her insides were burning now; blindfold as she was, she wanted whatever he could give her. With a quick movement, she knew he had opened his breeches

155

and, as he deftly lifted her legs, she moaned as he wrapped them around his slender hips. Now she knew the import of his song. Castrati were not neuters. They had cocks like any man. The next moment, that belief was a certainty as the hot tip of his undoubtedly rigid manhood jabbed eagerly at the inside of her thigh. With a cry of pleasure, she felt him part her hot and silky flesh as he manoeuvred to make his entry, standing before her with his breeches open.

'Angelicco! Are you having fun?'

The voice was Anton's. Clara froze.

'You little worm! I wondered what you were up to, behind Barberini's back.'

She could hear him walking towards them. Hurriedly, she did her best to pull down the layers of her skirt, but it was no good; the dreadful bells heralded every frantic movement.

Suddenly she felt his grasp staying her hand.

'Stay still, Clara.'

When she reached up to pull Angelicco's stock from her eyes, he also prevented her from removing it. Agitated and embarrassed, she waited to hear what he would say. Surely he would be furious to find her like this, with her legs wrapped around the boy?

Anton appeared to settle down comfortably behind her, sliding his arms around her waist. She was aware of Angelicco still standing before her, though silenced by the presence of the count.

'So, how are you finding your lesson?'

'My lesson?' She was perplexed. 'I thought – you would be angry.'

He dipped his head and kissed the back of her neck, where her hair was lifted and pinned. 'Well,' he said warmly, 'if I was angry with anyone it would be this pretty tart Angelicco, but when I try to get angry with him, he always thinks of something to improve my mood. Do you know how I found you? I could hear the rustling of your gown. Not just the rustle and jangle as you walked. The steady beat of your sex. The jigging of your hips straining for this eunuch's cock.'

Clara blushed warmly and he laughed at her.

'You have had quite an effect on our young friend,' he whispered conspiratorially, his breath hot in her ear. 'Even now, he has not lost his vigour. Do you not want to test it?'

With this, he took her hand, and next moment she felt the tight, slender heat of Angelicco's cock within her grasp. The boy sighed and she felt him squirm a little against her thigh.

'Go on. Play with it. I know you want to.'

Trying to hide her eagerness, Clara began to explore its length, caressing the long ridged shaft.

'Here, work your hand up and down.'

Her insides cramped as she followed the count's detailed instructions. The boy, too, began to make little impatient sounds as she touched the swollen end; she felt a hot, syrupy dampness in her palm. But then, as she moved down the blood-swollen length of it again, she hesitated as she reached the thickened base.

'Go on,' giggled Angelicco. 'I know you are curious.'

Very tentatively, she let her fingertips reach where she might have found a pair of fat, expectant testicles. Instead, she found nothing but a small and shrivelled fold of skin at the base of his cock.

'So you see,' the count laughed, 'he is quite safe to lie with.'

'When I think of the virgins I have had,' sighed the castrato with affected weariness. 'All so they can remain virgins evermore.'

She could feel, meanwhile, a growing bulge against the back of her waist. As she returned her attentions to Angelicco's delightfully hard member, she discovered that the sight of her stroking the boy was clearly arousing the count. Shifting a little behind her, he reached around and began to fondle her breasts, running his hands over the naked arcs of flesh, slipping inside her bodice to find her stiffening nipples. For a while they continued like this, Clara still blindfold but rapturously content between the two questing cocks.

'I can hear your skirts jangle again,' the count whispered, with a little less control of his breath. 'What sweet music. I think we should complete your lesson indoors.'

If she had thought that she was aroused before, now Clara felt weak with excitement. The broad swelling that nuzzled against her dress made her tingle and squirm. And then there was Angelicco too – if he was to come with them as well, she eagerly wanted to finish their little business off. The lad was potently stiff now, knocking against her thigh.

The count stood, guiding her forward. Still he would not remove her blindfold; so, between Anton and Angelicco, she staggered into the cool shade of a room at the back of the villa. The count told her that the room was used as a storeroom for musical instruments; no one would disturb them there. Now he pulled her towards a hard seat and bid her sit down beside Angelicco. In front of her, when he pulled back a dustsheet was what proved to be a harpsichord.

Clara felt a twinge of disappointment.

'Now, Clara, what has Angelicco taught you about the power of your sense of hearing?'

She thought a moment.

'He barely touched me,' she confessed. 'I think it was all done by sound. His singing, the melody, the story.'

Beside her on the stool, Angelicco began to play phrases on the harpsichord.

As his fingers lingered on a grand, dominant chord, he said artfully, 'I personally find it is always best to begin with the upright firmness of the root of the scale.'

Clara felt Anton's fingers sink on to her shoulder. He was standing behind them; she guessed he had slipped his arm around both of their shoulders.

'Ah, that is always necessary, Angelicco,' Anton replied in a bantering tone. 'There must be firmness at the centre. A good, firm root at the base. From then, it is all in the relationships of parts – of tones, rhythm and timing, of course, Clara.'

Playing a little melody, the boy conjured a moment's sadness, a passionate motif and then returned to the firm tonal root of the piece.

'Like scents, Clara, or like colours, there is a complex palette of sounds,' said the count. As Angelicco began to accompany his playing with his lovely voice, the count explained the way in which music carries the sensitive mind through expectation, discovery and satisfaction.

'And all the best music – like the best pleasure – builds and builds upon expectation,' he added, with a little laugh. 'So that the final satisfaction is all the more gratifying.'

'Expectation,' added the boy, 'is achieved by timing. As Clara found, if I sing slowly, the emotion is greater. With my little game I can affect even the rate of her heartbeat. For, in manipulating time,' added the boy, playing a strong, percussive beat, 'the repetition of two beats is used because it echoes the beat of our own breath and our own hearts.'

'And even the blood in the deeper organs of the body. So sound travels into the senses and directly affects the body,' maintained the count. 'The myriad tones and rhythms and keys affect our different organs. So, Clara, the chime of a silver bell on a winter's morning is similar to the circling of the palm of your hand very, very slowly with my fingernail.'

Lifting her palm, he carried out the latter movement, and she felt a sharp fire shoot straight to the top of her legs.

'I think it is time for some different music,' the count suddenly announced. 'Angelicco, fetch me a pair of those violin strings.'

Bemused by all of this, Clara sat as sedately as she could and waited. What had the count said about expectation? She was drunk with it, her centre still damp and unsatisfied from Angelicco's little foray.

'Clara, would you kneel? So we can give you a little practical demonstration?'

By now only pretending reluctance, she let them lower her to the carpeted floor and she knelt with her arms extended over the stool.

'Bind her.'

It was the count's voice. She could feel Angelicco's soft hands grasping first one and then the other of her wrists. She could feel something rapidly wrapped around them. Pathetically, she pulled at it, but it held her as tight as any set of iron manacles. She guessed that she was bound by lengths of the strong wire used to string a violin.

From the direction of his voice, she could tell Anton was standing above her. She waited for him to move to her, so was surprised when instead he gave Angelicco an instruction.

'Take her, my friend.'

'Anton!'

She was incredulous. Blindfold as she was, she raised her head to where she guessed he stood. 'You are just going to – watch?'

'I am indeed,' she heard him reply suavely. 'And of course, listen. For this is the music I like best.'

It was too late to do more than put up a meagre struggle, as she felt the boy drop behind her and slide his breeches to the ground. Then, with much delicacy, he lifted the musical hem of her dress for a second time.

There was no time to think. Angelicco's stiff cock prodded against the back of her thighs.

'I tell you, I would bet a gold louis she is ready.' The count's voice was sardonically cool.

Blindfold and bound as she was, Clara wished she was unable to hear as well. To hear herself discussed like this – she was mortified.

Holding her breath, she felt the boy's soft white finger push between her parted cleft and slide, effortlessly, into her wet entrance.

'Oh, yes, Count,' Angelicco sighed triumphantly. 'All

160

this reluctance is just on the outside. Inside – oh, she is ready.'

She could feel the boy grasping his cock now, as he moved closer to her upraised rear. I should protest, she told herself, but in truth she could barely wait for him to get to action. As the moist head of his cock probed against her entrance, she cried out involuntarily. Closing her eyes tight, she felt her thighs open slackly.

With a grunt of pleasure, Angelicco worked the head of his cock inside her. Blissfully, she felt her muscles close around it, burning with molten pleasure. With a swing of his delicate pelvis, he thrust again, forcing his prick harder and faster into her.

It was impossible to stay silent. Clara was being pushed hard against the immobility of the stool as Angelicco fucked her with long, powerful thrusts. Slowly, he was pushing deeper, arousing sensations she had barely guessed at. With cool assurance, he reached up from her waist to find her breasts. Struggling with her bodice, she was aware suddenly of Anton approaching.

'I'll unlace her,' he said throatily. 'You concentrate on your work. *Brillante*, my friend. Your timing is exquisite. You play the man with style.'

As the boy got into his rhythm, extending his cock now deeper and more fully inside her, Anton hurriedly unlaced the back of her gown. With a rapid tumble, her breasts spilled from her stays and, as she felt the count reach beneath her and seize her warm breasts, she struggled not to cry out to him.

'Oh, I cannot bear it,' she moaned. The lad's honeyed cock slid effortlessly now, faster and faster, in and out of her like a slippery rod. Beneath the count's hands, her breasts were so sensitive, she felt her nipples judder sharply against his palms. When he began to rub their jutting stiffness, she wailed wordlessly.

'Oh, if you cannot bear it, think of me,' he whispered hotly. 'I can hear the slap of your wetness, smell the sweetness of your juice. I can see you, Clara, but I will not take you.'

Greedily, then, he reached down between her legs and began to fondle her widened lips. With a spasm of fire she felt him exploring, finding that place where Angelicco's cock pumped ceaselessly into her and gripping it with his hand.

His fingertip was rubbing in a slow, circular movement on her maddened clitoris. In a second, she was thrown over the edge of self-control. Barely aware, she cried out as her hips convulsed, squeezing the boy's burning cock, wetly nuzzling down on to the hardness of Anton's fingers.

When she recovered a little, she found Anton was next to her, caressing her, kissing her spine.

'Do you know what it means, not to take you?' he whispered.

In the darkness behind her blindfold, she felt barely conscious. But, from Anton's scent, she knew that he was wildly aroused. She could smell his sex, the first drops of his semen. Her mouth hung slack. Angelicco had paused, though she still felt him as hard as a candle, all the full length of her, from her wet entrance to the tantalising tip buried deep within her.

She became aware of Anton panting, of him struggling to throw off his clothes. Yes, she thought abandonedly, I am ready for him now. He moved behind her, and she waited for him to dismiss the boy and take his place.

'I need your honey,' he murmured. He was behind the boy, who was using this interlude to reach around her and work at her hanging breasts. It felt good as he massaged the crimson points of her nipples. Already she could feel her muscles tighten and clutch at him again. His cock pleasurably kicked back inside her.

Anton's fingers were again caressing her wet entrance, squeezing around the base of the boy's cock. In reply, Angelicco groaned happily. Again, Anton's hand returned, spread across her slippery lips and then retreated. She was aware of his broader cock now, pushing against her rear. Slightly puzzled, she wondered why he was rubbing himself with her slippery fluids.

'Excuse me, my friend,' she heard him murmur to Angelicco, 'but this wetness will oil me a little.'

'Yes, only do it fast. I cannot wait forever.' Angelicco was half-strangled with arousal as the count's weight fell on to him.

'Do not worry. We shall arrive *presto*, my friend.'

Clara's wave of shock rapidly turned to frenzy. Now, as the boy's cock bore into her, she felt the guiding rhythm of Anton above him. He seemed quickly to penetrate the boy's raised backside and began to pummel into his slender form, ceaselessly pushing him further into her. As he took the length of Anton's cock, so Angelicco too grew almost painfully rigid as he pounded inside her.

Lost in her darkness, feeling every judder and spasm of the brutish act being performed against her body, Clara soon reached again that simmering plateau of pleasure. Now she felt that the fierceness of every thrust of the boy's cock originated in the count's fiery loins. Moaning, with her cheek pressed against the wooden stool, she felt her heartbeat quicken. Someone – she no longer knew who – was squeezing and pinching at her nipples. Another hand lifted her groin, pulling her back on to the boy's rapidly twitching member.

Angelicco was muttering, breathlessly clutching her as Anton delivered a series of long, swift blows to his pummelled rear. The uplifted dress was ringing and jangling in a continual, frenzied note. With a strangely musical cry, Clara's climax erupted. Through it, she still felt the double blows of their cocks, brutal and unrelenting. Then she felt Angelicco clutch her, crying out as his prick jerked dryly.

Still, as she panted hotly beneath him, she could feel Anton finish, she could feel his broad hands clasping the boy's narrow hips tightly, his breath getting faster. Suddenly his hands slipped down over her saturated sex, working into her, then rubbing what was left of Angel-icco's wilting cock. For a few moments, Clara and the boy simply lay there battered and supine, feeling his climax begin from a series of muted cries in his throat. Then, as it roared through his muscles, he pounded into them, squeezing the breath from their bodies with the force of his final blow.

Clara felt a strange, slow smile break across her face as she lay beneath them both. She knew she would not be allowed to get up and see them, to see Angelicco's lovely golden body as he stretched and yawned, no doubt vainly parading in front of Anton as he dressed. No, Anton would certainly not let her see him still glowing and wet from his exertions. That would be too – uncivilised. All would be back in order before they untied her and lifted the blindfold from her dazzled eyes.

She was correct. They left her for Tresa to find.

'Clara, what has happened? No, do not speak. Let me untie you.'

The girl felt dizzy as she rose. Tresa did her best to gather up the back of her dress but it was useless to pretend Clara could return to the company. Somehow, it had become ripped and stained.

'Tell me, did he finally have you?'

Clara shook her head and shamefully wiped the wet-ness from her thigh that was the only sign left of him.

'Ah.'

'Where is he?'

'He has gone. He has borrowed a horse and left.' Tresa shook her head as she inspected the reddened rings still throbbing at Clara's wrists.

'Where has he gone?' Clara asked.

'On to Prague. I am sure he will have left by the time you get back to Rome.'

Clara felt a sudden anguish but was not sure why.

'Come along, put this on. I will tell them you have fainted and must return to Rome.'

Clara nodded, happy to let Tresa face the others for her. Wearily, she slipped on Tresa's warm pelisse.

Back at the Albergo, Clara listlessly bathed. Closing her eyes, she lay back in the warm water, drifting in her mind. Each time she heard the clatter of hooves in the yard or the door to their apartment slam, she felt herself jump and listened carefully for Anton's return. But of course he did not return. She told herself she was greatly relieved at this, for what she would have said to him she could not guess.

The message was quite clear from the driver; the count had ridden on ahead to do business at the court in Bohemia, and the ladies were to follow next day more slowly in the carriage. That, at least, was the count's will in the matter. She closed her eyes, feeling tender bruises on her body stinging in the water, her mind still numb from the extremity of her encounter with Angelicco and the count. While it was happening, yes, there was no opportunity to think or judge the situation. But later – reflecting, she was as appalled as she was excited.

Wearily, as she rose to soap her body, her eye again caught sight of the letter on her dresser. She could remember almost all of the words; indeed, they rang in her mind like the jangling of a cymbal.

After continuous deliberation since our meeting, I have at last set pen to paper. It is impossible for me to watch unmoved as you are led unwittingly into the life of corruption that all those about you sadly predict.

In writing to you, neither am I entirely innocent of a selfish motive. Since our first meeting in the Dutch Provinces, I have harboured an affection for your person that was further magnified when again we met in the shadow of Rome's great ruins.

I am of the fixed belief that you believe yourself honourably obliged to complete your contract of marriage to the Italian gentleman. In this matter, I can only set forth my own logical deduction, that you hope thereby to relieve your family of some unfortunate liability.

I am a gentleman of comfortable means with a property and woollen business in the vicinity of Nottingham. Frankly, Miss Fairfax, I am in want of a wife, and should you be willing to know me better, I am assured you would find me honest, steady and not without respect in my locality.

There, it is said. Perceiving your difficulties, I assure you that with the utmost speed a carriage could be hired and we could be at the port and on our way back to England forthwith. A communication to 302 Piazza di Spagna will suffice. I will be here in Rome another month, should you need to consider but, I truly beg you, do not endanger yourself so long.

Your servant,
John Palmer Esquire.

Chapter Eleven

'Why do you sit all day with your nose in a map? Come out into the air.' Tresa appeared at the window to their little cell, her parasol twirling in her fingers.

It was cool and shady inside. Clara liked the bare plastered walls of the Italian convent where they had put up for a few days; it was still and light, unlike the breathless confines of the carriage. Outside, it was a torrid Italian July. Already well into July, she sighed – then August, September and finally October. The end of the summer. Time to come to a decision about the count was running out.

'Yes, yes. I will join you soon.'

She is like a child, Clara thought, always needing attention.

Alone again, she rolled on to her stomach on the bed, her eyes devouring the map she had borrowed from the driver. So, they were now halfway. With her fingers, she traced the distance between Rome where Palmer still waited and Bohemia where she expected the count had already arrived. So many times she had been tempted to turn back and take up the Englishman's offer. Yet here she still was, suspended halfway across the map.

Soon they would cross the border of the Veneto into

the Empire. Today the men were anxiously engaging extra horses and new guides to make the perilous journey north. All good sense told her to turn back now, before they passed into uncivilised territories. Yet still her eye strayed along the black line of the road as it surmounted miniature mountain ranges and forests, until at last it reached a diminutive picture of a walled city studded with churches and castles. That was where the count waited: the famous Habsburg city of Prague. Reluctantly, Clara moved from contemplation of the past and future to the jarring experience of the present.

Outside, in the balmy Italian sunshine, she found Tresa sitting on a bench beneath the trees, watching the men reinforce the carriage. They had been staying some three days now at the convent of Santa Maria in Sylvix, in the heart of the flat landscape of the Veneto. The sisters were gentle and hospitable, generous with their local honey and produce from the kitchen gardens. In return, Clara knew that Tresa was empowered by the count to leave a generous offering towards their many good works.

'You look pale. Here, eat. Who knows what we will find further on?'

Tresa offered her some soft cheese and the salty ham of the province but Clara shook her head. Closing her eyes, she listened to the gentle rustle of the trees that surrounded the lovely worn walls of the old convent and the chattering cries of the martens swooping around the tower. If only I could stay here alone and think, she reflected.

'Do you miss him?'

'Who?' She had said it quite without thinking. Opening her eyes, she saw Tresa's frown.

'The count will be thinking of you, I assure you.'

'Ah, yes. I forgot you know him so much better than I do,' Clara yawned. 'By the way, have you shared his bed recently, or am I supposed to be blind to your little intrigues?'

The question hung unanswered in the air for a long time while the martens circled, crying forlornly.

'He has not noticed me since Amsterdam. Does that assuage your jealousy?'

Gently, Tresa moved towards her, taking her hand into hers. 'I do not know how to explain this. The count is a proud man, used to the mastery of his own emotions. I know he wants you; it is like a torment to him.'

Clara stared resentfully at their two hands. Next to her own, Tresa's was slender, bony, elegant. In truth, she believed Tresa had an honest and guileless side to her character and that was the aspect she liked. The comfortable trust between them had not returned since the day at the Villa Barberini. In her worst moments, Clara feared she was a valuable pawn in a peculiar game of which she alone was ignorant of the rules. If only she could trust the intimacy of Tresa's gestures and confide something of this agony to her. But, despite Tresa's approaches, a timid instinct held her back – they had not shared a bed since before their arrival in Rome.

'Tresa,' she suddenly exclaimed, surprised at the force of her own curiosity, 'do you ever question the rightness of what you do? Do you never want a nice steady husband and a quiet life in one place?'

The Italian woman's response was a *glissando* of glassy laughter that she quickly attempted to stifle when she saw Clara's dismay. 'Oh, my dear Clara, you do not know me at all,' she smiled, squeezing her hand. 'How I detest dullness, how I tire of a lover after barely five minutes. It is how I am and, may God be praised, it is how I am fortunate enough to live my life. Such a dull life is – how shall I say it – for the necessary breeders of this world. Yes, someone must produce the children to grow the wheat and barley to bake the bread, but please let it not be me!'

She must have noticed the increasing exasperation in her friend's face.

'Right and wrong – what are they but the signals of

the heart? If, let us say, for the sake of an example, you were at this point to abandon Anton – Clara, that would be both cruel and wrong.'

Clara did not give herself time to wonder how it was Tresa guessed such a thing.

'Do you love Anton?' Clara asked.

Tresa smiled her lovely smile. 'Of course I love him. I first met him when my aunt died and I was attached to his household at the age of nineteen. He was wild and beautiful even then, and we were devoted for some years. And since, he has aged well. Then again, I love a man in Lucca, a man in Rome, I even love you when you smile and kiss me and are not so dreary. Why, today I have again fallen in love. Have you seen our new postillion? A Teutonic god, I should call him. Yellow hair and the shoulders of Hercules. Look, here he is almost carrying the carriage axle with one hand.'

Clara could not help but laugh, especially when the young man came into view and she could see that Tresa had described him to perfection. He was a young giant, bursting with energy and no doubt with animal vitality too.

'He is called Otto,' Tresa whispered. 'He is travelling home to Saxony and with us as far as Prague. At last – a little amusement.'

Otto was obviously aware of his rapt audience. A tall, muscular youth, he was nailing a brace to the back of the carriage. His battered leather jerkin showed every swelling of his well-developed form as he lifted and swung a heavy mallet. But, each few moments, he would cast a hooded glance over to the ladies and sweep back his shoulder-length flaxen tresses.

Tresa was watching him with the careful eye of a connoisseur. Clara shook her head and looked away. At least, she thought, Tresa will be distracted, so I might have time to myself. But a moment later, she too found herself watching the young Saxon, unable to drag her eyes from the compelling performance taking place right before her eyes.

Finally she rose, unable to bear the youth's conceit as he tackled his work, always with the best view for the ladies in mind. 'I suppose we must begin to pack,' she said dolefully.

'Yes. Only this time, we must put all but our hardiest clothes into the leather chest. There will be no one to see our finery.'

'But Tresa, this is not like you. Surely even for yourself, or even Otto, you would never travel *à l'Anglais*?' she smiled.

Tresa shook her head.

'You have been staring at that map all morning, no doubt wondering whether to undertake the next part of your journey. But you do not know at all what will be there. In fact, that is the problem. I have never travelled this road either, but my new friend here –' and here she fluttered her fingers towards Otto '– tells me it is not at all like what we are used to. Once we reach Bohemia, we will find very few travellers and precious few inns, never mind hotels. I think, my dear Clara, we must prepare to miss a few of our creature comforts before we feast at the Empress's court in Prague Castle.'

At first, all of Tresa's dire warnings appeared superfluous. After crossing the border into the Empire, they were pleasantly surprised by the order and civility of the Austrians. Some of the inns, indeed, were of the type where the guest might as soon share a dining room with a small herd of cattle as any gentlefolk, but on the whole the beds were clean, the milk fresh and the maids not unhelpful.

Some of the larger cities were even a pleasant surprise. At Salzburg, Clara begged the driver to unload their boxes so that they could unpack dresses for the opera. There, in that many-spired city, where the houses were painted with every bright colour and the mechanical clocks rang each quarter-hour, they heard the music of the German composers. Clara secretly considered it even better than the Italian opera for, though the language

171

was more difficult, the melodies were sweeter, and any lack of expensive settings was more than made up for by better stories and characters.

It was with even greater reluctance that they left the delicious chocolate and pastries of Salzburg to encounter the privations of the range of mountains that stand like a great white wall around the city. Soon, as the carriage jolted and swung up and up the winding, rutted roads, Clara could no longer bear to peep out of the windows. Even without seeing the vast, jagged precipices outside and icy snow-topped peaks, her heart jolted at every slip of the wheel and groan of the springs.

Yet, after a few days, even she tired of her own annoying thoughts. Now they had left the civilised delights of Salzburg it seemed even harder to imagine turning back. Each day she swung from thoughts of John Palmer to quite different ideas about the count, until her head swum like an unsteady pendulum. But it was only when she turned to her fellow traveller for companionship that she realised Tresa was also completely absorbed elsewhere.

Clara's first intimation that Otto was exerting more than a merely flirtatious influence upon her companion was when they stopped at a wretched inn past Linz. Finding no maid in the household – only dirty, ragged manservants – Clara went in search of the Italian to ask for assistance with her hair. Tresa had claimed to be in need of some fresh air and, although the forest air was not particularly pleasant, Clara followed the path through the trees in the direction in which she had last seen Tresa disappear. Clara knew it was not wise to wander alone in the thick forest but, all the time, as the pine-needles crunched beneath her sensible travelling boots, she was aware of a strong sensibility that Tresa was indeed ahead of her in the trees. This assurance grew as she heard not only the sound of twigs cracking in the undergrowth ahead, but also the low, murmuring sound of voices.

With a start Clara recognised Otto's guttural laugh.

Tresa's melodic Italian murmured in reply. Hesitating in the shadows, Clara for the first time became aware that she might be about to intrude upon some private interlude. What was she to do: creep off back to her room and wait? A little bubble of anger rose in Clara's mind. Maybe they were only walking together. Why should she not catch up with them? Stealthily, she crept forward and peered through the trees.

In a little clearing of felled logs where the broad pine branches formed a kind of shady roof, Tresa was sitting on a thick trunk as broad as a sofa. Wearing only her shift, for her travelling gown was hung on the branches, Tresa was wrapped in the arms of the Saxon, who was eagerly pulling at his clothes. In a sudden attempt to help him, Tresa laughingly knelt and began to tug at his breeches. In response, the youth pulled her face against his flat belly, stroking her hair.

Clara was utterly astonished, although later she wondered how she could have been so unobservant. Indeed, she guessed she might be the only one of the party not to have noticed the liaison taking place beneath her nose. Each day now, she recalled, Tresa had taken to strolling at dusk while Clara rested alone with her thoughts. Certainly, Clara had observed that the atmosphere did Tresa's complexion good, for she often returned with a healthy glow and lighter step. Only last night Tresa had replied that the mountain air certainly made her feel more lively. Clara pursed her lips bitterly at the deception and watched.

For two people used to meeting each evening for love, they were certainly eager, she observed, as the Saxon threw off his jerkin, revealing a broad, bronzed chest which Tresa clung to. Deftly, he slipped behind her to unlace her corsets, all the time caressing her long flanks and curving bottom. He was pressing against her back, kissing her ears and neck wildly; Tresa's long black hair tangled with Otto's golden curls. With a sigh, he drew the last lace out of her corset and it fell to the ground unheeded.

Now, as Tresa turned and knelt before her lover in only her shift, Clara wondered if she should leave. There was certainly no possibility of speaking to them. But instead of turning and going, she found she was transfixed, curious to see how it would end. Silently parting the branches, she watched.

Tresa's dark eyes flashed as she slid off the last of her clothes and knelt in the clearing, naked as a wood nymph with tumbling hair and smooth brown skin. Proudly, she threw her hair back over her shoulders and let him see her beauty. Then she reached out and took one of his calloused hands and placed it on her upturned breast. Eagerly, he reached out for the other, too, fondling her dark brown nipples, reaching down to kiss and lick her swinging breasts. Exultantly, she drew away and perched on the edge of the log, her legs brazenly apart. Clara could see her pull her lover's head down there, his yellow head disappearing between her upturned knees. She began to writhe pleasurably, squeezing her own breasts, gathering every drop of pleasure from the experience, guiding the youth as he explored her most sensitive cleft.

Captivated, Clara watched as Tresa approached a powerful climax; her hips thrusting towards the youth's pleasure-giving mouth, her bottom raised to gain the best access, her own hands rubbing and squeezing at her elongated nipples. With a great gasp and spasm, it was over.

To her surprise, Clara found that she, too, had breathed faster and at the consummate moment had held her breath, trying to conceive how it might have felt. Then, a moment later, she felt a flood of shame. How could she be jealous of them? It was her own fault if Tresa ignored her, so apparent had she made it since Rome that their intimacy was over. As for the German youth – handsome he may be, but even she, who felt she now knew Tresa well, had been surprised at her choice of lover. Tresa was beautiful and elegant – in every city they visited, men were charmed by her. And this Saxon

– why he was no more than a postillion who probably could not read or write.

Hearing yet more whispering, Clara again peered into the clearing. To her surprise, the couple were not dressing; instead, Tresa was kneeling before the youth, pulling from his breeches quite the largest, liveliest cock Clara had ever imagined, never mind seen. Large-framed the Saxon might be, but even he was somewhat dwarfed by his swollen appendage. Sighing and cooing, Tresa was rapturously playing with it, stroking its length and head and fondling the heavy, swinging balls. The youth's eyes were closed as he surrendered to the pleasure, crying out as Tresa rubbed her face against it, trying to cram it into her narrow mouth.

Suddenly alarmed, Clara felt her own legs grow weak and she reached out to steady herself against a tree. What must that feel like? The size of it? Tentatively, she pressed her hand against her mouth. If only, she suddenly thought, I was not encumbered by these self-destructive restraints. Tresa's philosophy did not harm her – she benefited from her libertarian views considerably. Quite plainly, she had all the fun.

As if to illustrate this point, Tresa chose this moment to slide up her lover's body, pressing against him hard as they kissed. Next moment, he had lifted her to his waist and, with her legs wrapped eagerly around his torso, he gradually impaled her on his cock. Clara watched open-mouthed as the youth carried Tresa, as if she were a piece of thistledown, across the clearing to lean against a conveniently wide tree trunk. Once there, he merely braced his legs apart and set to, with such speed and gusto that Clara's eyes grew wide. What had she condemned about Tresa's choice of lover? The man was superb; every cry and gasp of pleasure from Tresa testified to that. Only when Clara grew tired of standing did she turn to go back to their lodgings. Still they did not show a sign of finishing as she left them to the privacy of the woods.

* * *

175

'Did you enjoy your walk?'

Tresa really was as cool as the icy peaks all around them. The question didn't even make her blink. 'So, so. The sights were much the same as ever.'

'Ah. Yet you look so well exercised. Your colour is up. Perhaps the path was steep?'

Clara could see her quickly consult the mirror in their meagre little room.

'Oh, I think I merely look well,' she grinned with self-satisfaction.

After a long silence, Clara remembered to ask about her hair.

'Yes, I will do it. Perhaps I can braid it like these peasant girls.'

Clara sat before the grimy mirror, watching the Italian as she first unloosed and then began to brush her hair with her own silver hairbrush. It was something she loved, to feel the long tresses of her hair lifted and smoothed as the brush ran from root to tip. As Tresa stood behind her administering the brush, she felt her eyes occasionally flicker and close with pleasure.

'And you,' asked Tresa softly as she parted Clara's hair and then brushed each portion until it shone. 'Why do you not join me for a walk?'

Clara looked up with alarm. 'Join you? You know I do not much care for exercise.'

Tresa began to braid her hair quickly and neatly. 'You do not like to walk in the woods?'

Clara wondered if there were some cryptic meaning to the phrase. 'No. Of course not.'

'Ah.' She continued to braid and pin, coiling the pale hair around Clara's head. Clara watched her in the mirror but her face was intent and closed. At last the hairstyle was in place.

'That's beautiful.'

Tresa's reflection smiled down on her; for a long moment they both stayed as they were, watching each other warily. Then Tresa's hands suddenly dropped gently on to Clara's shoulders. 'You are stiff, Clara.' She

176

began to knead Clara's taut shoulders, deliciously relieving all the pent-up tension of the last few weeks.

'There is no need,' she murmured, but was glad when Tresa continued. Slowly, the insinuating fingers worked up towards her neck. With a deep sensation of relief, Clara felt the fingertips began to penetrate the strained muscles.

'Why will you not come to the forest with me?' Tresa whispered.

'I do not understand,' she replied, though her voice was a little thick.

Very softly, she began to trace circles on Clara's temples, a feeling Clara loved. 'You know what I mean. Visit the forest.'

Clara's eyes were closed. She felt passive and malleable in Tresa's hands. Very gradually, she felt the fingers return to her shoulders, her stiff upper arms, and then drop to her breasts. Tresa's fingertips burnt through the thin fabric of her gown, squeezing and kneading in the way she knew Clara could hardly bear. Almost immediately, she wondered if it were possible, given just that pressure on her breasts, to be completely satisfied without even removing an article of clothing. In only a few moments, her nipples were so stiff they prodded through the fabric, beneath Tresa's touch.

'Ah, I hear it is time for dinner.' Coolly Tresa withdrew her bewitching fingers.

As Clara stood, Tresa faced her. The breach in their intimacy was restored. Quickly and casually, Tresa kissed her. Clara returned the kiss, questing with her tongue, having to hold back the force of her need.

'There is nothing to do up here in the mountains,' began Tresa with a smile. 'Maybe I could show you something after dinner?'

Clara nodded silently, finding it hard not to fall back into her friend's arms. But, as she turned to go down to dinner, Tresa could not resist a parting shot. 'And before we reach Prague you really must brush down your skirts. Those pine needles do stick so persistently to the cloth.'

The dinner was poor but the local wine was better. Picking at a tough ragout of unidentified meat, Clara decided that it was easier to follow Tresa's lead and take comfort in the jugs of drink. The wine was as dark as blood, rich and spicy and, although Clara tried to chew on the hard, dark bread of the region, soon she felt her head swim as she pushed her plate away.

'Do you need some air?' Tresa asked thoughtfully.

In reply, Clara pushed back her rough chair and together they walked, somewhat unsteadily, out into the dusk.

'Where are we going?' Clara found herself asking. They were crossing the clearing towards the dark shadow of the forest. Recently, her mind had been so full of tumultuous impressions it was hard to find any coherence in her muddled thoughts. The strong wine only made the night seem stranger.

'Look at the moon.' Tresa pointed to the full, silver disc of the moon rising above the pointed spears of the pines. The stars, too, were beginning to appear, very clear and close, so high up above the clouds.

'Can you not feel it in your blood? The power of the moon.'

Clara was silent, though she too could feel the magical silvery rays dance upon her and see the mysterious shimmer of moonlight playing amongst the branches of the forest, giving the appearance of an insubstantial faerie landscape. At last, they reached the first overhanging boughs and smelt the sweet sharp scent of pine resin.

'Can you not feel it?' Tresa asked again, suddenly. Then, stopping, she pulled Clara towards her and suddenly Clara knew why she had allowed herself to drink so freely.

Without a care, she drank at Tresa's lips, tasting the bitterness of the wine, greedily pressing hard against her mouth, seeking her tongue. Both were breathless when at last they came apart.

'In the centre, we can see the moon.'

Hurriedly, Clara followed her as they stumbled along the path, cracking twigs and snaring their gowns on spiky branches. Then at last they were at that clearing Clara had seen earlier in the day, where the logs lay carelessly felled like giant's furniture. Here, it was almost as light as day; turning to Tresa, she could see Tresa's eyes glinting whitely and her skin shining as pale as a ghost. Immediately, Tresa began to pull at Clara's clothes, opening her bodice and kissing her flesh. A great wave of well-being erupted in Clara's blood. Instinctively, she joined her friend, dragging off her clothes, eagerly watching as both were transformed into silky, silvery figures in the dark openness of the wood. Finally naked, they clutched at each other, thrilling to the sensation of naked skin against naked skin, trying to achieve contact with every inch of their bodies.

'Let us be wood nymphs,' cried Tresa, suddenly breaking free and clambering on to a wide trunk. Now her ripe breasts and narrow waist were out of reach, Clara felt bereft. In a moment she was beside her, pulling her back towards her craving body.

'How do we become wood nymphs?' she whispered, trying to reach down and press her mouth to Tresa's delicious breast. Closing her eyes, she felt bliss as the long nipple hardened sweetly in her mouth, springing back when she lapped at it with her stiff tongue.

'We should follow the god Pan. Seek oblivion in pleasure.'

In reply, Clara's hand caressed the smooth firmness of her buttocks and then slipped inside the parting at the top of her legs. She was pleasurably damp and heated. Clara's probing fingers parted the silky lips to press and press until there was no more resistance, only a little cry of delight from above. Clara pulled her gently downward. Soon they were both prone on the rough bark, Clara still easing her fingers back and forth, feeling

Tresa's hips pleasurably shudder and twist. As they lay entwined, she felt Tresa reach and grasp her breasts, burying her face there, sucking hard and fast until the fire built up so high in Clara's stomach she thought she might ignite from that ceaseless stimulation. Then, with a wordless cry into the night, which some might have mistaken for the exultant shriek of a bird soaring up into the darkness, Tresa shuddered in release, her body squeezing Clara's slippery fingers in wave after wave of gratification.

Greedily, she raised her head and kissed Clara on the lips. Then, with a long, sensual gesture, she ran her fingers down Clara's smooth white body, rubbing against her rigid nipples and golden-haired sex.

'First, a little game. Run, my sweet: and, when I catch you, I will have you.'

Clara laughed. She wanted it now, for sure, but to run – that too would be exciting. In a moment she was up and off, stumbling off down the path, careless of the prickle and sharpness against her feet.

In a moment she heard Tresa catch up behind her. With an exhilarated scream, she crashed on into the undergrowth, feeling now only a floor of pine needles, as soft as any carpet, beneath her feet. Behind her Tresa was laughing, intent to catch her, only a dozen paces back. With a sudden spurt, Clara reached a clearing, glorying in the naked power of her limbs. Not since she was a child had she run like this, unencumbered by corsets and hoops and petticoats. With a little cry, she took another path, but not before she heard Tresa darting up behind her, almost catching at her ankles.

This path was even darker, and now Clara had to stoop and push low branches out of her way. Still she could hear Tresa laughing and panting just behind her. But now, for the first time, she thought she glimpsed another shape off to the left, moving alongside. But, when she looked that way, there was nothing there.

In that moment of distraction, Tresa crept upon her and grasped her waist. With a shriek of laughter, Clara broke free, pelting down the path. Again, she wished she was indeed a dryad, born to a life only of pleasure, without a care for morals and manners. This time Tresa had her scent – however fast she tried to run, the woman was gaining on her. As she felt Tresa's fingers grope around her waist she made a last dash, trying to make her legs go ever faster. It was no good. Her foot caught in a branch and, the next moment, she tumbled, unhurt, to the ground.

Unceremoniously, Tresa grasped her ankles and pulled her backwards until, with a giggle, Clara felt her face push between her thighs. With her last breath she began to struggle, wriggling to escape Tresa's firm grasp.

'Don't struggle. Surrender!'

Tresa pulled herself up astride her hips, holding Clara's upper arms down. Clara could just see the glinting smile at Tresa's mouth and the twin points of her breasts.

'I do not!' Still she feebly struggled, although the ache in her loins now, to be taken, was growing to an agony.

'Surrender – or I will send the god Pan to sort you out,' Tresa threatened.

'Do your worst.'

'I will.'

Then she submitted once more to the heat and pressure of Tresa's kisses and the urgent seeking of her fingers as she squeezed her breasts. Easily, their two hips locked together and Clara felt that exquisite pressure of Tresa's pubis, scorching back and forth against her own nakedly shining fissure. In the pitchy darkness they clung to each other, hands probing and parting, tongues teasing and rolling. Soon Clara's first wave of pleasure approached. She could feel Tresa's mouth rubbing sensually back and forth along her slippery sex. It was driving her wild, making her push hard downwards, craving to be filled. Then, tentatively, a long tongue slipped inside her, making her gasp.

'Oh, yes,' she groaned, even more excited as her

nipples continued to be rubbed and squeezed. In the darkness, Tresa was a masterly lover, attending to her every desire, her fingers seeming to probe and fondle each sensitive place, guiding her expertly to a shuddering release. Fingers were inside her, thrusting back and forth like a little cock – uncontrollably, she writhed and moaned. That mouth, too, still sucked and teased. She felt delirious with want.

Then she felt it – something hot and taut against her skin. Her hand slithered down her own smooth flesh. Where she had thought it was only Tresa beside her, there was another. A man. She did not ask who it was. Only a white lightning flash of delight ripped across her body. Her hands closed around the massive weight of his cock and she dissolved with pleasure.

'It is Pan, come to pleasure you,' teased Tresa.

Wordlessly, she felt there was enough of herself to share with any number. Greedily, she caressed the long phallus, from its tight rounded tip, along its veined length, to the thick base. She could hardly breathe with excitement.

'Not inside me,' she whispered, though she barely knew who it was she spoke to. Then she guided the hard pole of flesh between her legs. Her wetness drenched it with sweet juice. Still holding it carefully, she pressed the rounded end against her swollen clitoris. She could hear the man now, groaning as he felt the welcoming heat of her cunt. Impatiently he rocked it a little.

'No. Only outside.'

'You must do as she says,' murmured Tresa. 'Let me down.'

Then she wriggled downward and continued to rub and kiss Clara while, at the same time, the head of the cock pressed insistently back and forth against her sex.

Deftly Clara reached down and explored the strange cock, feeling the hard-knotted veins, the wide base as broad as a slender arm, the swollen balls that felt so heavy and tight with desire. Panting, she squeezed the rounded head against her, feeling drops of hotness mix with her own needy wetness. It was enough. It did not need to be inside her. It was enough to feel it nudging and rubbing. Then she could bear it no longer. With a cry she squeezed her thighs around it, riding it, jerking against the fleshy phallus. As she did so, Tresa's fingers found her entrance and pushed inside. For an intoxicated moment, it felt to Clara as if two cocks were at work and, the next second, she surrendered to a wave of release, screaming out into the night. Her mind was swimming with pleasure, her entrance squeezing drop after drop of sweet honey over her lovers.

With a sigh, she lay back and saw the distant stars twinkling above the black silhouette of the trees. Then she felt Tresa clamber on all fours above her, kneeling astride her with her long hair brushing her breasts. A moment later, Otto – for now she knew it was Otto – mounted her friend, groaning as he slid inside Tresa's ready sex. Lying beneath the pair of them, Clara could feel the swinging of Tresa's soft belly and the hard brushing strokes of Otto's legs. Curiously, she reached down, finding the soft shadow of hair at Tresa's cunt.

She could see Tresa smile as Clara explored her distended lips, her entrance so stretched by the girth of Otto's hammering cock. Her hands grew wet as she felt the long hot phallus slithering back and forth. Gently she cupped his swinging balls, eliciting a groan of frustration from Otto. Above her she felt Tresa's hard nipples graze her own breasts. Ecstatically, she lifted her hips and rubbed against Tresa's open cunt. Again and again Otto's cock bore down, squeezing their lips together.

Clara's mind swam, wanting to feel the three as one. Suddenly raising her legs she lifted herself, locking her ankles around Tresa's hips. Now she could feel the rapid quivering of Otto's cock just above her as it pumped in and out of Tresa. With a final effort, she lodged herself just below the grinding power of his cock. Suddenly he felt her and realised what it was she wanted. Moving slightly closer, he pressed against her, too, abrading back and forth as he fucked Tresa. Now Clara, too, could feel the whole inward and outward journey of his cock against her slippery lips as well.

In the confused darkness she felt lips kiss her, felt Tresa's nipples jutting hard against her own. Clara could no longer tell cunt from cock. Heat, friction, wetness – something was frantically rubbing against her own stretched and swollen cunt. Cries of pleasure broke into the night from her two lovers, along with the delicious sound of flesh striking slippery flesh.

They were one. He could stand it no longer. With a shudder she felt him jab, impaling Tresa, scorching Clara's greedy lips as well. Then she felt him quiver as he delivered his load, pulling out to saturate both women as hot milky liquid seeped on to them. It was not the physical sensation, but the idea that made Clara involuntarily buckle and climax. The three, in their moment of climax, were one. Somehow all three had made love. Throwing her head back on to the grassy carpet, feeling the moonlight bathe her smooth skin in magical shadows, Clara laughed deliciously and was satisfied.

Chapter Twelve

*T*hey had stopped to water the horses at a ford. Stretching her legs, Clara wandered a short way along the dusty road. There, in the distance, was the walled city on a hill she had only before gazed at on the map. The distant tower of St Vitus's cathedral glinted in the sunshine, surrounded by the massed storeys of the castle and then the rest of the city with its domes and spires beneath. The journey had taken many frustrating weeks. She was unkempt, dirty and exhausted. All she longed for was civilised food after the liver dumplings, black bread and sauerkraut provided in the filthy inns. That, and a warm bath and huge, luxurious sheets.

Clara turned around and looked back the way they had come. Tracing the long white road back to the mountains, she suddenly spotted a rider on a dark horse making steady progress towards them. Quickly, she drew the driver's attention to the horseman.

'Come along, quickly,' he cried to the rest. 'This road is plagued with bandits who pick off solitary travellers like flies. If this fellow has pistols, we may still never reach the city.'

And so, as many times before on these dangerous roads, the two women, the driver and postillions piled back nervously into their dusty, creaking carriage. It had been the same through all the barren mountain roads of Bohemia. Any stranger had to be treated with suspicion. Bandits commonly attacked isolated travellers and merchants; the lonely valleys were infamous for murderous highwaymen. The driver cracked his whip and the horses wearily accelerated to their fastest pace.

Anxiously, Clara peered back out of the window. It was the pace of the rider that alarmed her. An honest traveller might just as easily take this road but would be loaded with panniers and would proceed at an even pace. There seemed no alternative but to do what the driver was already doing – driving the horses as fast he could, so they might reach the city gates first. Clara gripped the edge of the window and silently urged the horses on. But their own horses were tired, and pulling a heavy carriage besides. Soon the horseman on his fresh steed gained on them. As Clara stared back she could see the animal's hooves flashing in the dust and the long mane flying.

'It is hopeless,' she said to Tresa. 'I am sure we will be robbed.'

To her surprise, Tresa began to rifle through her bags, pulling out little pouches and cloths and hiding them about her person. Clara guessed she held all her wealth in that most easily transportable of forms – jewels. She, on the other hand, had nothing to hide. Only my dresses, she thought, are my treasures. The lovely gowns created in Amsterdam, Paris and Rome – and, most precious of those, the lilac dress. She would be truly sorry to lose that.

With a rumble of hooves the dark rider pulled alongside the clattering coach. Clara had time only to see that the man was swathed in a billowing riding cloak pulled up high across his mouth and above that a black tricorne hat. Then, to her alarm, she heard the driver pull in the reins. Gradually the carriage ground to a bumping, shuddering halt.

'No,' she cried. 'Surely we should try to escape?'

Tresa, meanwhile, was crossing herself, though Clara

186

thought that the saints would do little to protect her hidden cache. They could hear muffled voices from the front.

'I dare not look,' she whispered.

'No, no, stay still. Listen, we must say all our valuables were sent ahead with the count.'

'Yes,' she agreed, but was already thinking she would far rather hand over any earthly goods than not arrive safely in Prague. They were so close – and yet might never reach the city. Privately, she cursed the highwayman or robber or whoever he was, not for taking any valuables but for putting her rendezvous with the count in the slightest jeopardy.

The door opened, letting a blaze of light into the gloomy compartment.

'We have nothing!' cried Tresa, before Clara hushed her with a squeeze of her fingers.

'Anton!'

In a moment, Clara was up and out of the carriage, standing beside him by the side of the road. He took her hand in his and, for a long moment, all she could think of was how happy she was to see him.

'I was hunting at Karlstein when a messenger told me he had seen you out on the road. I hope I did not scare you.'

He looked quite the same – still handsome, if windblown and dusty – yet different, too. He seemed less formal, almost eager behind his haste and dust. His fingers affectionately caressed hers and, in that one small movement, she knew she had made the right decision. The bond between them was even stronger now.

'Yes, yes. It is wonderful to see you.'

Then she blushed, for she was not used to telling him such things. When she raised her eyes, his dark eyes were still drinking in her face. With a tender smile, he cupped her face in his hands and kissed her quickly on the lips. She felt overwhelmed, as if she might uncontrollably laugh or cry, she could not tell which. However hard the journey, it was now worth every difficulty.

Suddenly, she saw Tresa appear at the door and her heart sank. But, instead of rushing to greet her, the count only nodded quite civilly and asked how she was. Then he turned back to Clara and stroked her cheek, as if she were his greatest treasure.

'Do you want to ride with me into the city? You could ride in front, on my horse. It is much more pleasant than sitting in that airless carriage.'

'But I have never ridden a horse. I should be terrified.'

He pulled her tenderly towards him and kissed the top of her head. 'There is no need. I will see you come to no harm.'

In a few moments, he had lifted her up in front of him. Then, with a click of his heels, they moved forward down the road.

'It is very high.'

'Then I must hold you tighter,' he said warmly.

So he pulled her even closer around her waist, carrying the reins loosely in his other hand. They talked quietly of nothing in particular – the weather, the journey, the countryside. As Clara nestled against his cradling body she felt an overpowering peace. She had never been quite as happy before. It was a peculiar happiness. It made her eyes prick with tears, just to feel him so close beside her.

'It is good you have arrived early,' he said as they neared the city. 'For tomorrow is a great feast for the Empress. She is here, you know: Maria Theresa, with all her court. It will be a very interesting evening.'

'But I have nothing to wear. I am sorry I have come in these old rags; it is just that the travelling has been so hard.'

'Oh, always complaining,' he teased. 'Of course I have arranged a court dress for the occasion. The Austrians are very formal in these matters and it is only right that you wear court dress. I think you will like it, when you see it.'

'I am sure I will. Did you know, when I feared our

goods would be stolen, my greatest concern was the loss of my lilac dress? I wish never to be parted from it.' She surprised herself, talking to him like this, but something between them had changed. She felt like the hero of some ancient tale who has braved many ordeals to reach his goal. She had not chosen John Palmer's safe haven, but instead made this difficult journey to Prague. She had no doubt that her reward was here, in some mysterious change in their feelings towards each other.

'The feast will be a fitting occasion for your next lesson,' he murmured, pulling her close against his body. 'Are you ready, Clara, to explore the fourth sense, the sense of taste?'

She turned a little, so she could just see his face. He looked so serene, guiding the horse upwards now, towards the massed buildings in the city wall. She felt an excited hunger ripple through her body.

'I should like that.' She smiled, leaning her head into the crook of his shoulder. 'I have developed quite an appetite for your scheme of education.'

Next morning broke blue and bright upon the shining turrets of Prague Castle. Clara awoke in her high, airy chamber and thought that all her dreams had come true. The vast sheets were sparkling white and crisp against her newly bathed skin. Above her were ruffled peacock-blue hangings gathered in thick golden cords. At the side of her bed was a silver tray set with a jug of steaming cream-topped chocolate, fragrant brioche and fruit-studded Viennese pastries and strudel.

After a lazy breakfast reclining amongst her bolsters and pillows, she rose and took a look around her apartment. The walls were painted with elaborate frescoes and hung with tapestries depicting gardens and hunting. Besides her huge wooden bed, there were trunks and tables and rich Turkey carpets beneath her bare feet. It was so different from the filthy rooms and straw pallets of her journey that she wandered about, touching the sumptuous cloths and polished wood. She found her new gown in a separate dressing room, displayed on a faceless wooden mannequin.

It was so magnificent, it was almost frightening. The skirts were as broad as an arm's length, stretched on panniers to reveal every inch of the sumptuously patterned gold brocade fabric. Ruffled in gold and silver lace, the skirts were slashed at the front to show an ivory silk moiré petticoat worked with the most delicate gold embroidery in a pattern of roses. The tight narrow bodice was also of gold brocade with a v-shaped stomacher panel set with dozens of pearls inside silver rosettes. Even the lace ruffles at her elbows were double layers of finest, frothy Valenciennes lace.

Tentatively, Clara ran her fingers over the dress. It was a masterpiece of artistry and fine needlework. Every accessory was also laid out on cushions around it: narrow diamond-buckled shoes, an ivory fan depicting the Habsburg crest on silk, a long ostrich feather on a diamond clasp to wear in her hair. For a long time, Clara gazed at the objects, finding exquisite little images in the embroidery, new lace underwear rolled in a silken bag, even a painfully narrow gold satin corset worked with a pattern of birds and fruits in silver thread.

'Magnificent, but rather dated, don't you think? The waist is so low; but then, they say the Empress is rather stuck in her ways.'

It was Tresa; she had let herself in quietly.

'And what will you be wearing?'

'Ah, I am afraid I must make do and mend with my blue silk. But it will not matter. I shall be sitting at the lowest of low tables with the rest of the Italian riff-raff.'

It was Clara's moment of triumph but she felt nothing, only a little sadness that they would not share the occasion, as had previously been the case.

'Come along. What a dreary face. It is not for such a day as today. Do you care for a stroll in the gardens?'

'Yes, if you wait while I dress.'

* * *

An hour later, they emerged from a covered bridge into the enchanting Palace Gardens, deep within the walls of the castle. On the one side were the high-turreted towers with conical red-tiled roofs and, to the other, acres of orchards and formal Italian gardens. For some time they wandered, looking at the fat carp in the ponds and taking cover beneath the shady pergola.

'So, Clara, only weeks now until your wedding.' Tresa eyed her mischievously, fishing for information as the carp lazily quested for food with their sharp rows of teeth.

'Yes. Oh, I do feel sure now, Tresa. I am so glad I came to Prague.' She pressed Tresa's hand, knowing her eyes shone brightly and a smile played across her lips. 'Anton says our wedding itself is unimportant. If we are still travelling, any wayside church will do. But yes, only six weeks left. I never guessed for one moment when I left England I could truly love him. But I do, Tresa; now I am sure of it.'

With an expression of affectionate concern, the Italian touched her arm. 'Clara, I know you love him. So you must be strong. He is not a usual sort of man. Sometimes what he does – it may not seem loving. But it is, my sweet, it is.'

But before Clara could ask Tresa for an explanation for her cryptic words, her companion stood abruptly, noticing the count appear at the other end of the garden.

'Ah, there he is: the man himself,' Tresa announced.

He was waiting on the terrace of the Belvedere, a graceful summer house topped with a roof of green copper. He greeted them with a broad smile as they approached.

'I have just played a game of what they call tennis with Count Galinski,' he told them, looking all the more vibrant for his exertions. 'It involves hitting a rather small ball with a racquet which we have both cursed thoroughly. Now I deserve my reward in sitting and resting in such delightful company.'

He was still dressed for his game, in a loose white

191

shirt and white breeches and stockings. Clara watched him shyly as he lounged in his chair, so unaware of his animal allure. A servant brought some glasses of iced sherbet decorated with fruit.

'Do you like it?' he asked Clara as she tried the sweet confection. 'Like so much here, its origin is in the east. Now,' he said, enthusiastically sitting up, 'I am rested. I can show you the tulips. Long before they were grown in Amsterdam, they were cultivated here, when they arrived from the east. Shall we look?'

Clara took his arm, but Tresa had spied the Austrian Count Galinski crossing the gardens towards them. With a conspiratorial smile, she said she would prefer to stay in the shade of the Belvedere and write a letter.

'We are rather late for the best. In the spring there is every colour, from palest yellow to sky-blue and the famed black tulip.'

He picked up a single scarlet bloom which had bent in the wind and presented it to her. With mock graciousness, she accepted it, admiring the glossy petals and yellow powdery stamen. But, in truth, as they paraded along the rows of gorgeous flowers, she would have admired a collection of fleas, so happy was she to be pressing on the count's arm.

'You know so much,' Clara said. 'I have learnt a great deal since I left England.'

'This programme of education,' he confided. 'It began as a foolish conceit of mine. But now it is my passion.' He hesitated, then continued less certainly. 'Sometimes I think that, in setting tests and traps for you, I have only succeeded in snaring myself.'

'To me, it is as if you have woken me from a deadly sleep. Until I met you, I was a sleepwalker, blindfold and deaf, buried in dullness.'

'And now you are woken, what do you want?' He smiled mockingly, turning towards her and pulling her close, raking his fingers through the back of her hair. He smelt of pomade and healthy perspiration and she could feel the strength of his warmed muscles through the muslin of his wide-sleeved shirt. Silently, she promised herself that, this time, she would have him.

'I want so much,' she confessed. 'Sometimes my mind is maddened by it.'

His hands ran possessively up the back of her gown, pulling her closer. She could feel the hard outline of his body. She could feel the hardness, too, of his stirring sex, pressing close to her groin through her dress.

Lifting her face with his fingertips, so that his eyes were close to hers, like black pools of hunger, he said what she had been waiting to hear, all these months. 'I love you, Clara.'

'Yes,' she whispered.

'But sometimes my love may feel cruel. Can you bear it? Do you truly want to complete our journey?'

She felt she would do anything, anything in the world to have him.

'Yes, teacher,' she murmured, opening her lips to surrender to his kisses. 'I will travel with you, wherever our journey takes us.'

The long self-indulgence of dressing for dinner was marred by only one thing. She had been interrupted by one of the castle's servants, bearing a letter. Immediately, she had recognised the writing and torn it open.

I confess I am here, Miss Fairfax. Here in this same wretched city where fate has transported you in the cruellest manner. I could not, for the sake of my eternal soul, watch you leave Rome alone and unbefriended. My excuse to my friends was a journey into Saxony but, by my conscience and before God, I could not help but follow you.

Reiterate I must, my offer of help and also far more than that, should you be able to accept my proposal. I beg you, reflect on the precarious nature of your existence with these manipulative fiends. Neither can be trusted, the Italian nor his female companion. I implore you to trust the servant Joseph. He will bring you to my inn at the sign of

the Iron Horseshoe by the bridge. Think on it, I beg
you for, by the Sabbath, I must return to Rome.

Your friend and protector,
John Palmer Esquire

There is no fool, she considered, like a sad fool who
believes himself in love. Irritated, she threw the letter
down into the empty grate.

The banquet was held in the cavernous Vladislav Hall,
where row upon row of tables were laid out, resplendent
with golden tableware.

'There is no need for us to sit here with all the court,'
Anton whispered, as they walked arm in arm into the
candlelit hall. 'Once you have seen the Empress, we can
retire to one of the side rooms and eat in peace.'

'Why would we do that?'

'You will see.'

They stood back beneath one of the great arched
windows as the members of the court began to take up
their places. Clara could not help but recollect that Tresa
considered the Habsburg court old-fashioned. It was
true, for unlike the new lightness and elegance brought
to Louis's French court by Madame de Pompadour, the
Austrians were still addicted to heavy powdered wigs
and sombre braided coats; the ladies were encumbered
by panniered brocades and velvets in the dullest bronzes
and purples.

As a fanfare played, all rose for the arrival of the
Empress herself, Maria Theresa of Habsburg, Empress
of Austria and Queen of Hungary. Clara watched keenly
as the Empress walked regally down the centre of the
hall. Whilst only a woman of middle height and middle
age, her presence nevertheless exerted an arresting
power. Heavily powdered white hair topped a rather
plain, self-satisfied face which occasionally deigned to
nod at some fortunate as she passed them.

Yet much of the effect, Clara thought, derived from
her dress. It was a vast, cumbersome creation of cloth of

gold encrusted with jewels. Now she had seen it, Clara realised that her own gown was but a faint copy of this costume. Where her own dress was sewn with diamonds, the Empress wore a hundred. Besides, her waist was circled with a dozen strings of large pearls, and ermine trimmed her bodice and scarlet ceremonial cloak.

No sooner had the Empress reached her throne at the highest table than again all the court stood, as her priest proclaimed a grace.

'It will be like this all night – up and down for one speech or tribute after another,' whispered the count. 'Shall we disappear while their eyes are closed?'

Clara nodded and, in a few moments, they slipped through a finely wrought door into one of the small chambers off the hall.

'This is much more to my taste.'

Anton looked around at the sumptuous tasselled hangings and ornate carved furniture, the sconces full of burning candles and damask-covered tablecloth awaiting their food. They settled down together on a richly brocaded sofa.

'So, tell me, what did you make of the Empress?'

'She looks as if she is that rare kind of woman who could rule an Empire.'

Anton nodded. 'You are right. Beneath that pink face, she is no fool. A turn of the card has brought Austria this great chance and she intends to stay in the game until the end. I hear she even has great plans for marrying her daughter Marie Antoinette to the French dauphin. So, what will happen to your Protestant England then?'

Once, Clara would have been affronted at such teasing. Now she only smiled placidly. 'Sir, my travels have left me quite liberal. If our imperial hostess wants to marry her daughter to the King of the Elves, who am I to contradict her? I am afraid I am quite drunk on luxury.'

'Drunk on luxury,' he mused, with his chin resting on his elegant fingertips. 'I should prefer something even stronger.' Getting up, he served her himself with a deep goblet of wine. Throwing off his heavily embroidered golden coat, he sat back in his waistcoat and ruffled shirt.

'The Empress allows seven hundred of the best Viennese families to grow Heurigen wines. Let us begin with this: a young white, a Weissburgunder. Do not swallow it: roll it around the inside of your mouth. Taste the crispness of the grape.'

Trying not to laugh, Clara did as she was told, releasing a warm, peachy fragrance from the cold wine. Swallowing, she pronounced the wine 'very nice'.

The count took a mouthful and shook his head. 'I can see you do need a lesson in the development of taste. It is not enough to eat and drink for sustenance, my sweet, it is essential to taste as well. It is not the throat, but the tongue that is your sensory organ. Ah, here are the *fruits de mer*.'

A liveried servant had slipped in and out, leaving their first dish. It was filled with crushed ice tinted in various hues of green and blue.

'Firstly, the appearance of food,' said Anton, 'is intended to stimulate the appetite and appear beautiful in itself. It is not enough for the dish to please only when it reaches the mouth. The best chefs – such as Gareme, who has prepared this banquet – first of all teases the palate with superb appearance so that even the most languid gourmand will be tempted.'

Clara was looking somewhat nervously into the gold salver. She had never eaten a living creature before.

'Here, do not look, then.' With his arm around her back he brushed her eyelids shut with his fingertips. Then she felt something soft cover her eyes – a ribbon or scarf.

'Firstly, the aroma.'

She could smell the sea and also something rich and piquant.

'This first is a *belon*, small and plump and white. A little lemon juice.'

She could hear him lift a fork. 'Now, mouth open.'

Instead of a cold oyster, she instead felt his mouth press against hers and a flicker of his tongue. Then, laughing, he kissed her forehead. 'I am sorry, now I will feed you the oyster. Taste it only momentarily, then swallow.'

Then she felt it, icy cold and savoury, tasting of the fertile depths of the sea. In a moment, it had gone and she was ready for another.

'Ah, not yet. As the French say, "*Poisson* without wine is poison". Now, a different wine. A sip of Riesling. And next, a nice pale-green *marennes*.'

As soon as she had swallowed the second oyster, he asked for her opinion.

'The second was sweeter, more juicy and fragrant.'

'Very good. A little more wine.'

She felt deliciously acquiescent as he fed her on oysters and wine, parting her lips and slipping the cold mouthfuls down her open throat.

'Here is a large one. A *pied de cheval*, or horse's hoof oyster. When I touch your throat, you must swallow.'

Now, as she felt the delicious slippery frost of the oyster pass between her lips, he gently caressed the soft skin of her throat. As she swallowed, he kissed her again; his tongue, hot and sweet, quickly followed. This time he did not pull back so quickly and she clung to him. She decided she liked the taste of him too.

Suddenly, he whisked the scarf from her eyes.

'Now, we must not be too greedy,' he said, with grinning eyes. 'For there is much to learn from the balance of Gareme's menu. Tell me – are you hungry?'

She nodded enthusiastically.

'It is the intended effect. The oysters are merely a stimulant for our appetites. Just as a kiss,' and here he again pressed his mouth to hers, 'is but a taste of the entire promised pleasure.'

At the ring of a bell, their next course appeared. As the golden lid was lifted, the dish burst into a mass of blue and golden flames. As these died away, Clara could see a delicate stew of braised fish.

'Ah, one of Gareme's special dishes. *Matelote Canotière*, a dish of eel, tench and bream flambéed in cognac dressed with gudgeon and crayfish. Taste a little with this Rhenish wine.'

The braised fish was so tenderly cooked in the finest wine, it fell apart in flakes of creamy flesh. It looked delightful too, dressed with rosy crayfish and a sprinkling of fish-roe.

'Tell me why this is a great dish,' she asked. 'For I know it is but cannot express it in words.'

The count let his fork rest and dabbed at his mouth with a napkin.

'Like a painting there are darker notes and lighter, or like a sonata, deeper chords and higher ornaments. Here, taste the richness of the fish *fumé*, a *court-bouillon*, to which has been added the best wine; it has been thickened with the blood of the eels. Balanced with this is the sweet delicacy of each different fish, each quite separate in the lexicon of the *poissonnerie*. But the perfection is also in Gareme's eye to select only the finest produce, at the best season, prepared in the most delicate fashion to reveal, once again, the true essence of the creature.'

Next was *Juive Polonaise*, a dish of delicious Danube carp spiced with honey and almonds. So delicious was this, aromatic with a stuffing of ginger and cinnamon, that Clara longed to eat the whole portion.

'It is wiser to take only a morsel, to savour and then retire,' Anton advised. 'For we have barely sampled the first courses.'

He filled her glass again from one of the dozen bottles in gold coolers on the sideboard; Clara felt her head swim a little as she sipped the chilled wine.

'So, what do you say?' he asked. 'Are the pleasures of the table the greatest of the pleasures?'

She shook her head in bemusement.

'I cannot say. Each pleasure you unfold before me seems the greatest at that moment, overpowering all my other senses. To see is to be confronted; to hear, to be transported; to smell, as you so rightly said, communicates the essential essence of a thing. But to taste – do we not then consume the very thing? What could bring us closer than to ingest that which is not us?'

'Wisely spoken. Mankind, some say, begins by feeding at the breast and never loses that desire until he dies.'

At this, Clara could not help but notice that he looked admiringly at the fullness of her own breasts, forced upwards by the flat stiffness of the gold bodice.

'Some would say,' he added, reaching out to appreciatively caress the ivory fullness of her bosom, 'that is where we get our rapacious desire to taste flesh.'

As his fingertips lingered, tracing the curve of her breasts, then drawing together where he knew the sensitive nipple lay beneath the silk, she wanted it never to end. But he maddeningly withdrew and rang the bell for the servant.

'A change of direction in our menu,' he announced. 'So you must play a little guessing game.'

The scarf appeared again and Clara willingly allowed herself to return to the dark arena of the senses. Now, when the lid of the dish was removed, she was assailed by a rich and pungent scent. The count parted her lips with his fingers. Teasingly, she nipped him with her teeth.

'I shall pay you back later for that.'

Then he slipped a morsel into her mouth. Lusciously tender, it dissolved in her mouth with a burst of vigorous, gamey flavour.

'It is some kind of flesh, but so pungent – I cannot say.'

He fed her another titbit.

'There is fragrance too – of summer orchards, apples drying in the sun.'

'Very good. You have a sensitive palate.'

Again he kissed her and again she thought, whatever delicacies this man feeds me, I crave the taste of the man himself.

'Here, some more,' he said, drawing back. As she ate again he told her what it was.

'It is one of the Empress's favourites from Vienna – marinated goose livers in Calvados and cream. The scent of the monk's apples is subtle, so you did well to detect it.'

Now the dishes arrived thick and fast. The scents were of savoury roasted meats, prepared to perfection. Each dish wore the seal of a master. Like the written symbols of music, the count told her, the trained palate can taste differences of seasoning, ripeness, spicing, even a bare second's difference in roasting. There were the darker, earthy notes of black diamond truffles studding a roasted Styrian capon and the ruby depths of chamois venison stewed with marrons glacés and armagnac. To Clara's palate, the most delectable was a small, succulent cock of the woods poached with fragrant pomegranates in a pool of savoury claret.

The count removed the scarf from her eyes. The candles were burning low as a servant removed the array of salvers. Looking about her again, she realised the room, the count, the whole evening swam in her head like a dream. Momentarily, she wondered how she would get to bed, whether her legs would even carry her. Oh, she was sure Anton would sort it all out as usual. She was undoubtedly getting drunk.

'Now I hope you can manage just a little more,' he teased. Again, he offered her a glass of strong wine.

'Not a drop,' she insisted. 'Or I may embarrass you.'

She looked at him teasingly, with expectantly raised brows. But he only laughed and poured himself another glass of wine. 'Very well. For the dessert course, I will allow my pupil something lighter. Just one glass of champagne. Surely you can manage that?'

'I think so,' she said, though her voice seemed to echo rather distantly in the recesses of her head.

As she sipped, a golden tray of desserts appeared. Austrian tortes of every hue and flavour – nut, chocolate, peach, mocha. Mountains of Mont Blanc, luxurious ices piled with chestnuts and meringues.

'Look, they have sent to the convents for these speci-alities. I have always succumbed to the temptation of these Troubled Thoughts.' The count picked up one of the little sugar iced biscuits. 'And this great confection is a Triumph of Gluttony.' It was a vast dish of cream, *pasticchio* and green pistachios.

'And what are these?' asked Clara, choosing a little white cake with a cherry at the summit.

'I forget you are not a Catholic,' he laughed. 'There is a tradition at our convents for baking unusual offerings. You have just bitten into one of the Virgin's Breasts.'

Clara grinned wickedly. It was deliciously light and sweet.

'Here, let me try it.'

Enticingly, she fed him a bite of the cake.

'That is good, but let me compare it with the real thing.'

Deftly he reached out and eased her left breast above its constricting fabric. Clara giggled, stretching back into her seat as he lowered his lips to the reddened rosebud of her nipple. His tongue, when it met the sensitive nub of flesh, teased her unmercifully.

It must be tonight, she thought; I cannot wait for him any longer than tonight.

'Let me compare this,' he said, freeing his mouth for a second, leaving the crimson spike glistening and hard, 'with the other.'

Gently he freed her right nipple, too, and began to taste this, though now his fingers rolled and squeezed the first. Clara closed her eyes, feeling her body flutter with excitement. He is so skilled, she thought. As a lover, he will please me more than any man in the world.

Suddenly, he broke away, leaving her for a moment bereft and giddy.

'Ah, another delight from Gareme.'

Unnoticed by her, the servant had returned and left

another selection of dishes. In a moment, Anton turned to her with two little figures, each the size of a hand, of a man and a woman all decorated in court dress, made entirely of hard sugar.

'I think it is fitting that you eat me and I – at least metaphorically – eat you up, Clara.'

He gave her the figure of the man.

'Where would you start?'

She looked at it: at the blank little face, coat of gold leaf, and moulded legs.

'I should like to keep it,' she marvelled.

'But that is not the idea at all,' he baited. 'If you could eat a man, where would you begin?'

Smiling, she looked again at the figure. Should she bite off his head – no, that would seem barbaric. His legs? Again, it seemed severe.

'I should do this,' she announced, sticking out her pink tongue and licking the little man from his boots to his face. 'I should like to taste all of a man.'

'Would you, indeed?' he whispered, then pressed his sugary lips to hers. Drunkenly, she dropped the little figure on her lap. All she could think of was the flooding tide of her need. Hungrily, she opened her mouth to him, meeting his tongue with hers, feeling sharp teeth graze the soft inside of her mouth. His hands slipped the brocade from her shoulders so she could feel his fingers working against her flesh. Like a starving woman, she reached out to him, tasting the sweetness and heat of his mouth. Soon, he was pressed hard upon her and she felt herself descend into the ample cushions of the sofa, her eyes closed as she fought the fever racing through her veins.

Tentatively, she felt his fingers reach down and brush her ankle. Then, more confidently, he began to caress her foot, easing her silk shoe away. Lifting it, he raised it to his lips.

'Some nights I have even dreamed of repaying the compliment you paid to my boot with one of your pretty little shoes.'

202

At first she frowned to see him kiss the sole of her shoe, then suddenly realised the import of what he was saying.

'I fear it is too small for your purposes, sir,' she giggled. 'As your boot was almost too large for mine.'

'Oh, but I should have liked to see you try to accommodate it,' he said warmly.

Kneeling beside her, he carefully lifted her heavy skirts and raised her stockinged foot to his lips.

'If I were to eat you, I should begin here,' he murmured, kissing her silk-clad toes. She thought she might faint away with desire; her veins were pounding, and her sex throbbed and tingled with anticipation. She longed for him to continue, to move his lips upward and upward. Sighing, she felt her legs grow limp.

'So, as the nuns teach,' he murmured, 'the triumph of gluttony warms us to the glory of lechery.'

His lips pressed against her calf and then the inside of her knees. She was not even ashamed when she felt a tremor of passion in her legs as his lips ascended on their delightful journey. With a loud sigh, she felt his lips reach the point above her gartered stockings. His mouth scorched the naked flesh of her inner thigh. She could hear him breathing quickly from his position between her opened legs. With his hands he gently caressed the most susceptible skin inside her legs, but it was his tongue that drove her wild. Then, at last, it happened. With a groan from his frustrated body, he delicately parted her most private flesh with his fingers and sank his lips against the slippery inner lips.

'And so, for my dessert,' he murmured from below.

Intoxicated as she was, Clara's veins seethed with heated, molten blood. She knew she could not hold back. With a loud cry, she let her head fall backward on the cushion. With the utmost delicacy, he slipped his fingers beneath her buttocks and lifted her open sex towards his lips. Kissing and licking and probing, he touched again and again those most explosive cusps of her body. Slowly rolling his tongue, he found her entrance and made love to it, lifting her a little, rocking her back and forth on and off his tongue. It felt, for all the world, like a tiny, rasping cock working away to torment her. Beyond her control, she felt her muscles tighten greedily around it.

'And for your dessert.'

For a moment he broke away, reaching for the little sugar figure, which had tumbled to the floor.

'If I were this man,' he whispered wickedly, 'I should not be eaten, but eat you up instead.'

Very, very slowly, he pushed the figurine up, against her glistening inner lips. Then, as she gasped, he pushed it through the natural resistance of her opening. It felt very hard and rough inside her clutching entrance. She could barely breathe; she could feel her breasts rise and fall as craving spread like liquid fire through her body. Pushing her knuckle into her mouth, she did her utmost to stay silent, but it was impossible. It was hard and exquisite, rocking back and forth inside her.

Beneath her skirt, he again sank his face into her open cleft. She was aware of wetness, of an uncontrollable slow flow of sugared fluid being licked into his mouth. Still, he worked the little figure inside her, as she gasped. Twisting a little, she felt him suddenly force her legs as wide apart as they might go. Then his tongue pressed insistently on her clitoris. Uncontrollably she felt her thighs spasm; as she lifted her knees around his head, she felt herself begin to convulse around the tormenting hardness of the figurine. Rapture dammed up within her, until the moment before the highest peak was reached. Her fingers clawed at the fabric of her dress. Still, as he penetrated her with the little figure, his tongue played across her maddened labia, circling and pressing. Rapidly panting, she felt her hips arch, her muscles grip, her throat stretch backward. Then, just as she felt herself begin to drown, he pulled away from her completely.

For a few moments she lay back, eyes closed, panting, unable to believe he had left her like this. Her frustration was a painful knife twisting in her gut. Then she was aware of the count standing before her. He was looking down on her, on her raised skirt, her loose hair, her breasts spilling over the tightness of her gown.

'We must go,' he said.

'Go where?'

He was biting his lip as she stared at him. His face was flushed and his voice uncharacteristically hoarse. She could see it too, pressing against his clothes. He was massively, painfully aroused.

'We should be more private. I know somewhere better than this.'

'No, Anton, please.' She looked at him imploringly. Surely he could tell? She was aching with need. 'Please don't stop; I cannot bear to move.'

What made it worse was that she could see it, hear it in his voice. His pulse throbbed at his throat; his eyes were black with lust as he gazed painfully at her disarranged dress, her breasts still peeping over the gold of her bodice. His cock was rigid, pushing against his clothes.

Roughly, he grasped her arm and pulled her up from the sofa. Impatiently, he pulled down her skirt and swept her hair back over her shoulders. He slapped her lightly across her breasts.

'Clara, behave yourself. It is time for your lesson.'

Surprised, she found herself willingly compliant.

'I am sorry,' she offered. She was most powerfully aware, now, of his excitement.

'Very well, then. Are you ready?'

Already weak with desire, she nodded. Certainly, I am ready, she thought. But for what, she could only guess.

Chapter Thirteen

Outside, the feast had ended. The hall itself was still in disarray; tables and chairs were strewn about, the air thick with the scent of stale wine. Only by circumnavigating the whole of that gigantic chamber, larger than the precincts of a cathedral, did Anton at last lead her to the shadowy staircase at the furthest end. Now, as they descended, Anton held a candelabra aloft as it cast unsteady shadows on the walls.

Step by step, Clara felt they were leaving the airy lightness of the main castle buildings. There were no signs of apartments here, only unsteadily glimmering tallow burning low in wall sconces and the ever descending stairs.

At last they reached the bottom. High, nail-studded doors faced them, clearly leading to the stable yard. But in the wall behind them stood another, smaller door. When Anton opened this, they passed into a much lower, vaulted chamber. Looking about as Anton lifted his weak flames, Clara could see that it had once been a grand, richly frescoed room. Now it appeared to be used for storage – there were many chests and leather cases against the walls, and wooden cupboards with old-fashioned lettering in the curious Bohemian language.

A figure moved in the gloom. With a start, Clara

identified herself, momentarily caught in the glass of a shadowy mirror. Her face was so pale in the nest of her hair, her figure shimmering like a ghost in the dazzling carapace of the stiff court dress. Beside her, Anton was coolly intent on his purpose; his face was inwardly absorbed as he guided her onward.

Just then, a noise caught her attention. Standing stock still, Clara pulled back on his arm, peering into the deeper gloom at the far end of the chamber.

'What is it?' she whispered.

Someone is hurt, she thought at first. Perhaps they had fallen down here and been left to suffer alone. It was only that consideration which propelled her forward to peer into the darkness. Quickly, she was reassured that the sound was not actually in the room. It was an irregular whispering and moaning sound, undoubtedly human, suggesting great pain and anguish.

Anton remained silent. She gazed keenly at the walls and low vaulted arches. The noise was coming from the right-hand side of the room. Then, in the dimness, she suddenly saw an opening in the stone paved floor. Another descending staircase.

Clara froze. The alcohol had lessened in her blood; the cool air in these vaults shivered across her skin. Perhaps she should turn round? Despite her unspoken resistance, Anton wordlessly led her to the head of the staircase. Here the noise was even clearer: the repetitive sound of struggling and muffled cries of supplication.

'No, Anton. I am frightened.'

He was standing behind her. Silently, he slid his arms about her waist and kissed the pulse that raced at her neck.

'You will not disappoint me?' he whispered. His fingertips worked at the edge of her gown, pushing between the brocade and her naked shoulder. As he reached down and scorched the nape of her neck with his lips, she began to tremble noticeably. Violently contradictory emotions battled within her. Whatever lay at the bottom of the dark stairs frightened her – a part of her mind simply did not want to see what lay there. Yet, when he touched her, the lightest touch was all she needed to rouse the weakness in that great dam of wanting. So weak was she with need, she would do anything, anything, to please him.

'Clara,' he intoned softly in her ear, sliding his hands caressingly over her body from white shoulders over burgeoning breasts to her narrowly constricted waist. 'Your fear is good – it will magnify the experience. Do you want to feel such pleasure as you have never felt before? Do you want to feel the overwhelming power of your senses?' Suddenly, crudely, he slid his hand inside the opening of her gown where it was slit to show the rich petticoat. Suggestively, he squeezed the rounded mound of her pubis. 'Or do you want to turn back now?'

She found she was shaking as violently as if standing naked in the depths of wintry snow. Biting her lip, she turned to face him, imploring him silently with liquid eyes. Yet he was only excited by the force of her desperation.

'Oh, Clara,' he whispered, unable to suppress the thrill of power in his voice, 'your bones will shake this hour, even harder, in the oblivion of ecstasy, if you let me be your teacher.'

She could not challenge his will. Silently, she placed her foot upon the first stair. The stairway was dark but, as she descended, she was relieved to see that the room below was softly lit. The sound was growing louder, only now she could also hear a lower note, a constantly intoned murmuring of reproach. Yet each few seconds, as if in response, the louder voice would answer with a cry, a groan or pleading.

Shivering still, Clara tiptoed into the hollowed stone chamber. It had all the appearance of a fearful dungeon, with low burning torches set into the walls and scarlet embers glowing in an iron brazier. Scarcely daring to breathe, she turned her face to the source of those unearthly sounds.

For a moment, she thought she faced two devils, red-skinned in the glow of the fire. Then she saw a naked man and woman, though what demonic act they were engaged in, she could not at first discover. The woman, she saw quickly, was Tresa.

'Ah, Clara. Your timing is perfect.'

Stupefied, she walked towards Tresa's laconic voice. The woman was naked, her black hair flowing down her back, parting only around her pointed breasts. In her hand was a black leather scourge, its end split into a dozen finely fringed lashes.

Unwillingly, Clara raised her eyes to the man who was clearly her victim. Clara recollected him dimly as Count Galinski. He was stretched by ankles and wrists, held with four great coils of rope attached to apparatus along the ends of a wooden trestle table. Naked, his body glowed with sweat, his hair loose across his face. Crimson weals criss-crossed his chest and shoulders and stomach. From the black mass of hair at the pit of his stomach rose his cock, crimson and distended. When he raised his eyes to her through his straggling hair, he seemed an animal, a creature less than human. She could not believe this was the same man she had seen chatting so urbanely in the Belvedere.

With a swish of the scourge, Tresa aimed a blow at his stomach. With a cry of pain, he shuddered, then twisted slackly forward, only his bonds stopping him from sliding to the floor.

'Don't be deceived; it is what he wants. What he craves. Don't you?' With a skilful turn of her wrist, she aimed a stinging stroke to the top of his thighs. The man gazed at her beseechingly. With the swinging end of the whip, Tresa softly tormented his twitching phallus. Galinski cried out, arching his back to be relieved.

'I do not want to watch this,' Clara said, turning to Anton.

But he was transfixed, his eyes shining red in the firelight. He held her fast, fingers digging into her arm. 'Clara, I only ask that you watch awhile.'

Indeed, it was difficult not to watch now, as Tresa

climbed astride her victim. How well Clara knew that ripe, golden-brown body as Tresa tormented Galinski: rubbing her gorgeous, swinging breasts tantalisingly close to his transfixed face, sliding her hot and tempting sex along his writhing thigh. Clara did not want to watch, but there was something almost narcotic in the cruel sensuality of Tresa's baiting.

At the same time, Clara became aware of Anton silently undressing her. He pulled open the tight laces down the back of her gown; he unloosed the ribbons that held her skirts around her waist; finally, he dragged off the stiff brocaded corset. Now, she could feel his hard thigh and tumescent phallus against the sheer muslin of her chemise.

At last Tresa relented, mocking Galinski as she arched her open thighs above his tormented cock. Finally, she lowered herself and let him feel a taste – no more – of her deliciously receptive cunt.

'Do you want it?' Tresa hissed, momentarily lowering herself an inch on to Galinski's purple-engorged cock. Then, as he cried out with pleasure, she laughed, pulling off him, savouring the misery of his torment.

Impatiently, Anton reached to open Clara's thin shift. Momentarily thwarted by the seamless fabric, he ripped the chemise down the back, slipping his hands possessively across Clara's naked skin. Now, as they watched Tresa torment her lover, he rabidly squeezed her breasts, her stomach, her thighs, her incessantly throbbing sex. The strangely erotic performance, unfolding so close before her eyes, filled her with fiery desire. As she watched Tresa's lovely, rounded buttocks part across the man's prone body, she too felt a sympathetic spasm clutch between her legs.

'So – do you really want it?' Tresa laughed, taunting him as he bucked beneath her, twisting within his bonds.

Galinski replied wordlessly, his voice lost in an anguished cry of need.

'Well, then – perhaps I will let you have a little taste.'

With this, Tresa disdainfully lifted Galinski's distended cock and slipped the rounded head into her opening. The man looked as if he might expire with pleasure. Clara found herself holding her breath. Slowly, the Italian worked the crimson phallus deeper inside her stretched entrance. Clara could see the cock gaining a sheen of slipperiness as it worked slowly in and out of Tresa's opening. It made her feel sick with suppressed desire to watch. Anton, too, as he held her, was feverish with hunger; seemingly without being sensible of his actions, he rubbed against Clara's nakedness – she could feel him hard and hot through his rich clothing as his cock probed against her bare thigh, questing against her rounded bottom and damp cleft.

'Enough!' Tresa admonished, as Galinski began to cry out, jerking his hips towards a convulsive climax. Cruelly, she slid off his juice-soaked cock. Grasping the whip again, she teasingly let the fronds dance across him as he begged her for some satisfaction.

'Later – perhaps. Now, get up!'

Unloosing the cords at his ankles, Tresa yanked up the man by his wrists. He was sore and stinging from the punishment with the whip, yet even more so from the cruel treatment she had meted out to his unmercifully distended cock. Staggering, he stood, his hands bound as Tresa led him to an iron hook buried in the ceiling. There, as if it were an action she performed every day, she slung the length of rope around the iron and hauled him upright like a side of meat. With a last, tickling caress from the scourge, she left him there, hanging by his wrists, his body still painfully, poundingly aroused.

The count turned Clara about, so that she faced him. She was suddenly aware that, of the four of them, only he still wore his sumptuous costume. Pressed against the embroidered brocade of his coat, she felt vulnerably naked.

'Your lesson, Clara,' he coaxed. Cradling her tenderly in his arms, he kissed her softly and asked, 'Are you ready now?'

She closed her eyes. Her body hurt with wanting.

'Yes.'

Taking her by the arm, he led her to the wooden trestle. Suddenly realising he meant to place her there, she began to struggle against his grip.

'No, not here!'

'Clara, it is only a little test.'

He held her down, his fingers tight around the top of her arm. With his face so close to hers, she could feel his breath; he brushed across her lips with his, entreating her to be calm.

'It will be easier if you are here. The restraints will not hurt. They will only add to your pleasure.'

Tresa was there, too, gazing down on her with her dark eyes blackened and half-deranged with carnality. In her old, familiar manner, Tresa stroked her open hand down across Clara's body, over the swelling of her breasts and sensitive stomach to her golden-curled sex. For a few moments, Clara relaxed into acquiescence. But then she felt Anton wind the harsh coils of rope tight around her ankles. Struggling to get up, she felt Anton's grip fasten like iron around her leg. Then, with a horrified shock, she felt a burning lash sting across her stomach. Clara cringed – Tresa had struck her with the scourge.

'Be calm,' Anton entreated, stroking her hair. 'I know that for you there is pleasure as well as pain.'

Stunned, she let herself be arranged as they wished. The bonds at her ankles pulled her legs wide apart. Panting, she felt herself opening before them, rivers of shame washing over her as Anton gazed at her body, so immodestly spread to his view. She could not help but let a sob of humiliation escape her lips as the count gently wound thick ropes around her. She was utterly exposed, her body spread in a perfect 'X' as Anton licked his dry lips, admiring his handiwork as she squirmed beneath his gaze.

Even worse, Clara suddenly noticed that Galinski, too, was intent upon her as he hung from the cruel hook. His ribs rose and fell as he breathed slowly, his wild eyes taking in the vulnerable form of the young girl spread supinely where so recently he had suffered. Clara could see that his purple-veined cock was dripping slow drops of involuntary pearly fluid. She was ashamed to find that her effect on Galinski excited her violently. Though she barely knew the man, his feral discomposure made her veins run hot as he devoured her with his eyes.

'Tresa,' murmured the count. 'Why not begin?'

As she lay spread-eagled across the hard wood, it was Tresa, not Anton, who slid over her. Appalled to think that their pleasuring might be watched by the two men, nevertheless Clara could not help but respond to Tresa's touch. The Italian woman was hot – not only hot to the touch, her skin burning and slippery, but burning within, intoxicated with lust. As her tongue slid around Clara's, as her hip bone locked across Clara's pelvis, as their two vulvas slid wetly one against the other, Clara whimpered with excitement. She did not know how much of this she could bear. Even worse, through half-closed lids she could see Anton standing above them, drinking in this epicurean feast of lovemaking. His face was engrossed as he watched Tresa luxuriously lap and suck at Clara's tautly erect nipples. Only his hand, she noticed, gripped the edge of the table, working convulsively as if he wished it was he who stroked Clara's soft white flesh and not her female lover.

Almost immediately, Clara experienced the scorching acceleration towards her climax. Now the tight bonds left her no alternative but to lie stretched, with her clitoris exposed between her wet lips. She could stand no more than a few of Tresa's heated strokes with her grinding pubis before she ignited in quivering throes. Abruptly she struggled to raise her bottom, arching her hips as the first spasms began.

'Stop! Use the whip.'

Tresa was immediately obedient to Anton's orders. Pulling herself back off the restrained girl, she reached for the scourge. Clara quailed, crying out not to hurt her. But when the feathered fronds fell with a crack on her parted thigh, the pain was only momentary. More powerful was the afterglow of fiery heat. It was the strangest sensation – she was close to fainting, as if even her bones were melting in the incandescent fire of pleasurable pain. For long moments she bathed in the pure sensation of that afterburning. Then, recovering, she looked about herself, at the red-glowing vault, at Galinski, who watched her every spasm with wide lust-crazed eyes, and at Tresa, whose face was alight with triumph. Finally, she sought the count. His face was rapt with tenderness.

'When your moment finally comes,' he whispered gently, 'it will be so exquisite, you will never want to return.'

She could not understand him. All she could feel was sensation. This time, Tresa turned the long whip upside down, so that its thick handle, ridged with a handgrip, was lowermost. Hard and unyielding, it probed between Clara's legs. Guiding it deftly, Tresa pushed against the wetness of Clara's sex, causing Clara to cry out. She wanted it, certainly. Her muscles yearned to grip the stiff phallus-shaped handle. Unable to hold in a sob of frustration, she felt the rigid tip press a little way inside her. Tresa was rocking it gently, trying to work past the grasping muscles of her entrance.

'She is tight,' she breathed. 'Maybe too close.'

As Tresa pushed the end against her again, Clara could feel it stinging against her. She wanted to hide her face with shame at being discussed like this, while she lay so exposed in front of them all. Then the count suggested the next best thing.

'Cover her eyes. She must be ready now.'

'Ready for what?' she entreated him, feeling her rib-cage rise and fall with panting breaths.

'Calm yourself, Clara. It is only my little test. When you have proved your skill, you may retire.'

Fastidiously, he smoothed back a stray lock of her hair. Then cradling her cheek, he reached down and kissed her dry lips. Yet, all the time, she could feel a repressed tremor within his touch. It took great self-control, she could see, for him to reach down and touch her face without allowing himself to claw at her as she lay supine and submissive beneath him.

Tresa appeared with a cloth to bind around her eyes. Now Clara was wholly powerless. Around her, she could hear Tresa and Anton moving and whispering, but for some long time she was left with only her own fears and apprehensions. Then, with another tender caress to her cheek, Anton returned.

'What have you learnt this night about taste, Clara?'

She was too confused to deal with such a question.

Suddenly, he pressed his finger against her parted lips. 'You have a beautiful mouth,' he whispered. 'Often, I watch it.'

Involuntarily, she opened her mouth and felt his finger explore between her teeth, pressing inward until her tongue rolled deliciously around it. She remembered his tongue rolling her nipple, then his mouth nipping and sucking against her sex as the sugar figurine dissolved sweetly inside her. He withdrew his finger, tracing the outline of her lips with the wetness of his fingertip.

'What have you learnt?'

'That to taste a thing is almost to be the thing. That since we first suck at the breast we long forever to know a thing with our mouths.'

'Excellent.' He caressed her jaw and suddenly she began to shiver in expectation. 'All I ask is that you distinguish these few tastes. And then I will let you be.'

In the muffled darkness behind the blindfold, she wondered expectantly what he could mean.

'I have anointed these pieces of silk. I think you will recognise this first one.'

The next moment, a length of cloth was pressed to her lips. Tentatively, she opened her mouth and felt the dampness of it press against the soft skin inside her lips. Cautiously, she pressed the tip of her tongue against the fabric.

She could smell salt, and that was the taste that assailed her, too, when she probed it with the sensitive tip of her tongue. Suddenly, she remembered the semen-soaked lilac dress with a pang at her groin. But no – it was not Anton's taste. Musky and sweet: she drew a little of the cloth into her hot mouth and tasted it. It was familiar. It reminded her of long, dark nights pleasuring herself beneath the grubby sheets in countless inns. It was the peppery-sweet taste of the hot, smooth folds within Tresa's gorgeous sex.

'It is a woman,' she whispered. 'It is Tresa.'

'That is good. I said earlier, you have a refined sense of taste. And this?'

With a tingling in her tongue, she felt Anton press another cloth to her mouth. Bizarre as this activity was, Clara found it oddly arousing. She had not forgotten her secret delectation over the stained dress. Now, as she let her tongue penetrate the second cloth, she again sought that completeness that only the taste of a thing can achieve. But this – it was again a woman's taste, she was sure. Eagerly, she savoured the unctuous salinity of the taste. Again, it reminded her of her amiable lovemaking with Tresa. She had tasted this – on Tresa's mouth.

'It is a woman,' she repeated. 'But it is me.'

'Well done.'

As if giving a reward, Anton reached down and pressed his mouth to her parched lips. His mouth tasted still of wine as it pressed into hers, his nails dragging along her throat so that she gave a little yelp of pleasure.

'Oh, you are like a spring, my love, so taut and stretched to the edge.'

With the fringed end of the scourge, he caressed her, running the lambent fronds across her swollen breasts and midriff. No longer concerned, she cried out to him. Very gently, he grazed her parted sex with the tormenting tassels. Groaning, she lifted her hips for him to penetrate her with it.

Now, at last, she could hear his breath grow ragged.

'In a moment,' he shushed. 'We are almost finished.'

The next cloth was laid across her open mouth. This time, she pulled it into her mouth greedily. It was pungent with semen; a bitter brininess stung her tongue. If her legs had not been restrained, she would have drawn up her knees and squeezed her thighs together with pleasure.

'It is you,' she moaned. 'I know it. It is you.'

'Wrong!'

With a shivering blow, the scourge fell on to her thigh. Genuine irritation rang in his voice. Again the whip kissed her flesh with a stinging, smarting blow.

'Anton, no!' She reeled beneath his blows. In the darkness of her captivity she experienced again that surprising heat transfixing her. The scourge flayed the rawness of her nerves, so long had she been tormented at the edge of release. Pain illuminated her mind for long, convulsive intervals of time.

When she felt Anton loosen her bonds, she was scarcely sensible. Tresa was there, too, helping him turn her on her stomach. She felt the scratching ropes at her wrists pull her upward a little.

'Kneel up,' he ordered. Confused behind the blindfold, she let herself be lifted. She was aware, finally, that she was on her hands and knees, although the bonds at her ankles still held her legs fiercely wide. She could feel her hair falling in a curtain before her face. Then Anton was there again, before her. His sensitive hands cupped her face and, for the first time that evening, she felt his crotch near her face. It was there, jutting rigid beneath his silken breeches. She could feel the outline of his cock pressing momentarily against her questing face. She could smell it. Now she wanted to taste it.

'No!' he commanded, pulling away as her mouth eagerly nuzzled the rich fabric of his clothes and, beneath them, the solid bulge of his cock. 'Can you not tell me from another? Taste it, taste it fully, and then you will know.'

Shocked, she felt a naked, fiery penis push against her face. No – it could not be Anton. Undoubtedly it was

Galinski. She could imagine, although she could not see, that Tresa had quickly led him over to her. Now, to her horror, she felt Anton's elegantly strong fingers hold her jaw open as the man was thrust against her.

'Does it taste like me, then?' he hissed in annoyance. 'Go on, then, Clara, taste your victim. I can assure you, looking at his face, he can barely contain himself to have you suck on his throbbing cock.'

Disgusted, she struggled to avoid the swinging appendage. But the count was strong and had the advantage, too, of being neither blinded nor bound. Behind her, she could feel Tresa had climbed against her, holding her upright at her waist, or she might have simply collapsed down on to the wooden table.

Instantly, she felt the tight, rounded head of Galinksi's cock being forced inside her mouth. It was scorching hot and salty with sweat. Anton prised at her jaw so an inch more slid in. Gagging a little, she finally had to relax so that she could breathe again.

'So, Clara, how does that taste?' he snapped.

She was overwhelmed by it – she could hear Galinski panting, no doubt wild at the sight of the restrained girl compelled to take his ill-used prick. And Anton's hand as he held her chin – that, too, however controlled his voice might be – that, too, was trembling with excitement.

She felt hands – whose? – reach down and stroke her breasts. Behind her, Tresa pressed against Clara's buttocks, her fingers groping towards Clara's wetly parted sex. Unable to withstand her instincts anymore, Clara relaxed her jaw and rolled her tongue around the man's twitching cock-head. He tasted of bitter sweat and salt, but it made her cunt throb each time she sucked the juicy head. So, when Tresa tried once more to penetrate her tense entrance with the handle of the scourge, this time Clara pushed back hard like a bitch on heat so it penetrated her. Meanwhile, Anton gently rocked her mouth back and forth along the end of Galinski's cock. As he did so, she pushed wordlessly forward, wanting

218

more and more of it inside her. Taste, pressure, scents – all conspired to drag her into a greedy, ravenous frenzy.

With a violent jerk, she felt Galinski's cock spatter like a fountain against her throat. Deliriously, she pulled back in surprise as he twitched and jumped, delivering his brackish load against her lips, her chin and throat. For a second she hung there dizzily, feeling the phallic handle begin to slide back and forth inside her pulsing sex. Then Galinski was jerked away. Now it was Anton she could hear, his breath hoarse as he held her head to his crotch by the roots of her hair. With a pleasure so sharp it was a pain, she was aware of him finally pulling open his clothing.

'Now, taste this,' he groaned, extending his rigid cock from the opening in his breeches.

I must still be smeared with the other man's semen, she thought, but guessed that only excited Anton more. Yanking her mouth upward, he opened her jaw with trembling fingers. Excited by the long thrusts of the hard implement in her, Clara let her mouth open slackly. Eagerly, he crammed his bulging cock inside it.

'How many times,' he hissed, 'have I watched your lovely mouth as it pouted and smiled, wishing only that I could pull it on to this? Oh, that is good.'

It tasted sweet and strong; salty droplets dripped off the distended head. Ravenously, she rolled her tongue round and round the head. Between her legs, she could feel the heated thrusts growing sweeter and sweeter. Honeyed juice was trickling down her thighs.

'Remember,' whispered the count as he roughly pulled her mouth back and forth along his shaft, 'it is your tongue, not your throat, that is the organ of taste. When I fill you,' he groaned, 'taste me with your tongue like wine.'

His words alone made her quiver and buck. Now she could not stop her climax. It had been so long thwarted that every hair on her skin rose with excitement. As she was swept up and upwards, feeling the long ridged handle fuck her greedy cunt, she rolled her tongue lasciviously around the juicy end of his cock. The sensation of hard thrusting at either end of her drove her wild.

'Tresa,' she suddenly heard him shout, 'do it now!'

With a peal of anguish, Clara felt the handle slide out of her, just as her first convulsion gripped her abdomen. She knew she might have ridden four or five juddering paroxysms through her climax. But now, instead of the handle of the scourge, after the first convulsion, Tresa turned it about and lashed her buttocks with violent, stinging blows. At the same time, she at last felt Anton lose all self-possession. She heard him give an animal cry, then felt him squeeze the base of his cock and lodge the tip hard inside her open throat. Jerking the whole veined length, she experienced him flooding into her mouth. Just remembering his words for a moment, she let her tongue saturate with the hot, pulsing liquid.

Pleasure and pain knotted each around the other in her pelvis, her spine, the very ends of her fingers and toes. The lash continued in a raid of blows, igniting her senses and, though her spasming passage was empty, still she was wracked again and again with an explosive, molten climax. Pleasure burnt on her tongue, in her spattered throat, where Anton's seed pulsed and pulsed hotly. Feverishly, she was aware of a reeling pleasure, of finally slumping unconsciously on to the hard wood of the table. The pattern of the scourge burnt incandescently across her skin, setting off little afterflames of ecstasy as she sank away. Her mouth was piquant with his taste; she wondered if she were about to expire. She wondered hazily if it were possible to die of this – to die of pain and pleasure.

She came back to herself in the quiet of her apartment. With some difficulty, Clara turned, tormenting pain gripping her as the cuts from the scourge throbbed across her legs, thighs and buttocks. Trying to collect her thoughts, she lay watching the shadows of the clouds chase across the walls, knowing she could not sleep.

Now that her body was satisfied, the events of the night horrified her. She felt broken and used; a bitter taste filled her mouth. Never had she imagined such transports of pleasure were possible – and yet, she quailed at the price he wanted her to pay. Her perfect skin was cut; her limbs ached stiffly. With some wonderment, she recollected her crazed thoughts of death as she experienced the exquisite throes of that final, torturous climax.

She dared to take John Palmer's view. If he were correct, the count's only intention was to hurt and corrupt her. He had even abandoned her here, alone and frightened, to wake wracked with bodily and mental pain. She loved him. But where was this love taking her?

It took only a few minutes to pack her things, for she took only the barest essentials of clothes and luggage. The court dress hung disconsolately on its faceless mannequin, numberless luxuries were left in their places, and even the lovely lilac dress remained strewn across her pillow. The redoubtable Joseph quickly engaged her a carriage and, almost before she had got her breath, she was free of that tainted place and clattering down the steep cobbled lane into the narrow streets of the city. Yet the air she breathed now seemed to be that of freedom. The fetid atmosphere of that underground room, the smell of sweat and blood and semen, the wounding caresses of the scourge – it was these she needed to escape. Though her head and body reeled with shock and exhaustion, still she had the composure to face John Palmer as he rose from his bed to meet her in his nightshirt. His face was animated, overjoyed.

'You have decided?'

She fell into his surprised arms, weeping. 'Please take me away,' she begged.

And, as she expected from this stolid individual, within the half-hour a carriage and driver were engaged, horses found and all of their luggage and themselves safely stowed. As the horses trotted through the city gates, Clara had barely a moment to remember her triumphant arrival less than forty-eight hours earlier. A tear formed in her eye but was as soon blinked away as her eyelids dropped quickly and she fell insensibly asleep against John's shoulder.

The room where she woke was clean with whitewash and hung with bright peasant tapestries. Stretching, she found she was fully clothed beneath a thin blanket. With a shot of physical pain and mental anguish, she recollected the events of the night before. It was too much to bear to turn them over in her mind. Sitting up, she looked about. She guessed it to be some time after dawn, that maybe she had slept most of the day and into the night as well. It was a single room, the sparse accommodation of a country inn. Ungratefully, she was glad to find herself alone. Beneath her dress, she could feel the stripes across her skin had dried, leaving her body tender and stiff.

Rising, Clara took a look out of the narrow window. She recognised the endless pine forests, the steep undulations of the countryside, the rough and rocky road. They appeared to have made good progress from Prague. But, even as she stared out at the barren landscape, her heart began to gnaw on questions. What is he doing now? Does he know I have gone? Does he miss me?

To rid herself of these reproaches, she went in search of John. Creeping into his room, she found him still sleeping, curled on his side, his face at peace. She sat down in the chair by his bed and watched him. His broad honest face, fair hair and ruddy cheeks – all of these symbolised to her a calm and quiet life. Closing her eyes, she remembered the green meadows of England, the fresh scent of rain on cut grass, the sedate charms of its towns and village churches. She would be safe there, shrouded in respectability and long tradition. Soon the whole of her adventure with the count would pass into memory. She would like to have a ticking clock in the hallway and Staffordshire pots on the table. She would like a kitten. Perhaps, in time, they would have

222

children. They would never, never know about their mother's adventures. She would preserve their innocence as her parents had been unable to preserve hers.

Her future husband stretched and yawned.

'Clara, what are you doing here?' He was alarmed, sitting up in his night-shirt.

'I am sorry, John. I could not sleep. And I could not be alone.'

She reached out to him, but he did not take her in his arms, only took her hand. She felt some inner force in his grip holding her back from him.

'Clara, you must not come here alone to my chamber. I know how much you must dread being alone, how much we want to be together – but it is out of the question until we reach England and marry.'

She blushed, springing back. 'I am doing no harm.'

'But people would talk.'

'The people here are only peasants,' she protested.

'Clara, that is not a civil way to speak.'

His tone was sharp enough for her to feel a momentary wince of dislike. 'I am sorry. I have got used to – speaking as the thoughts tumble into my head.'

'It is the company you have kept, that is all.' He smiled and she felt she was forgiven. 'Now, if you get along downstairs, we can take some breakfast together.'

'Very well.'

She would have kissed him quickly, but something held her back. This English reserve. She had almost forgotten how to affect it.

Their journey was rapid, for John insisted that, by constantly engaging fresh horses, each alternate night could be spent asleep rattling along in the carriage. Their destination, he told her, was the Habsburg port of Trieste, from which many ships left to circumnavigate the peninsula of Italy. Clara sensed from this that he was apprehensive, even fearful, of the count pursuing them. His immediate goal was to get off Italian soil as quickly as possible. Yet Clara kept her own counsel. She knew the count would not follow her. He had left her, in pain and bereft. Why had he said he loved her? Was this anguish she felt – so much more cutting than the stripes from the scourge – the product of her love for him?

And so it went on – even when John doggedly clasped her hand in the darkness of the carriage, her inner eye danced with visions of Anton. She pictured him as she had first seen him, a black-cloaked figure against the dazzling snow, sitting at the breakfast table, peeling fruit as his dark eyes searched hers, or listening pensively to the Roman children sing, a rosary threaded through his fingers. At night she longed to stay with John in his chamber, just to banish the phantom of Anton, naked and heavy with desire from her restless dreams. She watched spectres perform their intense encounters, when his words and actions so powerfully reduced her to a willing, submissive creature of pleasure. But all of this she kept secret, and though her mind spun with memories, she practised keeping a demure little smile upon her face.

As they approached the imperial port of Trieste, John and Clara reluctantly fell in with some other English travellers. Sitting in the garden of an inn just beyond the city walls, it proved impossible to escape their enthusiastic affability. The Campions were a pair of stout and resolute travellers, both of middle years; he had a pigtail wig and she had greying, frizzled locks and a fiery face. Mr Campion was a clerk at Whitehall, who had occasional business of a record-keeping nature at the Saxon and Habsburg courts. Consequently, they were more familiar with the organisation of travel than most tourists, and immediately took it upon themselves to be personal advisors to the younger couple.

'Sir, you should have done better to head for Vienna and on through Germany,' Mr Campion announced, as soon as he had dragged the smallest details of their plans from John.

John appeared mortified, not daring to confide his

true reasons for taking the fastest route out of Prague. 'Nevertheless we are here.'

Clara had noticed that when annoyed he blinked rather frequently.

'And we will take this ship, the *Dragnet*, to Marseilles as you describe.'

Meanwhile Mrs Campion launched a sudden parry at Clara. 'And your fiancé, is he one of the Stoke Palmers?'

'I have no idea.' Then, as the silence lengthened, she added, 'We met in Amsterdam so I have not yet had the pleasure of meeting his family.'

'Ah.' Mrs Campion took a sip of tea. 'And what was it took you to Amsterdam?'

'I was on a trip for my education. A tour of Europe. Unfortunately – or fortunately, I should say, it has been interrupted by my forthcoming marriage to Mr Palmer.'

'And what of your family, did they continue this – educational trip?' Mrs Campion's small blue eyes peered at her inquisitively.

'My family are in York, Mrs Campion. I travelled with friends.'

'And your friends? Your chaperone? You did have one?'

Clara straightened her skirts, eager to leave. 'Of course I had a chaperone, Mrs Campion. I am afraid she was unavoidably delayed in Prague.'

The woman stood up as she did, and sauntered with her back into the inn. To Clara's discomfiture, she amiably took her arm in hers. 'Miss Fairfax, I must confide in you. I do not know how or why your family have set you adrift like this, but it simply won't do. You cannot travel with Mr Palmer like this – two young people alone! Listen, I have a suggestion to make. Why not travel with us, as far as Genoa, at least? There we can engage a companion for you and also – well, my dear, it must be said – find you some decent clothes.'

'What is wrong with my clothes?'

'I don't quite know how to say this,' the woman continued, nevertheless finding the words easily enough, 'but they are far too showy. They suggest something – well, it is certainly not English. No doubt they are foreign? Two rules you must learn, Miss Fairfax. Never, ever travel alone with a gentleman and secondly, always dress to avoid attention, not seek it.'

'Ah, now I understand,' replied Clara with cutting irony. 'Thank you for completing my education so attentively.'

'Your education? Yes, I forgot. A novel idea for a young woman. Did you learn anything useful, by the by?'

'Oh, I learnt more than you could ever believe.'

As Clara sullenly refreshed herself for dinner, in no good temper at the prospect of a further inquisition from Mrs Campion, John tapped at her door.

'Oh, I am so pleased to see you for one moment alone,' she cried, rushing to him with her hands outstretched.

'Clara, you are like a too fond puppy,' he smiled, though his hands, when they met hers, still seemed protective rather than inviting.

'Too fond of your company alone.'

'Yes, you refer to the Campions. They are useful, respectable people. I must not stay long in your chamber but, nevertheless, we must respond to this plan of theirs.'

Clara sat at the empty fireplace and fixed on her placid smile as she listened.

'They have a point, you know. Whilst we both know our intentions are perfectly honourable, that is not how it appears to the world. I think we should travel with them to Genoa, as they suggest. I am sure you are in need of female company, someone to confide in, to rid yourself of this restlessness.'

His voice, as ever, was the slow steady tone of common sense.

Clara gave a heartfelt sigh. 'I should rather we made our escape from them and were together. Alone.'

He did not know how to take her.

226

With a strained smile he patted her hand.

'All of these adventures, Clara. The whole of your life cannot be one escapade after another. Back in Nottingham, they would hardly comprehend even how we come to be together.'

'John, you are a good man.' She said it sincerely, but with a tinge of sadness.

'And you are a good woman, Clara, I am sure of it. Only you must not constantly seek the next drama. A few steady years in Nottingham and I am sure that all of this will seem like an unpleasant dream.'

The ship *Dragnet* stood above them, its towering masts and rigging seeming to obscure the sun. Now that she had reached a decisive moment, Clara felt herself withdraw from the battle. There was nothing to do but submit and comply. Mrs Campion had clearly adopted her and would at every opportunity describe to her those knots and tangles of civilised English behaviour that Clara knew would eventually strangle her soul to death.

Their luggage stood on the quayside and, as she smelled the fresh brine of the sea, she suddenly recalled that terrible, lonely voyage from Dover.

England. Now the word filled her with dread. Already she had weighed up the possibility of leaving John and returning to York on her arrival. But she could not do that to him – even she recognised the weight of her obligation. As she ascended the gangplank, she considered it might as soon be a walkway to the gallows.

With a heavy sigh, she escaped the attentions of Mrs Campion to rest in her cabin until the ship sailed at the next tide. So deep had her mood fallen that she barely looked around at the painted walls and rough-hewn furniture. But, as she stood at the mirror to loosen her hair, she saw it on the little bureau fixed to the wall. A letter addressed to Signorina Clara Fairfax travelling with John Palmer Esquire, Englishman. Its mark attested that it should be delivered by the Captain of the Ports to whichever vessel took the said lady as passenger. The handwriting was undoubtedly the count's. She ripped the envelope open in her eagerness to read it.

Chapter Fourteen

*S*weetest and best Clara,

Amora, I write to you by the fastest posts, only
because to ride ahead of you on the road is now
outside the physical bounds of possibility. If it were
not, I promise you I should now be upon my knees
before you, offering these words from my own pale
and contrite lips. *Cara,* imagine it thus. That my
letter speaks to you in my own halting, penitent
tongue.

She had to sit, dropping on to the edge of her narrow
cabin-bed with hands shaking so much she could barely
read his words. It was, indeed, as if he were here,
suddenly speaking to her in this confined, wooden
room.

My beloved pupil, this path I guide you upon is not
to be feared – it is built hard upon foundations of
love. Denial, submission, pain: I give you these only
as gifts, administered with the tenderest wish to
delight. Many, it is true, choose not to face the
harrowing possibilities of their true natures, taking
to the grave all of their rabid dreams unfulfilled.

The dust of the sepulchre is dry, my love: and you, I know for sure, are sublimely wet and yielding. Do not fear your own nature. I am here to hold your hand. Together we can take those courageous steps.

I confess it was wrong of me to leave you as I did, alone and unprotected. I can barely guess what fears and apprehensions must have haunted you when first you woke, that drove you to this rash action. My explanation – that, after carrying you in an insensible state back to the safety of your bed, I was hurriedly called away to affairs of business – now seems a paltry, pitiful reason. I should have kept vigil over you as you slept, my sweetest girl. Weak, you were, in my cradling arms, lost in that oblivion which only the true seekers of ecstasy ever find. All through the hours of that rapturous night, I should have kept watch, to be there beside you when you woke, to worship afresh at those crimson proofs of my love, to whisper that they are in truth quite easily restored.

Cara, I do confess that the best years of my youth have been spent in amusement and self-pleasure, thinking little of others beyond their facility to please. I have never even felt before, this beating of my own hardened heart. How have you ensnared me? To speak it plainly, I am utterly consumed by my love for you.

It was too much for her. As she read, she began to weep, tears rolling down her cheeks and dripping down on to her gown. Uncaring of being heard, she sobbed out loud, only pausing to wipe away the glassy tears from her eyes, so she might read on.

That bliss upon your face as I held you in your bonds was as beautiful to me as the face of an angel, carved in the purest marble of loving submission. You have been to that place, I know, where most fear to fly. I saw it in the irregular beat of your pulse, in the flutter of your translucent eyelids, in the cruel writhing of your beautiful, ecstatic sex.

I fear now that you cringe from me with horror; you cannot imagine what anguish that rouses – it is harder to bear than a thousand scourges. I can only beg, on my penitent knees, as I have never begged before.

I shall not pursue you and your English suitor. I know of him, from the letter discarded in your room. If that is your choice, to return to England, I cannot drag you back. From now onward, Clara, you must come with me of your own will.

I am with you in spirit. As I write these desperate words, I hold against my cheek – as if desire might fill it once more – that fragrant lilac dress. It still bears your scent, even your taste, tormenting me with its silken caress.

If you can return to me, I will cherish you until my final moment and beyond, into the eternity of our own sacred Eden. Even if you choose, as I dread you may, to flee from my memory, trust that I will always regard you as my angel, who has visited me in this great and empty darkness.

I am leaving this cursed city to ride for Constantinople and the house of my friend, the Pasha Daniz. Tresa will stay with Galinski, should you wish to communicate with her here. In foolish hopefulness, I enclose a written authority for you to board ship at Trieste and join me in Constantinople. *Volere è potere* – to desire is to be able. I know from my dreams, my visions – we can be united in love.

Rapidly, she searched the papers for that missive. It was there, like a golden key to her future. Tightly, she clutched it to her breast and read on.

To see your radiant face again, to know that you can bear my flesh beside you, would restore a blind man to the light of dawn in this impenetrable darkness. If you should not find it in your heart to return to me, I will continually pray that in spirit we may one day be joined under heaven's unsullied light, for I know, *mio amora*, you are my missing heart.

Il suo amore,

Anton

The sun played across Clara's back like the playful fingers of a lover. Even beneath the canvas shade on the deck of the ship, it was lazily hot. As the summer sun reached its peak, she discarded her heavy gowns, floating across the shimmering air in creamy muslin skirts. With her parasol shading her face, she strolled along the deck each morning, watching the rolling depths of the Adriatic split at the edge of the pointed prow. Then, after lunch and siesta, she would return to the rail, looking at the rocky outcrops of the shore or the grey silhouette of islands looming mysteriously from the dark green sea. It was her favourite time: the brilliant white ball of the sun would sink and glow behind the craggy shoreline, blistering red in a mass of luminous pink and golden clouds.

I am sailing east, she rejoiced. Towards the east, towards the glorious sun, towards Anton.

There were no other passengers: it was a working ship. Captain Treviso was a grey-haired Venetian, an honourable man with a loyal, profit-minded crew. That first evening, he had joined her on the deck and told her politely that she was welcome to join the officers at meals but, beyond that courtesy, all the men had strict orders not to speak to her.

'I shall deliver you safely to Count Malibran in Constantinople,' he added. 'And, until then, you shall be treated as if you were my own daughter.'

Carefully, he pointed out those few areas of the ship she had access to – her cabin, one short length of the deck. She smiled gratefully, happy to have no obligations for the ensuing weeks, to be left alone with her thoughts and fancies.

At mealtimes, the officers met in the cramped mess. Clara was comforted to hear their rapid, gesticulating Italian, though she soon detected that lisping dialect of the Venetian nobility. Their talk was of fortunes, of trading routes and products from the east – hides, furs, wines, spices. Having eaten, she quickly left them to enjoy their drink, slipping away from the table to watch her beloved sun setting behind the mountains or into the sea.

Sometimes she could not help but be haunted by that other sister ship, ploughing westward along the opposite shore of Italy towards cooler climes. Then she grieved for John Palmer, remembering his stricken face as she told him, quickly and resolutely, that she could not return to England with him.

'No! You must not go back.'

His hand grasped her wrist painfully. For a long moment she stared at it; her thin wrist encircled by his broad, reddened hand. So often had he seemed to repel her; now she looked quizzically into his pale eyes. Sadly, he let go. The claim had been blind instinct only. He could not answer her unspoken challenge.

'It will be better for you in the end,' she whispered, touching his arm.

As she disembarked the *Dragnet*, she necessarily had to pass Mrs Campion, who was watching the crew take on cargo. The older woman had opened her mouth to speak and then instantly seen Clara's luggage and also, perhaps, the resolution in her face. Like a trap, her mouth had shut and, with a sniff, she turned her weather-beaten face aside. Clara almost laughed out loud, to be cut dead by her so recent bosom friend.

She had little doubt, on reflection, that the redoubtable Mrs Campion would do her best to find consolation for John amongst the English community at Genoa. By the time he reached Dover, she was certain he would have a bride to share that quiet life in England.

The Captain of the Ports had effortlessly arranged her

transfer to the *Athena*, a Venetian merchantman docked at Trieste, on its way to the Sea of Azov.

'The ship will call at Constantinople as fast as the wind can carry her,' the official explained, pocketing the bill of exchange for a large sum, entrusted with Anton's letter.

This was not especially fast, Clara found, as they meandered down the coast of Dalmatia, calling at Split and Ragusa. By the time they docked at Corfu, it was early September and the men were glad to take shore leave on familiar Venetian territory. From the rail, Clara watched them ascend into the narrow tumble of streets enclosed within the massive twin forts guarding the town.

Growing restless and impatient, she was glad once more to feel the sea breeze as the *Athena* drew up anchor and eagerly nosed out of the safe harbour. Out on the open ocean, the sails cracked and filled and the tall ship sped south like a seabird, to the Morea. Rapidly they flew past lovely islands clothed in pine forests and tiny whitewashed villages clustered around distantly tolling church bells.

One evening, the captain pulled out a chart across the table, once dinner was cleared.

'Signorina Fairfax, you may see now that you are almost halfway to your destination.' His callused finger traced the undulating shores of Dalmatia, Albania and Greece along which they sailed. The names of the islands were sweetly poetical: Santa Maura, Ithaca, Kefallinia, Cerigo.

'Here at Zakynthos, the men are allowed a few days of personal trade before we cross the Aegean. Then we can safely deliver you here.' He pointed at the land bridge stretched across the entrance to the Black Sea. There, marked where two fingertips of land met at the juncture of Europe and Asia, was the city of Constantinople.

'I have come so far,' she pondered, looking back at the distance even to Italy. 'And where is England?'

'England is not on our charts.' He smiled. 'It is almost a world away.'

That was how it seemed when they docked at Zakynthos. In the shuttered coolness of the coffee house, the crew did business while Clara watched the townsfolk at their business from the ship's rail. No longer the same world as England, she repeated to herself. Whatever the captain said about these islands being a part of the Serenissima, still she felt they were leaving even Italy far behind. Even the scents were different: the mountains of glossy currants ripening in the sun destined for European plates, pungent sheep and goats, sweet-smelling white breads and spicy meats.

A few boys in white stockings and buttoned waistcoats passed by, holding up bobbin lace, rolls of rare Venetian damask, bottles of wine and glittering icons painted on wood. There she saw a battered copy of Homer and, paying a few Italian *zecchini*, took it back with her to her cabin.

During the long, final stretch of her voyage, the sun seemed to heat her blood. Languorous and lazy, she slept until the sun was high above the dark sea, lying naked in her cabin, dreaming of the meeting that shimmered and danced in her mind. It seemed to her that, just as he had written, they could indeed meet in visions and dreams; in the half-light of the tiny wooden room, she imagined his skin, his taste, his scent. Waiting was pain and pleasure, as anticipation and desire swam through her veins like golden ichor. For hours she lay outstretched, feeling the pull and tow of the ocean carrying her nearer and nearer to him, dreaming she was drowning, not in water but in warm and salty love.

Past the mainland of the Morea they sailed, skimming past Piraeus, Andros, Skiros, Lindos. Reading her Homer, Clara fancied herself also to be on a strange odyssey, travelling beyond the limits of her known world. She could barely remember the brisk and tiresome girl who had set off from England. England itself seemed no more than a grey speck at the back of her sun-dazzled memory. Before her, as the boat carefully manoeuvred into the Dardanelles, was a new existence as an entirely transformed being.

They approached Constantinople at night. As the *Athena* was guided into the Golden Horn, Clara was aware only of the dim shapes of the city and the occasional splash and cries from surrounding vessels. Standing at the rail, she watched the sun rise over the glittering minarets and domes of the mysterious city. Byzantium, Nova Roma, Constantinople – Clara mused over the rich and barbaric civilisations that had risen and fallen at this turbulent crossroads of the world.

A thin mist hung across the water, where turbaned boatmen loomed and disappeared in jostling *caiques*. On the shore stretched a mass of low buildings, seemingly piled one on another with tiny windows and carved shutters. Between these were alleys, gardens, stone medieval houses, arches, turrets and towers. But constantly her eyes returned to the great massy domes of the royal mosques and palaces shining in the dawn light, slender minarets and gilded banners piercing the azure sky.

'Here, Signorina Fairfax. This boatman will take you.' It was the captain, calmly overseeing the necessary work on board. He pointed to a beautifully carved craft, painted with flowers and gilding.

'If we leave now, I can accompany you,' he added gallantly, signalling for one of the men to pick up her luggage.

'There is no need,' she replied, touching his arm. 'I will always remember your kindness, but now I wish to meet the count alone.'

Having seen her safely ensconced in the vessel and settling the bill for the journey, the captain briefly shook her hand and, with a push of the oar, Clara began the final stage of her journey. Inside the boat, reclining on piles of fringed cushions, she watched the river world pass through richly curtained windows.

Soon they left the area of the port and passed a market place where a huddle of red-capped old gentlemen sucked contemplatively at huge waterpipes. Baskets were full of scarlet peppers, black aubergines, glossy lemons and watermelons. Across the water, spiced smoke drifted from street-sellers preparing sizzling meats and seafood; Clara saw huge sacks of coffee and pepper being unloaded on to the quay. Around the stalls and alleys, early risers in flowing robes and baggy trousers made their way, balancing great baskets on their heads or leading heavy-laden donkeys.

Soon the scene changed and the boatman was taking her along the wide waters of the Bosphorus. The rambling hubbub of the city fell away, revealing pine-clad hills embellished by massive grey stone fortresses marked with serried rows of battlements and glittering pennants. Astonished, Clara looked from one shore to the other, from the Europe she had crossed for more than half a year, to the edge of a new continent: Asia. The sun was rising now, ever hotter, shimmering across the broad river as if it were a great golden path.

Then, with skilful use of his oars, the boatman swept the craft towards the farther shore. Dusky foliage overhung the river; glimpses of cool and inviting boathouses flickered behind the trees. With a gentle push, the boat passed around a curtain of drifting fronds. A carved wooden jetty appeared; in a moment, the craft was secured and the boatman reached out to escort her from the craft.

Carefully, although it was still partly obscured by trees, Clara gazed up at the Pasha's residence. Before her was an elaborate stone archway, through which she could just see the rainbow-coloured tiles of the imposing entrance. With an impatient gesture, she dismissed the boatman and rallied her thoughts. An elaborate brass knocker hung at the entrance but this, she had already decided, was not to be the way she would arrive.

Quickly hiding the encumbrance of her luggage in the dark undergrowth, Clara began to circle the building, staying within the shadow of the trees. A few morning sounds could be heard through the closed lattice-work shutters – grumbling voices, the clatter of dishes, the laughter of a child. Behind the main frontage of painted stone walls, Clara found whole suites of smaller buildings: wooden summer houses and pavilions near the river, stables and stone cooking houses, a marble walled edifice she guessed to be a bath house. Where might he be? Clearly the most palatial part of the building was to the front for, at the very rear, the outbuildings were only wooden huts for animals or storage. With some trepidation, she approached a likely area, marked with pretty tiles in the shapes of roses and a heavy brass-bound door.

All was quiet inside.

Tentatively, she reached towards the thin painted wood of a lattice-work shutter. Standing on tiptoes, she carefully pulled it back to peer into the dimness inside.

A face met her face. Surprised, yes, but nevertheless calm, it was a round and serene face. The young girl suddenly smiled, her black liquid eyes shining. Startled, Clara smiled back. With a slender brown finger to her lips, the dark-eyed maiden motioned her to stay quietly where she was. Clara did so, although apprehension made her look nervously about. But all was silent and still.

'*Merhaba!*'

The girl was motioning quickly for Clara to join her at a small concealed doorway. With little choice other than to trust to her instincts, Clara picked up her skirts and joined her.

Inside, the rooms smelt of musk and incense. Clara followed the girl down a dim corridor decorated with heavy wall hangings where they met no one. With a broad smile, the dark girl turned, beckoning with scarlet coloured fingernails. Hesitantly, Clara followed as the girl's pointed leather sandals clipped noisily against the floor.

They emerged into a wide hallway where two massive Nubian slaves stood impassively, either side of a double brass door. Clara looked nervously at their swords hanging from broad jewelled belts around thick, ebony waists. Her new friend began to chatter girlishly to them, smiling and pointing at the European in explanation. Clara flinched as one of the black fellows eyed her with some suspicion. For the first time, it truly struck her how far she had come: the language, the manners, everything was outlandish. For a moment, as she was ushered through the heavy doors, she wondered if she would ever pass out of them again. What recklessness was she yielding to? She did not know if these were savages, nor even have any assurance that the count was here at this time. With a rapidly beating heart, she followed the dark-haired girl, hearing the doors boom solemnly closed behind her.

The rooms were lighter now, hung with embroidered silks and delicate brass lanterns. Clara followed her companion outside through a double door into a court-yard so delightful she touched the girl on her arm and smiled admiringly.

Around a central fountain surrounded by blossoming trees, a score or so women of varying ages sat or lounged with another dozen or so pretty children playing around them. The air was filled with the delightful babble of the fountain and murmuring laughter of the children and their mothers. All appeared to be peace and harmony. There is grace, too, Clara thought, as she admired their long silken tunics, wide trousers and embroidered short jackets. Such beauties as well, she reflected, all with waist-length tresses, braided and jewelled, and limpid eyes painted with smudgy black powder. Yet, despite her undoubtedly bizarre appearance, they did not stare or laugh, only cast a few shy glances at the pale woman in wide, light coloured skirts.

'Hanim!'

Clara hurried along to join her guide at a shuttered doorway. This time, Clara was bidden to remove her shoes. Leaving her French kid shoes neatly alongside a number of others, she slipped a pair of soft leather slippers on as she passed into even grander chambers. With a shiver of anticipation, Clara wondered if at last she would meet Anton. But no, they were still in the labyrinthine quarters of the harem. White gossamer curtains billowed at the windows and, in the stillness, gold and silver ornaments glinted against mosaicked walls.

Before them sat a very ancient lady, wrinkled and brown with age but painted nevertheless with scarlet at her lips and talon-like nails. Seeing her companion prostrate herself on the carpet, Clara bowed her head and curtseyed as low as she felt able.

The lady spoke to the girl quickly in her own language.

With head still bowed, Clara interrupted. 'I am Miss Clara Fairfax, a traveller from England.'

'Miss Fairfax, what brings you here?' she asked in curiously genteel English.

It was with relief that Clara found they could converse. The lady had learnt the language, she explained, when she had been a concubine to the Ottoman ambassador to London.

'I seek an Italian gentleman, Count Malibran.'

'He stays here in the palace,' the woman replied with a knowing smile. 'But today he is in Stamboul with my son, Pasha Daniz.'

An expression of gratitude must have illuminated Clara's face, for the Pasha's mother held out her heavily ringed hand. 'Am I speaking to his betrothed?'

Clara nodded. 'And how is he? Is he happy?'

'Come and sit beside me,' the old lady said in her soothing, strangely accented English, 'and we will talk of him.'

Ascending on to the luxuriously cushioned dais where her hostess reclined, Clara lowered herself as decorously as she might, given the encumbrance of her skirts. The Pasha's mother patted her hand and then began to describe in precise and cultivated terms the state of the Italian count.

'He arrived in Stamboul five nights since. At first he was exhausted in the body, but now I believe him to be also weary of the soul. Mostly he stays alone in his apartment. Some say he reads, but my spies tell me he

never turns a page from hour to hour. Every attempt
has been made to lift his spirits. Food, entertainments,
sensual pastimes. Even Sorayah, the Pasha's favourite,
could not tempt him.'

With this, she pointed at the dark-eyed girl whom
Clara had followed.

'It seems your count has given himself up to sadness.
Last night, my son told me his melancholy stems from a
great loss. He has lost a woman. Is that woman you?'

'I believe so. When will he return?'

'This evening.'

A thrill of anticipation must have flushed her face.
The Pasha's mother looked into Clara's face. 'Why did
you not simply ask for him at the door?'

Clara smiled mysteriously. 'On the long journey, I
formed a plan. But maybe it is foolish. Can I trust you?'

The old lady grinned, showing gold teeth. 'You are in
the home of secrets. The harem is a place of intrigue. All
dwellers are secretly sworn to powerful vows of obedi-
ence to me, the *Valide Pasha*. It is necessary for all to be
able to keep secrets, or terrible things may come to pass.
Do not fear appearing foolish. Perhaps I can help you
with your plan. If not, it will reach no other ears.'

With a tiny gesture, she dismissed Sorayah and they
were alone.

A little hesitantly, Clara began to explain her idea. 'I
have been on a long journey with Anton, the outward
purpose of which was my education. You can imagine
that meant an education in every sense of the word. I
have learnt so much, madame, in relation to every aspect
of life and how to truly experience that life. But another
part of our lessons, as Anton called them, was undoubtedly a set of tests. Not only was my learning examined,
but also I believe he latterly tested my loyalty, my
courage, even the strength of my need for him. This may
be fanciful,' she muttered, suddenly embarrassed.

'No, no, carry on,' she urged.

'Well, my idea was to turn the tables, to test him. I
believe that if I knocked at the door and announced

241

myself, he would be overjoyed to see me. But what if I could meet him under more mysterious circumstances? Would he sense it was me? Once, he tested my sense of smell – would he know my scent? Does he know my taste? The sound of my voice murmuring in his ear? And finally, after all this time and waiting, does he recognise my touch, when he finally feels it?'

The Pasha's mother clapped her wrinkled hands with pleasure. 'Miss Fairfax, you speak to the very person who can help you with your intrigue. I tell you, it is a most excellent plan, worthy of the mind of Queen Scheherazade herself. If he returns at sunset we have all afternoon to prepare you. I shall send you to him as a special gift – what do you say? Dressed as a *gözde*, a favourite: he will never know you.'

Clara took the old lady's hand and squeezed it with affection. 'Yes,' she said warmly, 'it will be the perfect end to my education.'

A short while later, Clara crossed a courtyard into the bath house. Following Sorayah, she found herself in a stone, dome-shaped building, where the other girl immediately began to pull off her silken tunic and trousers. With some reluctance, Clara began to loosen her skirts but, seeing her difficulties, the girl began to help her. With much laughter, Sorayah tugged at the heavy lacing of her stays until finally another woman, whom Clara took to be the *bagnio* attendant, arrived with a knife and quickly slit the ribbons to release her. With some relief, she felt the tight stays spring apart and Clara stood awkwardly in her thin chemise.

For the first time, Clara felt a sudden shyness. Sorayah stood quite unselfconsciously naked before her, unaware of the beauty of her ripe brown body. Even the *bagnio* attendant wore only a girdle around her gently flaring hips. In contrast, she felt she would appear quite ghostly and unattractively pale.

'*Evet, mamselle!*'

It was no use; these lovely innocents had clearly never

heard of bathing in a gown, such as was practised in Spa or Bath. With a tug, Sorayah pulled the thin shift off and, feeling horribly immodest, Clara followed her into the first chamber.

The floor and walls were built of dripping marble, surrounding three fountains which steadily dropped into shallow pools. With no explanation, Sorayah took her hand and, in a moment, Clara felt the refreshing warmth of the water falling on her stiff shoulders and back. Closing her eyes, she relaxed, feeling the spray work across her naked skin, washing away the grime and salt of her long journey.

With a start, she opened her eyes. Sorayah had begun to soap her shoulders. Grinning, she nodded that Clara should stand still. So again, she closed her eyes, this time feeling the long, sensuous strokes of the girl's hands working over the muscles of her shoulders and back. Onward the fingers moved, working their magic across her buttocks and thighs. So long had she anticipated physical release that Clara was immediately nonplussed to find her body tingling with pleasure.

Quite matter-of-factly, Sorayah turned her about and, still grinning, began to soap Clara's breasts. The girl's fingers were light and teasing, cupping the rounded flesh and rubbing quite methodically at her nipples. To Clara's anguish, she felt them grow hard and stiff, jutting exquisitely beneath the girl's arousing fingers. Yet she was too embarrassed to break away, even when the probing fingers delved to her waist and slid and slipped across the fluttering pit of her stomach. More rapidly, she felt the girl reach down to soap her thighs, a couple of times slipping her fingers into the damp juncture at the top of her legs.

As she reached for a ewer to rinse Clara off, it seemed Sorayah brushed accidentally against her guest. But when it happened a second time, when the girl's breasts pressed against her back, Clara guessed it was not completely accidental. Anguish began to grip her mind and body. It would not be surprising if, in this enclosed world of women, girls such as Sorayah turned to each other as lovers. Indeed, she could hardly bear to look at the girl's generous body – her tender, brown-tipped breasts, narrow waist and deliciously prominent rear. Her skin was flawless, of a delightful milky coffee colour against which jet-black hair framed her face and also fell in silky tangles at her pubis. Arousal spread through Clara's body like a fever – in any other situation, she would have simply leant forward and kissed the girl's carmined lips. But today she could not. Surely, her conscience told her, this is Anton's day. On the very doorstep of pleasure, it would be churlish to take satisfaction elsewhere.

Still, the ritual of the *bagnio* continued. Sorayah led her across to a narrow marble slab, upon which she was clearly meant to lie. With some qualms, Clara lowered herself down and did her best not to watch the girl's luscious form as she stood over her. Speaking softly in her own language, Sorayah began to wash Clara's hair, rubbing hard along her scalp so that again Clara felt her eyelids flicker and droop. For a while she drifted sleepily, feeling the warm water rinse her hair as the girl's strong fingers massaged her head and neck and shoulders.

Then the torment began again. Armed with a pair of rough mittens, Sorayah began to scrub her charge, pummelling her shoulders and then stretching her arms to cleanse every inch of her skin to the finest degree. With an expressive groan, Clara felt the mitts massage her breasts, the rough fibres creating an agony of excitement. She barely knew how she could wait until this evening. Half opening her eyes, she saw Sorayah bending over her, her lovely breasts almost brushing against her own. With a sudden wriggle, Clara moved down the slab and, for a moment, their breasts tantalisingly brushed against each other. The sudden smile on the girl's face was unmistakable. Clara noticed that her chocolate-brown nipples were pointed and stiff, too. Giddily, they both exchanged a long, dark-eyed glance.

As the harsh mittens worked across her hips, Clara considered sitting up and demanding an end to this. But the sensations were so lovely, the girl so clearly willing, that it felt impossible. At last, the implement reached her pubic bone and, with a long, bristling stroke, Clara's thighs were brushed apart. With a cry, she felt the rough fabric work its way from front to back, pushing insistently at her entrance. Deliriously, with eyes closed, she thought of Anton. Anton's cock, long and hard, pounding against her. Anton's hands on her shoulders, pulling her yielding body down forcefully on that hardness, like a stake hammered into soft earth. The mitt was tormenting her, rubbing back and forth until, with a gasp, Clara felt her thighs squeeze around it. She wanted more; she wanted it inside her, if only it could be pushed that far.

When she opened her eyes shamefully, Sorayah only giggled. Then, with tentative fingers, she reached out and gently ran her fingertips through the golden hair of Clara's sex. Murmuring in her own tongue, she twisted the pale curls around her fingers in a manner Clara found most provoking. Then, in explanation, she slipped on to the slab beside Clara with great agility. Laughing, she ran the fingers of her other hand through her own luxuriously jet growth.

'Yes,' whispered Clara, feeling the girl's fingers deftly probe the inner lips that covered that most sensitive spot. Surely she could recognise her willingness now, for the girl's fingers met no resistance; in fact, her body betrayed her at every move, welcoming and lubricating Sorayah's little sortie. Cautiously, Clara reached out and met her friend's other hand. Gently, she led Clara's hand to the wiry luxuriance surrounding her own sex. As her fingers slipped into it, Clara gasped ecstatically. It was impossible, now, to hold back. Sorayah's fingers, too, were rubbing expertly at Clara's open sex, occasionally dancing around to tease the rim.

There was a clatter at the doorway. Instantly the two girls stopped their mutual pleasuring. Looking up, Clara could see it was only the attendant, filling the bathing ewers. With a tug at her arm, the dark girl pulled Clara up and signalled for her to follow her into the next chamber. In an instant, they were surrounded by steam, pungent with the sweet scent of eucalyptus. Lazily, Clara sat down on a padded sofa and Sorayah emerged from the clouds of vapour to climb astride her thighs.

Uncontrollably, their lips met with a passion and force that surprised her. She could not get enough of the girl, as she slid her hands over her naked shoulders and back, deftly exploring the round firmness of her writhing backside. Now their breasts pushed hard against each other and, instinctively, Clara broke away from her lover's mouth to slip her lips around as much of the luscious brown breast flesh as she could take into her hungry mouth.

The steam was overpoweringly hot. Sorayah's body was slippery, her wet legs straddling her, her heated cunt rubbing against the skin of her thighs. Clara's fingers worked into the fissure, rewarded by a little cry of pleasure as she found the tight grip of her entrance.

'Stand,' she whispered.

And though Sorayah did not know a word of English, she staggered to her feet so her hungry sex was raised just above Clara's greedy face. As her fingers delicately parted Sorayah's lips, Clara began to kiss the purplish-coloured cleft, tasting the sweet saltiness, exploring each fold and ripple of that satiny inner skin. Drunk on lust and woman's juices, she made love with her tongue until she felt Sorayah's legs tremble and little panting cries call out from above her. Hearing a cry like a wailing bird, Clara felt the girl spasm against her face, rubbing involuntarily as she cried out, her legs almost buckling. Then, weakly, she climbed down, her dark eyes lazily flickering like a well-fed cat.

'*Mamselle*,' she murmured, pulling Clara off the sofa. In the next room, she smilingly bid Clara lie again. This time, Clara thought, I will not be able to withstand any additional provocation. Like dry tinder before a match, she felt that only the barest touch would ignite her.

Languorously, Sorayah began to cleanse her again, this time with a soft and silky sponge. But now, as she rubbed Clara's stomach, the girl leant over and kissed her navel, making her shiver with anticipation. And as the cloth teased her thighs and parted lips, Sorayah's mouth dropped exquisitely on to her breasts and began to suck slowly and hard on the engorged scarlet of her nipples. Delirious with lust, Clara was barely aware when the girl produced a slender stone bottle of perfumed oil. Removing the rounded stopper, she dribbled a little stream on to Clara's stomach. With a gasp of pleasure, Clara felt its coolness turn to heat as the girl skilfully rubbed it into her painfully sensitive stomach. When Sorayah began to pay attention to her breasts, Clara groaned at the piercing pleasure of the warm oil driving her to distraction. Rolled between Sorayah's skilful fingers, her nipples had never felt so solid. Looking down, she could see they were almost dark red with excitement, the areolae wide and flushed, the nipples thick and spiky between the girl's fingers.

The oil dripped between her parted legs. Almost embarrassed by the maddened state she was in, she could feel her engorged clitoris protruding, eager to be rubbed. With fingers like featherdown, Sorayah began to massage the oil into Clara's parted cleft, stopping to pour yet more into her excitedly widening entrance. Trembling, Clara knew she could not hold back. The girl's rhythmic strokes were building to a crescendo. She knew, suddenly, that she would as immediately be ready for Anton. Again and again she could take this, would want it, want it even more. This was merely a mouthful before the banquet. Still the girl massaged her heated opening, dropping her dark head quickly to suck on Clara's tormented breasts.

Feverishly, she imagined Anton astride her. As she had done many times in her imagination on the ship, she lifted her thighs to finally yield to his heavy, swollen cock. Then, with a gasp, she suddenly felt something part her convulsing entrance. Something hard and

247

rounded. With her head flung back, she let her mind believe it was indeed Anton's cock. There was more – something wide and thick was being pushed inside her.

With an anguished glance at Sorayah, she felt herself grip that hardness longingly. With a gentle nod, the girl continued pleasuring her until, with a gasp of delight, Clara recognised the phallic stone hardness of the oil bottle. Closing her eyes, she felt the rounded head parting her, delving deep into her hot and syrupy flesh.

Expertly, Sorayah began to work the device, gently thrusting backwards and forwards, teasing her until, with knees raised, Clara cried out wordlessly. Then, with great speed and force, the girl pushed the whole delicious length of the bottle into her, fast and hard so Clara could feel it tormenting her deepest senses. Feverishly, she pictured Anton naked inside her, pushing and driving, ready to release that great tide of pent frustration. Breathing hard, she felt Sorayah reach down and deftly squeeze her lips together, burying the stone phallus its full length inside her. With a wordless cry, a spasm of fire rushed through her veins. As if it were Anton himself, her body gripped the hard length, throbbing and squeezing the rigid stone again and again.

Then she was aware of Sorayah panting above her. With a nodding smile, the girl seemed to ask if it was good. Wiping perspiration from her brow, Clara smiled back. Then, reaching up, she kissed the girl and for a while they lay together, until Clara's racing heart slowed and she no longer heard it pounding in her ear. Together, then, they returned to the fountain to rinse the salt and sweetness from each other's skins and make preparations for the long sultry evening.

The *Valide Pasha* came to see Clara, once she was dressed.

'Stand,' she commanded.

To the accompaniment of much rustling and jingling, Clara walked to the centre of the dressing room. Sorayah had dressed her hair in long braids plaited with strings of pearls that hung heavily down her back. A fillet of worked silver-and-blue diamond flashed across her forehead.

'This *yelek* fits well.'

The old lady passed her bony fingers over the gorgeously embroidered white tunic made of silver samite, that clung to her breasts and hips and fell to her ankles. Beneath was a simple silk chemise with wide, loose sleeves. From waist to ankles, beneath her skin-tight *yelek* were wide silver gauze trousers. At her waist was a fringed silver girdle and, over all, another fitted Levantine gown, open at the front and trimmed with luxurious white fur.

'Do you like the clothes of our favourites?'

'They are truly beautiful.'

Clara stared in the mirror. The woman staring back at her was exotic, opaline, made for pleasure. The costume glittered mysteriously with filigree jewellery at her neck, wrists, ankles and waist. It felt light and yet clung to her body, jingling as she moved.

'I have told the count I am sending a special gift to him tonight.'

'And how did he reply?' she asked eagerly.

The Pasha's mother shrugged. 'I believe he is still reluctant to share his bed. So that is flattering to you – and yet also makes your task more difficult.'

'I am glad he is reluctant,' she sighed, circling in front of the mirror to the music of silk and chiming jewels. 'It will be a true test. Where is he now?'

'He has just retired from dinner to his room. My son has given him his own pavilion by the river, the white pleasure house by a grove of jasmine. Yet still, he seems weary with sorrow.' Then, pursing her lips, the old lady signalled to Sorayah. 'If you wish to proceed with your plan, we must disguise you. Here, first of all, is the *yashmak.*'

A gossamer-thin veil of silver tissue was arranged over the bridge of Clara's nose and tied at the nape of her neck. The old lady laid a matching veil over her hair and attached it to the first. Finally, the all-concealing *çarsaf*, a cloak of richly worked taffeta, covered her from head to foot, tied with silver tassels.

'Now, we must leave you and pretend there is nothing afoot. You must wait here until I send the guard to fetch you. We will choose an opportune moment.'

'I will try to be patient,' she replied, though her limbs were trembling now, to be so near the end of her waiting.

Time seemed to stand still. Fretting in the small lamplit room, Clara rustled and jingled, cursing her own folly in not simply announcing herself to Anton and instead setting up this humiliating charade. As the afternoon had progressed, many of her sprightly certitudes had disappeared. Instead of judging Anton, she felt more as if it was herself who was about to step before a county judge and jury. A thousand horrible possibilities assailed her mind – that he had forgotten her, or only written the letter to flatter her, or that his refined sensibilities would be appalled to find his bride engaged in such a vulgar pantomime.

Clara had just decided to pull off her exotic mummery when a scratching sound attracted her attention from the shuttered doors. Annoyed, she eased back the lattice. Outside in the garden, one of the Nubian guards stood, beckoning her to follow him. With a few incomprehensible words in the Turkish tongue, the guard led her forward along the night-fragrant paths of the gardens.

The moon had risen and the gardens had lost their colour to reveal silver bushes and statuary shining against the black shadowy undergrowth. As she skipped along in her flowing gowns behind the long-legged guard, Clara had no time to fret over her nerves. Ahead was the white pavilion. Clara's mouth was dry with anticipation. Quickly, she dismissed the guard.

Chapter Fifteen

*H*er senses were acute. She could hear crickets singing in the grass, diving fish in the water, the lonely melody of a distant nightingale. She closed her eyes, breathing in the night-scented air. Jasmine. A lusciously sweet, green fragrance of jasmine blossom. Opening her eyes she gazed at the low white building.

The pavilion was constructed of wood, carved and fretted, then painted in lucent white. The thin drapes were down and all was silent as Clara hesitantly climbed the steps to the wooden terrace overlooking the river. But, within the gossamer drapes billowing behind the shutters, all was dark and still.

With her heart pounding, Clara listened at the door. There was no sound. The notion struck her that perhaps Anton might not be here. So it was with a flood of desperation that she nudged the door open. Stepping inside, she was immediately confused by the shadows and reflections trapped inside the long room.

He was here. Asleep on a low divan, his pale throat thrown back in sleep. Creeping across thick Turkish rugs, Clara drank in his presence, devouring the vision of him laid out before her. His black hair was undone, tousled about his sleeping face. He was breathing softly, his curved lips slightly parted, his face serene. He had

251

the air of someone who had merely lain down to rest, for he still wore his loose white shirt and black breeches. Beside him, rumpled and twisted, lay the empty lilac dress. The moonlight, tossed and fragmented by the trembling river, was the source of those confusing shadows. Across the walls and ceiling reflections danced, as if he was slumbering in some magical subterranean cavern.

As quietly as she could, Clara crossed the room, watching his tranquil face, hesitant to break the spell of the moment. But, as she knelt beside him, lowering her head to rest blissfully against his shoulder, the soft jingle of her jewels broke the silence. With a slow blink of his eyes, he stretched. Then, waking, he opened his eyes wide and saw her.

'I am a gift from the *Valide Pasha*,' she said, hoping her impersonation of a Turkish accent would disguise her voice somewhat. She had no need to fear.

'Ah, yes.' Sitting up, he ran his hands through his hair. 'I am sorry your visit is a wasted one. I do not want company. However, thank the *Valide* for her consideration.'

It took all her strength of will not to reach out to that slender, elegant hand and bury her mouth against his skin. 'I have other talents. I could bathe you, or massage you.'

Wearily, he reached for a candle and lit it with tinder. 'You do not understand. None of those things interest me. Shall I call the guard to escort you back?'

In the sudden amber glow of the candle-flame, her heart leapt as she devoured the delicate lines of his face, his glittering, dark-shadowed eyes, his skin still a little pale from sleep.

'No,' she cried. 'I beg you, let me stay a short while,' she rambled. 'What will the others think? It will be the worse for me, if I return so soon. Can I not amuse you in any way? I could –' her mind raced for a possibility '– tell you stories.' As he stretched his arms lazily, she surreptitiously admired the long leanness of his body.

'Well, you have woken me now,' he said a little petulantly. 'And sleep does not come easily to me. So yes, tell me a story if you will. A drink, first. There is some iced wine on the cabinet. Fetch it.'

So he really did believe her to be a slave girl. Obediently, she poured two glasses, then, in a panic, poured the second one back. Presumably a girl from the harem would not help herself to her master's drink!

'Take that ridiculous thing off.' He pointed at the voluminous *çarsaf*. 'It muffles your voice.'

But, as she slid off the all-concealing cloak he did not even watch her.

'Here,' he added, patting the divan next to him, 'sit comfortably next to me, so I can hear you.'

As she curled up her legs on the pile of cushions and bolsters, Anton reclined lazily, giving her not even a second glance. Conflicting feelings of relief and disappointment shifted through her mind. But, even more pressingly, she racked her brain for a story to tell him. Then she remembered the old copy of *One Thousand and One Nights* in the nursery at York. One of the less well-known stories, perhaps. Straightening her back and taking a deep breath, she began.

'Once upon a time, long ago in the land of Persia, there reigned a king who knew no happiness. Though he lived in a beautiful palace by the sea with many wives, and though hundreds of charming slave girls attended to his every want, they could not please him. After a time, he began to despair and to lament at the sickness in his heart and body.'

Suddenly, she could feel Anton playing with her braided hair. As she hesitated, he lifted the candle closer and inspected it in the unsteady light.

'Yes?'

'Your hair is very pale. It's beautiful. Go on with the story.'

Clara proceeded to tell him of the finding of a beautiful slave girl at the market whose skin was delicately pale and whose lips were as red as cherries.

253

'And your face?' interrupted Anton. 'Is it pale, like your hair?'

'Yes, your Excellency,' she replied, just remembering not to address him as 'count'.

'Like this lovely storybook slave girl, will you let your master see your face?'

'Your excellency, you do not want me. So I need not remove my veil. Only if you want me, must I show my face.'

'Ah, that is the rule, is it? Very well; carry on.'

'You are sure?' She turned her thinly veiled face towards him and, to her relief, he barely looked at her. 'I mean, you are sure my tale does not weary you?'

'Not at all.'

With this, he began to play with her ribboned braids as she spoke, which was most distracting. Nevertheless, she dared not ask him to stop.

'But when the king visited her that evening, in her own gorgeous chamber overlooking the sea, she kept her eyes fixed across the terrace where the first pale stars were just then rising from the sea. Even when he slipped his arm around her waist and kissed her lips, she answered not a word. And when he carried her to his divan and made long and tender love to her, still not a sigh nor a word passed her lips. So, firstly he gave her treasures: jewels of ancient workmanship, bales of silks, the finest paintings and craftsmanship wrought on this earth. But still, despite the glittering of the world passing before her eyes, she spoke not a word.'

'Surely you are too warm in that fur-lined coat?' The count was sipping his wine, eyeing her more appreciatively now. 'Take it off. You are allowed to do that?'

'Of course.'

For this she had to stand, and now he was watching her, with that old hungry look as she eased her shoulders back to drop it in a scented mass on the floor. But it was with mixed feelings she felt his black eyes run appreciatively over the voluptuously tight tunic below. As ever, he had spun her mind about, so now she was

254

uncertain whether to bask in his admiration or sulk at his plan to deceive the memory of Clara Fairfax by seducing a girl from the harem.

'But you will not remove your veil?'

'No.'

'Very well; continue.'

Settling back down, she took up the threads of the story once more. 'The next night, the king again could not stay away from her chamber. And this time, after he had taken his pleasure with his compliant but silent slave, he clapped his hands for attendants to bring food and sweetmeats. He thought that if she still would not use her mouth to speak, she might use it for eating. So he began to push morsels of the choicest food into her mouth. But still she stared at the ocean, never replying a single word.'

'You make me hungry,' he announced. 'Fetch me some of that food.'

She was aware of his eyes still on her shape as she crossed the shadow-lit chamber to the table set out with different drinks and dishes. Returning, she kept her eyes as low and modest as the heroine of her oriental tale. Setting the food down on a low table, she hesitated.

'What have you brought?'

Nervously, she looked at the dishes, then thankfully recognised a few of the sweetmeats she had eaten at lunch with the Pasha's mother. 'This is called a Lady's Navel,' she smiled, offering him a little fried delicacy dripping with syrup.

'You can feed me.' He smiled at her wolfishly. With a little tremor, she placed the mouthful between his lips, just feeling his teeth graze her fingers.

'And what do you have to tell me about the sense of taste?'

She shook her head stupidly. 'I do not know what you are talking about. I am only here to please you.'

With a sudden dart of his hand, he grasped her wrist, drawing her closer. Then, with the other hand, he slowly raised the candle nearer to her face. Mortified, she let him inspect her. His fingers traced the outline of her face beneath the veil.

'You have a look, sometimes, of someone I knew,' he said slowly. An expression of pain crossed his face momentarily. 'But if I pull off your veil, the illusion will be over. Just for this short time, I am content with deception. You do not mind, do you, if I imagine you are someone else?'

'Of course not, your excellency. I only wish to please you.'

But Clara's heart grieved at his sudden confession. For the first time, now, she longed to pull off the veil and tell him who she was. He spoke so sadly, his wish was so melancholy, she felt tears well in her eyes.

She held out another morsel of food. 'The Lips of the Beloved,' she announced, nudging his lips open. This time, as she deposited the mouthful, his lips closed around her fingers, sucking the syrup from them.

'Wait,' he murmured, licking her fingers. Quickly, she had to pull them away. They were trembling – so much did she quake at the warm touch of his tongue.

'Your eyes,' he continued, watching her, 'are very pale. Where are you from?'

'From the east. Past the Sea of Azov.'

'But you speak English?'

'I was, for a while, a concubine to the Ottoman ambassador to London.'

Again, his dark eyes looked disappointed.

'You are sad,' she ventured.

'I think it might be best if you leave. I am sorry I am such a disappointment to you, but I cannot pretend to want anyone but the one woman I have lost. Be comforted, if you will, that of all the girls your mistress has sent, you have pleased me most.'

'But if I look like her?' she asked desperately.

Reaching out, he caressed her face through the thin gauze and her heart shivered. 'It is worse, I think. If I deceive myself you are her, then, when you finally remove your veil it will be more cruel. I do not think I can bear the anguish of finding a different face. And yet, I am fascinated.'

Despite his words, he was creeping closer to her, peering all the time at her eyes, trying to trace the lines of her face behind the *yashmak*. Abruptly, his lips met hers through the gauze and they kissed as his fingers ran along both sides of her neck. She could feel the heat of his mouth through the thin fabric, his tongue like a beast inside a flimsy cage. His nails just grazed the sensitive skin beneath her ears. A little cry of excitement escaped her as he coolly pulled away.

'What is underneath that tunic?'

'A chemise.'

He seemed to consider.

'Perhaps you could just stay to tell the end of your story. Take that tunic off and we can sit here comfortably in bed while I listen to you.'

He wants me, I am sure of it, Clara exulted to herself, as she untied the white tunic. And at least, she considered, he wants me because I remind him of Clara. So, either way, I can be flattered.

Now, as he watched the silk costume fall to the ground, his interest was intense. The glaze of lust covered his eyes as he appraised her body through the sheer fabric of her chemise. The Turkish women wore no undergarments, so beneath she was naked. Glancing down, she could see the swell of her breasts below the fine fabric, the cloth clinging to the twin points of her nipples.

Inquisitively, he held up the single candle and surveyed her from tip to toe.

'Turn around.'

Obediently she did so, guessing the thin fabric clung to her curves.

'Which would you remove first – your chemise or your veil?'

'So you do want me?' she asked triumphantly.

'I did not say that. You are like her – but a little thinner, I think. I cannot tell without feeling you.'

He patted the space beside him again but, when she sat down, he only put his arm around her in a protective, brotherly manner. 'Carry on with your story. What did the king do next to awaken his mute lover?'

It was difficult to concentrate now, with the heat of his body next to hers: even the warmth of his breath against her neck.

'Next, the king attempted a cure with the most gorgeous perfumes from all the known lands – pouncet boxes filled with heliotrope, oil of jasmine, balsam of Mecca, attar of roses. It was the same when he took up his lute, for he was skilled in music, and sang to her of his desire. But still she spoke not a word. Finally, he drew up a marriage contract and offered her the whole of his kingdom. For, in all this time, whilst he had grown to love her, still he longed for her to speak, so that he should know if she, too, wanted him. Are you still awake?'

His stillness had suddenly struck her. Glancing around at him, she found he was lying back on the pillow, his eyes half-closed as he steadily watched her.

'I am listening to your voice. Go on.'

'Well, I am nearly ended. At this, the slave girl raised her great eyes and smiled, so that the whole room seemed to be filled with light. At last she spoke, and her voice was as soft and musical as a fountain. "Oh, King," said she, "your constancy has deserved that I should break my vow of silence. I am Jallanar, the Pomegranate of the Sea, who was cast up on your shores and sold to be a slave. At any time, if you had not made me your Queen, I could have thrown myself into the water from this terrace and gone back to my own people under the sea. But I have listened and watched as you showed me the pleasures of your strange kingdom. For, beneath the sea, there is no scent, no music, no delicious food, nor do we so value the beauty before our eyes. So, dear King, I have resolved to make my life with you here, in the richness of your world." And, at this point, the king stopped her voice with a thousand kisses. And as may be imagined, that night and every other night, the joy of the king was utterly complete as he held the sea princess in his arms and heard her soft words and cries as she made him, the king, into the slave of her very soul.'

Breathlessly, Clara paused after finishing the tale.

'That is a sweet story,' he declared, 'but I do think I have heard something similar in the west. It has a familiar ring.'

'Oh, many of these tales travel about,' she began, then lapsed into silence. Did he know her? Yet his voice was ingenuous, not calculating at all. Surely it was time to do away with this pretence? She had learned enough of his attitude to be satisfied.

Twisting around, she faced him and he slipped his arms around her shoulders. Clara almost whimpered with pleasure.

'What is your price to remove the veil?' His fingers reached out and caressed the gauze across her cheek.

'I should like you to be blindfold.'

'Then what is the point of removing the veil? I still will not know you.'

But she could see he was intrigued. His eyes were shining black, narrowing as he waited for her reply. She had forgotten his effect on her, this paralysing spell.

'You will see.'

'Metaphorically, I assume. For I will be blinded. Very well. I am in your hands.'

In a moment, she had lifted the girdle she had discarded from the floor and knotted it tightly around Anton's temples. With an increasing flood of exultation coursing through her veins, she also grasped a scarf and quickly, before he could protest, slipped it around his wrist. In a moment, his wrist was bound to the frame of the divan and, in another, she had secured his other wrist in the same manner.

'What are you doing?' he cried, struggling to loose his wrists.

'I am about to effect a cure for your melancholy,' she announced, surveying with no small satisfaction the sight of him bound and blindfold and helpless. She barely knew where to begin. With a tug, she pulled off the silken veil.

Pulling herself on to hands and knees across his body, she began to kiss him. After only a moment's reluctance, he let her slide her tongue inside his mouth and responded compliantly to her eager passion. Rubbing her fingers beneath his shirt, she gloated over his powerlessness. His skin was smooth and hard; the muscles rippled to his waist. Like a worshipper at a private shrine, she abandoned herself to the pleasure of tasting the salt on his skin, nuzzling his flesh, working her tongue across the hard presence of his body.

Revelling in her strength, she let her fingers glide down over his breeches. Whatever he might have pretended, his body was not indifferent. Her fingers curled around the width of his stiffened cock, her sex tingling with anticipation. Then, too greedy to wait, she unloosed it from the fabric, sobbing a little with excitement as at last she touched the hot, taut shiny skin. Gasping over it, she slid her hand around it, feeling its weight, easing back his breeches, so she could see it from the hair-clouded testicles up the long shaft to the swollen, glistening head.

'Oh, yes,' she whispered to herself. It was like a most wonderful plaything. Stiff but flexible, proud and sensitive. Running her fingers around the thick base, she felt it jump in a most satisfactory manner. As she ran her nails along the shaft, it twitched responsively. Panting a little, she eyed it greedily. Then, licking her lips to make them wet, she lowered her head and did something she had dreamt of for more than a long month.

Pushing his cock between her moist lips she closed her eyes, feeling the muscles between her legs grip with excitement. It was sweetly salty, so big between her eager lips that she had to stretch her jaw. Tentatively, she flicked her tongue around its head. As if in response, a few drops of briny dew were released and she began to suck a little harder, all the time rubbing the shaft with her hand. She could feel, beneath the chemise, her sex growing wetter, pulsing with desire. Self-indulgently, she pulled up her chemise around her waist and straddled Anton's thigh, beginning to rub her heated cleft against the exciting hardness of his leg.

'Stop! There is something I need.'

Irritated, Clara looked up at her blindfold victim. 'What?'

'In a moment, we can finish,' he gasped. 'Only I have something in my bag which can increase our pleasure tenfold.'

Her concentration was broken. She looked covetously from the long red cock to its master and back again. 'What is it?' she asked peevishly.

'You will see. I promise, you will thank me. It will only take a second. Do you see the leather valise over there?'

She could see it against the wall.

'In it, there is a little case. Bring it here.'

She was intrigued. Again, she looked at his delicious cock rigid beneath her wet lips. It could wait just a moment.

Still, it was with poor grace that she clambered off Anton's prone frame and walked across the thick carpets to the valise. Leaning down, she reached inside. There were some clothes, but that was all she could find.

'Are you sure it's here?'

Bending over, she reached further, groping into the corners of the bag. Now she was irritated. She felt weak with lust, her legs trembled as she bent over the bag with her bottom in the air. Yes, there was something there. It was rough and long, like a folded parasol.

With a massive lurch, someone sprang on her, knocking her, so that for a second she had no breath. For a panic-stricken moment, she thought the guard had run in and arrested her. But, the next instant, one hand sped across her breasts and the other seized her waist. Struggling, she whipped around and saw it was Anton.

'The look on your face!' He shrieked with laughter. 'I must teach you how to tie knots, one day.'

'What do you mean?' she cried, writhing like a snake to get free. 'Get off me!'

He was strong beneath his elegance; now his arms held her as tight as a vice. Clawing up her chemise, he raised his palm and suddenly administered a stinging slap against her wriggling backside.

'Get off me!' he mocked. 'What, after all the manhandling you've given my poor cock? It's time I gave you back what you deserve.'

With another swing of his arm, he executed a deliciously smarting blow. Her bottom burnt as his fingers lingered awhile, stroking the crimson flesh and then teasingly brushing her parted cleft. The next moment, he lifted her and carried her, kicking and struggling, back to the bed.

'What do you think you are doing?' she cried as he threw her unceremoniously on to the mattress.

In a second he was astride her, pinioning her down, grinning wickedly. 'Clara, I am so happy to see you. Only, before the social chit-chat, there is something I really must do.'

'You recognise me!'

'I am afraid –' he laughed '– I knew you almost as soon as I awoke.' With this, he began to lift her chemise and then, growing impatient, tore it from neck to hemline with a loud wrench.

'How did you know me?' she asked breathlessly, as he pulled her hard down the bed by her legs.

Again he laughed, tossing his hair back from his face. 'Oh, I knew you: of course I knew you. Your shape, your scent, the sound of your voice. And, I must add – of everyone I know, only one says things like "what will everyone think!"'

'Why didn't you say so?' she sulked.

With a tug, he pushed a pillow under her rear. Then,

taking each wrist at a time, he tied the two silk scarves tightly around them and fixed them to the bedhead. He found another two scarves and did the same to her ankles. Finally, he gazed appreciatively at his work. She was spread naked before him like a succulent feast.

'Because I was enjoying your little deception. Well done. By the saints, I am so happy to see you, Clara. But we can talk about that later.'

'Why, what is happening now?'

As if to illustrate, he pulled his rampant cock up in his hands and grinned at her.

He is not a tame sort of man, she suddenly remembered. How could she ever have imagined he was? No, that was the best thing about him. There was still an unpredictable savagery beneath that meticulous grace.

'Pupil, you have tormented my poor cock for six months now, across as many kingdoms. Now you finally arrive, it appears to be your idea of sport to torture the permanently engorged organ for an eternity with your delectable little mouth. Frankly, I can bear it no longer. No man could.'

Clara felt a quiver of anticipation as he ran his fingertips like teasing featherdown from her breasts over her stomach to her lewdly gaping sex.

'What are we going to do?' He mocked her startled voice again. 'My love, I am going to complete your lessons. Have you forgotten? There is still a gap in your education. What is the fifth lesson?'

Swallowing, she confided, 'Touch.' Then she closed her eyes, waiting.

A few moments later, she opened her eyes. He was no longer there.

'Anton?'

Still laughing, he appeared at the foot of the bed, with a cup of sherbet in his hand. Setting it down, he sat beside her on the divan. His eyes travelled over her and she felt her hips respond, rising imperceptibly to arouse him.

'How does that feel?' he enquired. 'Not to be touched?'

For a moment, she struggled to understand him. Then he raised his fingers and held them for a second, an inch above her parted cleft. Uncontrollably, she strained at her bonds, clamouring for him to touch her. But he did not.

'Unbearable,' she confessed at last.

His gaze upon her was palpable, his handsome face alive with pleasure and desire.

'The first step,' he confided, 'is to learn that the absence of touch is often the most powerful provocation.'

Still he only gazed at her, drinking in her rapt face, the arc of her ribs where her arms were stretched taut, the swell of her upraised breasts, widely parted thighs and the golden-curled lips stretched within.

'Like a composer's pausing with a rest in music, or the painter's use of the white canvas shining through, absence is as powerful a stimulant as presence. Do you agree?'

She could barely speak, so powerful was this lesson. Cramps of frustration worked within her stomach. Between her legs, she could feel a little dribble of wetness running on to the bed. Her temperature seemed to be rising, as if she were running a fever.

Panting, she nodded.

'All these months of my education,' she begged hoarsely, 'I swear it is the absence of your touch that has made me frantic. Please, touch me now.'

'Very well.'

His coolness maddened her. Yet, as ever, she guessed it was merely strength. Suddenly she noticed, with a sympathetic throb between her legs, that his cock was still stiffly standing upward outside his breeches. She wanted it, to the point of madness.

'Just to illustrate,' he added serenely, 'as our second step, you must experience the variety of touch.'

Leaning forward, he suddenly began to smear her left

breast with the ice-cold sherbet from his cup. It was so cold it burnt, forcing her nipple to shoot up beneath his fingers. Then, more slowly, he rubbed the coldness slowly in concentric circles around her right nipple. She could feel fast, fiery jabs of pleasure running straight to her protruding clitoris.

'Oh, you are hot,' he whispered admiringly. 'You need to cool down.'

Scooping a handful of the sherbet, he rubbed it into the furnace of her sex. The coldness made her gasp – it stung and burnt pleasurably, but did not numb her to sensation. No, she could feel the tiniest squeeze of his fingers, raking into the wet mixture of honeyed juices and melted ice. Tormentingly, he circled her clitoris with his elegant index finger. His face was intent, absorbed, as she writhed in a strange transport of icy fire.

'Heat, we will come to later,' he announced. 'First, we must move from this smoothness to a little roughness. You feel how smooth my fingertips are?'

She nodded, as he stroked her open cleft from the curve where her lips met her golden hair, over her quivering entrance to the pulsing of that second, hidden orifice.

'Yet, if it is a little rougher, it can be even more gratifying.'

She held her breath as his face disappeared between her thighs. This time it was the slightly abrasive tip of his tongue that made that same journey. Whimpering, she cried out to him not to stop. As his tongue worked its way back again, over her throbbing sex, she felt the beginning of her climax tense her muscles. But then, he had gone.

'And if it was even rougher than that?' he teased. Glancing up at him, she noticed him run his tongue over his juice-wet lips. His breath was faster, she noticed. Momentarily, he tugged at his foreskin, as if it were getting uncomfortably tight.

Then he disappeared again, and Clara was alone with the sick cramps of her frustration. If only, she thought, I was not bound, I would not be able to stop myself delivering myself with my own hand.

He returned. In his hand was the case she had grasped in the bottom of the valise. She saw it was a thick horsehair case that held the leather scourge she had felt in Prague. But now, instead of fear, she felt a glow of welcome. Deliriously, she anticipated that sublime ecstasy that only the burning kisses of the whip could bring.

He noticed her staring longingly at the long black fronds. Caressing her cheek, he turned her to face him. 'Later, pupil. Soon, I will let you feel those stinging kisses.' Suddenly he leant down and kissed her and she ground her body upward towards him, opening her mouth to feel his stiff tongue, pressing her thigh as far into his lap, as close to his twitching cock as she could.

'Oh, Clara,' he moaned, momentarily transported, as he pulled back, stroking her hair. 'You test me, pupil. I can barely stand this. Let me show you now, how roughness can be an even harder sensation to bear.'

He climbed above her, where she wanted him. Now his fingers dug into her soft arms and he dragged his body over her. Almost sobbing with need, she pressed her wetness up into his crotch. She was drowning now, under the wildness of his touch. Then she felt it – a harsh bristling presence between her legs. Uncontrollably, she shivered.

'Keep still,' he whispered. 'You will like this.'

It was long and wiry and the rough bristles made her hair stand on end. As she struggled to see what it was, he pushed upward towards her molten cleft, laughing wickedly.

'It is the sheath, my love, for your beloved scourge. Designed, I must say, to be a useful instrument in its own right.'

She could feel that it was coarse horsehair, rough to the point of pain in its design. The long, cylindrical shape was clearly made to pleasure a woman. She knew she should struggle, but her legs spread eagerly for it, ready to taste this new sensation.

As it pressed against her slippery entrance, she felt herself grip it. It was crudely hairy; she could feel rough little fibres stimulate her sensitive nerves. Then, as he pushed it further, watching her face all the time as he lay above her, she cried out loud.

'How many thrusts do you need, my love? You are close, I think.'

He pushed it further in. Hard and jagged, it seemed to swell inside her, parting the walls of her throbbing sex. Closely he watched her face, as her eyelids dropped and her lips parted dryly; she whimpered wordlessly to herself.

'Clara,' he demanded, 'how does that feel?'

She was too aroused, now, to answer. He had pushed perhaps six thick inches inside her and all her senses were focused on that burning, bristling rod that slowly impaled her. As her eyelids flickered momentarily, she noticed his face, now wet with a sheen of lust, glassily watching her throes as he directed her pleasure.

'How does it feel?' He was breathless, suddenly, and anguished.

She could barely speak. Soon, she knew, she would find release. 'Almost painful,' she moaned. 'Brutal. Crude. Like an animal.'

He groaned and reluctantly pulled the harsh instrument out of her.

'No!'

'We are almost there, pupil,' he reassured her. 'Only wetness now remains, before the final heat.'

Again he left her for long moments and she twisted feverishly in her bonds, aching with the pain of unsated need. He returned with nothing but a little jar of oil.

'I am going to unloose your legs for just a moment,' he said softly. With some relief she felt the blood return to her veins as he untied her. Quickly, he turned her over, on to her hands and knees, so this time her arms were crossed before her and she leant on her elbows.

She was aware that this raised her rear high in the air; her thighs were still partly stretched as the bonds held her ankles wide.

'The wetness will make it seem less,' he said, as she suddenly felt a dribble of cold oil drop between the cheeks of her buttocks. 'I think you will enjoy this more than you would ever imagine.'

Next, his fingers slid between her parted cheeks and began to rub back and forth in a most arousing manner. Whenever his touch brushed the quivering little orifice hidden between her buttocks, she gasped, feeling a new, violently heated pleasure. Slowly, she felt his long index finger slide inside her and she cried out, partly with pain but also at the fierceness of the invasion. She could feel it, burning back and forth, a long, slender fire sliding in and out of the exquisitely sensitive opening. Then, suddenly, it was not his finger but something broader and softer. It was the end of his cock brushing back and forth across her oiled and slippery entrance. Clara closed her eyes, feeling a red darkness drown her senses.

Then she felt it, a massive pressure at her second entrance, broad and heavy, nudging to enter. Reaching down, he grasped her buttocks and pulled them even more sharply apart. With a sudden thrust, he pushed inside her. Crying out, she felt him stop and grip her waist tightly. Then, again he nudged forwards, and she guessed perhaps a solid inch of him was inside her rear. It felt so much bigger than she had expected. A sudden fear made her struggle, but he grasped her tight at the shoulders and then pushed a little further. Now she could feel it, quite unlike anything she had known before, parting her inner flesh which tingled and smarted, resisting this intrusion but arousing at the same time previously dormant sensations.

With a groan, he began to work his fiery prick back and forth, not so deep, but maddening the entrance. Twisting her head from side to side, she wondered how much of this she could bear. At her crossed wrists, the bonds tightened as she struggled. From deep inside her chest, her breath was growing irregular. Her heart was pounding in her ears. Uncontrollably she cried out to him as he slid his cock back and forth, widening his way inside her.

She buried her face in the bedcover, her eyes barely focusing. With a sudden jolt, he pushed further until she felt a pain that was also pleasure. The sensations were fast and sharp, making her dizzy. Again, that rhythm grew stronger and faster but, this time, she knew she could not wait. She was aware of being pulled backward in his arms and the thrusting of his cock reaching a crescendo. Then he pushed further.

'No,' she cried weakly.

It was like falling fast, head over heels. She couldn't stop now, only hear herself panting. Then, with a jolt, he pulled his cock out of her.

She screamed with anguish.

'Shush, my love,' he panted, rapidly unloosing her and turning her around. Feebly, she rolled on to her back. He retied the scarves, but it was not likely she could have lifted herself anyway.

'Please,' she pleaded.

A sheen of perspiration covered his face and his eyes were black chasms as he watched her writhe and moan beneath him. His cock was shiny with oil, reddened in front of his abdomen.

'Very well. If that is what you want.'

With heavy, lust-filled eyes, she nodded.

As he clasped his crimson cock in his hand, she saw his testicles, fat and swinging below. All her senses were concentrated on that need – to have him.

'Very well,' he challenged. 'I am going to fuck you straightaway. I am going to fuck you good and hard, as I should have done many months ago. I am going to fuck you to the point, I boast, when I believe you will barely know the time or place or universe in which you reside.'

'Yes,' she panted.

Gently, he lowered himself upon her and already she

felt a kind of bliss as he wrapped her in his arms and she felt his nakedness melt into hers.

'Oh, and by the by, Clara, I do love you so very much.'

He was so beautiful. They kissed and she whispered back that she, too, loved him more than her soul could bear.

Slowly it seemed, she sank away into another world. At first, she was only aware of his caress, of his lips at her throat, of his mouth sucking her hard, maddened nipples. Then his hand reached down and roughly pulled her legs apart. She could hear him breathing now, tremulous in anticipation. She watched him through half-closed eyes; his face was still with concentration. Suddenly, he saw her watching him and kissed the tip of her nose affectionately.

'You have tasted me, smelt me, watched me, heard me. Now you must feel me. I have waited so long,' he murmured hoarsely. 'Now, I cannot wait.'

Tenderly he pushed his cock between her open legs. He was kissing her eyelids, her nose, her lips; she felt herself launched on a massive tide. She was euphoric to find him inside her, as his fingers squeezed her breasts, pulling at the nipples, skilfully drawing her into a place of wonder and sensation. Looking down, she could see his stiff cock jabbing in and out of her. Though she felt full of him, still she could see the thick base outside her, pushing and striving to enter her.

Gently fondling her breasts as he faced her, he made the fever in her blood rise again. Tenderly, he dipped his forefinger into his mouth and rubbed the slippery spittle on to the stiffened rosebuds at her breasts. Her nipples felt rigid, cool with drying saliva. Clara shivered, aware of the muscles between her legs clutching his cock with excitement.

'*Mio amora*,' he murmured, working his way inside her, burningly slowly. Whispering in Italian, he reached down and, with his fingertips, parted her lips as widely as they might open, nudging ever deeper inside her.

270

With a little cry of pleasure, she felt the tip of his cock graze a place inside her so sensitive she could barely stop herself from shaking. This time, as he reached down, he let his fingers brush against her inner lips, where honeyed wetness made every stroke burn with rapture.

'*Cara*,' he whispered in her ear, so close she could feel his heated breath, 'when we are both at one moment transported – that is the final lesson of the senses. Each sense builds on the next – the look of the lover, her taste, scent, sound. But when the mind can take no more, there is sweet oblivion. The absence of our senses. What the ancients called our "little death". Because, when our souls are joined, the senses fuse into one great illumination – that we are not alone.'

Suddenly he withdrew, pulling the length of his cock out of her, leaving her empty and thwarted.

'Soon it will be time. Only first, let me taste you again.'

Eagerly, he crawled downward, rolling her nipples in his mouth, kissing her midriff, licking her navel. With a shiver of anticipation, she felt him brush his lips across the fluttering pit of her stomach. Then slowly, ecstatically, he began to kiss and drink at her cunt, running his rasping tongue from one end to another.

'Yes,' she moaned, as his tongue worked into her entrance and her muscles gripped it, ready to explode.

But at this he withdrew, stroking the soft insides of her thighs.

Suddenly, she was aware of his cock only inches from her face as he straddled her. Reaching out, her lips met its hard, veined tautness. In bliss, she tasted the pungent stickiness coating its length, rubbing her lips back and forth along the shaft. This time, as Anton's mouth again dipped into her swollen cunt, she felt her hips rear involuntarily to meet him, and his touch was like burning fire. For a single second, he sucked her clitoris into his mouth and she felt the first spasm of a climax begin.

But then he had gone and she was left panting, again clinging to the dizzy edge.

Her attention returned to his throbbing cock. Bound though she was, she could just catch the tip in her greedy mouth. As her mouth was filled and she sucked gluttonously, again she felt her inner muscles spasm quickly, but no moment of release followed. Anton was still tormenting her with tender kisses and caresses to her thighs and rear, teasing every inch of her body except her ravening cunt which stretched with anticipation.

'Please,' she moaned.

'Tell me, pupil. What do you want?'

'Anton, please.'

His tongue momentarily flicked across her. She was a second away, a mere moment's delirious rubbing away. To her surprise, she felt a stinging blow to her upraised buttocks. Tensing, she felt the blood burn below the skin.

'Say it,' he whispered.

Again he administered a little pain with the scourge, this time opening again that strange conduit of pleasure. As he stroked and then stung her open thighs, she felt an upsurge of ecstasy course through her veins, as potent as any opiate. He was using pain to take her higher and higher – ever further along the path that she had barely known existed.

Feverishly, she rubbed her face against the heat of his cock, feeling it massively hard against her cheek. It pressed against her eyes, her nose, her mouth. She was suddenly aware of a bubbling stream of heated juice running down her thigh. She wanted to scream. Helplessly, she pulled on the silken bonds. This time, as he struck her, she felt only scorching desire, like a knife twisting in her gut.

'I want you inside me.'

'The precise term, please.'

He was licking her thigh, licking the sweet runnel escaping her overheated cleft. As if to prompt her, he slid a long finger into her entrance. With a gasp, she felt the climax again begin, then ebb maddeningly away as his finger quickly disappeared.

'Fuck me,' she whispered, too quietly for him to hear her.

Grasping her raised bottom, he again slipped his mouth around her most sensitive spot, flicking his tongue back and forth fast, then infuriatingly pulled away. Almost dismissively, he struck her shivering thigh.

'Please,' she begged, feeling his cock twitch against her face. 'Fuck me, please.'

Quickly, he moved around and began to adjust her bonds. Their eyes met and she saw triumph intoxicate his gaze, as strong a drug as the juice of poppy.

'Just one last taste,' he murmured drunkenly as he straddled her. Then, with a brutal tug, he eased his cock into her mouth and she felt him tremble as his dark eyes watched her pleasure. Breathing fast, he watched her, tenderly stroking her hair back from her brow with one hand, with the other stroking his shaft, pressing the swollen head into her ecstatic mouth. She could feel it as he caressed her, this deep physical tremor as the floodgates of months of restraint were so close to ending.

With a groan, he pulled back, leaving her mouth yearning and empty. Lusting at him as he crouched before her, she greedily eyed the purplish mass of his cock and balls.

'Please,' she whispered, 'fuck me.'

Decisively, he turned her over on to her stomach again; then, yanking up her bonds, pulled her up on hands and knees. She could feel him behind her, feel the heat of his genitals and his hot breath on her back. His breath was fast and tortured; as she closed her eyes, all she could think of was the power of his frustration. His hands reached down over her buttocks, pulling her thighs apart. With a grunt of pleasure he parted her swollen lips and pushed the head of his cock against her entrance. When he bore down on her, it was no longer gentle, she could feel him seething, burning to explode inside her.

'Let me in,' he moaned: for she was so near to climax, her muscles were rigid with anticipation.

Grasping her waist he stormed against her, pushing hard until the pressure was too great. Then, pounding into her flesh, he penetrated her. Crying out, Clara felt exquisite pain grip her. Back and forth he swung, forcing his way deeper and deeper into her, cleaving into her softness. Like a man possessed, he mounted her, clawing the rigid nipples of her breasts, making Clara wail with delight. Deeper and deeper his cock buried itself, long thrusts taking it from tip to stem until she felt his balls banging against her trembling rear.

'How is that?' he moaned. 'Here you are, lady: my every inch, my every drop saved for you.'

His speed quickened now and he kept it deeper, pushing always for the deepest penetration. With a sigh, he bent and began to kiss the back of her neck, making her spine shiver. Then, with more passion, he sucked and bit the sensitive spot below her hair and she shivered with pleasure. She remembered the exquisite thrill of his ejaculations against her dress and in her mouth. His semen had been hot and fast, spurting again and again. But now, at last, he was pounding inside her: that was where she wanted it. He was giving her plenty of good measure for all her tormenting of him.

'Now you are not so prim. No, you must have it all,' he cried and, taking her hips, lifted them, pulling her back on to his bulky phallus. It seemed at that moment to impale her, driving deeper and deeper into her flesh, forcing her apart, throbbing and tormenting her intact flesh. With love, not hatred, he swung out with the scourge, administering a stinging lash to her sensitive rear.

'Take it all,' he intoned, as she felt his pelvis buck and drive. With a final groan he lifted her upright, pulling her back on to his full length. Clutching her swollen breasts, he sank his head against her neck and bit hard.

Ecstatic with pain and pleasure, she felt him jerk inside her. It felt so good and deep. He was panting, overcome.

Then it seemed all thinking ceased. He was still pulling her hard back on to his shuddering cock as her own climax exploded. Exquisite ripples of pleasure began and jolted through all her body until she was, for long and glorious moments, unconscious in a blind, otherworldly oblivion. Then, with a sigh, she returned. He was still inside her, his chest rising and falling rapidly as he caught her in his arms. He was kissing her spine, calling her his love. She was flooded with love and pleasure.

Dawn rose on the river. Opening sleepy eyes, Clara found the room flooded with dappled light. Then, above her, she saw Anton gazing down upon her, watching her as she woke from the sweet oblivion of their lovemaking. His arms were comfortably stretched around her, his hips locked easily against hers, their legs snugly entwined.

All night, they had swum the tide of that strange country – drifting in the lingering shallows of touch, feeling the grazing fire of lips and tongue. She had loved his power and strength, the force of his muscles, the heaviness of his body forcing his way inside her. With each climax had come a new recovery, a new insistence that it should not end. No longer did she tingle with anticipation as she felt his cock harden against her thigh; she burned incandescently, her body swimming in feverish juices, sweat and semen.

Through the heart of the night, he had fucked her. In those darkest hours, he had shown her the beauty of attendant pain and pleasure, each time she climaxed adding a stinging spasm to her flood of sensations. With wrists and ankles bound, she was at his mercy, pulled and pushed into the shapes of his desire, her reflexes tested as he slapped her buttocks or thigh with the palm of his hand, or lashed her with the scourge, or bit her sharply with his teeth.

Coasting the twin pinnacles of pain and pleasure, she had tumbled again and again into the deepness of oblivion, clutching at his hair, his rhythmic muscles, the thick base of his cock as it slid ceaselessly back and forth into her. His eyes blackly devoured her, his long fingers reached sensuously into her aching cunt, the sudden hot saltiness of his semen burst on to the back of her throat. It was then she had felt herself almost drown in the flood of desire: a tremor shaking her bones, her climaxes jaggedly ripping through her flesh as he pulled her roughly astride his cock and slapped her hard down on to it.

Now, he tenderly cradled her in his arms. Outside, they could hear the first birds rise and begin their song. The river, too, sang outside their window, rippling and tumbling on its way to the sea.

'Today marks the end of the summer. Our journey is over,' he whispered.

Looking up into his face, Clara could see his eyes were serious. Gently, he reached down to kiss her brow.

'At last,' she replied, 'I have reached my destination.'

And, as she nuzzled her head against his shoulder, her last thoughts before sleep were of her journey. Her route seemed like a great river, winding across the maps and charts of Europe, propelled forward always by love and desire – once secret, but now at last naked and exposed. Yawning, she clung to Anton and let go of wakefulness. It was difficult now to tell where one of them started and the other ended. Now, she thought sleepily, my journey is over. We are together. I am home.

BLACK LACE NEW BOOKS

Published in December

A SECRET PLACE
Ella Broussard
£5.99

Maddie is a locations scout for a film company. When a big-budget Hollywood movie is made in rural UK in the summer, she is delighted to be working on-set. Maddie loves working outdoors – and with a hunky good-looking crew of technicians and actors around her, there are plenty of opportunities for her to show off her talents.

ISBN 0 352 33307 3

A PRIVATE VIEW
Crystalle Valentino
£5.99

Successful catwalk model Jemma has everything she needs. Then a dare from a colleague to pose for a series of erotic photographs intrigues her. Jemma finds that the photographer, Dominic, and his jet-setting friends have interesting sexual tastes. She finds their charms irresistible, but what will happen to her career if she gives in to her desires?

ISBN 0 352 33308 1

SUGAR AND SPICE 2
A short story collection
£6.99

Sugar and Spice anthologies mean Black Lace short stories. And erotic short stories are extremely popular. The book contains 20 diverse and seductive tales guaranteed to ignite and excite. This second compendium pushes the boundaries to bring you stories which go beyond romance and explore the no-holds-barred products of the female erotic imagination. Only the best and most arousing stories make it into a Black Lace anthology.

ISBN 0 352 33309 X

Published in January

A FEAST FOR THE SENSES
Martine Marquand
£5.99

Clara Fairfax leaves life in Georgian England to embark on the Grand Tour of Europe. She travels through the decadent cities – from ice-bound Amsterdam to sultry Constantinople – undergoing lessons in pleasure from the mysterious and eccentric Count Anton di Maliban.

ISBN 0 352 33310 3

THE TRANSFORMATION
Natasha Rostova
£5.99

Three friends, one location – San Francisco. This book contains three interlinked and very modern stories which have their roots in fairy tales. There's nothing innocent about Lydia, Molly and Cassie, how-ever, as one summer provides them with the cathartic sexual experi-ences which transform their lives.

ISBN 0 352 33311 1

To be published in February

MIXED DOUBLES
Zoe le Verdier
£5.99

Natalie takes over the running of an exclusive tennis club in the wealthy suburbs of Surrey, England. When she poaches tennis coach, Chris, from a rival sports club, women come flocking to Natalie's new business. Chris is skilled in more than tennis, and the female clients are soon booking up for extra tuition.

ISBN 0 352 33312 X

SHADOWPLAY
Portia Da Costa
£5.99

Daniel Woodforde-Ranelagh lives a reclusive but privileged existence, obsessed with mysticism and the paranormal. When the wayward and sensual Christabel Sutherland walks into his life, they find they have a lot in common. Despite their numerous responsibilities, they immerse themselves in a fantasy world where sexual experimentation takes pride of place.

ISBN 0 352 33313 8

If you would like a complete list of plot summaries of Black Lace titles, or would like to receive information on other publications available please send a stamped addressed envelope to:

Black Lace, Thames Wharf Studios,
Rainville Road, London W6 9HT

BLACK LACE BOOKLIST

All books are priced £4.99 unless another price is given.

Black Lace books with a contemporary setting

ODALISQUE	Fleur Reynolds ISBN 0 352 32887 8	☐
WICKED WORK	Pamela Kyle ISBN 0 352 32958 0	☐
UNFINISHED BUSINESS	Sarah Hope-Walker ISBN 0 352 32983 1	☐
HEALING PASSION	Sylvie Ouellette ISBN 0 352 32998 X	☐
PALAZZO	Jan Smith ISBN 0 352 33156 9	☐
THE GALLERY	Fredrica Alleyn ISBN 0 352 33148 8	☐
AVENGING ANGELS	Roxanne Carr ISBN 0 352 33147 X	☐
COUNTRY MATTERS	Tesni Morgan ISBN 0 352 33174 7	☐
GINGER ROOT	Robyn Russell ISBN 0 352 33152 6	☐
DANGEROUS CONSEQUENCES	Pamela Rochford ISBN 0 352 33185 2	☐
THE NAME OF AN ANGEL £6.99	Laura Thornton ISBN 0 352 33205 0	☐
SILENT SEDUCTION	Tanya Bishop ISBN 0 352 33193 3	☐
BONDED	Fleur Reynolds ISBN 0 352 33192 5	☐
THE STRANGER	Portia Da Costa ISBN 0 352 33211 5	☐
CONTEST OF WILLS £5.99	Louisa Francis ISBN 0 352 33223 9	☐
BY ANY MEANS £5.99	Cheryl Mildenhall ISBN 0 352 33221 2	☐
MÉNAGE £5.99	Emma Holly ISBN 0 352 33231 X	☐

THE LION LOVER	Mercedes Kelly ISBN 0 352 33162 3	☐
A VOLCANIC AFFAIR	Xanthia Rhodes ISBN 0 352 33184 4	☐
FRENCH MANNERS	Olivia Christie ISBN 0 352 33214 X	☐
ARTISTIC LICENCE	Vivienne LaFay ISBN 0 352 33210 7	☐
INVITATION TO SIN £6.99	Charlotte Royal ISBN 0 352 33217 4	☐
ELENA'S DESTINY	Lisette Allen ISBN 0 352 33218 2	☐
LAKE OF LOST LOVE £5.99	Mercedes Kelly ISBN 0 352 33220 4	☐
UNHALLOWED RITES £5.99	Martine Marquand ISBN 0 352 33222 0	☐
THE CAPTIVATION £5.99	Natasha Rostova ISBN 0 352 33234 4	☐
A DANGEROUS LADY £5.99	Lucinda Carrington ISBN 0 352 33236 0	☐
PLEASURE'S DAUGHTER £5.99	Sedalia Johnson ISBN 0 352 33237 9	☐
SAVAGE SURRENDER £5.99	Deanna Ashford ISBN 0 352 33253 0	☐
CIRCO EROTICA £5.99	Mercedes Kelly ISBN 0 352 33257 3	☐
BARBARIAN GEISHA £5.99	Charlotte Royal ISBN 0 352 33267 0	☐
DARKER THAN LOVE £5.99	Kristina Lloyd ISBN 0 352 33279 4	☐
HOSTAGE TO FANTASY £5.99	Louisa Francis ISBN 0 352 33279 4	☐

Black Lace anthologies

PAST PASSIONS £6.99	ISBN 0 352 33159 3	☐
PANDORA'S BOX 2 £4.99	ISBN 0 352 33151 8	☐
PANDORA'S BOX 3 £5.99	ISBN 0 352 33274 3	☐
SUGAR AND SPICE £7.99	ISBN 0 352 33227 1	☐

Black Lace non-fiction

WOMEN, SEX AND ASTROLOGY £5.99	Sarah Bartlett ISBN 0 352 33262 X	☐

‐ ‐ ‐ ‐ ‐ ‐ ✂ ‐ ‐ ‐ ‐ ‐ ‐ ‐ ‐ ‐ ‐ ‐ ‐ ‐ ‐ ‐ ‐ ‐

Please send me the books I have ticked above.

Name   ....

Address   ....

               ....

               ....

               .... Post Code ....

Send to: **Cash Sales, Black Lace Books, Thames Wharf Studios, Rainville Road, London W6 9HT.**

US customers: for prices and details of how to order books for delivery by mail, call 1-800-805-1083.

Please enclose a cheque or postal order, made payable to **Virgin Publishing Ltd**, to the value of the books you have ordered plus postage and packing costs as follows:
   UK and BFPO – £1.00 for the first book, 50p for each subsequent book.
   Overseas (including Republic of Ireland) – £2.00 for the first book, £1.00 each subsequent book.

If you would prefer to pay by VISA or ACCESS/ MASTERCARD, please write your card number and expiry date here:

....

Please allow up to 28 days for delivery.

Signature ....

‐ ‐ ‐ ‐ ‐ ‐ ✂ ‐ ‐ ‐ ‐ ‐ ‐ ‐ ‐ ‐ ‐ ‐ ‐ ‐ ‐ ‐ ‐ ‐